NYX

A DARK & DIRTY SINNERS' MC: ONE

SERENA AKEROYD

NYX

PLAYLIST

If you'd like to hear a curated soundtrack, with songs that are featured in the book, as well as songs that inspired it, then here's the link:

https://open.spotify.com/playlist/1DUSGULSE0AXqm715QTLIP

AUTHOR NOTE

When I originally published Nyx, my trigger warning was not what it should have been and now that my series is complete, I need to do better as I have grown as a person and an author and I recognize that my previous trigger warning let you down.
I'm so sorry for that.
In this book, you will find:
Sexual assault of the heroine but not by the hero.
Graphic violence
References to past sexual assaults.
Enjoy my Sinners!
Love
Serena
xo

UNIVERSE READING ORDER

FILTHY LIES
FILTHY TRUTH

RUSSIAN MAFIA
Adjacent to the universe, but can be read as a standalone
SILENCED

PROLOGUE

NYX

"WHY THE FUCK are you doing this to me?"

The scream had me frowning at Steel and demanding, "Is this guy a dumb fuck or what?"

"It's the blood loss," Steel reasoned. "It's all leaving his head, meaning he's more stupid than usual."

I scowled at the logic. "Isn't that how an erection works?"

Steel shrugged. "Same difference."

As I eyed my handiwork, I muttered, "Not sure this goes under the same caption as an erection, bro."

When he snickered, I grabbed one of Haune's hands and selected a fat finger. "These filthy fucking paws have touched something they shouldn't have. That's why I'm doing this, you cunt."

His eyes widened. "No! No! I've been good. I haven't done anything!"

"Bullshit," I snarled. "Little Jessie Dresden? She's *nothing*, huh?" When he blanched, I whispered, "To you, I'm God. I see all, hear all, *know* all."

I pressed the blade to the digit and sliced it off. Blood instantly spurted, drenching me in the spray, but as he writhed, screaming in agony, all I could do was smile.

"Unluckily for you, you have nine more fingers to go," Steel noted, looking up from his phone. The irritating soundtrack to a game sounded, but I blanked it out.

Haune's screams reached a peak then. "Help me!" he shrieked, his desperation culminating in a wet patch on the front of his pants.

"Ain't no one gonna help a sick fuck like you, Sammy Boy," I told him, satisfaction loading each word. "Just like no one can help Jessie now. No one except *me*."

And with that, I grabbed another finger and sliced off the fat chunk of flesh and bone.

My night's work was only just beginning.

Fuck me, I had the best job in the world.

ONE

NYX

"TODAY, City Hall revealed that the police are treating the death of Samuel Haune as a homicide. This is the seventh murder of a known sex offender in three years within the state."

When the news came on the big screen TV in the bar, an immediate hush settled over the room.

Sixty bikers—most of them so drunk they were wobbling on their feet—made a fuck ton of noise, but the second Link switched on the news that had a "Breaking Story" banner running along the bottom of it, everyone shut the hell up. A miracle in itself, but nothing compared to what I left behind in the tiny town of Bridgeton, New Jersey.

One less fucked-up piece of shit walked the streets tonight.

Because of me.

Sure, Satan's Sinners were involved too, and all the work that went down, all the logistics prior to the main event, weren't organized by me, but the kill?

That was all mine.

"Mr. Haune was a known pedophile, whose release from prison triggered public outrage. He refused police protection, ignored advice against returning to his hometown, and had received several death threats since his release from incarceration.

"The Chief of Police confirmed the authorities are seeking a link between the murders, and are also conferring with other states for similar vigilante-style homicides. As it stands, detectives are looking for witnesses who might have been in the vicinity of the Johnson Reeves playground yesterday around 2 AM.

"A few people spoke with us today and recalled the gruesome sight of what they could only call a lynching—"

As the story switched to videos of interviews with witnesses, the silence remained for a second before a bunch of hollers soared around the bar. I grinned at the noise, then let Rex, my Prez, grab me by the arm so he could pump our fists into the air as we celebrated our twenty-ninth slaughter. Twenty-two of which hadn't been linked because they'd gone down all over the US, with only seven here in New Jersey.

Sure, we'd get arrested for our crimes if we were discovered, but I considered it a fate worth testing, and knowing what they did about my past? The Sinners did too.

We were an MC. A one-percenter club that was bad to the mother-fucking bone, but we didn't fuck with kids. Kids were sacrosanct within our ranks, and we protected them. Didn't matter if they belonged to one of the brothers or not, we defended them when the legal system didn't.

As the party started up again, Rex mumbled in my ear, "You need another tattoo."

My smirk of satisfaction widened. "Sure as fuck do." My back was a patchwork quilt of tattoos that were linked to the deaths of twenty-nine monsters who'd raped, abused, beaten, and/or killed children.

The first one represented my own monster. Well, mine and my sister's. I'd survived that cunt, but she hadn't.

And I'd made that fucker pay. Just as I made them all pay. The thought alone had me cracking my knuckles. Survivor's guilt had morphed into a rage that would never be appeased, forged from a grief so strong that more than twenty years after her passing, I still mourned her as much as I had the day I'd found her swinging from the rod in her fucking closet.

"You're going to run out of space soon," Cruz pointed out from behind the bar. He was pouring beers as fast as my brothers were shoving their glasses at him, while Sin was 'helping' by handing out tequila shots, except for every two shots he poured, he took a guzzle from the bottle too. Not that I begrudged the fucker his poison—he'd been the one to help me string Haune up. He deserved a little respite.

"That's a problem I can deal with," I stated grimly, staring down into my shot glass. When Rex slapped me on the back, then gripped my shoulder, I asked him, "Did everything else go down alright last night?"

He cocked a brow. "Did I call church?"

I winced at the quiet reprimand. "No."

"Well then, all's good, man." The handsome bastard's grin twisted along his jaw. "Enjoy your success. You earned it, bro. That fucker..." He whistled. "Squealed like a pig."

"I know." Satisfaction sang through my veins. "Made him pay."

"You make them all pay." Rex cut me a look, and I knew, deep in his eyes, there was concern buried within those baby blues.

"I'm okay, man," I assured him quietly, uneasy at the sight.

I knew he cared, but his concern, today at any rate, wasn't necessary.

Of course, it wasn't like you could switch that shit off and on. We weren't kin, but we might as well have been. Rex loved me like we were family, and in a way, we were.

Rex, Steel, Link, Storm, Maverick, and I had all been raised on the compound at one point or another. We'd grown to be brothers, and it was only a twist of fate that saw us all sitting on the Sinners' council, but that twist meant that every man in the MC, be they on the council or just a regular brother, had my back where this crusade of mine was concerned.

"You're the opposite of okay, man," Rex argued with a grumble as he eyed the deep amber of his beverage of choice—JD. Neat. No rocks. He could put away a bottle of that without feeling the pain the next day. "But you're nowhere close to rabid, so I'm cool with that."

Unable to stop my snicker, I slammed back some tequila and retorted, "You going to put me down if I go wild?"

"Depends on your definition of wild." He arched a brow as he leaned forward, shoving his elbows on the peanut-strewn bar. As his gaze drifted over Cruz and Sin, I saw him take note of the stock in the bar, and had to shake my head at the sight.

The bastard seriously never stopped working.

Because concern wasn't a one-way street, I questioned, "You going to fuck off and get fucked? I don't know about you, but Cammie wants to suck my cock, don't you, darlin'?" I hollered the last part so my bitch of choice knew to get her fine ass over here. With a flick of her long blonde hair, she leaped up off the sofa where she'd been chilling with a couple of the other whores, her tits jiggling as she did so.

Eying her, Rex snorted. "Since when did you mind having an audience?"

As the sweetbutt sauntered over to me, swinging her hips for all she was worth, I muttered, "Everyone knows Cammie is shy and timid." Rex and I stared at one another before bursting out laughing, because describing Cammie as shy and timid was like saying a fourteen-year-old virgin boy didn't have wet dreams... but for all her sins, she was, for all intents and purposes, mine.

I hadn't claimed her, never would, but every brother in the MC knew I didn't share my spoils. It was just how I worked, and because no one wanted to get on my bad side, they steered clear of the sweetbutt.

I was well aware Cammie thought that gave her Old Lady privileges, and used it to one-up the rest of the whores, but I didn't really give a fuck. She wasn't my woman, never would be, and if it made her feel better for her to think she was more than just a trio of holes, then I wasn't enough of a dick to make her feel shitty about herself.

See, that was me. Being a good person.

Wasn't I just a fucking angel?

Even though she was off limits, even from him, it didn't stop Rex from appreciating the view, and it was definitely a good one.

She had the face of a saint and the body of a sinner—exactly how I liked my bitches, and Rex, entertained by the show she put on, grinned at me before he slapped me on the back and strode over to some other brother he needed to pester—dude was worse than a mother hen—and I let Cammie come to me.

She milked the moment, but with a pussy as tight as hers and tits that bounced with every thrust? I'd let her get away with it.

Leaning back against the top of the bar, I didn't care that it was wet from spilled beer and tequila, didn't give a damn that there were peanut shells on there either.

Honestly, I was already way past my own personal limit of alcohol. I never drank. Only on nights like tonight.

Nights where I celebrated.

It was why they called me Nyx.

I was a creature of the night, of the dark, and these moments, in the aftermath, were when I could let myself loose. When the demon inside me had been sated, I could take a few hours to enjoy the peace.

I knew for a fact Cammie had been avoiding me all evening. Knew it because my rep preceded me. It was why she'd stayed over with the others before I called her over, why now, she was nuzzling into me, cuddling me... she was trying to temper me.

Yeah, because that worked. When affection came from a bitch I didn't really give a fuck about, from a woman who saw me as her bread and butter, it didn't really mean anything, did it?

The night after a kill, the night after I made an evil cunt beg at my feet, I was pretty much a beast, which was why Rex had looked at me all concerned.

He knew what I was like.

He'd been checking on the sweetbutt's behalf, making sure I wasn't a danger to anyone. He'd meant it when he said he'd been checking that I wasn't rabid.

I didn't know if he'd ever be able to tell if I *had* turned. He knew me well, probably more than most, but that didn't mean he knew everything.

A part of me *was* rabid, I just hid it deep.

That was what happened to a man's soul after what had happened to me and my sister *happened*, and after so many kills.

Something like that changed you, made you see the darkness in people that others never noticed. Made it harder to trust and more difficult to have faith.

With Cammie trying to hug me, the desire to push her away reached a peak as my throat grew thick with thoughts of Carly, thoughts about how fucked up I was and how much I'd enjoyed making Haune suffer, and for a second, I didn't just mourn my sister, I mourned the loss of *me*.

The promise that had been in me, in my future, all gone because of one person.

My personal demon began to stir once more, and because I couldn't deal with it, not so soon after a kill, I reached back to grab the bottle from Sin's hand, needing to drown out the ever present rage with the numbness only alcohol could diminish.

Not even coke or dope took it away, and I'd tried, several times, but only tequila did it. Only that gave me any rest when the monster was on edge.

Sin grumbled at losing his bottle, but he knew to back the fuck off. Not just because I was the club's Enforcer, but because of why we were cele- brating.

Our run had just netted us a cool three million bucks, but what we were truly partying over was Haune's death.

Sin flipped me the bird before he cracked the lid on a new bottle, and as I poured some of the burning liquid into my mouth, Cammie shimmied against me.

She'd been all confidence as she'd strutted over to me, but in her eyes, I saw her caution. She knew she was playing with fire tonight, but although she was feeling wary, she wouldn't say shit. She'd do whatever the fuck I wanted, *whenever*.

Another reason I liked her.

I looked deep into her eyes, then demanded, "Open your mouth."

She obeyed. Instantly.

Everyone knew to obey me.

From the whores to the brothers, even most of the council did as I asked because they knew, where business was concerned, my brain was screwed on right—most of the time anyway.

I was good at hiding the real me, to the point where I'd reached a position of power when I should probably be locked up in some asylum or something.

With her mouth wide open, I poured more tequila into mine then leaned over and trickled the alcohol between her lips. They were painted a ruby red, and as liquid splashed onto them, they gleamed.

In a weird way, it reminded me of Carly's favorite Disney movie—*Snow White*. The poison apple looked less shiny than Cammie's lips though, lips that were about to be around my dick.

As she swallowed my offering, I challenged, "You been avoiding me, Cam?"

Her eyes flared wide, and she instantly shook her head, fear slithering into her bright green gaze, and I reached up, enjoying her fear and knowing I was sick because of it.

I wasn't a monster, but I was a predator, and Cammie knew she was my prey. I wouldn't hurt her, wouldn't dream of it, but she didn't have to know that, did she?

Aside from Maverick, who'd served overseas, I had the most kills, and I wore the proof of that on my spine. That gave me an edge that all the sweet-butts knew to be wary of.

Reaching up, I tapped her chin. "You lying to me, Cammie?"

A hand slammed onto my shoulder. "Don't fuck with her, Nyx."

I cast Steel a look, but smirked when he rolled his eyes at me. Apparently, he wasn't up for dealing with my shit tonight.

"Cammie likes it, don't you, babe?"

"Y-Yes, N-Nyx," she stuttered, making me scowl.

"Well, that sounded convincing," Steel commented dryly.

Huffing out a breath, I ordered, "Get on your knees, get your tits out, and suck my dick."

"Thought you might want to take this somewhere private?"

The instant the words slipped from her mouth, she knew she'd made a mistake. She kept pulling this shit. Trying to take things to another level, which was never going to fucking happen. She was a clubwhore. Nothing more, nothing less.

Without another word, without my even having to cock a brow, she slid to her knees and unfastened the bralette she wore. As her tits spilled free, I turned my attention to Steel who I knew was eying up Cammie.

She wasn't mine, but every brother knew to back the fuck off her. I didn't share. And I expected no one to watch if I pulled a move like this out in public.

"You want to watch the show or something?" I growled.

"You're at the bar. Free country, ain't it?"

My brow puckered at that, and a memory prodded into being thanks to those two words—*free country*. "Ain't seen Mav around."

"He's in his room."

"Was hoping he'd get some pussy tonight. He was as integral to tonight's celebration as any of us."

Steel shrugged. "You know he won't come down."

Yeah, I'd known, but Haune was one of the worst fuckers we'd targeted, and Mav, more than anyone, knew what the bastard had done.

We didn't just slaughter these cunts without researching them. We made sure they deserved the punishment, and that involved Mav having to do some shit I'd never be able to thank him enough for.

See, if they came out of prison rehabilitated, we left them alone. Mav monitored some of them, had watches on the agencies that were keeping their eyes on the sex offenders' list.

But the ones who were released and went straight back to their vile ways, we showed them the true definition of vile.

If anyone deserved a bottle of tequila and a blowjob tonight, it wasn't me, it was Mav, but he, of course, was too fucked in the head from his own wounds to even enjoy the celebrations of one less sick fuck roaming the streets.

My mind veered off course when Cammie's hand began to roll down my zipper, but just as she slipped her fingers inside my fly, headlights flashed into the window of the bar. I grabbed her hand, well aware that all the brothers were in here tonight, partying.

Which meant anyone who came to the gate wasn't welcome.

Not tonight.

Maybe not ever.

Shoving her hand away, I almost walked into Cammie in my haste to figure out what was going on, then realizing she was there, I grabbed her and set her on her feet.

She tottered around a bit, wobbling on the too high heels all the whores wore and couldn't walk in, and I left her to Steel's care. Not that he'd touch her, but entertaining these bitches was just as much of a drag as it was when fucking an ordinary woman.

The compound was right on the outskirts of West Orange, situated smack in the middle of a triangle that had three swanky country clubs at each point. We were the mother chapter of four other MC chapters around the States, and I knew the Originals—one of whom was Rex's dad, Bear—had set up shop here simply to piss off the locals.

Close to Caldwell, we were in the middle of money. Money talked, but we had more than even the richest country clubber, and the sheriff and his deputies were all in our pockets. Regardless, we had to be vigilant.

We never stored drugs at the compound.

Ever.

That was our main source of income, that as well as a protection racket that defended some local storefronts from the fucking Bratva who were trying to elbow into our turf, and the transporting we did for a couple of Families in New York. So the money we earned was never kept here either.

I knew we were safe if the sheriff came armed with a search warrant, because one of the local rich fucks decided to get his panties in a twist over having scum too close to his eight-door garage loaded with classic cars, but just because there was no risk to us didn't mean I appreciated the inconvenience, especially when they fucking destroyed everything during the raid. Tearing up our beds and other soft furnishings, dragging everything out front on the hunt for our hiding places...

Because, yup, apparently we looked so fucking stupid that we'd keep shit stored in our fucking sofa cushions.

Dumb fucks. And they said we were the rednecks because none of us had more than a high school diploma among us—yeah. *Right.*

For all we were close to the ritzy areas in town, we had about three acres, and the building was a purpose built clubhouse, complete with bedrooms for the council, some for the whores, and a few others for families who, for whatever reason, couldn't afford to live off site. There were kitchens, living spaces, a dining area, and more offices than the local council probably had in their town hall.

Our MC was big business, and that was why it took a lot to protect our home. It was also why I was vigilant at all times, especially on nights like tonight where my family had gone to bat for me in a big way. I showed my appreciation by making sure that no one fucked with us.

It was my job, but it was my honor too. Nothing and no one meant more to me than these bastards, and I showed that by keeping them all safe.

As I pushed between brothers, who hadn't realized our security might have been breached, I forcefully shoved my way through the crowd. Bros wanted to congratulate me, and I just smirked at them and slapped them on the back, because it was quicker than explaining why I was in a rush.

When I finally made it to the front door, out through the wood paneled hall, it opened wide, and Jaxson, the Prospect I'd put on the gate tonight, was there, ready to step in.

"Just coming for you, Boss."

My road name was Nyx, but to the guys on security, they all called me Boss. I guessed it was a badge of honor. Only Rex had a different 'label,' and he was the fucking Prez.

"What's going on? Who's at the gates?"

Jaxson pulled a face as he reached up and rubbed the back of his neck. I'd known him since he was a kid. Had watched him grow up around the place. His dad, a loyal brother to the end, had died in a stupid bar brawl in a honky-tonk on Route 66 of all fucking places.

I'd been there when the bastard had bled out, and with his last, dying breath, he'd made me promise to watch over his kid.

Trouble was, watching over Jaxson meant trying to protect him from club life, and there was no way I could do that. Ironically enough, Hills wouldn't have wanted me to keep his kid from club life either, so it was a pointless deathbed promise. But I figured a man who died a violent death was allowed to talk pointless shit in the vain hope that his son wouldn't have a similar end.

Because I knew Jaxson well, I saw his discomfort. He was about eight or so months away from earning his patch, and he was good on security. Good enough that I'd be keeping him with me once he got his cut.

"Remember Lizzie Fontaine?"

The name had me narrowing my eyes as I released a whistle. "Fuck. Haven't heard that name in a long time. Don't let Dog hear you mention it. He's still bitter as fuck—"

"She's dead," Jaxson blurted out.

It took a lot to surprise me, but his declaration did. "She is? That's a fucking shame." Lizzie wasn't the slut Dog painted her as. If anything, she'd been good people, and this fucked-up shitter of a world was a worse place for her not being in it. Although... "How do you know that?" I inquired warily.

Lizzie had left when Jaxson was around ten. No way he'd know something like that when he probably didn't remember her all that well, so where this conversation was coming from, I didn't know.

After looking over his shoulder at the path he'd just taken, he pulled a face that set me on edge. "Lizzie and Dog's kids just pulled up at the gate. They want to come home."

TWO

GIULIA

EXHAUSTION TUGGED at my last nerve, as did the overpowering scent of Cheetos, which made the cabin of the cage I was in smell like feet.

Still, for a better life, who was I to complain?

Getting away from Salt Lake City was the best thing for my whole family, even if my brothers initially had to work hard to get me to move, I knew being back here was where I needed to be right now.

Coming back to the Sinners' compound was bittersweet. This was where I'd started my life, where I'd spent a good chunk of my twenty-four years, and yet, it was loaded with a shit ton of bad memories too. Salt Lake City had been better, I guessed. No arguments between my mom and dad, no violence, but I'd missed this place.

It was and always would be, I recognized, home.

And what that said about me and the kind of dip shit I was, well, hell, I wasn't sure.

As the engine idled, making our crap in the truck bed vibrate, the two hogs my brothers had secured on there shake in their moorings, I drummed my fingers against my knee. As I fiddled with the hem of my shorts, I also yanked at a strand of hair that had fallen free of the topknot I'd shoved it into when we started this trek. Touching it made me feel icky, and it reminded me that I really needed a shower.

Four years of going to school here had drilled it into my head that I needed to be clean, because being associated with an MC meant everyone thought we were dirty. I wasn't dirty. Neither was I OCD, but I was really aware that my brothers and I had skipped staying in motels the past night to save money.

North and Hawk had refused to let me drive on my own. I was a better driver than they were, but who was I to complain when they were the ones willing to trek across the country, all two-point-three thousand miles of it, without me having to do shit? I'd spent the journey with my AirPods in, music on, and a book on my kindle while they chatted about all the crap we were leaving behind and all the great stuff we were going to find on the other end.

None of us had admitted that our father might not want us here. They weren't willing to accept that might be the case.

Me? I'd never liked my dad, so I wouldn't put anything past him, but I'd be gutted for them if he turned his back on us.

I'd also feel lost, because without Mom? There was nothing for us in Utah. Nothing except for a POS stepdad who'd eyed me up more times than I could count, all while dissing me by calling me a fat bitch—as he silently panted over me—and who'd judged my brothers for wanting to follow in our dad's footsteps.

Sure, becoming a one-percenter wasn't everyone's dream, but it was Hawk and North's. And what could I say? If I had a dick, I'd want that too. As it stood, nothing with a cunt was allowed to wear a cut, so my options were few. Well, unless I wore a 'Property of...' cut and tat.

My nose wrinkled at the thought, every feminist sensibility jerking to attention at the idea of being someone's property. Look how that had turned out for my mom. Dad had beaten on her just as much as she'd beaten on him. But, and it was a huge but, it wasn't like my dick stepfather had been a much better catch.

Sure, he'd had legit money flowing in through his used car business, but he'd been just as much of an asswipe.

I was under no illusions that my father was great. Biology didn't make for a decent man, but being back in West Orange felt right, and he was our in to getting back into the clubhouse, to being allowed to stick around the MC.

Because he must have sensed how nervous I was, Hawk slipped his hand around the back of my neck and squeezed it gently. "I promise, Sis, things will be better back here."

We weren't really a touchy-feely family, so I had to wonder what I was projecting if he thought I needed comfort. Because of my past, both my brothers tended to keep a wary distance from me. I couldn't blame them. If I owned a pair of balls, I'd worry for them around me too.

"We've only made it to the gates," I said dryly, and I awkwardly patted his leg. "Don't get too excited," I cautioned, not wanting him to be disappointed if they didn't let us in. "They could still toss us out."

"Dad wouldn't let them," North stated confidently, making me want to shake my head at him.

Dad, AKA Dog, wasn't much good at the whole parental responsibility thing. Though my twin bros were six years older than me, it felt like I was the only one who really remembered how crappy Dog had been as a father.

Still, we weren't here for him. We were here for the Sinners. Most of the Old Ladies were like second mothers to me, and when Mom had forced us to leave, dragging us halfway down the country to a part of the States where the MC had no reach, I'd probably been more devastated about leaving the Old Ladies behind than my own father.

Nerves flickered inside me as I wondered who was still around. Some Old Ladies were in it for life, others less so. It wasn't an easy existence.

With all the pussy on offer, with zero expectations, the threat of the cops knocking on your door at any moment, as well as the likelihood that part of your relationship would go down with your Old Man in jail, leaving you saddled with however many kids he stuffed in your belly... yeah, women tended to smarten up real quick.

It was hot at first. The danger, the excitement, the adrenaline. Then life got in the way.

North tapped his fingers along the steering wheel, muttering, "Come on. How long does it take to get approval?"

The Prospect guarding the gates he'd spoken to had scuttled off to the clubhouse about five minutes ago. I wondered if his absence meant we weren't even going to be told to fuck off before we just left on our own devices.

It surprised me how much I hoped that wasn't true. I really didn't want to travel anymore tonight, and I just...

Sighing, I reached up and rubbed my eyes. Not only was I tired, I was still hurting. Mom had only died three weeks ago, and leaving everything behind, packing up our lives to come on a wild goose chase was just going to make this month even shittier than it already was.

Toward the end, we hadn't been close, but that didn't mean I wanted to be in a world without her. She was young, and I'd always thought we'd have time to make things right. But that hadn't happened. *Fucking life.*

"It's okay. They're probably just finding the Sergeant-at-Arms or the Enforcer." Hawk tipped his chin at the clubhouse. "They're having a party."

"You always were a genius, Hawk," I remarked wryly. Anyone with ears could hear they were having a party. Not only from all the whooping and hollering, but the music that would make a death metal concert look like a ten-piece classical orchestra.

"I try, I try," he mocked, nudging my leg with his. "Cheer up. Things will get better now that we're home."

I shot him a look, wondering how he could be approaching thirty and still be so fucking naive. But I kept quiet because I didn't want to crush things for him. There was only room for one pessimist in the truck.

In the distance, the compound sat there, as unchanging as ever. It was custom-built, two stories high, and ugly as fuck with its clapboard fronting that had been gunmetal gray when I'd last been here. The doors and window frames were still white though—I could see that much in the flood-lights that randomly popped on and off if something moved in the yard. From what I could view in the dark, it looked like there were a lot more bikes than there'd been before around the side of the property, and from the racket that throbbed through the walls of the clubhouse, I had to assume the Sinners had done well in the years of our absence.

As I stared at what had always been my second home, the front door opened, and in the backlighting from the hall, I saw two men appear.

One was the Prospect, who was a little thin, a lot tall. Kind of reed-like. The other was the opposite. Tall, sure, but thick, every inch of his frame muscled. The two men approached the gate, and in the headlights, I saw the other guy's cut.

Enforcer, just like Hawk had predicted.

Except, this wasn't the same Enforcer as before. Buddy's beer gut had exploded out of his cut, and he'd also been a good six inches shorter than this guy. He'd also had a kind of greasy comb-over.

This brother had short hair, about two inches long, all of it standing up like Bart Simpson, except he made it look good. At least, I thought he would when half the spikes weren't sagging all over the place from what looked like him raking his hand through it too many times.

In a cut and a Henley, he packed out both to full capacity, and his jeans clung to him like he'd been born with them on as they formed to his legs as if painted there.

He kind of reminded me of Luke Perry back in *Beverly Hills 90210*. Except Luke was skinnier, and this guy? Not a bit of him was skinny.

Especially not the log he was carrying between his legs, because, yup, the dude was sporting wood, and that wood looked like a fine piece of timber. Which told me exactly what we'd interrupted, and my nose curled at the thought. Fucking bikers. Their parties were a euphemism for a goddamn orgy.

Refusing to drool—over his face, body, and cock—because that's what these brothers were used to, blind adulation from the club sluts, I stared right at him, aware that he was looking at me and not my brothers through the windshield. Even as I wondered why, I soon had my answer. He tipped his head to the side, like he was reading me in the play of light and shadow from the dash, and I knew he was trying to see my mother in my face.

My throat closed at that, grief sucker punching me. I'd never get over her death, never get over the loss of what might have been. Reconciling wasn't possible when you were fucking dead, which meant that was it. Our unfinished business would forever be that. And though, for these past few years, she'd been a bitch, before that, she'd been a good mom. A little hands-on when it came time to punishments when we were younger, but nothing like what had gone down between her and my father.

Still... Lizzie Fontaine was a good person. She'd have been the best if she hadn't gotten knocked up by Dog, but that wasn't something you could roll back the clock on, was it?

When the guy finally stopped studying me, he moved to the gate, which began moving now that the Prospect had pushed a button in a shelter just off the driveway.

The Enforcer rounded the cab to North's side, and my brother rolled down the window, letting the hot air spread into the cab.

Hawk reached up and clicked on the inner light too, and I squinted, the brightness painful after traveling in the dark all night long.

"You Dog's kids?"

For a greeting, that was pretty polite. Especially since we'd interrupted something personal. His erection was proof enough of that.

"Yeah. Lizzie Fontaine was our mom," I stated, giving my mother ownership of us and not that dumb fuck of a sperm donor.

His mouth tightened, and regret shaded his eyes. "I remember her. How did she die?"

"Heart attack," I choked out, dipping my chin as I clenched my hands into fists.

"Fuck. She was only... what? In her late forties?" he exclaimed, sounding genuinely sad.

I cut him a look, surprised by his dejection, and whispered,

"Yeah, she was forty-eight."

"Too fucking young."

North and Hawk didn't reply, but then, they were taking Mom's death weirdly. Honestly, I sometimes wondered how it was that they were the eldest siblings and I was the baby. They acted like toddlers most of the time, and the way they were grieving only backed up that theory.

"Yeah, she was," I whispered, my pain ringing through each word.

"What brings you here?"

North cleared his throat and finally deigned to speak. "This is home, Nyx—"

My eyes widened at the name. Nyx? Sweet fuck, this was *Nyx*?

"You got a good memory on you, kid," Nyx rumbled, his eyes darting over North's face, searching for what, I had no idea.

"Helps that my dad writes me often, tells me some of the shit you get up to."

Well, that was news to me.

Nyx's eyes narrowed at my brother's statement though. "That a threat?"

North stiffened, aware he'd put his foot in his mouth, as per fucking usual. "No! Not at all. I just mean, he told me about the crazy stunts you pull. Extreme sports shit, you know?"

The tension surged in the cab, and for a second, it combined with my fatigue, my grief, and the fact I hadn't eaten properly since we'd set off, making me feel lightheaded. Reaching up to rub my forehead, I massaged my temples. Nyx caught the movement—fuck, I felt like he caught every movement—and murmured, "There's a party going on at the moment. You're welcome to sleep in the bunks until Rex can decide what to do with you."

"Rex is the new Prez?" I asked, eyes widening, because I remembered him too. Maybe this wouldn't be so bad after all. Not if I knew all the brothers and the Old Ladies.

"Yeah. He is. For the past four years. Why?" His mouth twisted. "You got a problem with that?" His tone told me he didn't give a shit if I did or not.

In an effort to be polite, which wasn't something I did often, I countered, "No! Of course not. I just remember when he was a Prospect, that's all." My smile was genuine. "He was nice."

Nyx snorted. "Nice. Yeah. That's Rex. All heart." The Prospect was hovering by the gates, and as Nyx turned around and began to walk back, he told him, "Drive the truck into the nearest parking bay. I'll take our guests to the bunks." The word 'guests' didn't sound all that cordial or hospitable to me, enough so that I frowned at it.

"Nyx?" I called, aware that there was a quiver in my voice, and hating myself for it because these bastards thrived on weakness.

Just because they were, essentially, family, didn't mean I didn't know how shit worked around here.

"Yeah. What?" he demanded impatiently, twisting back around to stare at me.

"You do know it's us, don't you?"

"Wouldn't be letting you through the fucking gates if you weren't the spitting image of your momma. Now, I don't have all goddamn night. Do you want to come in, or stay out here until Rex wakes up tomorrow?"

THREE

NYX

IT HAD BEEN shitty of me to talk to Giulia like that, especially when, later on that night, I found out from her brothers that they'd been traveling from Utah, hadn't stopped much on the journey, and that their mother had only just died a few weeks ago.

I felt like a cunt. But then, I usually felt that way.

No change there.

But I felt even worse than usual about it when I woke up the next morning.

Staring at the ceiling, I thought about the way her eyes had darkened at my gruffness, thought about the fact I might have hurt her feelings, and wondered why I gave a fuck.

I'd granted more a 'buck 50' smiles than I could count on two hands, and lynched monsters without blinking, but putting a woman down when her momma had just died somehow felt like my biggest sin.

Especially when I'd compounded it by ignoring her as I'd walked the trio over to the bunks. Though she'd tried to ask if I was okay—me? Okay? I wasn't okay. I was the exact opposite of okay. But she'd tried to be nice, and I'd blatantly ignored her, mostly because the sight of her reminded me of a time I really wanted to forget. I'd had the biggest crush on her mom, and sometimes, that crush had been the only thing that got me through the fucking days.

Cammie moaned at my side, reminding me she was there. I'd fucked her hard last night, hard enough to make her scream—not necessarily in a good way. She'd come though, clenching down on my cock like she was a vise... which diminished some of the guilt I felt on that score. What was left wasn't enough to stop me from shoving her arm away and muttering, "Go back to bed."

She mumbled, "In bed already."

"Wrong bed," I retorted. When she started to close her eyes so she could fall back asleep, I shook her harder. "Cammie, fuck off back to your own bed."

She squinted at me, then pouted. "Don't be mean, Nyx. I can make you feel good later," she whispered, more sleepily than sexily.

"I don't want to feel good later," I told her dryly, then I smoothed over my harshness by tapping her on the ass and saying, "Go on, get."

With a huff, she rolled off the bed, grabbed her shit together, and barely took a moment to slip into her shoes—couldn't blame her, only a fool would walk about this place barefoot—and limped off toward the door.

Without a backwards glance, she disappeared into the hallway buck naked and shameless. But then, why would she feel ashamed? She wouldn't be the only clubwhore wandering the halls at this time of the morning.

Rubbing a hand over my face, I yawned and stared at the clock. Rex was a sicko. He liked to be up and about before eleven—didn't matter if we'd been partying hard the night before or not. And because I was on the council, that meant I had to be up too.

In fact, I was so fucking used to his dipshit ways that my own circadian rhythms knew to be awake at this time—it was ten-forty.

Grunting as I rolled into a sitting position, I scrubbed a hand over my hair as I scanned my room. A lot of my brothers were pigs, but not me. Everything in here was spotless, except for the clothes I'd tossed on the floor last night and the wet condoms that hadn't hit the trashcan.

If anything, that was what had me shuffling off the bed. I tied knots into them before shoving them in the trash, and yeah, I knew it was weird, but I grabbed the packet of disinfectant wet wipes I stored in my bedside table for just this occasion, and bent over to clean that mess up.

The rest of the house might gleam under a black light, but not this fucking room. I was too accustomed to keeping shit clean after a kill to let my DNA out on the loose.

Making a mental note to get Cammie to change my sheets later on, I headed for the bathroom. After I took a piss, I shaved, then dove into the shower. I hadn't shaved in at least five days, and I didn't even want to think about why shaving was suddenly imperative.

Ten minutes later, I was just in time to make it to Rex's office. His was the biggest in the place, and it had a conference table in there. It was where we held council meetings. Church, on the other hand, went down in the bar.

Around a yawn, I headed for his desk where a large tray had been placed. There was coffee, Ibuprofen and aspirin, a few cinnamon buns, and some bottles of water.

Ignoring some of my brothers who were already at the table, I grabbed a coffee, some aspirin, and a bottle of water, but stared at the cinnamon buns with definite surprise. They not only looked freshly baked, but they smelled it too, and no one, as far as I knew, baked around here. Certainly none of the skinny bitches we fucked on the regular.

"I'm sweet enough," I commented, eying the treat which, I had to admit, would have been appetizing if I hadn't been shitfaced from the night before.

Rex grunted. "As far as I'm concerned, you could eat a thousand of them and not be sweet enough. Maybe that's the key to getting you in a better mood. We need to force feed you baked goods." He laughed. "Like in *Seven*?"

I grimaced at the memory of watching that movie back when we were twelve and had to sneak around to watch that shit. Even I wasn't sick enough to force feed someone until their stomach exploded. *Go me.* "You're all fucking heart," I retorted, then eyed the door when I heard some squeaking sounds out in the hall. Knowing what they meant, I muttered, "Mav's late."

"Ain't he fucking always," Rex grumbled, casting a glance at the clock.

A few minutes later, the sound of swearing hit us loud and clear, followed by a few bangs as Mav used his crutches—crutches he only used as battering rams to get about inside the clubhouse—to push the door open before quickly wheeling inside the room.

He wore his usual scowl, a cut, and jeans. With his chest on show, I could see scars and tats. Because he could have worn a clown suit for all I gave a fuck, I never asked him why he always had his scars out on display, just wasn't surprised at the sight of them anymore.

First time I'd seen them? My initial reaction had been shock—not at the sight of them, but that he'd survived in the first place.

Fucker always had been stubborn, and if there was a God, I'd thank him for that. Maverick was one of the best.

Even if, ever since he'd come home, he'd been ornery as fuck. And when I said ornery, I meant it. He'd make a bear who'd been disturbed mid-hibernation look fucking cheerful.

"When are you changing the fucking door?" Mav growled at Rex.

"Why do I need to change my door? Nothing wrong with it."

Rex folded his arms across his chest, standing there like Solomon, like he could wait forever for Maverick to change his ways without having to move an inch.

"Would make my life a lot easier if you made it a swing door."

"You're in that chair by choice," I pointed out. "The second you start pulling your weight with physical therapy is the second you'll be back on your feet."

Mav didn't reply, just scowled at me, then wheeled over to the desk. He grabbed himself a cinnamon bun and took a bite that was close to defiant.

"I ain't the one who's gonna get fat sitting down all the time," I told him cheerfully, enjoying his glower while everyone else was still settling into their positions.

Making Mav feel *something* was number one on everyone's to-do list. The poor bastard had PTSD from his time served overseas, and if we let him, he'd just curl up and die.

That was why he was Treasurer.

As soon as he'd woken up after his last surgery in Bethesda, Rex had dumped the role on him and told him to get better, because the club's books were a mess after Boney had been looking after them—a lie because Boney was one shrewd motherfucker.

Four years later, he was still in the fucking chair, though the doctors said there was no physical reason for him to be handicapped, and while Boney had ceded the role to help a brother out, he'd never asked about taking the position back either—even though being on the council earned him forty percent more of a cut in earnings.

Everyone knew being Treasurer was the only reason Mav got up in the morning. That, and the shit he did for me too. We were both on a mission, didn't matter that it wasn't government sanctioned... Someone had to take out the trash.

"Who made 'em?" Link asked, gracing us with his attention as he looked away from his phone.

From the smirk on his face, he'd been sexting. Only God knew about what. Link was unusual where sex was concerned, and that was being goddamn kind. We'd all heard the rumors, and I didn't need confirmation. Even if he had a habit of oversharing when we were in the gym.

Rex pursed his lips. "That's a long story."

"I don't need the fucking recipe." Link's eyes lit up at almost the same brightness as his phone which pinged with a notification. "Just a name."

"That's exactly it," Rex retorted crisply. "We had some visitors last night. One of them made us the buns."

My brow puckered at that as I figured out who was behind the baking. The twins had come with me to party, and I had no doubt they'd be gracing the porcelain God this morning, which meant... "Giulia made them? When the fuck did she have time to do that?" I knew she had to be exhausted after that trip, but not only that, from the shadows under her eyes—eyes I'd done my best to avoid during most of our interaction last night—it looked like she hadn't been sleeping that well for a while. The idea of her jumping up and pulling a Stepford wife routine put me on edge.

No one did shit without a motive in mind.

What was her game?

Rex shrugged. "This morning. I think she's trying to prove she can be useful."

"Well, they're a fucking wet dream," Mav growled around a mouthful, his eyes bright sparkling dimes as he chowed down. "If she can bake like this, she's more than fucking useful."

"I'll be sure to tell her she has your vote," Rex said, making me laugh into my coffee.

"Why does she think she has to be useful? She's family," I pointed out. "Not like we're going to toss her out."

"Wait, wait, wait," Link interjected, finally turning his phone face-down and giving us all his attention. "Who the fuck is Giulia?"

"Dog's daughter," I informed him. "She and his boys came in last night during the party. I took them to the bunks, told Rex about them, and that's about as much as I know."

Well, that and she was the spitting image of her dead mom. The woman I'd jerked off to more than once when I was a teen.

Except, if I was being honest, Giulia was like a pimped up version of Lizzie. She had bigger tits, a smaller waist, and rounder hips. Her skin was that Italian olive that was close to gold, and her eyes were shielded by the thickest fucking lashes I'd ever seen.

Cammie had those beetles she got stuck on the lids every month. Giulia was the opposite. Everything about her was natural, from her curves to her features, which had been makeup free last night. Her hair wasn't dyed, and unlike her mom's, it was longer, and it had a curl to it that made me think about wrapping it around my fist, which led to thoughts I had no right to be thinking.

Not about Lizzie's girl.

Rex rubbed his chin as he leaned farther against the side of his desk so he could cross his feet at the ankle. "Where the fuck are Storm and Steel? I'd prefer not to have to tell this twice."

"I'm here! Sorry I'm late. Tink wanted to suck my cock, and who am I to disappoint a lady?" Storm came swirling in like the storm he fucking was. His grin was as wide as the Cheshire Cat's, and he clapped me on the arm as I moved toward the table, jostling my coffee.

"Fuck off, man, some of us didn't have enough time to get blown," I snapped at the pain in the ass who, as usual, was oblivious to the chaos he left in his wake.

Storm just started whistling, which irritated me even more. He fist-bumped Rex—he had to lift Rex's fist to bump it—and grabbed a coffee, which he slurped halfway down, before topping it up and beaming another grin at us.

Motherfucker was just asking to be punched.

"Jesus, since when was Tink good at oral?" Steel complained as he shuffled in, squinting at the window. It didn't surprise me when he headed over to it and closed the blinds.

When we were sitting in the semi-dark, almost everyone but him and me began to laugh.

"How the fuck are we supposed to discuss business in the goddamn dark?" Rex retorted, but he was amused too. That much was clear from his tone, as well as the fact he didn't undo Steel's work and left the room in a haze of shadows.

"Don't care," Steel grumbled, slumping over the table and dragging his arms over his head, "but fuck if my eyes are going to work in the light."

Rex huffed but switched on his desk lamp. Always made me laugh when he did. Hard ass Prez of a biker with a fucking banker's lamp of all things gracing his desk. The one with the gold stand and the green glass?

I shook my head at the sight, especially when he twisted it around so that Steel, who'd slouched against his chair, was in the spotlight. Rex just grinned at his groan, then tipped it back down so there was a golden glow in the middle of the floor.

"Now that we're all here... Late is better than nothing, although you know I'll fucking dock your goddamn cuts if it happens again—"

A chorus of "Yeah, yeah, yeah" sang at that. Not because we knew he wasn't good for his word, but because sometimes, it was worth being goddamn docked. Even for me, this was way too early.

"We have some news."

Steel peeped out of one eye. As the MC's Secretary, he needed to keep his finger on the pulse—well, when his brain wasn't full of vodka, the fucker's drink of choice. "Of the good or bad variety?"

Rex hitched a shoulder. "Neither, really. Just information."

"During the party last night, Dog's kids showed up," I announced to the table, keeping my eyes on my coffee just in case I revealed something I didn't want to. I could be found in the dictionary under the definition of expressionless, but Lizzie and Giulia were a match made to fuck with me. It was like my past and present were combining into one explosive package, and I hated explosives.

They were Sin's forte. Not mine.

Storm raised his brows as he sipped his coffee. "Dog's and Lizzie's, right?"

"Good memory," I murmured. "She's dead. Heart attack."

"So they came home?" Link rubbed his chin. "Can't blame them."

"Why? Dog's an asshole," Storm said with a snort. "Even more useless a father than he is a brother."

While he wasn't totally wrong, I was compelled to defend the fuck just because he'd worked on my hog last month and it was now purring like a tiger.

The run this past week had been bliss—and not just for the wet work I'd undertaken.

"That's not fair. Dog's good at some stuff," I argued.

"Yeah? Like what?" Link retorted.

When he looked like he was waiting for an answer, I just rumbled, "Grunt work. Someone has to do that kind of shit. Plus, he can tune up a bike better than some of the mechanics." That last part I said tongue-in-cheek as Link was the best mechanic the MC had.

When he flipped me the bird, I just smirked.

Rex input, "He has you there, Link. Dog's a fucking wizard with my hog."

Steel agreed, "Anyway, what's the problem?"

"The boys want to patch in."

"They old enough?" Link asked, brow furrowed.

"They're nearly thirty. I think they're fucking old enough," I commented wryly.

"How the fuck was I supposed to know that?" Link flipped me the bird.

"But what about the girl? She wants to be a sweetbutt?" Steel questioned, sitting up slightly. His eyebrows bobbed with his interest. "She hot?"

"Fuck off. She ain't gonna be a clubwhore," I hissed, before Rex could even get a word in.

There was no way in fuck I was going to allow that. When I thought of those big, chocolate-brown eyes that had stared at me from an angel's face, there was no way I could—

Everything in me rejected the notion of her lying flat on her back and thinking of her grocery list just to get through the next fuck.

"Since when do you have a say in this?" Storm retorted, biceps bulging as he started to get mulish—the dickwad had such a shitty attitude that sometimes, I didn't know why Rex put up with his ass. He'd been worse since Keira, his Old Lady, had fucked off. Not that I could blame her. "Fuck, that might be her lifelong dream. Taking after her—"

"Don't say another fucking word," I growled, aggression lacing every single word. "Lizzie wasn't like that."

"She wasn't, Storm. You know that, so don't start shit."

"From the way Dog used to whine—"

"Dog wouldn't know how to piss in a straight line," I countered, angrier than the subject really called for. "Lizzie would be doing the fucking salsa in her grave if she thought her daughter was whoring her snatch out for the club."

Link pondered our argument for a second. "Wasn't that why she took off in the end? She got sick of the clubwhores, right? I was only fucking twenty-something, so I don't remember that much, but I think I remember that... the blonde. Big tits with nipples like she'd painted them in red lipstick. That huge eagle tattoo on her ass."

Despite myself, I had to laugh. "Yeah. Cherry."

He clicked his fingers. "That's it. Cherry. She took mine—"

"She took everyone's," Steel joked, making most of the table snicker.

"And she and Dog were a thing for a while," I pointed out. "Remember? Lizzie found out, and there was that huge clusterfuck—"

"Christ, yeah." Steel slid his hand over his head. "Lizzie trashed his bike when she found out, didn't she?"

"Yeah, and he nearly fucking throttled her. I remember now!" Link declared.

I slouched in my seat because I remembered that morning like it was fucking yesterday. "She took off later that day."

The urge to make Dog pay had been heavy, but I'd been a kid, and he was a brother. You didn't kill brothers. Even if you really goddamn wanted to.

"Okay, less of the reminiscing," Rex growled. "I don't need a history lesson, and I sure as fuck don't need to know who sucked your virgin cocks this early in the morning."

"You'd be down for the dirty later on though?" Steel hooted, then instantly grabbed his head and held it as though the throbbing in his skull was going to split it in two.

"Fuck you," Rex retorted, but there was laughter in his eyes. "Anyway..." He extended the word. "Giulia doesn't want to loan out her cunt to the club. I never said she did."

"What does she want then?" Storm queried, like there was only one use for females around the MC—snatch.

As much of a dick as I was, I wasn't that fucking bad. Keira was better off without this fucker.

"She wants to feed us." Rex snickered when everyone eyed him like he'd just pulled on a Santa outfit and started 'Ho, ho, hoing' all over the fucking place.

"Feed us? What are we, a soup kitchen?" Steel replied with a scowl.

"I'll tell her I'm homeless if she'll feed me more of those buns," Mav added hopefully.

"Trust me, she made me breakfast this morning. She's good, guys. Fucking good, and I don't know about you, but I'm sick and fucking tired of JoJo's sloppy eggs, and the shit the other sweetbutts serve ain't much better."

"How anyone can fuck up sandwiches, I don't know," Maverick groused, rubbing his abdomen like he was a starving man.

Anticipation welled in me.

If Giulia had a purpose here, then she'd be able to stick around, and that was a topic I didn't particularly want to broach. Not even in my own head. Because I wanted her to stay, and yet, I didn't.

Trying to hide my nerves, I eyed Rex and asked, "You down for that?"

"I am. She's family. I shoved her into the kitchen, told her to make the best of it—"

"Shouldn't we have voted on that?" Storm interrupted, scowling at the Prez like he really wanted his ass kicked today. And that was something *I'd* be down for.

Hell to the fucking yeah.

The dick had a date with my fists.

Only the fact he was VP meant I hadn't beaten the shit out of him before now. We'd always butted heads, but ever since Keira had kicked him out he'd been worse than a bear with a sore paw.

Temper clearly stirring, Rex narrowed his eyes on Storm. "Since when do I have to discuss shit like that with you? *She's family,*" he repeated. "Dog might be a useless turd with MC business, but as we've already said, he's good with the bikes, which as far as I'm fucking aware is how we run most of our businesses," he growled, his scowl darkening when Storm looked even more belligerent rather than apologetic as he should rightfully be. Then he continued:

"I threw her in the kitchen, told her to write down whatever she'd need to make us a decent dinner, and then we'd finalize things tonight.

"If her food is anything like what she made me for breakfast, then we'll all be piling on the pounds."

Steel snorted. "Maybe that's why the whores feed us junk... so they can keep us ripped."

"Could be." Link chuckled. "More like they want to keep their own asses skinny and have no idea how to make jack shit in the kitchen."

Nodding, Rex rubbed his chin. "There's only one problem."

"Only one?" Storm questioned.

"Yeah." The Prez scowled at him. "Okay, scratch that. Looks like we have two problems. One being the fact that you woke up in a piss-poor mood. You can either fuck off back to bed or I can kick the shit out of you." He balled his hands into fists. "Whichever would suit me."

Storm sniffed. "Bad hangover."

Like that was a fucking excuse when Steel was evidently suffering after last night, and he wasn't being a dick.

"Worse attitude," I retorted, stirring things up and not even giving a fuck. I only sneered at him when he shot me the bird.

"What's the second problem?" Mav demanded, his attention on Rex.

"We need to tell Dog they're here."

FOUR

GIULIA

I'D NEVER WANTED to cook. Ever. It had just been one of the only chores I could do, something that made sense without me having to think about it. When it boiled down to it, I could either cook or clean, and I hated cleaning more than I hated cooking.

Then, of course, I'd learned I had a knack for it.

Wasn't life a bitch?

Where creative shit was concerned, I couldn't paint, didn't know how to write anything fancy like poetry, and sewing? What was this? The eighteenth century? Who the fuck sewed nowadays? Cooking was the one creative thing I could do, and I hated it, but it was useful. Always had been, always would be.

When Mom had tossed me out, I'd found work in a diner, and it had kept a roof over my head before I'd started temping. So, with it being something I could fall back on and with my brothers wanting to prospect for the MC, I'd known one way to stick around them. They wanted to get back into the life because, to them, this was what they'd always wanted to do. And me? I just didn't want to be far from them. Not so soon after Mom's death, at any rate.

They were dumbasses, but they were mine.

Trouble was, in an MC, there were literally two roles for women. Either be a biker's bitch or be their cook and maid. Neither notion filled me with glee, but I was, I'd admit, on shaky ground.

With only a small amount of money saved up, getting an apartment near my brothers would cost a fortune I didn't have. Here at the MC, I could stay rent free, bills free, and if I was good—which I was—then maybe they'd pay me, and I could save up until I could get away from this place.

The Sinners' compound was my brothers' dream, and there was no way in fuck I was going to let them leave me behind in Dipshit, Utah, when they were all the way over here.

I knew them. Well... knew that in barely any time at all their weekly phone calls would diminish to monthly, and then yearly, as the life creeped up on them and took most of their time.

They were the only family I had left, and they loved me and I them—even if they were forgetful as fuck.

So, I compromised.

I, Giulia Elisabetta Fontaine, compromised by agreeing to cook the council a decent meal.

And from the state of their fridge? They fucking needed it.

"Who are you?"

The whiny voice was more than just irritating—it was rude. The sneer was audible, and fuck, it had me gritting my teeth, even as I ignored the bitch and kept my focus on what I was doing.

God, I'd always hated clubwhores. They seemed to think their pussies were made of gold when they weren't. If anything, they were disease-ridden slatterns who caused more shit than anything else.

My mom had always hated them too, and I knew most of the Old Ladies merely tolerated them because it was part of the life.

'Part of the life' was one of the sayings you heard often in these shit-holes. Those four words excused every biker's bad behavior, not just to their women, but to society itself, because it was the way of it.

It was 'part of the life' to beg, steal, and borrow. 'Part of the life' to kill and deal drugs. 'Part of the life' to fuck around on the woman who loved you, and 'part of the life' for said woman to just deal with that shit as though it was their man's right, hell, his *privilege* to be a cunt.

My jaw clenched as I remembered just how often my mom had argued with my dad when he'd come back covered in the scent of some other woman or his cheek dotted with lipstick—yeah, I wasn't predisposed to like any of the bitches, but them sounding like a snotty PITA wasn't going to make shit easier.

Rather than take my head out of the fridge where I was running an inventory on the scraps they had in the industrial-sized behemoth, I carried on with my work.

"Hey! I'm talking to you. Who the fuck are you?"

If they'd just carried on being bitchy, I wouldn't have done it.

I'd have behaved.

This was my first day, and I didn't need the MC to know I had more attitude than height... not until they tasted my pasta *puttanesca*, at any rate.

But she didn't just bitch at me. Nope, she made things physical. So when she grabbed my ponytail, I froze, especially when she pulled my head back and tried to turn me around to face her in the same move.

I let her roll with it, let her think she had me, but the second I could, I twisted around and gave her the same shit back. Smashing my forehead into hers, I headbutted her like she was a soccer ball. The second our skulls bounced off each other, she burst into sobs and began wailing. Me? I just reached into the freezer and grabbed a packet of peas that I placed against my crown.

The plastic burned where it touched, but it was worth it.

Round one to me.

"What the fuck is all that wailing about?"

I didn't need to turn around to see that Nyx was here. That voice. Fuck. It was deep and raspy enough that he could have been a smoker, but he was a biker and therefore, off limits.

I wasn't about to end up like my mom. Knocked up at seventeen, three kids in tow when she finally realized her dumb fuck of a husband was never going to change.

It pissed me off that I recognized the voice period. And it pissed me off even more that a quick glimpse of him over my shoulder, scowling and grumpy but still so goddamn pretty, made butterflies take root in my stomach.

I didn't get butterflies over anything. Not a job interview, and certainly not over something with a dick.

The attraction I felt for him came as a massive surprise to me, and it was totally unwelcome. He was everything I didn't want in a man.

Well, kind of.

Take off the cut, and I'd date him in a heartbeat because, dear God, the man was fine. In a 'my ovaries hurt' kind of way. In a 'come to *mami*' kind of way.

Sheesh.

"S-She h-hit me, Nyxy."

My lips twitched, and I couldn't stop a laugh from escaping. *Nyxy?* Fucking Nyxy? When I thought about the bruiser I'd met last night, the one who'd scowled at me for most of the time he'd had his eyes on me, I didn't think he'd appreciate being called 'Nyxy.'

I stopped hiding in the cooler, and instead, with glacial eyes that I knew would express just how little of a shit I gave about this bitch's opinion of me, I stated, "She pulled my hair to get my attention. This isn't grade school. If I don't want to talk to the club snatch, then I don't have to."

Nyx's eyes narrowed and, fuck me, if he didn't look even more beautiful. His hair was rumpled again, but this time, it was more like he'd gotten out of bed and hadn't had time to style it.

There were shadows under his eyes from a lack of sleep, and it didn't take much to figure out why that was... Some bitch was probably walking around bow-legged thanks to him. He wore his cut, another Henley like last night, dark jeans, and heavy boots. Standard MC brother fare, but holy hell, there was just something about him.

Maybe it was the sharp cheekbones and the carved jaw that looked as though it were made of stone—hell, make that diamond because his jaw tensed even harder the longer I glowered back at him.

That razor-thin nose that led to an expressive mouth... or those eyes. A beautiful green that made me think of shamrocks and emeralds. Even when they were laced with a warning that his temper was close to breaking. Whatever the reason, all I knew was he was beautiful.

Truly beautiful.

A work of goddamn art.

He cocked a brow at my prolonged stare, but I didn't blush—I'd lost the ability around my stepfather years ago. His come-ons and insults had made me grow a thicker skin than most women usually had. "She shouldn't have pulled my hair," I stated calmly.

He cut a look at the slut who was only wearing a goddamn G-string and a tee she'd knotted at the waist. *In the fucking kitchen.* Her stringy hair was showing all the extensions, and she had that in a loose topknot.

Despite the fact she looked cheap as hell, she was beautiful. There was no evading that. Even with the blossoming bruise on her forehead, she had the face of a china doll, and there was no way in fuck she should have been selling herself to these guys for room and board.

My throat tightened as I likened my situation to her.

No way in hell would I sleep with any of these bastards.

No. Way. In. Hell.

"She didn't answer me, Nyxy!" the bitch whined.

"Shut the fuck up, Kendra."

They might have sounded like it, but I knew those harsh words didn't mean he was on my side.

He wasn't.

That much was clear from his considering stare.

"That how you deal with people who ask who you are?"

"When they talk to me like I'm trash, then physically assault me?" I bared my teeth at him. "Yeah." I jerked my thumb at her. "I remember all the snatch from the old days. If you let them get away with shit early on, then you're fucked. I'm not an Old Lady, but I'm a brother's daughter. Straightaway, that means that cunt over there shouldn't even be talking to me, let alone—"

He didn't let me carry on. "Your momma let you talk like that?"

Brows lifting, I laughed. "My momma taught me to talk like this. Especially around guys like you."

He stared at me again, considering me *again*. "Kendra, get the fuck out of here."

"What?" The whining bitch glowered at me. "It's my turn to make lunch!"

"Yeah, well, it's your lucky day. Someone else is here to do that. Now fuck off."

Kendra pouted, and rather than look pleased at shedding the chore, she glared at me and trounced off.

Nyx, the bastard, took a second to watch her ass flounce off, but I couldn't really blame him—she had a nice ass. I'd even go so far as to say that I wished mine looked like that in a G-string instead of cheese wire around a ball of mozzarella. With more dimples.

Folding my arms across my chest, I waited on the lecture. On the 'if you can't play nice, then get the hell out of here' card, but when he'd stopped eyeballing her butt, instead of reaming me a new one, he turned to me and murmured, "You sure this is the right place for you?"

I cocked my hip against the counter which, surprisingly, was a damn fine piece of marble—hell, the rest of the kitchen was nice too. All of it stainless steel like a commercial kitchen in a restaurant or something—and inquired calmly, "Answer me this, would you allow someone to treat you like shit on the first day in a new place?"

"No," he replied simply. His eyes would never be considered kind, but they weren't mean either. So I took that to be a positive.

"Are you, or are you not, aware that sweetbutts are skanky-ass hoes with attitude problems? They're all cats in a bag hissing and trying to fuck one another over." I didn't wait for him to answer, just steamrolled on. "If I gave her an inch, she'd take a mile. You know it, I know it."

He tipped his head to the side. "You've caused yourself a whole heap of shit with the other girls. One and done with these bitches. You should remember that."

I snorted at that. "I was always going to get shit from those witches. If you don't believe that, then you're naive." My lips curved as I eyed him up and down. "One thing I doubt, Nyxy, is that you're naive."

His eyes narrowed, and he leaned forward, pressing his forearms onto the counter. As he did, his pecs bulged, making his Henley bunch up. Instead of focusing there, I looked at his throat, which was covered in a tattoo of a songbird with "Carly" inked there in a scroll font. It wasn't the first time I'd seen it, but in the light of day, it was the first time I realized that the banner that streaked out from behind the vintage bird, housed a chick's name.

Bikers only had one name on their bodies—their Old Lady's. Did it sting that he'd evidently claimed a woman? Yup. And did I feel stupid for feeling stung? Yup.

I didn't want him. He, like the rest of the brothers in the MC—mine included—were bad news, and that was the last thing I needed in my life. Or my bed. Still, he was hot.

And he fucking knew it.

Instead of hiding the fact that I'd been checking him out, I arched a brow at him, stacked a smirk on my lips, and folded my arms across my stomach in a way I knew had my boobs bulging.

When his gaze dropped, just like I'd known it would, I drawled, "You got something to say, Nyxy?"

"Yeah."

"What?" I prompted when he didn't say another word.

"It's Nyx."

"Only people you've fucked can call you that, huh?"

He smirked. "Wouldn't you like to know?"

"Actually, I'm fine as I am." My sneer turned into a wry smile. I decided to drop the BS, and told him, "Look, I'm not here to cause any shit, but that doesn't mean I won't protect myself. I know how to handle any of the crap those bitches can throw my way—"

"They're not all bitches," he interrupted, his brow puckering at my statement.

"They are to anyone who isn't like them. Even the Old Ladies." Because dicks like him let the skanks get away with that.

His scowl deepened. "You say that like it's my fault."

I hitched a shoulder. "My mom left this place because my dad never put any of the sluts in line. Never said shit if they disrespected her, never did a fucking thing." My mouth tightened. "I'm not about to let them treat me that way. Ever."

My words held more emotion than I liked, but he didn't call me out on it, instead, he just stared at me some more—and why wasn't that irritating? Why wasn't his regard annoying as hell?

If anything, it made me tingle, and that was not a good sign.

"You spoken to your father yet?"

The question surprised me. My eyes rounded for a second before I controlled my reaction—something he also took note of. But then, how could he understand how adept I'd become at hiding my expression from the world?

How could anyone, other than someone who'd been through the same shit as me, ever get it? And the bitch of it was, of course, that I was one of the lucky ones. I'd gotten away. But that didn't mean I didn't have scars.

"Why would I?" I replied easily, turning my back on him to look into the fridge once more.

I'd already figured out what I was making for dinner—steaks.

What other way was there to men's stomachs?

At least while I was trying to impress them enough to keep me around until I got my things together and could leave this place with some funds in my bank account.

The pasta *puttanesca* could be for another day. Steaks would reel them in, even if my signature dish was close to a masterpiece.

"Because he's your father," Nyx reasoned, for the first time sounding surprised.

"Some father," was all I groused. "If he wants to see me, he can come and find me."

Nyx grunted. "If you don't give a shit about him, then why are you here?"

I peered over my shoulder. "Because my brothers were moving. I wasn't about to stay in Utah when they were here."

"So you came for them?"

"I just said that, didn't I?" I muttered irritably.

"And do they hate Dog too?"

"I don't care enough about my father to hate him," I told him, meaning every fucking word.

He hummed under his breath, though I knew I'd surprised him again with my candor.

"But, to answer your question, no. They idolize him. Fools that they are," I mumbled, and deciding this conversation was going nowhere, I stated, "Anyway, I need to start marinating these steaks."

And with that, I dismissed him from my mind and got on with my chores.

FIVE

NYX

TWO DAYS LATER

THE KNOCK at the door had the council meeting coming to a halt. Everyone knew not to disturb us, so that someone had, made me get to my feet and walk over to open the door myself, rather than just hollering at whoever it was to fuck off.

When I saw Giulia standing there, I cocked a brow at her. "Do. Not. Disturb," I told her gruffly, pointing at the sign on the door.

"This is important," she said, sniffing at me as she barged her way into Rex's office.

Her confidence didn't surprise me. I knew she had more balls than her father, even with our limited interactions, but that she faced down the council when Dog would have been pissing in his pants had me wondering what she was up to.

"I need a Kitchen Aid mixer."

At first, I thought I hadn't heard her right.

Had she really, *truly*, just walked into a council meeting, interrupting important shit, to ask for a mixer?

When Rex's brow lowered, his scowl making his entire face darken, she blustered on, "If you want me to make pasta and cakes, then I refuse to make it for the lot of you when I don't have a stand mixer. You can't expect me to do that shit by hand."

Not unsurprisingly, Maverick's ears fucking *twitched* at that, and in his wheelchair, he straightened up and, with a hopeful tone, asked, "You want to bake us cakes?"

"Cakes are easy desserts," she replied with a huff, folding her arms across her chest in a move that was self-protective.

That move right there was the only indication it had taken her some nerve to burst in here.

I wondered why she hadn't just asked me—I was spending enough time in the kitchen with her after she dealt with the sweetbutts in her own particular way, after all.

Or was that exactly why she hadn't?

Was this her way of saying that she didn't need my input?

Ha.

I was the only one between her and the rest of the council at the moment. Everyone was sick of the sweetbutts bitching about their bruised eyes, sprained wrists, and broken noses.

Only the food she made, meals good enough to serve in a fucking restaurant, kept the guys from turning into jackals.

We weren't stupid.

We didn't bite the hand that fed, and with the few meals we'd had, we knew she was *good*. Not just good, but italics *good*.

"What kind of cakes?" Steel inquired, evidently getting in on this too.

"What is this? A bake sale?" I grumbled. "Just buy the fucking stand mixer. Why did you have to ask?"

"Well, they're expensive." She bit her bottom lip.

"How expensive?" Maverick questioned, his Treasurer side coming to the fore as he eyed her up.

I half wondered if he was about to haggle with her on the price.

"They're about six hundred dollars with all the attachments. And I need those to make pasta."

"Six hundred?" he repeated, his brow furrowing.

"Yeah." She shifted on her toes. "But it will make preparing food a lot easier—"

He raised a hand. "Buy three. If it means we get cakes and fresh pasta, buy fucking four, and I'll cover it with my own wages."

Her eyes widened at his statement, then she eyed his abs, the scars that covered his torso, and muttered, "At least I can see where you put all my meals."

Mav gaped at her. "Did you just tell me I'm fat?"

I laughed at that. "Ain't this the first time she's seen you? How would she know to compare?"

Giulia blushed. "I didn't mean that. I just... I overheard Jingles saying how you never ate before and now you do."

"Fucking women," Maverick rumbled under his breath. "Can't goddamn win. Get bitched at if I don't eat enough, get bitched at if I eat too fucking much."

"I wasn't complaining!" Giulia explained. "I was just saying it's..." She blinked. "Well, you're all very much on display, aren't you? I mean, all your muscles and things."

Steel snorted out a laugh. "I think she likes you, Mav."

The Treasurer squinted at her and, ignoring Steel, asked, "Is that what you're saying?"

"Well, I'm not calling you fat," she retorted with a huff. "Anyway, if I can get four mixers, I'll get four. I'm out of here—sorry for disrupting you."

I could have hauled her back, but I didn't. Instead, I watched her go. Her ass bounced in her jeans, and I watched the motion until the door slammed to a close.

"Maverick has an admirer."

I clenched my teeth at Storm's statement and shot him a warning look. When I realized he was staring straight back at me, I knew he'd said that to twist the knife.

Jerking my chin up, I ignored his jibe, and grated out, "Can we get back on topic here? Some of us have shit to do with the rest of our day."

Maverick sniffed. "I didn't realize she was that pretty."

Steel scratched his chin. "She was flustered. That must be a minor miracle considering every time I've seen her, she's scowling."

"Must be because she was in front of the council."

I laughed at Link's remark. "What? You think she was shaking in her shoes about that? You didn't watch her with Kendra."

"I'd probably have paid to see that shit," Maverick commented. "Can you imagine the pair of them in a kiddy's pool full of Jell-O?"

"Is this what you do with your time?" Rex retorted. "Watch weird as fuck porn?"

"Get Jingles to suck you off later," Steel advised. "It will do you a world of good."

"I don't need sucking off."

"Every man needs sucking off," I said dryly. "It keeps the world in order."

Maverick rolled his eyes. "Yeah, yeah." Then, he paused. "Do you think she meant it about baking?"

"This is what happens when you avoid sex," Link lamented. "You start appreciating food more than fucking. It's weird, man."

Maverick flipped him the bird. "I think Nyx is right. We need to get shit back on track."

The rest of the meeting didn't take long, but when I headed back out into the clubhouse, I'd admit to wanting to break something when I heard the arguing in the kitchen.

Fuck's sake.

While I was pretty sure the woman could argue with a corpse, I didn't get why the whores kept on returning to the kitchen. Why were they being possessive of a task they'd always fucking moaned about? Bitches made no goddamn sense.

But, the weirdest thing of all? More than the annoying sweetbutts and the brother's daughter who put the sass in sassy?

The strange buzz that filtered through my veins as I thought about heading into the kitchen to spar with her. Sure, it sucked having to referee a caterwauling bitch and a babe with an attitude problem, but it was almost worth it coming face to face with Giulia, and wondering what the hell she was going to say next.

One thing was for sure.

The place wasn't goddamn boring with her around.

SIX

GIULIA

THE NEXT DAY

"WHO'S CARLY?"

"Huh?"

When Steel eyed me like I'd lost my marbles, I just repeated, "Who's Carly?"

"We don't have a Carly around here."

Beside him, Link moaned as he took a bite of my pasta. "Fuck, this is good shit, Giulia. I mean, I think this might be better even than the damn steak."

Steel's brows rose. "You're kidding me. Better than the steak?"

"Yeah." As Link slurped up some more food, he moaned like he was having an orgasm, and even though I was used to hearing my brothers mid-sex, which was a level of TMI that I hoped few ever had to understand, my cheeks burned hotly at his reaction.

For the first time in my life, people were appreciating my food instead of just grunting at it or taking it for granted.

It was weird.

I liked it, liked *that* more than I liked cooking at any rate. At least it made it more bearable.

"Where's mine?" Steel demanded, eying the pots in front of me with a hungry look that had inspiration hitting me.

"You don't get any until you answer my question." I tossed the pasta that I'd boiled for sixty seconds into the frying pan. As I let it get coated in the *puttanesca* sauce, I smiled at him. "Answers for food."

"You do know that's not how shit works around here, don't you?" Steel growled, eying the bright red sauce as I flashed it in the pan, letting the homemade *sghetti* get drenched in it.

"Isn't it? Far as I can see, I have a lot of hungry mouths to feed. *First*."

He frowned. "I'm on the council!"

Link cackled. "She's got you by the balls, dude. Just answer her."

"A-Are you bribing me for my dinner?" Steel sputtered.

"Finally, he gets it." Link grinned at me. "Can I have some more sauce?"

"Sure." I reached over and ladled some into his dish. "There you go."

He moaned again when he took another bite. "This stuff... it's fishy. Why?"

"Anchovies," I explained, but my attention was on Steel. Mostly because he'd messed with me yesterday in the council meeting.

I got the feeling Link would tell me who Carly was, but messing with Steel did no harm.

As far as I could tell, he and Link were the most easygoing of the council.

At least, I was hoping that was true. Or my ass was about to be tossed out, all because I wanted to know who the fuck Carly was.

I mean, it already stung my pride that I'd been on the watch out for an Old Lady called Carly just so I could eye up Nyx's woman, but when that had revealed nothing, I knew I was left in the lurch.

I shouldn't give a shit about whether he'd claimed a bitch or not, and yet, I really fucking did. Why, when the brother was a grumpy pain in the ass, I didn't know, but tell that to the butterflies that took up residence in my stomach whenever he made an appearance.

Steel groaned. "I love anchovies."

"I know," I told him sweetly. "I heard your pizza order the other night."

That wasn't why I'd made the dish today, but it helped.

He folded his arms under his chest, and I knew he was thinking he could outwait me, so I called out, "Jingles—" God, I hated her. "I have the tray ready for Maverick."

When I thought about the brother who, from what I'd heard, hadn't left the clubhouse in years, I determined to bake him a cake all his own.

From my perusal, a perusal that had gone awry, he still needed fattening up, and if I *had* to cook, I might as well get it right.

I figured it was my service to the nation. Helping one military vet at a time.

Steel grunted as Jingles headed over and snatched the tray off the table the second I dished up the plate for the councilor. He didn't even take the opportunity to study her ass, instead, he studied me as I poured more pasta into the boiling water in front of me.

"Did you really hand make that?"

"Yeah. I did."

Because I was one part insane, and one part eager to impress.

He whistled under his breath as he watched me flash some more sauce into the pan. I was doing this individually because the councilors were served first, which meant I had ample time to torment Steel into answering me, as Nyx was usually the last one in to eat.

"There is no Carly around here," Steel explained, his gaze on the sauce.

"Nyx has an Old Lady brand on his throat—"

Link wagged a finger at me. "Nyx is off limits to little girls like you."

That had me gritting my teeth. "I'm curious."

"Been asking questions about all of us, have you?" Steel retorted, brows high in disbelief.

If my cheeks burned, then fuck it. "I'm *curious*," I repeated.

They both snorted as they shot each other a look, then Steel's smirk disappeared. "Carly's his sister. She died a long time ago."

"Oh."

I hadn't expected that answer, and it made my relief all the more awful.

It was weird to eye up a taken man, made me no better than a club-whore. Still, I mourned for Nyx, even as I wondered why I didn't remember Carly's name.

Having been raised around here, I mostly recalled the kids of my generation and the Old Ladies. Nyx was a good fourteen years older than me, which put him in a different sphere, and while I remembered his name, and knew most of the council from memory, the details were vague.

And it irked me to no end that I didn't want the details to be vague about *him*.

When Steel's dinner was ready, I put on extra sauce and muttered, "Will that buy your silence?"

Link drawled, "Yeah. From Nyx. But if you think we're not telling the rest of the council, you're dumb."

When they wandered off, equally sniggering and moaning, my lips twitched.

"What are you smiling at?"

The bark had me jerking in place, and I glowered at Nyx. Mostly because he was a dick, mostly because even though he was glaring right back at me, my stomach was in knots.

"Not a crime to smile, is it?" I sniped at him.

He studied Steel and Link's backs. "What did they want?"

"Food," I retorted waspishly. "That's why you're here, isn't it?"

Squinting at me, he folded his arms across his chest. "What are we eating today?"

"Pasta *puttanesca*," I mumbled.

When he tapped the floury Kitchen Aid mixer that stood in a place of pride on the counter, he asked, "This what you burst into our council meeting yesterday for?"

I nodded. "It makes it easier to cook."

I'd only bought one in the end, but it was bigger than the one my mom previously had in her kitchen.

"In the future, ask *me*. Don't be bothering the council with that shit."

"Since when would the Enforcer need to get involved with this stuff?" I retorted.

"Since when does snatch interrupt a council meeting?"

My cheeks burned even as I heard a kernel of truth in his statement. "I wanted an expensive piece of kit. I wanted to go straight to the council to plead my case for it." With that justified, I glared at him. "Don't you dare call me that again. I'm not—"

"You're not what?" he challenged with a smirk that made me want to throat punch him.

"Don't you dare tar me with the same label you give the other sluts around here." I sniffed at him as I tossed pasta into the water, then got to work with his sauce.

Unlike with Steel and Link, I didn't bother conversing with the prick. He'd gotten my back up. So why the fuck did I feel hot under the collar? Because I knew he was watching me? Because I could feel his eyes burning into me wherever they touched?

Jesus.

My flush had nothing to do with the heat from the stove.

But I hated that I was so weak. Weak in the face of his insults.

How could my body respond to him when my mind rejected everything that he was? Was I just a walking pussy? That fucking weak that I—

I wasn't like Mom.

I refused to be like her. Attracted to the danger, to the wildness in a brother. Enough that I left sense behind and threw caution to the wind.

When I almost threw the dish at him a couple of minutes later, I twisted instantly around so I was no longer facing him, and asked myself why my eyes were stinging with tears.

God, how stupid was I?

I heard his boots thumping against the floor, and relief filled me that he'd gone.

"Nyx is Cammie's," a voice sneered at me. "You need to back the fuck off."

"She's welcome to his disease-ridden dick," I snarled back, twisting to look at the skank I knew was called Peach—the weirdo had dyed her hair that color. "What the fuck do you want anyway?"

"Food. What else, bitch?"

I glared at her. "You can make your own." My top lip twisted into a snarl. "Unless you want me to spit in yours, that is."

I wouldn't. I wasn't *that* gross, but she didn't need to know that, and the sweetbutts all knew to act warily around me by now.

She narrowed her eyes on me. "You'll regret talking to me like this. I'm Rex's favorite."

Snorting out a laugh, I scoffed, "I regret nothing, and I regret everything."

"What does that even mean?"

"It means I don't give a shit if you're his favorite or not. Fuck off."

And with that, I returned to cooking because I still had a lot of men to feed, but I'd admit, I felt better after sniping at Peach.

Nyx's words had, for some stupid reason, cut deep and that, along with this crazy need to know more about him, was something I had to cauterize now before the damage was too late.

Before I turned into my mom, and was left with a world of regrets.

SEVEN

NYX

AS I SLAMMED my fist into the punching bag, I tried to imagine it was the weird hold Lizzie's girl had on me. It needed more than a throttling, that was for fucking sure.

"What do you want?"

I could still hear her disinterested query ringing in my ears, which still stung two fucking hours later.

I wasn't used to being dismissed, and she kept on goddamn doing it. It was not only pissing me off, it was doing something else—making my faint interest in her morph.

Ever since she'd arrived a few days ago, I'd had this strange awareness of her. I was always on edge anyway, but something about her made me worse. It was like I knew when she walked into a fucking room or something.

Sure, the bitch was hot. And yeah, I'd wanted to fuck her mom when I was a teen who thought only with his prick, and maybe Giulia made her mom look fugly—that was how goddamn gorgeous she was—but I didn't think with my cock all the time anymore—only half the fucking time—and this wasn't an option. Obsessing on a bitch like this... that wasn't how I rolled.

Slamming my fist into the heavy piece of leather-covered sand, I let the adrenaline rush through me, as well as the aggression and irritation.

I'd have preferred to be fighting some fucker but no one, except Giulia, had pissed me off today.

"If you missed breakfast, that's on you. Not me."

Nine words.

Nine. Fucking. Words.

And they couldn't have stunned me more if she'd tried.

No one said 'no' to me. No one. Except for her. And she kept on goddamn saying it.

With a couple of jabs that I followed up with an uppercut or two, I pounded on the punching bag some more, trying to figure out what it was about her that got me so riled up.

I could feel my sweat flick and bead onto the mat beneath me. All around, the air began to thicken with humidity at the perspiration I was letting fly, and as good as it felt, it wasn't enough.

It wasn't that I wanted to rain my irritation down on her. It was the fact that she pissed me off, and I still kept on heading into the kitchen for more of her insults.

From never going into the damn room to visiting at least twice a day whether or not the clubwhores were starting shit.

Things were getting weird.

Even for me.

"What's got your goat?"

I ignored Rex, who was handling some free weights like they were one of the clubwhore's tits.

How the fucker's biceps were that big when he was a pussy around dumbbells was a piece of magic, and he wasn't willing to share the spell with anyone.

"Nothing's wrong with me," I muttered, punctuating each word with a jab that made the *thwacking* noise reverberate around the custom-built gym that ran along the full length of the basement.

"You're not normally this antsy after a kill." He cocked a brow at me through the mirror on the back wall as he tightened his stance and began to pull a bicep curl. "Not for a good month or so."

I scowled at the bag. "I'm not antsy."

I'd have throat punched him if he wasn't the Prez.

Antsy?

Six-year-old girls were antsy before a piano recital.

Fifteen-year-old boys were antsy before the homecoming dance they thought their date would put out on.

I did *not* get antsy.

"Fucking antsy," I sniped, finding myself to be more pissed about that than Giulia, who was fucking with my head without even uttering more than ten words to me at a time.

What the fuck was that about?

All the bitches wanted my time. They were all vying with Cammie for a place in my bed. But Giulia just ignored me.

"Looks like it to me," Rex grumbled, then he grunted as he raised the weight, held it a second, then slowly lowered his arm. "And the punch bag attests to it."

"Who's been eating the dictionary?" Link called out from the treadmill.

Rex just snorted. "Don't buy me 'word a day' toilet paper for Christmas, and I won't have a better *lexicon* than you."

"Fucking Kendra," I groused. "No Christmas gifts this year. We're fucking outlaws. Buying Christmas gifts, my ass." I gave the punching bag a cross then another jab before I snarled, "Secret Santa was a fucking joke."

Link laughed. "I kinda liked it."

"That's because Sugar bought you a butt plug," Rex said dryly.

"Hey, can I help it that I appreciate my G-spot being massaged?"

"Nobody gives a fuck," I snapped, "until you keep mentioning it all the time."

"That's because it's a revelation. Best orgasm ever."

"I know. I'm next door. I feel like you're finding Jesus every time you get off," Storm retorted as he taped up his wrists. The sound of the tape had my ears pricking up like a bloodhound on the alert for steak.

I stopped smacking the shit out of the punching bag, only grabbing it a hairsbreadth before it connected with me. As I absorbed its momentum, I wondered how the fucker had stayed connected to the ceiling without falling off.

Maybe Rex was right.

I was on edge.

On edge.

Not fucking antsy.

I eyed Storm and asked, "You want to spar?"

"Do I look like I have a death wish?" he responded wryly. "No way in fuck am I fighting with you when you're in this mood. What's bitten you on the balls today?"

I narrowed my eyes on him. "Nothing."

"Yeah, nothing my butt plug-filled ass."

"See? What's with the fucking references to the butt plug?" I growled, before I scowled. "How the fuck can you run with that shit in there anyway?"

"Mini orgasms."

"Bullshit," Rex countered, but he eyed him through the mirror. "If I even think that's true, I'm taking your cut from you. No way do I want to be anywhere near your cum."

Link chuckled. "You were ten feet from it yesterday when I was boning Lottie on the pool table."

"That's different. I expect to be close to way too much DNA in the bar. But in here? Fuck that shit."

"That's what I told Lottie last night," Link replied with a laugh.

"If you're supposed to be putting me in a better frame of mind, you're failing. The lot of you," I grated out.

"What's wrong with wittle Nyx?" Storm mocked, making me squint at him.

"Be grateful you're too much of a pussy to spar with me."

He just grinned, but I turned away with a sniff to beat the punching bag up some more.

I tuned out the fuckers who were chatting in the gym like we were a bunch of chicks getting our hair done at the local salon, and when I was finished, I flipped them the bird and hollered, "Later," at the group of them.

Pussy-assed douchewads.

Especially Storm.

Dipshit was too much of a goddamn coward to spar with me.

Fucker.

As I strolled out of the gym, I headed upstairs to the first floor, but I paused when I heard arguing in the kitchen.

For a second, I hesitated over elbowing my way in there. For a bunch of cunts who hated cooking, the snatches were all super territorial over the fact that Giulia had taken their place. That was probably why I'd seen more of her these past few days, now that I came to think of it.

It had nothing to do with me *wanting* to visit her in the kitchen, nope, no sir, it was down to the fact I'd had more of the sweetbutts coming to me over broken noses, pulled hair, and sprained wrists after they'd gotten physical with Giulia and she'd defended herself.

Christ, I'd been dealing with them more than ever before.

Most of the whores were bitchy. That was almost a given, and something we dealt with because bitchiness was better than having to fuck our fists.

But violent? Not until recently.

Giulia might have been pint-sized, but she put Floyd Mayweather to shame when it came down to getting ready to throw a punch.

That the snatches thought I'd chastise her over the shit they pulled was a testament to the fact they knew I hated violence against women. But that meant I had more of the bitches whining at me than anyone else, and when you were the Enforcer, people whined at you a helluva lot.

I just preferred it when the brothers complained over the club snatch and not the snatch about our new cook.

The raised voices got even louder, and though Giulia was the last person I wanted to see today, especially after her dismissal this morning, I stormed into the kitchen and glared at the four sluts who were eying Giulia like she was prey.

And they said the males were the deadlier of the species.

Right.

Rubbing my hand over my hair, I took in the fact that though Tink, Lottie, JoJo, and Enya looked on the brink of pouncing, Giulia was handling her knife in a way that told me she wasn't above slicing and dicing.

Because that made my cock ache, I shoved down the thought of her using that knife with intent, and ground out, "Why the fuck am I having to umpire shit between you again?"

Giulia's eyes flared wide. "I haven't done shit! I'm trying to make a fucking pot roast for dinner, and these fucking skanks come in here, acting like the Big. I. Am as though they rule the goddamn roost—"

I held up a hand to stop the tirade which, in fairness, had been somewhat deserved, because I'd sounded as though I was blaming her when I wasn't.

Centering my attention on Tink, I scowled at her. "I want it known that you need to back the fuck off of Giulia, Tink. I'm sick of this shit, and I don't need you starting crap either."

"She's hurting the girls," the other woman whined, and I only put up with that tone of voice due to the fact that she was the oldest and the de facto leader of the clubwhores.

I hated whiners.

With a fucking passion.

Gripping the back of my neck, and praying for patience, I stated, "No more of this shit. Giulia is defending herself against the sweetbutts who come in here looking for trouble. As far as I'm aware, anyway, you bitches hated cooking, so why the hell you're arguing over this—"

"It's the principle," Enya hissed.

"What principle?" I growled, a tic pinging at the muscles at the side of my mouth. She gulped at the sight, aware I was pissed at being interrupted.

"She gets paid." Lottie ducked her head to avoid my scowl.

"So?"

Giulia smirked. "I think they're pouting that I get paid for my job, whereas they have to suck dick and fuck ugly bastards like you for room and board."

The other women drew in a breath, but there was anticipation in their eyes, an anticipation that was founded in the belief they thought I was going to ream her a new one.

Instead, I focused on them and explained, "She's Dog's daughter. She isn't a slut like you. Fuck off out of here, and the next time you question the Prez's word or order, I'll make sure he knows about it."

When they scampered off, I didn't watch them go. Even if Enya was wearing a G-string that I knew from experience framed her butt to perfection, I kept my focus on the pain in *my* ass who'd been getting under my skin since she'd arrived.

What with her scowls, her perfect goddamn food, and an attitude worse than mine, she had no right to be getting under my skin at all.

She eyed me right back as I stared at her, unashamed, unflinching. Fuck, she had balls. Maybe that was why she had mine in a twist.

Every time I thought of her slamming Kendra's face into the counter or spraining JoJo's wrist, I'd get a hard-on. How couldn't I?

The demon in me that liked shedding blood appreciated her willingness to defend herself.

Instead of moaning about the sluts who were trying to make shit difficult for her, instead of coming crying to me like they were, she handled shit.

She didn't need me to protect her.

And fuck if that didn't make me want to protect her more.

It was a paradox worthy of a square on Rex's 'word of the day' toilet roll.

"If you're done staring," she sneered, "I have vegetables to prep."

"You have a shitty attitude," I informed her, careful to keep my tone bland.

She shrugged. "It's twenty-four years in the making."

"Can't teach old dogs new tricks?" I retorted helpfully.

A sniff escaped her. "You wanna call me a bitch, just let it rip."

I shrugged back at her. "Bitch." I let the 'B' pop. I peered at the counter, saw all the detritus on there, and inquired, "You need help in here?" It was only then that I realized how much work it was to feed us.

Storm had been in charge of scheduling, and I knew for a fact he had four to five girls making meals at any given time, yet here we were, expecting her to do it on her own.

"I prefer to be alone."

I frowned at that. "There's no point in doing it all and running yourself—"

She frowned back, and somehow, was still beautiful. But, for all that she was a joy on the eyes, her fucking personality was more like vinegar than honey. It was no wonder the only people I ever saw her talking to were her brothers.

"Have you seen those women?" she demanded, breaking into thoughts I had no right to be having over her. "I floss my teeth with strings bigger than the ones they have between their butt cheeks. It's a wonder you didn't have pubes floating around in the food you ate."

My stomach began to ache from just how serious she was and how hard I wanted to laugh.

Me.

Who never fucking laughed.

"Let me get this straight... You won't ask for help for hygiene reasons?"

"Damn straight. Only fuck knows what they're carrying." She sniffed. "In fact, you should get out of the kitchen too before your bacteria floats into my food. Once it's in the dining hall, it's No Man's Land."

"That's twice you've insulted me today."

She didn't flinch at my cool tone. "Then that's two times too few." When I saw her swallow, I knew she was all show. If she'd had an Adam's apple, it'd have been bobbing at that.

Because I could appreciate her front, I hitched a shoulder. "You saw how they reacted when you insulted me the first time."

"I did."

"Yet you repeated the insult." I reached up and rubbed my chin. "You must have been hell on your mom."

For the first time, she reacted—jerking back as though I'd hit her. Instantly, she twisted around, giving me her back. Not to piss me off further, but to hide her expression from me.

Scowling at the sight, especially when I knew she was upset about my referencing her mom and not the fact that all the sluts knew to watch my temper, I sighed. Hurting her by reminding her of her mom hadn't been my intention.

For a second, I just stood there, hovering.

Me.

Fucking hovering.

What in hell was even happening here?

I tried not to think about the fact that if she was any other bitch, I'd have stormed out of there. Instead, with her, I wanted to wrap an arm around her goddamn shoulder and ask her if she was okay.

Okay.

Fuck me.

Since when did I even care how anything with a vagina was?

Because it was a concerning development, since I didn't give a shit about anything other than my club, I just muttered, "If it gets to be too much, get a Prospect in. They can't fuck the sweetbutts, so they should be clean enough for your standards."

I didn't wait for her to reply, just got the fuck out of there.

Because if that sniff I heard as I left was her crying then I really would have to go over to her, and...

My jaw clenched as I thought about the last female I'd comforted, and when I thought about how shit had turned out for Carly, that made me want to start planning my thirtieth tattoo, not just my twenty-ninth.

❖

EIGHT

STORM

"HE'S got the hots for her."

I snorted at Rex. "You only just figured that out?" Arching a brow at him when he glared at me, I just flexed my hands in the tape before I contemplated putting on some gloves.

The last thing I wanted to do was work out, but it was the only way I had to beat off this aggression. There was only so much sex a man could have before it started feeling empty, before it started feeling like he was goddamn procrastinating.

And that, right there, was proof I was thirty-seven and not twenty-fuck-ing-seven.

Jesus fuck, I hadn't given a shit back then about how often or who I'd fucked, just so long as I'd gotten my dick wet. Now? Things were different. I was supposed to have a goddamn Old Lady to slake my thirst on, instead, she was the one behind my goddamn frustrations in the first place.

"I figured it out when I saw him daring her to watch while he practically chewed Cammie's face off."

I blinked at him. "And they say romance is dead."

Link chuckled. "It is in this place."

I shook my head at the weirdo with a butt plug up his ass while he went for a jog. "Doesn't have to be. But the way to a woman's goddamn heart isn't to have a bitch suck your dick or chew your mouth off while your boo is watching."

"Boo's a little strong, isn't it? They barely interact!" Rex countered, frowning at me in the mirror.

"Sometimes it's in a look not a conversation." I swallowed at how fucking real that was.

Back in the day, that was all it had taken for me and Keira. A long look, and I'd known where she was at, how she was feeling, what was going on with her.

That was how I'd felt sure she was supposed to be mine.

That a single glance at her could be loaded with such meaning had made me feel sure that things were different with her.

Now, even after all the crap, I couldn't say that didn't hold true. She was mine, always fucking would be. Convincing her of that might be a difficult feat, but I was slowly coming to the realization that life without her was—

"Storm?"

I gaped at my Prez. "What?"

"You doing okay, man? You were just standing there, staring into space."

Link snorted. "Maybe he was checking out your ass."

"Since when was I into guys?"

"I dunno, but you've been a dipshit of late. Maybe you're into compounding your mistakes by coming onto Rex."

Gradually, with each word uttered, my eyes widened until I was pretty fucking sure I couldn't look more stunned if I tried.

Link snickered at me. "Cat got your tongue?"

"No, but it should have yours," Rex ground out, glaring at Link. "Where the fuck is your head at talking to him that way?"

Link shrugged. "You try dealing with a call at four AM from someone's Old Lady..."

"What?" My entire body grew tense at what Link was inferring. "My Keira called you?"

Link let the treadmill slow down, and as it whined to a halt, he grabbed his water and took a deep sip. All the while, he milked the fucking attention until I wanted to rip off his goddamn head.

"Funny how she's your Keira when—"

Rex was suddenly there, his hand on my shoulder, holding me back. "You know not to fuck around with Old Ladies, Link," he grated out, shooting me a concerned glance.

"Fucking around with them?" Link frowned. "Fuck you, Rex. She was upset."

"Why was she?"

"Apparently over something she didn't feel comfortable talking about with you." He sniffed. "What she told me in confidence can't be repeated."

I narrowed my eyes at him. "Are you looking to have your ass kicked?"

"You could fucking try," Link snapped. He folded his arms across his chest, his sweat-flecked biceps bunching as he tensed them. "Get your head out of your ass, man. That's all I'm saying."

"You have no right to make any opinion about what I do."

"I have every right when Keira's the one calling me."

My gut churned at that. Why would Keira call another brother? I'd never realized they were close. Hell, Keira had never spent all that much time here. None of the Old Ladies did. Mostly because of the sweetbutts...

Okay, that was the only reason.

I didn't really blame them. As great as it was for the brothers to have pussy on tap, and to have a walking strip show wherever we went, for the Old Ladies, it wasn't exactly a fun time, was it?

I knew they had their own get-togethers. Parties or some such that they held every week at their homes, but Link wouldn't have been invited, would he? The entire point was to be in a brother-free zone, wasn't it?

"I can see I got your mind ticking over," he said dryly, "but as always, Storm, you don't see the trees for the fucking woods."

Rex huffed. "It's the other way around."

"It doesn't matter," Link argued. "Either way, it's right. He's focusing on the fact that she called me, that I'm the one she spoke with, not the fact she was crying."

"Mostly because you threw it down like a goddamn gauntlet to make him jealous, dumb fuck." Rex squeezed my arm. "What's going on with you, Storm?"

"Nothing."

Rex scoffed, "Keira kicked you out months ago. You've been fucking everything that moved ever since."

"You'd better not have fucking told Keira that," I snarled at Link, concerned over what my brother had told my Old Lady when everything that went down on the compound was sacrosanct.

"Like she doesn't already know." He arched a brow at me. "In fact, I think she might be getting some action of her own. Last time I visited her and Cyan, she was talking about a date."

My blood surged in my veins until I could hear my pulse throbbing in my ears.

Keira was fucking dating? I'd heard or seen nothing about that.

What had started out as a break, just some time to get our heads together, had morphed into something else.

Something that had me fearing there'd be no getting back together. No resolving our differences.

Christ.

What the hell had we done?

We should never have taken a break, never put distance between us. How the fuck could we fix things if she was in our family house and I was staying here at the compound?

I wasn't ashamed to admit that I felt shaky. Shaky as fuck. For a moment, Rex was the only thing keeping me upright, and I knew he knew it because he muttered, "It's okay, bud. You can still fix things."

My jaw clenched. "How can I if she's fucking someone else?"

"You've been fucking all the sweetbutts," Link pointed out, ever goddamn helpful. "Do they matter to you?"

"Keira isn't like me. She doesn't sleep around unless it matters."

"Maybe she changed." He shrugged. "You can't condemn her when you've done much worse."

While he was right, I wanted to.

How fucking dare she be dating some fucker when she was mine?

Like he felt the aggression surge inside me, Rex put both his hands on my shoulders and ground out, "Calm the fuck down, Storm. Don't do anything rash. You make another mistake, and it's all it will take for this break to become permanent."

Because he was right, I backed off, backed down. But I still felt like I was torn between puking and ripping off either Link's head or the head of the guy Keira was seeing.

I pulled back and staggered toward the wall so I could lean against it. As the bare brick cut into my skin, I let it ground me. For a while, I stared ahead, not really looking at anything, not even thinking all that much.

Thinking *hurt*.

Had I lost Keira?

Forever?

I scrubbed a hand over my face, and in that second, Link was there. Pushing his fucking luck as per goddamn usual.

"Link," Rex warned, but the faint clank of the weights told me he'd gone back to working out.

"What?" he sniped, just on the border between insolence and respect for Rex's station. "I'm telling him to pull his head out of his ass. We should have done it a while ago."

With his attention split, I let it rip.

A single punch let some of my aggression flow free and had Link coughing up his guts as he cradled his stomach.

I didn't surge forward, though. Didn't flow into a fight. I'd just needed to pay the SOB back for telling me this the way he had.

Link glowered at me, and the fact he didn't come after me and that Rex didn't stop what he was doing, told me they knew I wasn't going to take this further.

I was well within my rights. A brother knew not to fuck with another man's Old Lady. He should've known not to get in between them too, but Link couldn't keep his nose out of shit.

"Why was she upset?"

"Some kid in Cyan's class is picking on her."

My eyes flared wide. "She's being bullied?" I blurted out. Why the fuck hadn't Keira told me that?

"Don't get your panties in a twist," Link grumbled.

"No? My woman calls you about my kid being bullied, and you don't think I should be pissed off?"

"He has a point," Rex said.

"You're so helpful." Link winced as he straightened up. Rubbing his gut, he glared at me as he said, "They weren't tears of sadness. They were angry tears."

Either way, they were tears. My woman was crying. And she didn't think she could come to me.

More than anything, that made me feel surer than ever that we were over.

If she couldn't share her sadness, and wouldn't share her anger, then what the fuck were we?

Nothing.

That's what.

I ground my teeth as agony speared me in the chest.

Holy fuck, it hurt.

It hurt so fucking bad.

More than when she'd made the suggestion in the first place. More than when I'd sunk my dick into a pussy I didn't even want, but had used to alleviate some of my frustrations at a situation I hadn't even proposed.

I couldn't stop myself from sinking down into a crouch, because suddenly, the world just felt like it was all too much, and my life was crashing in around me without me even being able to do anything about it.

"Storm, go to her, man. Stop this shit."

Link's earnestness rang true then. He'd been trying to help. All along, that had been his intent.

But...

"It's too late for that," I rasped.

"It's never too late, and if you don't do something now, then you're a bigger fucking asshole than I already thought." From being earnest to being disgusted, it hadn't taken much to morph Link's opinion.

But I ignored it and him and just focused on the perspiration-dotted mat around the punchbag Nyx had been reaming a new one. The same urge hit me.

Nyx had been working off his frustrations of feelings he didn't understand. I knew my brother. Nyx and emotions weren't alien, but where a woman was concerned, they were. He was used to saving their butts, keeping them secured and out of danger, but that was easy. He didn't have to care about the individual woman. Didn't need to think about her hopes and dreams, her wants and needs.

He could be selfish.

Could lock himself down and never let anyone in.

But, for all the pain in the ass that she was, Giulia wasn't like that.

I knew because I knew what it felt like to fall. I knew the signs, and I was seeing them in Nyx and Giulia. In the sniping and the bitching, in the glares and hot stares when they didn't think the other was looking.

That had been me and Keira back in the day. Back before it had all gone wrong.

Heart in my throat, I got my equilibrium back, but the second I could stand without falling over, I toddled over to the punch bag on shaky legs and, ignoring the weakness in my bones, beat the shit out of the equipment.

It didn't help, but it was better than hunting down the fucker Keira was trying to replace me with and gutting him.

❖

NINE

GIULIA

FUCK, I hated this place.

I really, truly did.

It was everything I remembered loving as a kid, but it was somehow worse as an adult.

As a little girl, it had been somewhere to escape my mom and dad's constant arguing. There'd been a play area, and I'd been able to hang around with my friends all the time.

As a woman, I just saw everything my mom had despised about the clubhouse, and understood, totally, why she'd left. Seeing my brothers get absorbed in everything, pretty much like my father, made me glad Mom couldn't see them, and it made me regret all the times I'd given her shit for making us leave.

Nyx had been spot on.

I *had* been a pain in the ass to my mom. I'd railed and rebelled and given her nothing but shit. Fuck, no wonder...

My throat closed as I thought about her heart attack. About how we'd argued the day before, and I'd slammed the fucking phone down on her like the bitch I was.

My last words to my mom were hateful, and there was no getting away from that. No getting over it either.

I pulled in a breath because I felt like I was suffocating, felt like I couldn't get any air into my lungs, and then, he was there.

Awkward, but there.

I wanted to pull back, jerk out of his hold. I'd heard him head out of the kitchen, had thought I had some privacy, but no. He was there. The scent of him was overwhelming.

Sure, it was sweat, but it was clean sweat. And, unlike a lot of the bastards around here, he didn't stink of the beer that was seeping out of his pores in the aftermath of a heavy drinking session the night before.

When his arm slipped around my shoulders, I didn't think anything of turning into him. I didn't know why, wasn't even sure why I hadn't slammed my foot into his instep... okay, so I knew.

Because it was Nyx.

I knew it without having to look.

Anyone else, and I'd have done worse than slam my heel into their instep. I'd have kneed them in the fucking balls.

But...

Nyx...

He was the one who tended to come into the kitchen when the harpies from hell were whimpering over my attacks. He never shouted at me, just shot me an impatient glare, and usually sided with me in the end. He called me out on my shit, but he never got nasty. Not even when I talked crap and gave him more snark than I should.

There was something about him.

Something hot, sure, but more than that. Something that I liked.

He was a dick.

I'd seen his cock already because that fucking Cammie slut was always chewing on it like a dog with a goddamn bone, and he was mean and snarled a lot, but— *But what?*

I didn't know, but it didn't stop me from turning into him, sweat be damned, and pressing my face into the tee he'd donned since he'd left the kitchen the first time. I appreciated the gesture, but when my tears soaked into the fabric, I whispered, "I'm sorry."

He didn't reply. I didn't expect him to. He was a man of few words, and that was something I'd seen from not just watching him around the place, but also from his forays into the kitchen too.

He got more done with a glare than most guys did with a yell, and I appreciated that. After a childhood of hearing my parents shout at one another, I hated guys who yelled. It was an instant red card to a boyfriend who, during a fight, raised his voice.

I shuddered, thinking about how cruel I was with words because of that. I didn't even raise the volume when I wanted to be cutting. I just said the meanest shit.

"Mom died thinking I hated her," I murmured, not wanting to explain, and also not wanting him to think I was a pussy.

I got the vibe that he appreciated how strong I was, and sure, I was, but I was a pathetic priss too sometimes.

"We'd argued the day before she had her heart attack, and—"

"She didn't die thinking you hated her," he replied, his voice gravelly but free from expression.

Hell, his entire *being* was free from expression. He wasn't even holding me. Not really. He was standing there and letting me drape myself over him.

And, God help me, I appreciated that he was letting me be his scarf, because I was literally clinging to his neck.

I'd be ashamed tomorrow, as it was, I could hear my mom's voice in my ear, and I just felt like a bitch.

"How do you know that?" I whispered.

"Because when she was here, Lizzie did nothing but raise hell. I highly doubt that changed in death."

"We were mean to each other," I admitted.

"What about?" He hesitated. "You don't have to tell me that."

I sensed he regretted his curiosity getting the better of him, and because he regretted it, and being the contrary bitch that I was, I muttered, "She was giving me shit."

"About what?"

"She said by my age, she had a man and my brothers."

He snorted. "That's it?"

"Yeah, that's it." I pulled back so I could scowl at him. "This isn't nineteen eighty-five. A woman doesn't have to be shackled at fucking eighteen to feel like she's hit the peak of her life."

"Never said she did, but I'm laughing because I agree."

That was laughing?

He wasn't exactly rolling on the floor pissing himself, just a little snort and a twitch of his lips constituted full-blown amusement?

It felt like an eye-opening moment, so I just blinked at him for a second. "Anyway, I was tired of her shit, and I gave her a double dose back."

Another snort. "Why doesn't that surprise me?"

I sniffed. "I take after her in most things."

"Yeah. I know." When his eyes dropped to my tits, I wanted to die.

Jesus.

Was he comparing my tits with my mom's?

I covered my face with my hands. "Don't tell me you had a crush on my mom when she was here."

He cleared his throat, and that was answer enough.

"Great. Just fucking great."

I twisted back around to avoid his stare because, sure enough, I'd inherited my mom's massive tits, except fate had granted me a bigger set by one cup size and a round ass.

Motherfucker.

Literally.

"I'm okay now," I said woodenly.

"I didn't mean to hurt you," he blurted out. "I was only commenting on the fact your attitude is bigger than your—"

"Don't you dare say my boobs," I hissed.

"Do I look like I have a death wish?" he grumbled. "Look, can we not focus on your breasts?"

That had me blinking, because whatever word I expected him to say, *that* wasn't it.

Hooters? Sure. Melons? Maybe. Breasts? Nah.

"I wasn't. You were. You were thinking I'm like my mom, well, I don't spread my legs for bikers."

His nostrils flared at that, and when he took a step forward, I wasn't sure whether to be scared or turned on. My heart began to pound, and my throat felt thick as I stared at him, aware that I'd awoken a beast I wasn't sure I knew how to handle, and then, someone blurted out, "Giulia, I'm hungry."

It took me a second to realize it was my brother. He was the only one who would ask me for food outside of mealtimes, because North thought the sun rose and set on him, and because he was the apple of our mother's eye, he usually thought he could get away with shit with me.

He was wrong.

I wasn't sure if my throat worked or not, but I managed to garble, "There's a fridge over there. You can open the door and make yourself something to eat."

"You know I like your BLTs."

My eyes were still on Nyx's, still trained on him, and his on me, and fuck me, if my body wasn't singing with adrenaline. I felt like the proverbial deer in the headlights, only, a part of me wouldn't mind getting rammed down.

My cheeks flushed, and my entire body felt overheated, and then, he threw water on the flames by stating, "I think I could go for a BLT too."

And if there was one rule I was picking up on, it was that I couldn't push my luck with the council, even if I had more leeway than the club-whores because I fed them good stuff. But at that moment, I figured my luck had run dry.

So, even though the last thing I wanted to do was make my dick brother a sandwich, I shuffled away from Nyx's fiery hot stare and headed to the refrigerator I'd just directed North to so I could pull out the fixings for a BLT.

All the while, I felt as though I'd had a close call, so why the hell I was disappointed was something I'd have to figure out later.

When my lungs weren't burning as though I'd run a race.

TEN

STEEL

THROUGH THE CLOUD of smoke that always permeated the bar area, I watched the showdown with interest.

"Can't believe he didn't bring Katy to meet her," Cruz muttered from behind the bar.

I shook my head. "Old Ladies don't come to this kind of event."

"And that's exactly what's wrong with the MC."

"What do you mean?"

"I mean, look at this place."

I frowned at him but took a quick peek around the vicinity. As far as I could tell, everything looked normal, and because Cruz was usually too pie-eyed to walk in a straight fucking line, I had to wonder what he was seeing and what I was missing.

Over by the pool table, Jingles was...

"Is she plopping pool balls out of her ass?"

"Seeing is believing," Cruz drawled, but he wasn't as pious as he'd like me to believe.

He was semi-watching that show as well. Jingles was crouched into a squat, her toes curled around the side of the pool table as she looked out onto the crowd.

Every few seconds, a dull thud was proof that a pool ball had popped out into the world and onto the green baize.

As impressive a feat as it was, I still said, "Remind Jingles to fucking Lysol the shit off those things."

Sin, at my side, snorted. "Literally."

When I carried on with my perusal, I saw that Dog's girl was either trying really hard not to look at Jingle's display which, of course, went down totally naked, or fighting to avoid her father's intent glare from the other end of the bar.

As far as I knew, the twins had greeted their father like the prodigal sons returned. Everyone was chattering like old hens about how the girl, Giulia, had more of her mother's fire than anything else, because she hadn't said a word to her pa.

As I scrubbed a hand over my chin, I saw I wasn't the only one watching Giulia.

Nyx was too.

That didn't come as much of a surprise as it might have done usually. It was getting quite clear to everyone that Giulia fascinated Nyx. That was the only way we knew how to describe it.

Nyx had obsessive habits, and Giulia, for whatever reason, was catching his eye.

He'd be boning her soon.

If I didn't think Nyx would garrote me, I'd have put bets on it.

"He's noticed you looking at him," Cruz muttered as he poured a few shots of tequila into waiting empty glasses.

Because he was right, I smirked at Nyx who narrowed his eyes at me in warning, then took a look at a few of the guys who'd lit up a couple of joints and were busy giggling over Jingle's asshole.

From there, I saw two large clusters of very drunk bikers arguing about whether the Knicks could make it all the way this year, and another set bitching about the Patriots.

It all looked very normal to me—well, except for the scene by the pool table. There was nothing normal about that. Not in any way, shape, or form.

"You see it yet?"

"See what?" I groused at Cruz.

"That the only women here are fucking clubwhores."

"So? It's a party. We drink, we fuck, we party."

"Yeah, but our women are supposed to be here, aren't they?"

That had me squinting at him. "You ain't even got a woman."

"No, I don't. Not at the moment."

"Anyway, there are town bitches over there," I pointed out, eying the fancy snatch who definitely didn't belong here.

Sin, wiping off Tink's pussy juices from his fingers onto his jeans, froze when one of the fancy bitches eyed him like he was a sirloin steak.

Unsurprisingly, he got to his feet and stormed after her when she made to leave.

"Like they count." Cruz sniffed at me. "But none of the Old Ladies are ever around. You seen that yet, dipshit?"

When I thought about it, I knew he was right. Growing up around this place with most of the council, the Old Ladies had been an inherent part of the compound. Always there to watch over the kids, always there to keep things semi in line. They cooked and cleaned, and the clubwhores usually stayed in the bar area, rarely allowed to leave unless it was to go to the bedrooms.

Now I thought about it, the Old Ladies had stopped with the cooking and cleaning duties back when Rex's mom had died about eight years ago. Rene's death had been the precursor to a *lot* of changes, though, so it was no wonder that had fallen under the net.

She'd been killed in a hit-and-run, and Bear, her Old Man, hadn't been able to cope with her death. That was why he'd retired earlier and Rex had taken over the position about fifteen years too young.

Without Rene, shit had changed, and apparently, not for the better.

Because most of the council were single, it figured we hadn't noticed things weren't going in the right direction. But a few of the brothers were with Old Ladies now, and I barely knew them.

Digger's bitch, the reason we were getting so many epic contracts from New York, had hardly been around the clubhouse. Then Keira, Storm's woman, had never hung out around here all that much either, when I came to think of it.

"What made you come up with this?"

Cruz, apparently seeing that I'd recognized what he had, shrugged. "Noticed it a few weeks ago. Weird, isn't it?"

"It's not like when we grew up," I agreed, then grimaced. "Nothing's like back then. Nothing at all."

"Rene's death changed shit."

"Bound to," I pointed out, but it was definitely food for thought.

What was more food for thought? Watching Nyx shrug Cammie off— the bitch truly had a vacuum for a mouth—and slouch over to the bar.

Not right beside Giulia, but close to her.

Close enough for my brows to rise.

"Want a shot, Nyx?" I asked, slinking closer to the action. Not just because I wanted to listen in, which I did, but because I wanted to monitor the sitch as well.

Nyx was a dark motherfucker. We all were in our own way, but Nyx?

Nah, he was one of the darkest. He had more monsters in his closet than would give a five-year-old nightmares, and they tortured him.

I'd never really known a man as tortured as Nyx be so high-functioning. Of course, I wasn't sure if it could be considered high-functioning, considering he had to keep killing pedophiles, but fuck, we all had to have a hobby, didn't we?

"I'm not drinking," Nyx rumbled, staring at me like I'd grown a pair of horns.

I knew why. Nyx didn't drink. Unless it was the party after a kill.

"First time for everything."

"I imagine Nyx has very few first times still remaining," Giulia inserted snidely, her finger running around the rim of the Coke can she was drinking from.

"You'd be surprised," Nyx groused, glowering at her to which she, of course, instantly glowered back.

Because I was amused, I sank back against the counter, just in earshot but away from their attention—this was going to be a good show.

Nyx, for all that he looked pissed, had an energy about him that hadn't been there just a few seconds before.

His eyes were bright, even if they were narrowed at Giulia, and he looked... fuck, he looked excited.

I'd seen him look like that for only a couple of reasons. The moments before we set off on a run and headed off to slay one of his demons, and another? When he went off and did something batshit like bungee jump or something. He didn't do that often, though, because it involved heavy travel, and the club wasn't often able to spare him.

Last time, he'd gone canyoneering in Bali, and before and after, he'd been walking around like there was air beneath his feet.

As it was, the air around him was charged. And the fucked up thing was that Giulia was just as bad. She'd been staring into her Coke like it held all the answers to life itself, anything, I figured, to avoid looking at her father, but now, she was just as buzzing.

It was painful to behold in a strange way.

Nice, too, but painful.

It was earnest and honest.

A simple connection.

Like looking at something before the promise it held had a chance to be born.

The poetical thought had me wincing, because my flowery days were long gone, but still, I saw something in them that had my heart aching.

It'd been a long time since I'd given enough of a fuck about a woman to give two hoots about what she did, but at that moment, I realized what I'd been missing out on.

Of course, they had to spoil my musing by sniping at one another, which, I swiftly realized, was their version of foreplay.

"What you ignoring your dad for?"

"Because he's a dick." Giulia's lips curved. "Takes one to know one."

"That mean you have a cock, then? Suddenly, everything makes so much sense," Nyx retorted.

My lips twitched as Giulia reached down and adjusted herself. "Shit, my secret is out. Yes, I have a dick, and I warn you, I know how to use it."

"Now, that's just frightening," North, her brother, retorted at her side. But he was snickering. "Trust me, Nyx, she doesn't have a dick, but balls? Yeah. She's got them."

"A dickless set of balls?" Nyx shuddered. "Sounds revolting."

"Sounds like I could kick your ass," she countered, her tone sweeter than honey.

"Nyx might look docile, but he's a bear with a sore paw."

"Bet I could still knock him on his ass," she said proudly.

Even though I knew for a fact that Nyx would be pissed at anyone else making this claim, he looked just as amused as every other brother in the place who was near enough to listen. And amused on Nyx just looked fucking *weird*. Like the sky being green weird, or bread tasting like fucking flowers weird.

Just *wrong*.

"Yeah? We'll have to spar sometime."

"Spar?" Her brow puckered. "I don't do shit like that." She made it sound like it was dirty.

Laughing, I hooted, "Your face. He wasn't asking to fuck you."

"I didn't think he was," she sniped. "But I ain't about to fight in no ring or something. You bastards would watch and take fucking bets." She wagged a finger at me. "You forget, I was raised around you dicks. I know how this works.

"I'd lose to Nyx in the first round, and then you'd have me fighting some of the club sluts in the next." She huffed and folded her arms under her tits, plumping them up, and if I happened to notice, then that was between me and God.

And Nyx, apparently.

Considering his glower at me.

If he was trying to keep his feelings on the downlow, then he was failing. At least, he was if he wanted to keep it from the people who gave a shit about him, because to us, he was transmitting—loud and fucking clear—that Giulia was hands off.

"I can see it now. You tossing fucking Jell-O at us, and me in a wet white tee and G-string."

Nyx blinked. "This sounds like your fantasy, not mine."

She wrinkled her nose. "Fantasy? That sounds like a fantasy? What kind of woman do you think I am? Watching you and Steel kick the shit out of each other... now that's my cup of tea."

With a snort, I poured myself a glass of tequila and sank it back. "Everyone knows to avoid fighting with Nyx. Unless you want your nose reset, of course."

She sniffed. "Well, that's no fun, is it?"

"Your idea of fun and mine are completely relative," I said dryly.

"She always was a twisted little bitch."

Dog's doom-and-gloom declaration sank like a mine into the ocean. As much as we'd been cutting with one another, his words, his tone, were different.

He was staring into his tumbler of scotch, his focus on that, which was his first mistake. If he'd seen the power of Nyx's glare, then he'd have known to shut the fuck up.

Instead, he compounded his idiocy by grumbling, "I should have taken her in hand when she was a girl."

"Shame you were too busy back here at the clubhouse fucking everything in a skirt."

Giulia's mockery was powerful. Mostly because she wasn't hurt. Not one bit by what her daddy had said in public.

If anything, her brother looked uncomfortable, not Giulia, which told me they weren't about to attend no daddy and daughter dance any time soon.

Even if Giulia was about eight years too old for that shit.

"If your mom hadn't been such a—"

"Dog, you shut your fucking mouth," Nyx growled.

Seeing the danger that was about to hit the bar, and knowing that I'd be the one who'd end up having to fix the fucker if Nyx started on Dog—the last time I'd fixed the counter was because Nyx had grabbed the bar stools and hit some brothers over the head with them, inadvertently destroying the thick wooden countertop—I glared at Dog, "If you ain't got nothing nice to say, then don't say anything at all."

"What is this? Sunday School?" Dog retorted, glaring back at me, which told me he'd had one too many fucking drinks, because even though I was one of the lighthearted councilors, everyone knew not to piss me off.

I was called Steel for a reason, after all.

Nyx wasn't the only one with a steel plate in his skull.

"You want to watch your fucking mouth?" I hissed at him. "Dumb fuck," I carried on, watching as he sniffed, then heaved himself off the counter and slouched off to watch the show at the pool table.

Looked like Jingles no longer had any balls up her ass, but that wasn't stopping Link from loading her up again. Weirdo was obsessed with all things butt.

In fact... I made a mental note to ask him if he'd been the one to put the damn balls in her ass in the first place.

Nyx watched Dog go, glaring at him all the while, and North earned his glare next by muttering, "Why you always got to get him mad, Giules?"

Now, she looked sad. Nothing about what her father said had hurt her, but North's disapproval? Yeah, that hit her. Hard.

"I only have to breathe to piss him off," she rasped, shoving off and away from the bar to get to her feet. "Thanks for the... entertainment, guys." Her mouth twisted in a wry smile as she pushed away and made to move from the bar.

Only, when she did, she collided with Nyx, who'd moved directly into her path. Nothing Nyx did was accidental, I knew him well enough to know that, but seeing was really fucking believing.

Sweet fuck, the sparks that pretty much exploded into being reminded me of sheet metal being cut. And when they looked at each other, Jesus, it made me want to grab a pen and start writing shit I hadn't wanted to write in a real long time.

As far as I knew, the two of them just carried on sniping at one another. Just arguing and the like. But it figured that would be Nyx's idea of flirtation.

A smile twisted my lips at the thought, then they twisted harder when North stared at his sister with confusion.

Giulia was looking up into Nyx's face, her head tilted back as she peered deeply into his eyes. It was a vulnerable moment for both of them, and it touched me. Yeah, *me*. The guy who usually helped Nyx when he was slaughtering his demons.

Even killers had hearts.

Not big ones, maybe, but mine was there. Still beating away.

Still waiting...

Giulia swallowed, her eyelashes swooping down to shield her eyes. "Night, Nyx."

"Night, Giulia," he repeated, his voice husky.

She licked her lips before darting around him and heading on out. For a second, I didn't say anything, I didn't need to. Then Nyx's gaze caught mine, and I saw the panic in them.

The recognition.

I smiled at him. Not to agitate him, not to irritate him, but to calm him.

What he was feeling was probably the most normal thing he'd ever felt in his fucking life, and Jesus, I wanted something normal for my suffering brother, something that would make shit better, that would ease his ever-present guilt.

Nyx blew out a breath at the sight of my smile, then he nodded, before twisting back around to return to his seat. When Cammie tried to climb onto his lap, he growled something at her that had her scampering away, and amid the chaos of the party, he just sat there, staring into space.

Nyx wasn't someone who was easy to understand, and most didn't bother.

But then, I wasn't most people, was I?

Not even Nyx knew about our connection, and if I had it my way, he never fucking would.

ELEVEN

NYX

TWO DAYS LATER

I'D HOPED that things would change after that *look* two nights ago, but Giulia had been back on fighting form the morning after. So much so that her pisspoor attitude was impossibly worse, to the point where it was actually starting to amuse me.

As well as irritate me into doing shit I'd normally never do.

Having never been dismissed so much in my entire fucking life, and never having been insulted as much, not since I first earned my cut at any rate, I had to admit to being intrigued by the little bitch.

That first steak meal she'd made for us with two types of potatoes, two types of sauce, and two types of veggies had satisfied every brother on the council, and as I'd savored the good grub, along with every other meal she made being pure gold, it was evident that everyone was going to be A-Okay with her staying on and cooking.

After the dog crap the sweetbutts tried to pass off as food, it was safe to say that everyone was a lot more cheerful in the light of what she was feeding us.

This week, we'd had everything from a casserole that melted in my fucking mouth to a goddamn cherry pie that, aside from being delicious, had stained her lips a cherry pink.

A pink I wanted to lick off that smart-assed mouth of hers.

What was it Jerry Hall had said about marriage?

A good wife should be a lady in the living room, a slut in the bedroom, and a chef in the kitchen?

Well, some crap like that.

All I knew was that I didn't need a fucking lady, but a slut and a chef would suit me perfectly. Especially if she made BLTs like Giulia did.

She'd been around for just over a week, and I swore I'd never thought about a woman as much in my life. Carly didn't count. She was my sister. The woman I'd let down. Giulia? I didn't have a fucking clue what she was to me. I just knew that no one—*No. One*—had the ability to annoy the hell out of me like Giulia did.

As I scratched the scruff on my chin, I let Cammie suck me off. Not because I wanted her mouth around my cock, not because I even wanted to get off, but because I wanted to piss Giulia off.

I wanted to give her a fucking reason to have an attitude with me which, I knew, made no sense, but fuck me, neither did her logic.

When Cammie started to fidget, I knew it was because I was taking longer than usual to get off, and I knew her jaw had to be aching, but being the cunt I was, I didn't let her up.

If anything, I tightened my grip in her hair and made her work even more for my cum. She'd been fluttering around me more than usual, and that was pissing me off too.

Cammie wasn't dumb. She knew my interest in her was waning, but the way to my heart wasn't through hovering around me. If anything, I was glad for her to be on her knees so I didn't have to listen to her talk about how 'good' we were together.

As she slurped me down, and as I appreciated the silence, I watched Giulia with her brothers. She didn't spend that much time in the bar, and I figured it was because her dad, after staying away for the first few days, was usually in here at this time of night. He'd left earlier, which was why she'd come in, but I had to wonder why she'd even bothered because I wasn't the only one being sucked off, sex in here was par for the course, and her disapproval was evident.

James Dean—his legit road name—was fucking Lottie against the bar, just a few feet away from where Giulia was sitting with her goddamn nose in the air. Then there was Enya, who was being eaten out on the pool table by no less than two brothers, when that was *technically* against the rules.

Everything about the scene irked her.

I saw it, registered her tension, her disgust, and despite myself, I felt my irritation grow.

The weird thing was, she wasn't sanctimonious. If anything, she was easygoing. I'd heard her joking with a couple of the brothers over meals and, with her siblings, she was funny when she didn't think anyone could actually hear her. So what rubbed me the wrong way, I couldn't say. Just that she did.

Badly.

How could I appreciate her spunk and fire one minute, then want to take that pious glare of hers and make her see something that really would fucking disgust her, I didn't know. But she got under my skin worse than anyone I'd ever goddamn come across.

I didn't like feeling as though someone was looking down on me, and Giulia was doing exactly that.

These bastards were my family, and we didn't need no snooty, snotty piece of skirt coming in and looking at us like we were trash.

When Heather moaned a few feet away from her, Giulia jerked in place, her cheeks burning a bright, red-hot pink that had to be fueled by anger. I watched as she punched one of the twins in the arm, then leaned up on tiptoe to kiss the other on the cheek.

That didn't take much guessing. North had already charmed most of the snatch in the club, and even though he was still only a Prospect, which made the sweetbutts off limits, the bitches were going to be happy as fucking Larry when he could bone them. Hawk, on the other hand, was a miserable cunt. Even I thought that, and I was a miserable cunt too.

Without a backward glance, she scurried out of the bar, and I had to admit it pissed me off that she didn't look at me.

I knew she was aware of where I was sitting.

When I'd hollered at Cammie to come and suck me off, her eyes had glanced over me, her top lip curling in disgust before she'd darted her gaze back to her brothers and kept her attention fixed on them.

One of the reasons I hadn't come yet was the fact that I'd been willing her to look at me. To watch as another bitch sucked me down. My motives were suspicious, even for me, but all I'd known was that Cammie's Dyson mouth hadn't done shit for me tonight.

Not when she was in the audience.

Not when she was the reason I'd had the clubwhore go down on me in the first place, but it was the wrong mouth. The wrong eyes staring back up at me.

The second she'd gone, tension filled me, and I shoved Cammie off me. She staggered back, reaching up to wipe her mouth, but I ignored her as I got to my feet, zipped up, and stormed out the room without a look behind me.

It didn't take a fucking genius to figure out where Giulia was going, so I followed her, wanting her to know that her piece of shit attitude wasn't going to cut it. She didn't have to approve, we didn't need her goddamn support, but no way in hell was I going to let her cut into my mood again.

At that moment, she was to blame for my failure to come, global goddamn warming, and the melting ice caps.

As I practically ran through the front door in an effort to catch up with her—those short legs of hers were surprisingly quick—I came to an abrupt halt at the sight of Dog, who I'd thought had gone home for the night, with his hand on her arm.

It was the first time I'd ever seen them alone together, and I scanned the situation quickly, trying to figure out what was going down, because this was no daughter-daddy reunion.

She was scrabbling at his fingers, trying to get him to let go, and when she released a sharp cry as he tightened his hold on her, my jaw clenched, all my anger at her forgotten as I ran toward her.

"Just leave me the fuck alone," she ground out, her voice as loaded with vinegar as ever. "You didn't have any trouble forgetting I was your fucking kid when I was in Utah, so don't trouble yourself over me now."

My eyes widened when Dog raised his hand, twisted it around, and made to backhand her—I got there just in fucking time.

She flinched, jerking back in preparation for a smackdown even as she raised her forearm in an attempt to block his hit.

With me around, she didn't need to.

I grabbed his wrist, held it tightly in my grasp, and as I crunched it between my fingers, I shoved his arm behind his back then kicked his knees out from under him.

He cursed at me then cried out as I dropped my hold on him so he landed with a dull thud in the gravel driveway.

Uncaring that I'd just maimed a brother, I hissed, "Exactly what the fuck did you think you were doing, Dog?"

As he cradled his wrist, he spat, "Fuck you, Nyx. She's my daughter. I can do what the fuck I want—"

"No, you goddamn can't," I growled, somehow more livid now than I'd been with Giulia back in the bar. "You think it's okay to smack women?"

Giulia, because she had no fucking sense, sneered, "Why not? He did it to my mom all the time."

My eyes narrowed into a thin squint at that. "You beat Lizzie?"

"What the fuck do you care?" Dog snarled. "She was my bitch. I could do whatever the fuck I wanted with her. And this little cunt is just as bad as her momma. Never did know when to control her tongue—"

"You really shouldn't have said that," I spat, and rolling back my arm, I slingshotted my goddamn fist into his fucked-up face.

Even the snap of cartilage, the blood busting from his nostrils, and his wail of pain didn't make me feel better.

I wanted to pound on him. Really. I did. I wanted to kick his fucking face in. But in front of Giulia? No.

A man had to have standards.

Granted, mine weren't that high, but I wasn't about to do that shit in front of her.

Later?

Yeah, that was another matter.

I'd seen her grief. Even beneath her disgust at the way we all led our lives here at the clubhouse, I knew she was hurting, so beating the crap out of her POS father wasn't on my to-do list tonight.

Dog crumpled in on himself as he shielded his face, and his voice was a garble as he cried, "My nose! My fucking nose! You broke it!"

"Say shit about Lizzie around me again, and I'll do more than fucking break it."

God, I was beyond tempted to kick him in the gut while he was down. Let's face it, I'd done worse in my time, but I grabbed Giulia by the wrist, and began dragging her toward the bunkhouses.

After twenty or so feet, she began tugging at my grip. I glowered, whirling around to pin her with my irritation. "We got a fucking problem or something?"

"You're hurting me," she snapped, but it wasn't a whimper.

Wasn't even a mutter.

She'd just seen me break her father's nose, and while she didn't know me, she didn't cower. She fought the fuck back, and if that didn't do more for my cock than Cammie had while she was sucking on it trying to get me off, then hell if I knew what was going on with my body.

I hadn't intended on hurting her. If I had, shit might have been different. Still, I instantly loosened my grip, but I didn't let go.

I couldn't.

Don't ask me why, but that wasn't something I could do.

When she stared at me, half glower, half look, I watched her accept the difference in my hold on her with a wryness that had her eyes twinkling.

"You're an ass, aren't you?"

My brows shot up. Whatever I'd expected her to say, it wasn't that.

"I've been called worse, so I'll take 'ass' as a compliment."

"You've no idea how much that tells me about you, do you?" she grumbled dryly. She peered over her shoulder where her father was still on his knees, still wailing about his goddamn nose, and her smile beamed at me. "Thank you for that."

Her gratitude was genuine, and for this past week, though I'd known she was hot as fuck—how could Lizzie's daughter be anything else? As a teenager, I'd have fucked Lizzie faster than I'd have tried to steal some smokes from one of the brothers—but that smile? Goddamn. It floored me.

When I said floored, I meant it was like a fucking revelation.

All the bravado, all her sass, all her orneriness, all of it disappeared in that moment, leaving behind the real woman. Leaving behind a Giulia I wanted to know. Fuck, more than that. *Needed* to know. More than I needed my next damn breath.

My entire fucking life seemed to flash before my eyes, a life that had happened before her. What I saw wasn't pretty, but it was me.

All of me.

Flaws and sins and all, and fuck me, I wanted her to know it. Know every dark and depraved thing about me so that she could push me away, run from me, take herself away so I wasn't tempted to taint her with my poison.

For a second, I could do nothing more than stare at her. Wishing I wasn't a selfish cunt, wanting, for Giulia's sake, and her mom's, to be a better man.

But I wasn't.

I was a Satan's Sinner, and we took what we wanted.

We didn't relent, we didn't concede, and we didn't step back.

With that one smile, Giulia had sealed her fate, and she didn't even fucking know it.

I wanted her, and I'd take what I wanted.

Like she realized I wasn't following the conversation a hundred percent, she frowned at me. But even that frown was different. She didn't scowl at me like usual, or glare or glower. If anything, her eyes were gentle as she asked, "Are you okay? What's wrong?" Then, she bit her lip. "Why are you looking at me like that?"

I swallowed, my Adam's apple bobbing with the force of what I was feeling.

I was no pussy, but what I'd just felt pummeled me worse than any of the brothers could even dream of during a sparring session. And sweet fuck, I wanted to be the one gnawing on her bottom lip. Not her.

"No reason," I told her, when I got my voice back, but I still sounded like I'd just smoked a packet of cigarettes. "Let me take you to your place."

Her frown deepened. "No. It's okay, Nyx. I'm good from here. It's literally two minutes to the front door."

"Apparently not, if your fucking father thinks it's okay to accost you on the way to your room." My jaw tensed as outrage swelled inside me, overtaking even the most overwhelming of emotions she'd triggered in me. "I'll deal with him."

She shook her head, letting a chestnut lock drift over her forehead. I watched as the tip collided with the rosebud mouth that was beginning to fascinate me.

I'd seen it pursed in disgust, revulsion, and all kinds of other shit that pissed me off to think about, but mostly, now, I just thought about that rosebud around my cock.

I wanted that. So goddamn badly.

Giulia reached up and tugged at the piece of hair that had gotten stuck in her lip gloss, and her fingers drifted over her cheek—touching skin I wanted to feel against my palm.

Temptation burned inside me.

Fuck, it did more than just burn. It scorched me, but I was used to the pain. Used to it, and even embraced it. It grounded me. Kept me sane.

"It's okay. He won't hurt me. I've been ignoring him all week. That was a culmination of the ignoring I've been doing." Giulia grunted. "Guess that didn't work out too well for me, but I don't think he'll give me any more shit. He wants me around as little as I want him around."

I narrowed my eyes at her. "He's been giving you shit?"

She snorted. "Why would you care? He's a brother, isn't he? Aren't you on his side?"

"I'm on no one's side. But, and it's a big fucking but, I liked your mom. I don't want to hear shit about him beating the fuck out of her."

Those mocha eyes stopped twinkling, and sadness graced them. "To be fair, if he hit her, she hit him back. Usually twice as hard."

Because I could easily see Lizzie doing that, I barked out a laugh.

Suddenly, I felt better.

Dog hadn't gotten away with shit because Lizzie hadn't let him.

She jerked back at my laugh, then muttered, "Not sure that's something to laugh at."

"Isn't it?" She shook her head, so with the hand that wasn't still around her wrist, I touched the skin my fingers had been craving to caress since she had. Tension filled her as I dragged my thumb over her cheek. "To me, it is. Lizzie was a fireball."

Christ, I hoped Giulia had her fire.

From what I'd learned of her so far, she did, and I couldn't wait to be razed to the ground in her inferno.

TWELVE

GIULIA

THE WAY he looked at me?

I'd never been looked at like that before. Like he wanted to devour me. Consume me.

And Jesus, how I wanted to be consumed in his fire.

I'd never wanted that before. Ever. I was still young, but I'd been popular at school. I had more tits and ass than I knew what to do with, and half of the football team had spent most of high school trying to get into my panties.

Not one of them had managed it.

Why?

Because I saw what the kind of looks I had did to a woman. I saw it because I looked like my mom, and knowing what she'd gone through, it didn't make me predisposed to easily let a man between my legs.

I wasn't a virgin, far from it, but I'd always been selective about who I fucked, and guys like Nyx... that wasn't going to happen.

Not only because he was a brother, and I knew what they were like with women—shit, only a few minutes before he broke my dad's nose he'd had that slut's lips around his dick—but because Nyx was exactly the kind of man I didn't allow into my body.

He was hard, dark, twisted even. I saw that in his eyes. Saw it in his face. There was a pain there that I hated because it called to me. That stupid feminine part inside me, that integral part every woman had since we were cavewomen running around after hairy Neanderthals, wanted to fix him. Wanted to help heal him.

But I knew better.

There was no healing this kind of man.

No fixing him.

Whatever he was, he was fucked up inside, and I saw that, recognized it in him, and knew to back away.

Or, at least, to try.

Trouble was, when a man like Nyx got you in his sights, there was no getting away from him.

One thing I'd noticed this past week was just how barbaric these guys were. Not that it was news to me, but it sure was a reminder.

It was like going back to medieval times.

The women were there for sex, food, and cleaning. And as far as I was concerned, there was barely any cleaning going down, and the food, well, what they'd eaten before I wouldn't have fed to pigs. But the sex was like living in a frat house that had a brothel incorporated into it. I'd come across more couples fucking in the past seven days than I'd seen in porn.

And I'd watched *a lot* of porn in my time.

No one needed to pay for porn in this place. Fuck, they should set up a studio and get paid for it!

Which was even more of a confirmation why I should back the hell away from Nyx, run kicking and screaming for the hills because he was one of them.

A frickin' Viking, who didn't care that he went around pillaging because that was his right...

Well, he had no rights to me.

I lifted my chin and pushed back so he'd drop his hand and stop touching me.

Of course, that would have worked on any other normal guy in the fucking universe, just not this one.

His eyes narrowed, and I saw temper flash in them. A temper that should have scared me, but instead, had me narrowing my eyes at him in retaliation.

Most of the brothers treated me with indifference. I was, to them, the kitchen sink. Except more useful because I made edible food. They nodded at me, didn't talk the same shit about me as they did the club sluts, and basically let me be a ghost around them, and I wasn't about to complain about that.

But Nyx?

He didn't do that.

He watched me.

Maybe I should have anticipated this. Maybe I should have taken notice of the way he watched me.

But I wasn't a possession.

"Your cock is wearing another woman's lipstick, Nyx. You need to think about that before you take a step closer to me."

His lips curved—that came as a surprise. I'd expected anger.

"You watched. I knew you did," he murmured, sounding pleased.

His tone had me frowning. "I saw a lot of sex going down in that clubhouse. Of course, I noticed."

"What color lipstick is my dick wearing?"

A bright, trashy as fuck pink.

"I wouldn't know," I told him stonily.

"I bet you do," he breathed, bridging the gap between us by taking a step closer to me, until he was in my face, in my space, and I had no alternative but to back off. When I did, I wanted to groan in irritation, because it pushed me up against the clubhouse wall, which meant I had even fewer places to go than I had before.

"Nyx—" I started.

"Tell me, Giulia. Tell me what color lipstick I'm wearing on my cock."

I sneered at him. "Hot pink." I sniffed. "It isn't your color."

When his thumb tapped my tacky bottom lip, I wasn't surprised when he replied, "I'd prefer it was wearing clear gloss instead."

"Vaseline," I retorted. "I don't do makeup."

His eyes scanned over me. "You're lucky, you don't need it."

"Maybe."

I pushed my hands against his chest—sweet Jesus, how were his pecs that hard?—and tried to shove him away, but there was no moving him, no ducking out from under his arm and getting the fuck out of dodge.

No.

I was here until he let me go.

The weirdest thing of all was that if any other guy had me pinned like this, I'd have worried about what was going to happen. Rape was something every woman had to fear. But I knew I wasn't in danger. I knew Nyx meant me no harm, if, for no other reason than, I was Lizzie's daughter.

I clung to the thought with both hands. "Why did you defend my mom back there?"

The emotion in his eyes changed, shifting from hot and heavy to irritated. "What?"

"You heard me," I insisted, relieved to see that irritation. "Why?"

"Because I liked your mom. She was cool." His chin jerked up. "I was sad when she left, and I was sad to hear that she'd died so young. She didn't deserve that."

"No. She didn't." I bit my bottom lip and, even though I was relieved I'd toned things down, the way my bottom lip trembled wasn't feigned. "I miss her."

He released a sigh, and his hand—loaded with calluses, and all the better for it—rubbed against my cheek, raising more gooseflesh and making the hairs on the back of my neck leap up to attention. "I'm sorry, Giulia."

God, the way he said my name made me want to melt.

My smile was tight. Both from the grief and the weird attraction I had for a man who was so far beyond wrong for me. "Thanks."

He shrugged. "Come on, let's get you inside." The charge in the air had gone, but I still felt the effects of it, even knowing I'd been the one to calm things down.

When he pulled back, I missed the heat of him against me. He'd pushed his abs into mine, his hardness into my softness. Was it weird that I was disappointed about not feeling his cock?

In fact, screw that. Of course, it was weird.

I'd only just been thinking about Cammie with her stupid mouth around his dick, so I had no reason to want his hard-on butting up against my body.

Apparently, I was a contrary bitch because yeah, I was mad at that.

When he dumped me at the bunkhouse, muttering a churlish, "Goodnight," I was relieved because I hadn't thought I'd— *That I'd what?*

Escape him?

Was that what I meant?

He wouldn't force me. I knew that like I knew my face in the mirror.

Every sordid act the brothers did to the clubwhores was consensual, and it was all the more mindboggling for it. I'd come across women being assfucked over the bar, on their knees sucking someone off in the yard—it was endless. But it was all with consent.

That went unspoken.

The clubwhores wanted it. Loved it. Even seemed to crave it.

I didn't understand, but then, I didn't want to. That was their course, not mine, and yet, to have a man like Nyx in your bed, it figured that some women might go to any lengths.

When I shut the door behind him and turned to look at the bunkhouse where I was staying with my brothers for the interim, I thought about just how beautiful Nyx was. All darkness, all power. All damn man.

Gnawing on my bottom lip, I pressed my back into the wall beside the door to keep myself upright. My legs felt shaky, and nothing had even happened.

I reached up, cupped my chin where he'd touched me, then whispered to myself, "You just crossed into Narnia."

Hell, Narnia couldn't be any more fucked up than this place.

Blowing out a breath as I traced where he'd touched me, I looked at the simple armchairs that had seen better days, and the worn futon, table, and chairs that this place pretty much consisted of.

Nyx had told us, that first night, this was where visiting clubs, as well as other Sinners' chapters, lodged while they stayed at the compound, and where they'd be residing until Hawk and North earned their patches. As for me, I wasn't so sure. I'd be here until I'd either earned enough to get a place in town or if I had to save more to go further afield.

We weren't far from New York, and I had to admit, I was tempted to stay here for a while. Maybe not forever, but at least for a few months. The city that never slept after Buttfuck, Utah sounded like heaven.

Still, the notion of leaving this place, of being without my brothers, was just too hard to handle at the moment. I had shelter, I had a wage—quite a generous one too, considering all I did was cook—and I was safe.

Yeah, *safe*.

Like a gazelle amid a pride of lions, but, and it was nuts, I knew I was the only gazelle that the lions wouldn't touch.

All except for one.

Apparently.

I closed my eyes, and thought once more about why letting Nyx anywhere near me was a bad idea. There were a thousand reasons, and the major one was—

The door rattled to my left, and I jerked in surprised when it pushed open. Half expecting my father, because I knew my brothers would be partying all night long, and only the hell knew what they'd be getting up to in the bar, I started to shove it closed.

What was I just thinking about being safe?

Stupid. Stupid, stupid, stupid.

Then, I blinked when I saw it was Nyx.

He was wet.

At least, his hair was wet, his skin dewy, and I stopped fighting because damn, he was pretty. Like beyond pretty. Like so fucking crazy pretty that I just stared at him for a few seconds, unable to process why I'd been telling myself it was stupid to even think he was this damn gorgeous.

As he crossed the threshold, I staggered back, because it was either that or get trampled.

"Why are you wet?" I rasped, unable to clear my throat enough to get rid of the frog currently taking residence in there.

"I took a shower." His lips twisted into a smile so fucking hot, it about made my panties melt. "My cock is no longer wearing lipstick."

I'd been in a stupor long enough for him to take a damn shower?

And, what? He wanted me to be pleased about the fact there was no other slut's DNA on his penis?

I narrowed my eyes at him. "You better not be here for what I think you are."

He hitched a shoulder. "Maybe I am, maybe I'm not."

"What's that supposed to mean?"

His lips twisted. "What do you want it to mean?"

"God, I hate non-answers."

Even if I *was* the Queen of them.

Grunting, I swirled on my heel and headed past the shitty table and chair set, and toward the wall of cupboards and the counter space that made up the kitchen.

"What are you making?"

"Hot milk." I smirked. "Do you want some?"

When there was no reply to my question, I turned to look at him over my shoulder. When I found him gaping at me, I had to laugh. In fact, I had to more than laugh. I chuckled so damn hard that I almost peed my pants.

"Milk?" he blurted, glaring at me like I'd offered him cyanide. "Hot milk? I have a reputation."

"So do I," I retorted.

He narrowed his eyes on me, taken aback by that. "What kind of rep?" he questioned warily.

"I don't put out."

Instead of making him back off like I'd thought, his eyes burned as they traced over me. Not one inch was spared from his perusal and, God help me, between my legs and deep in my belly, I felt the pressure of that look. I didn't even need to touch myself to know I was sopping wet, my body preparing itself for his touch.

Nyx was bad news, but my body didn't give a shit.

"That's good to know," he rasped, his voice low and husky enough to make me whip my head around and carry on to the kitchen just so I could close my eyes and process how fucking hot he'd sounded.

Mouthwateringly hot.

I hadn't even known a voice could do that to me.

"You should work on a sex line," I muttered.

More silence, then, way too close to me for my own good, he choked out, "Is that supposed to be a compliment?"

"I guess." I twisted to look at him, saw he was barely a foot away, and groused, "You take up a lot of room."

That didn't prompt him to move, if anything, he carried on eying me as though I was a new species of wildlife and he was a zoologist that needed to write a paper on me.

Blowing out a breath, I dove into the fridge to grab some milk. Was I surprised when his hand cupped my ass as I bent down? No. And though it made my core clench, I whipped around to glare at him.

"Hands off, Nyx."

He shrugged but—and I wasn't sure whether this came as a surprise or not—he backed off. "Can't blame a man for touching something that pretty."

"Remember the rep? I don't put out. Now, do you want some hot milk?"

"I'd prefer something stronger. Like water."

While I was mad at him for touching me without my permission, I had to chuckle. "Water, I have."

Once I poured some milk into a mug and shoved it in the microwave, I grabbed a bottle from the fridge, but instead of bending down, I tucked my ass in and kind of shuttled downward then back up so he couldn't touch my butt again.

When I passed him the bottle, there was mirth in his eyes, and I shook my head at the sight as he cracked open the lid.

"What are you doing here, Nyx?"

He took a sip of water, which had me focusing on his throat for way too long. "I'm not sure, but I figure I'll find out soon enough."

His words didn't put me at ease. "I. Won't. Put. Out," I repeated, trying to get the message across. "I don't care if you bleached your dick or not, it's not going to happen. Not now, not ever."

The second I uttered those last four words, I regretted it.

What the fuck had made me say that?

Why had I been so goddamn stupid?

A challenge?

A fucking challenge?

I might as well have thrown down a beef sirloin in front of a pack of hungry dogs.

At my statement, he laughed, but I saw the intent on his face, and knew it for what it was. "We'll see about that."

THIRTEEN

NYX

"I HAVE A QUESTION."

I cocked a brow at her as I slouched back into the too small sofa. This place was uncomfortable as fuck, but in all honesty, my room wasn't exactly comfortable either. It consisted of a bed and that was pretty much it.

Bikers didn't tend to worry about soft furnishings.

But Giulia? She was female, and females and furniture went hand in hand.

I half wondered how long she'd put up with the rudimentary digs she had, but rather than ask that, I muttered, "Shoot."

"Don't tempt me."

"Didn't realize you were armed."

When her eyes twinkled, that thing happened again. That whole punch to the gut shit. Since she'd arrived, we'd been in a verbal war, and yet, after that scene with her asshole of a father, she'd calmed down some.

I had no idea how long it would last, just knew I wanted the ceasefire to continue.

"I know how to handle myself."

Interest piqued and cock hard at the idea of her with a gun in her hands, I asked, "You carry a gun?"

"Not anymore."

"Why not?"

"Because I moved to New Jersey. I'll get my license when things are more settled."

"When you're ready, tell me. I'll take you to a decent gun range."

"You'd do that for me?"

To keep her safe? Damn straight.

Armed, I wouldn't have to worry about her so much. She'd at least be able to protect herself.

"Of course," I said gruffly, not liking my reaction to her breathless words. She was all big-eyed at my statement, which told me how little she was used to being helped.

"Thank you, Nyx," she whispered, tugging at the hem of her shorts, plucking at some loose thread that was coming away from the denim.

"Like I said, no problem." Clearing my throat and eager to change the subject, I questioned, "Anyway, what did you want to ask?"

"Is it true what I've heard about you and extreme sports?"

"Where the fuck did you hear about that?" Then, it dawned on me. "Oh. Your father."

She nodded. "Well, the twins told me. Not him. Dog used to write them a lot about this place."

"And I was included in his letters home? Because we're so close," I mocked.

Shrugging, she admitted, "He didn't write often, but when he did, they pretty much scoured every letter and learned it word for word."

"I don't get it." I didn't. Dog wasn't much to look up to.

She snickered. "Neither do I, but their hero worship is on them, not on me. I'm not blinkered."

"If they loved him so much, why didn't they come back?" I queried, twisting the cap of the water bottle she'd given me before, to stop myself from reaching for her.

I had to fight the urge to touch her leg, to stroke where she was stroking. The way her fingers danced along her hemline was both enticing and a fucking torment.

"Because Mom made them promise they wouldn't become bikers."

"So? They listened?"

"'Course they did. You remember my mom. She wasn't a woman to be messed with."

I tipped my head to the side, butting up once more with that strange wistfulness in her tone. Because we were talking without sniping at each other, I felt like I could ask, "Why do you do that?"

"Do what?"

"Talk like that about your mom. I can tell you're grieving, that you miss her, but equally, it's almost like—"

"I have a lot of regrets where she was concerned. I told you already that we argued before she died."

"Kids and parents argue. A lot."

"True. But this was a bad argument, one after another bad argument we'd had a few weeks before that. We weren't close at the end, and I think that might be what you're picking up on. I can't change shit now. I've run out of time. She's run out of time. I regret that."

Because that did fit with what I'd heard in her voice, I asked, "Why didn't you get along? Were you too alike?"

Her lips curved, and a glint appeared in her eye. "You asking if I'm as ornery as she was?"

"I'm not asking that," I scoffed. "I already know you are."

She snickered, shoving me in the arm and pushing me away. She packed some punch, so I shifted in my seat, smirking as I reached for the bottle and took a sip.

"Lance, her new husband, didn't like me. We didn't get along, and because she took his side all the fucking time, I stopped getting along with her too." Her smile faded. "Simple."

"Nothing that you just said is simple."

Her lips twisted. "True dat."

Because I'd made her somber, when that hadn't been my intention, I muttered, "I don't do the extreme sports thing that much now."

"But you did it before?" I could practically feel her clinging onto the change in conversation with both hands.

"Yeah. When I could. I prospected as soon as I fucking could, and when you have all the shit to do to become a full brother, and then when you're patched in, it's not like you have time for hobbies.

"But I did some stuff. The best shit I did was in Bali, actually. There are a lot of waterfalls there, a lot of extreme sports, and things where you're pitted against nature." I pulled a face. "It was something I wanted to do, so I did. That trip is probably what Dog was talking about. It's all anyone was talking about for a while."

"Why?"

I grunted. "Most brothers don't even have a passport."

Her eyes widened. "Oh. They thought you were risking it by leaving the States?"

What she was really asking was if I had a warrant out for my arrest.

I just cocked a brow at her. "I had no problems getting in and out of the country."

Curiosity throbbed through her. To the point where she started fidgeting. If it hadn't been so fun to watch, I'd undoubtedly have told her what she wanted to know, instead, amusement firing me, I watched her suffer in silence.

After a while, the peace settled between us, and fuck, if it didn't make me feel rested. I wasn't sure that had ever happened, outside of the moments where I'd just killed a cunt, and, I'd admit, it was fucking nice.

Only, nice felt too lackluster a word for what I was feeling.

There was a serenity inside me that I wanted more than I needed my next breath, and the best part? As I felt all this, I could watch her.

And she could watch me.

What was it about her?

What was it about us when we were together?

Sniping and snarling like two pissed off cats sharing the same bag, and yet, when it boiled down to it, capable of sitting here in silence and just being.

I wasn't surprised, a few minutes later, when she released a shaky breath and stated, "I'm going to bed."

"You do that," I informed her, watching her brow pucker.

"You going to leave?"

I kicked my feet out and crossed them at the ankle. "Nope."

And so it went.

That was how I spent the night in the bunkhouse with her, but without her too.

It was why I was happy—fucking *happy*—enough to whistle when, the following morning, I walked into the council meeting, and happier still to laugh at the state of my brothers when I caught sight of them.

Only Mav didn't have a hangover, and that was because the bastard never left his fucking room unless it was for council.

Jingles always took food up to him, and I hoped for his sake that he slaked off some of his bitterness inside her pussy too. Though I doubted it.

Rex had told me once that Mav refused to have sex. Why, I didn't know, but if he couldn't get a hard-on thanks to what had gone down overseas, I wasn't sure why he asked Jingles to bring his dinner.

Talk about punishing yourself.

Jingles had the biggest titties among the clubwhores, and she had these little bells on her nipples. When she was naked—which she was, a lot—they always jingled.

Hence the name.

With everyone else groaning, and the room in the semi-dark again, it was, I'd admit, quite nice not to wake up with cotton mouth. I rarely drank, but even a couple of shots of tequila made your breath stink worse than dragon piss, but not today. Not for me. Because I'd had water after I'd returned to Giulia's place, and had watched her drink hot milk.

Hot milk.

What the hell was she? *Ten?*

I'd half thought she'd done it as a joke, but when I'd watched her swallow down the drink and hum as she did so, I realized she liked that shit.

Actually liked it.

There was plenty of other crap that was weird about her too. Things that weren't as disturbing as a preference for hot fucking milk. But that was the most concerning in my opinion.

Back before she'd left, Lizzie had been as much of a Sinner as Dog, and Giulia's twin brothers looked to be just as bad—or good, depending on your inclination—as the people who had spawned them. So, the question was, where the fuck had she come from? And why did she both irritate the shit out of me, and make me want her harder than any of the other bitches at the clubhouse?

"Okay, everyone, let's get our shit in line," Rex declared, his tone just an edge over strident, which had everyone groaning.

Of course, he did it on purpose.

He and I, as well as Mav—but I didn't include him in the mix—were pretty much the only ones who never let themselves get totally fucked every evening. Rex mostly because he'd never forgive himself if something went down and he was pissed out of his skull.

In our world, that wasn't an impossibility, and to be fair, it was one of the major reasons I didn't drink every night too. But after I purged a sick motherfucker off this Earth? I partied. Hard. I partied, and I reveled in the life I had that could never be normal, thanks to my own demons in my closet. Demons who'd torn Carly from me way too early. Demons who wanted to kill again and again, even though I knew from experience that spilling any amount of cunt blood would never make up for losing my older sister.

My heart began to pound as the ever present need to make someone pay throbbed through my veins. It was all the stronger for those feelings of happiness I'd just felt. It was like I wasn't allowed to be content without having to pay for it with the guilt that tore at me. Sometimes, it was to the point where I felt like I was goddamn possessed. Like that need inside me belonged to someone else, and I was only along for the ride. But the only thing that made me recognize it as bullshit was the delight I took in hurting those who hurt the innocent.

I might be sick.

I might be twisted.

But I wasn't as sick or as twisted as they were, which had to count for something.

"Fuck's sake. If you're not listening either, Nyx, then I might as well talk to the goddamn wall."

Rex's complaint had me blinking as I realized he'd started the meeting, but at his words, I shifted my focus to him. "Sorry."

"Yeah. You sound it." He sniffed, looked at the others, then rolled his eyes. "We have shit to discuss. I need you to bring your A game."

"Can't that Giulia girl bring some food in?" Maverick whined, scratching his abs like he hadn't been fed in a week. "I'm hungry."

I scowled at him. "She ain't your slave."

"She is." He sniffed. "I've gained six pounds because of her."

"Is that a complaint or praise?" Storm asked wryly.

Glowering at him, I muttered, "Considering Mav is skin and fucking bone, dipshit, I'd say it's a positive."

Didn't mean I liked the idea of him calling on Giulia for food all the fucking time. Even if I was glad—

What the fuck was happening to me?

Not only was Giulia *not* mine, she was here to feed everyone. Even if I thought she needed help for that mammoth task, her job was pretty much to make sure anyone who wanted something to eat had something in their stomachs, so it wasn't like I could bitch at Mav for being hungry.

"You know how often we've been talking about food in these meetings because Giulia started cooking for us?" Rex grunted.

"We've only had two since she arrived," I pointed out.

Eight days she'd been here.

Eight.

What would I be like when she'd been here ninety?

I really fucking hoped I'd be bored of the sight and sound of her, but I knew that wasn't going to happen. Knew it like I knew my name was Nyx.

No, I didn't want to claim her. No, I didn't want to make her my woman. But that didn't make me feel any less possessive about her.

No one deserved the fate of me claiming them. No one deserved to be tied to a sick fuck like me forever. And if that killed the small part of my soul that was still alive and kicking? Well, that was just tough shit. Protecting women and kids was what I tried to do, even if it meant protecting them from myself.

"Yeah, well, all we do is talk about food. The steaks she made, that whore pasta she—"

I scowled. "*Puttanesca*," I corrected. "Not *whore* pasta." I almost tutted at the sacrilegious label, because my experience with eating that dish had been close to holy.

"Since when were you Gordon goddamn Ramsay?" Storm sniped.

Link elbowed him in the side. "I think Nyxy is in wuv."

Because that made my heart pound again, I kept my face expressionless and flipped him the bird. "Nyxy is going to ram this up your ass if you're not careful." Goddamn Kendra and that fucking nickname.

"That wouldn't be a punishment," Steel remarked dryly. "Not when he likes things up there."

Link laughed, smacking his hand down on the table as he chuckled like a fucking hyena.

"Wasn't that funny," I retorted.

"Your face was a fucking picture!" Link hooted, then he made a big show of wiping down his cheeks from tears of laughter.

"How did shit derail more than it already had?" Rex mused, more to himself than anyone else, I figured.

I cut him a look. "I think you were intending on talking about our diversification plans."

"So you were listening." He hummed. "Good."

We'd been earning too much of late, and while that wasn't a complaint, it sure as shit wasn't as great as it sounded.

The more we earned, the more we had to launder, and until recently, that had never been an issue, but we'd opened up some channels for distribution that had been quite profitable.

One of our newer Old Ladies was related to a Five Pointer over in Hell's Kitchen, and because to the Irish, blood was everything, and because Mary Catherine was one of the upper ranks' daughters, that meant they put us on probation.

It had only been thirteen weeks since we'd been approached, but ever since, we'd had six runs and fuck, the money? We could use it to wipe our asses, that was how much was coming in.

"Okay, so for the boring shit. The bar is almost finished, so's the diner and the strip club. We have the garage kitted out, and the doors are due to open within the next few weeks, and then that microbrewery idea of yours, Mav, worked out perfectly. I'm sloughing off a couple mil into that project."

Mav, ever sober, slipped him the 'peace' sign. "If only you always listened to me," he intoned, and though he didn't grin, most of the council did. Hell, even the corners of *my* mouth twitched.

"If he did that, then we'd be really fucked," I commented, "considering you won't leave the clubhouse and haven't had your cock sucked in only fuck knows how long."

Mav, used to my digs and knowing that they came from a good place, merely stated, "If you're that interested in my cock, you can suck it yourself."

Because Mav swung both ways, the threat wasn't idle, but I still snorted and sniped, "I'll send Cammie up. She's better at it than me."

A certain stillness overtook my brothers, but I didn't know why.

Mav either didn't notice it, or just sandblasted through it, as usual. "If you do, make sure she brings some food. I'm more interested in that than the black hole between her thighs." He sniffed as though bored with the subject which, as per fucking usual, blew all our goddamn minds.

Mav, before Iraq, had been like a stallion in perpetual heat.

Seriously, the dude couldn't keep his dick in his pants, and now, it was like he wore some kind of fucking chastity belt or something.

It was weird.

Disconcerting as fuck to have the old Mav back, while still missing half of the man we'd known for so long.

Rex, clearing his throat, his desire to change the subject evident, muttered, "*Anyway*, I'm going to need you all to take these places under your wing." He scrubbed a hand over his chin. "All of this has come about quickly, too quickly, I know, but I see no reason the money won't keep rolling in, so long as we don't fuck up."

"And we won't," I reassured him.

The Satan's Sinners' MC had been on the up and up for a while, but getting the connections we had was a stroke of luck.

That Digger had fallen for a Five Pointer bitch was fortuitous as fuck, and we were all reaping the benefits of their deal with the Russians—even if those Bratva cunts did make our blood boil with how they kept swaggering over into our territory. We just had to make sure that Digger treated Mary Catherine well, because if he didn't, he'd fuck everything over for all of us.

In fact... would Giulia like Mary Catherine? I'd only met the Irish-American girl twice, but she hadn't been as bland as I'd imagined.

Being raised in Families like the Five Points tended to make dull bitches who were scared of saying boo to a fucking goose. Probably because their fathers whipped them or some shit straight after confession. Goddamn Catholics.

Giulia, on the other hand, was the complete opposite of dull and obedient, but was she too much for Mary Catherine? Or would she help ease the other woman into the life?

MCs and the Mob were two different entities entirely.

Just because you came from one didn't mean you could adapt well in the other. Plus, Giulia had been born and raised in the Sinners. Even if she'd left for a while, she knew the score. That was how she knew how to treat the whores.

I rubbed my chin at the thought of introducing her to Mary Catherine, and decided it wouldn't altogether be too terrible an idea.

"I'm going to assign you each to one of the businesses, and you can take control over how many men you need from then on out," Rex was saying, dragging me from my thoughts with a bang. Even knowing this had been the direction we'd been heading down for the past few months, didn't make the notion any less annoying. And I wasn't the only one. All the councilors were bitching under their breaths, and Rex, ignoring their mutters, forged on, "I have enough shit of my own to be handling, so I need you to pull up your big boy pants, stop getting fucking wasted every goddamn night, and do your jobs. You hear me?"

When everyone just squinted at him, he growled under his breath. Though this was the last thing I wanted, instead of siding with them, I sided with the club and slammed my hand against the table. Rex didn't need my backup, he was as much of a crazy motherfucker as the rest of us, but I had his back.

Always.

And the council knew that.

With a couple of faux yawns, they all began a circle of nods that had Rex grunting. I knew he didn't like it when I pulled shit like that, but if they were scared of Rex, then they were terrified of me. Even Maverick, and the fuck only knew what he'd seen overseas. But that was just my level of crazy.

When you saw a man smile as he sliced another fucker's throat and pulled out his tongue through the gaping hole, you knew something was wrong with them. That was the least of my crimes, and all my brothers knew it.

That they'd all started joking around me the past few days, wasn't a development I appreciated, but fuck, I'd been acting differently, and I didn't even know why or how. The only change in my life was that Giulia and her siblings had returned to the clubhouse, but there was no way in fuck I could see any causality in her being here, and my brothers suddenly deciding to make me the butt of their shitty jokes.

"I'll take the diner." If I had to do this shit, then fuck, I might as well have a nice view as I did it.

"You?" Rex scoffed. "You can't cook for shit."

"I know. But I reckon Giulia might come in handy."

"Leave that snatch alone. The last thing I need is Dog and you duking it out over her," he grated out.

I shrugged, even if a part of me was surprised Rex hadn't seen how Giulia and Dog had barely interacted since their arrival.

Rex usually noticed everything that went down around here... that he was distracted was a point of concern that had me eying him carefully as I said, "Already happened last night. He went to slap her." As my brothers grew tense around me, I reassured them, "I just hit him a few times."

"Thank fuck for that. I thought I was going to have to arrange a funeral." Steel made a show of wiping the sweat off his brow in relief.

Hitting women wasn't allowed on my watch, and everyone knew it. Dog had forgotten last night, but he wouldn't again. Not if he valued his kneecaps.

Even if a lot of the guys got handsy with the women, I overlooked it, so long as they never came to me and complained about any ill treatment.

I wasn't about to gut a man for spanking his bitch during sex, after all. They had to come to me or be sporting bruises for me to get involved in something that wasn't my business.

I was a mean bastard, and most people were scared of me, but the women—Old Ladies and sweetbutts alike—knew that I was a safe haven for them.

I'd slice and dice any of the fuckers I called brothers if I learned they inflicted pain on their women.

Jesus, I couldn't even think about it without my hands curling into fists so tight, they ached.

A hand slapped down against my shoulder, and Rex muttered, "He'll have learned his lesson."

"He'd better."

"That why you want Giulia's help with the diner?" Storm queried, his head tilted to the side in consideration as he studied me.

Like I was some kind of anthrax strain on a petri dish.

I fucking hated when he looked at me like that. Like I was a puzzle he wanted to solve.

No one could solve me. No one could fix what had been broken so early in my life.

"What? To make sure he doesn't chase after her?" I frowned. "You questioning my efficacy as Enforcer?"

That stunned him. He jerked upright and shook his head. "Of course, I'm fucking not."

"Then you should know that Dog is terrified, and that Giulia will be okay. I want her because she's the only one of us who knows how to fucking cook, and we have a team of sweetbutts who can feed us, but she could do that shit at the diner instead of here."

Rex laughed. "You have it all worked out, don't you?"

"Not exactly."

And it was probably a good thing I said that, because when I found Giulia knee deep in tears from all the onions she was cutting and told her my plan, she ground out, "Fuck that. I'm not cooking shit in a diner."

After last night, had I hoped things had changed? Had I hoped we'd be closer? Maybe?

We'd talked about a lot of things, things I wouldn't normally be interested in, not when I could be throat-fucking Cammie again.

But stay, I had.

Listen, I had.

Until she'd tried to toss my ass out.

I'd ignored her, of course. On principle. I'd bedded down on her sofa, and had woken up to her tight ass in a pair of sleep shorts waggling around the kitchen as she made some coffee.

In fact, even as she currently glowered at me, I thought of those moments. They'd been silent, like something from a movie. At least, I'd only ever seen shit like that in a movie.

A woman in the kitchen, a man watching her bustle around as she started the day. I'd half wanted to watch her get dressed and shit, and not because I wanted a front stage view of those tits of hers either, but because...

Fuck.

I felt like a pussy, and I wasn't used to that. Not one bit, but there was no denying how the intimacy of the moment had hit me.

I'd never been intimate with anyone before. Sex and fucking weren't intimate. Even Cammie was just a hole for me to plug. I treated her right, maybe rougher than I should, but I never fucking hurt her, aside from her gagging around my dick.

But that was just release.

Sex wasn't intimacy, and it stunned me that it had taken me nearly thirty-eight fucking years to figure that out. What was even more of a revelation, was that it had taken meeting Giulia for it to hit home, and I was nowhere near ready to think about why that was.

"Nyx?" I rejoined her grumbling to find her waving her hand in my face. "Thank fuck, I thought you were having a seizure or something."

I narrowed my eyes at that, then tensed when I zoomed in on the knife she was waggling around. "You know how to use that?"

She scowled at the weapon. "To cut onions? Sure. And that's why I'm not helping in the diner."

Okay, she hadn't been threatening to stab me. The tension in my shoulders lessened some. Then, her words hit home.

"Wait. You don't want to help out because of onions?"

"You can't make shit without onions."

"It's a diner. You make bacon or Canadian ham and fucking eggs. Waffles. None of that shit needs onions."

"You have no idea how to make sausage gravy, do you?" She stabbed the knife at me again, and it was a true testament to how much I'd appreciated the view this morning that I didn't grab a hold of it and slam it into the wooden board she was using. "Or how to make burgers or—"

"I know how to make burgers."

She scowled. "Whoop-de-do. How dare you put me forward for a position I didn't even ask for!"

"You're part of the MC now," I growled, jutting my chin out. "You do as you're fucking told."

"I'm not wearing a cut. I'm working hard for the money you pay, and the second I can, I'm out of here."

Whatever I'd anticipated her saying, it wasn't that. "Where the fuck are you going?"

"That doesn't matter."

It fucking mattered all right.

I scowled at her until her eyes stormed up, and she hissed, "The city, okay?"

"New York?" I grunted. "It's not as great as you'd think."

"Says someone who's been, and I've been no-fucking-where. Here and Dipshit, Utah. That's it."

Okay, so I'd been questioning where the rebel in her was, but this fit. Lizzie had loved riding bitch with Dog.

Even if I didn't remember much about her in the grand scheme of things, I remembered that, mostly because she'd had the longest hair that whipped behind her whenever Dog rode out with her at his back.

I remembered watching them drive off through the gates as a kid, standing in the clubhouse, just dreaming of the moment I could be like them.

Huh. Nostalgia.

I was seriously starting to wonder if I had a brain tumor or something.

"It's expensive as fuck over there," I grumbled, folding my arms against my chest.

Sure, the gesture was defensive, but so were the words.

NYC was dangerous, and Giulia had a mouth on her. She'd get stabbed or shot when she pissed off the wrong person, I just fucking knew it. If New Yorkers were dicks, then fuck me, Giulia was Queen Dick.

Why did the thought of her being anywhere but West Orange, in this clubhouse, send me into a tailspin?

"So? That's why I'm here. Save up some money, get myself a stuffed bank account, then—"

"Fuck off outta here."

When she just huffed, then twisted around to get some shit from the fridge, I wanted to shake her.

She was going to walk away from family, all for what? A visit to the Big Apple?

"It's less than an hour away, dammit. You can visit NYC without moving there," I reasoned, trying to remain calm when I had the worst feeling about her leaving.

She'd die.

I knew it.

Like some fucked-up premonition.

Some people needed a keeper, and Giulia was one of them.

Someone would gut her just to get her to shut the hell up. Here, she was safe. Sound. She was Dog's, so we'd protect her to the end. In NYC, she was just another rat racing around trying to make sense of the world.

"Why would I stay?" she countered. "This place isn't my home."

"Your family's here." I clung to that argument, because I knew how much family meant to her. Not her dad, but her brothers. Sometimes, her mom, with a wistful tone that spoke of a story she didn't want to share. They were all she really talked about.

"Dog isn't much family, and I love my brothers, but they're big boys. They don't need me hanging around, watching them eat out sweetbutts." Her mouth twisted as she returned to the counter with a couple of bell peppers.

"The MC is family. If you let them be," I told her stiffly. "But you haven't let anyone in. You haven't even tried to make friends."

Fuck, and now I knew why, didn't I? She didn't intend on staying.

Something she confirmed with her next statement: "No point. Not going to be here long enough. Everything's different, anyway. None of the people are the same, and the atmosphere has changed. It's more like a frat-house than a community."

Panic clawed at my insides, and I couldn't reason it away, not when the truth was that I didn't like Giulia, but she'd gotten under my skin.

Always watching, always judging.

You didn't have to like someone to want them, did you? And that was where I was currently at.

It fit, really, that she wanted to leave, that she would try to get away as soon as she fucking could, but—and it was a big but—that made me want her to stay all the more.

I didn't want her to be as intrinsically miserable as I was, but damn it, I didn't want her to go. Not yet.

Maybe not ever.

"On what you're earning, you'll be working for a decade before you can afford to stay in a rat-infested shithole in the city," I stated, instead. She wanted to think rationally, then I could be fucking rational too. "You'd be better off feeding us here and working somewhere else."

"I won't work at a diner."

Because there were options, I mumbled, "There's a bar. A garage. A brewery. A strip joint."

Her brow puckered. "What the hell? You giving me a list or something?"

"New business ventures," was all I said, not sharing shit with her, not just because she evidently didn't want to be here, but because bitches were never told shit about business.

Didn't matter if they were sweetbutts, Old Ladies, daughters, or mothers, we never shared that kind of stuff with anything in possession of a cunt.

She tipped her head to the side. "New business ventures? I'm sure I don't even want to know what they could be if, all of a sudden, you have so much money in need of... *laundering*," she mocked with a sniff. "I'd prefer to work in a bar than the diner. How about the garage? I'm good with admin. I did a lot of temping back in Utah."

"Nah, the bar would be better. I hate working in body shops."

"What the hell do you have to do with where I work?"

"Don't you know?" I told her, baring my teeth at her. "I've taken responsibility for you."

FOURTEEN

GIULIA

THE ABSOLUTE FUCKING nerve of the man.

Take responsibility for me?

Like I was a goddamn stray dog who needed a home?

"Since when is this the Dark Ages?" I replied, fighting the urge to take my knife and throw it at him. "I don't need anyone to take responsibility for me."

"No? Well, tough shit. It's happened. Where you go, I go. So, make your decision. Diner or bar? Which is it?"

I wasn't altogether certain why, of all the options, those were the ones he was interested in, but considering I had no desire to work at a strip joint —even if it was interesting at first, there were only so many tits a girl could see without getting bored—and the idea of cooking even more than I already was broke me out in hives, didn't seem like I had much of an option between the bar and the microbrewery—and I knew shit about beer. Liked it even less than I liked cooking.

Yeah, that was how much I didn't want to work there.

"The bar it is," I muttered, but I scowled at him as I said it. "I don't get why you're a part of the decision."

"Because every unattached woman that ain't a sweetbutt has to be taken in hand by a biker," a new, deep voice informed me.

The statement jolted me from my glowering session at Nyx, but when I saw Storm, I relaxed some. Sure, he was as much of a pervert as the rest, but he was always really cordial to me.

Yeah, cordial.

Go figure.

Plus, he always complimented my food. The bastard had manners.

Again, go figure.

"I don't need anyone to take me in hand."

"Just how it works, darlin'," Storm stated as he swooped in, and curved an arm around Nyx's shoulder that I knew the brother just wanted to shrug off. They shared a look I didn't get, one that had Storm smirking and Nyx tensing up even more, before he returned his attention to me once again. "You got any of those sandwiches left from earlier?"

"Nope," I told him succinctly.

"Make me one?" he wheedled.

I smirked at him. "Nope. You want a sandwich, get one of the sluts to make it for you."

Storm snickered. "You say the meanest things."

"I'm sure." I rolled my eyes. "In a clubhouse of dirty fuckers, I'm the one with a potty mouth. Anyway, I told you to get a sandwich before you went into council." I shrugged. "You snooze, you lose." It was a bittersweet fate that, though I hated cooking, I was really fucking good at it.

Even that miserable piece of shit, Maverick, always sent his trays down completely empty, and I'd learned that was a first, as he hadn't been eating right since he'd returned home from the frontlines four years ago.

"When did you see him before council?" Nyx groused, making me scowl at him.

"In here. Where I was making breakfast."

Was the guy deaf or something? Or dumb?

If I wasn't in the kitchen, I was at the bunkhouse, and we'd left there together this morning because he was a stubborn asshole.

Storm snickered out a laugh, saying, "I gotta get me a bitch who can cook," as he turned away, evidently going on the hunt for a slut who could make a sandwich as well as she could suck cock.

"You've already got one, dumb fuck," Nyx muttered, and I watched with interest as Storm tensed up, his shoulders hitching a second, before he headed on out.

I had no idea what that was about, but as far as I could tell, the cock sucking was more important than the eating. It was probably why all the brothers were so fucking slim. Well, except for the ones with Old Ladies, of course.

When Storm strutted out on the hunt for a cocksucker sandwich maker,

I turned my attention back to Nyx, who looked both pissed off and confused.

"What is it?" I asked, unsure why he was looking like that and well aware I didn't want his focus on me.

Just because we'd talked last night, just because we'd... *No.*

No way.

I didn't want this shit.

I wanted to work hard, earn some honest bucks, get the fuck away, and leave my brothers in semi-safe hands. I'd undoubtedly be visiting them in jail within the year, but fuck, that was their fault and their problem, not mine.

I didn't want a biker to be looking at me like he wanted to be inside me. Especially one who had half the evil cunts in this one-percenter club backing off when he approached.

I wasn't sure what Nyx was, but it ran deep. He had labels. Biker, brother, Enforcer, and yet, there was something running underneath the surface. Something that should probably have scared the piss out of me, but didn't.

Why?

Well, apparently, I had a death wish.

Because what had the brothers dashing out of his way, and what had that slut Cammie quivering on her too high, stacked heels when he summoned her like a dog, didn't scare me.

Not one bit.

Nyx wasn't bluster, he was cold reason. He was precarious safety in a dangerous world. He was a harbor in a storm, but even harbors came with splinters.

I saw him, but the issue was, I didn't know what I was seeing. Not really. Maybe if I did, I would be scared, but the truth was, Nyx would never hurt me. He'd have let my dad slap me last night, if that was the case.

He might break my heart, and if I let the fucker between my legs, might wreck my pussy—I'd seen what he was packing—but physically? I was as safe as I could be, and I wasn't sure why every other bitch in this club didn't recognize that.

He wasn't a kitty cat, never that, but if a one-percenter could and would protect a daughter from her father, that meant they had a twisted moral code that meant anything with a pussy was safe from danger.

Unless said pussy betrayed the club, I figured, and since I didn't feel like getting my throat slit, that definitely wasn't going to be an issue.

"What are you staring at?" he growled at me.

"I'm staring at you staring at me," I retorted with a sniff. "Anyway, the bar? I'll take that over the diner."

"Fine," he grunted, twisting around on his boot before he strolled off to only fuck knew where.

Shit, if I'd known that would have worked, I'd have told him that earlier.

Nyx was Trouble. Capital T necessary. I knew it, my body knew it, my heart knew it, but most importantly, my brain knew it. And while I was many things, no one could ever accuse me of being stupid.

That was why I avoided him.

Which wasn't easy.

The only time I talked to him over the next few days was when he showed up for something to eat, and while a part of me was okay with that, another part of me wasn't.

The other night, as I'd drunk hot milk and he'd glowered at my mug as though I was drinking poison, I'd started to think he was more than just a grunt. Sure, he'd barely said more than a couple of sentences at a time with large pauses in between, as though he wasn't used to speaking frequently, but I'd thought he wasn't as big of an asshole as I'd initially assumed.

Then had come the assumption that I'd be willing to work my ass off in a fucking diner.

A few days after the 'incident,' when he came into the kitchen, he grunted at me, "Time to get to the bar."

Eyes narrowed, I demanded, "Excuse me?"

"Have you gone deaf?" he growled. "It's time to get to the bar. We're opening in a few days, and we need to hire staff."

"We? No. You. I thought I was one of the staff." I wasn't just being ornery for the sake of it either, I was genuinely confused.

He was talking to me like I knew what was actually happening, when I seriously didn't.

"We're going to do this shit together."

"We are? Why is this the first I've heard of it?"

"Maybe if you hadn't been avoiding me—"

"Me? Avoiding you?" I half shrieked, wondering if I'd fallen through the rabbit hole, not just down it. "You're the one who's barely been around."

He frowned at that, folded his arms over his chest, and grated out, "I don't have time for this conversation. We need to get to the bar, now."

He sounded like he was trying to be patient, but he was failing.

Miserably.

Because I'd been short with him practically since the first morning, and well aware that I was earning pretty decent pay for making three square meals which, in my mom's day, had been handled by the Old Ladies for free, I decided not to be a total bitch.

"I have no experience in running a bar," I told him truthfully, wanting to be straight with him before I got myself into deep shit.

"Neither have I. How hard can it be?" he replied, totally unconcerned.

Shrugging, I said, "I don't know. That's the problem with having no experience. *I don't know.*"

"Our rep precedes us. We're opening up, and in a few hours, we'll have people head in with their resumes. Rex arranged for some breweries to come by and speak with us today and tomorrow, and—"

"Wait, there's no beer on tap? In a bar?" I stared at him. "You said it's going to open soon."

"It will."

"Won't it take a while to get a beer line set up?"

"Not if they want our business." His grin would have made a shark shudder. "Anyway, I don't have time to hold your hand. We need to get there, and we need to sort shit out."

I huffed, not appreciating his tone, but seeing as he spoke to me like I spoke to him, it wasn't like I could complain, was it?

"I need to grab my things."

"Go. You have ten minutes. I'll meet you outside."

With that declaration, he headed out of the kitchen, leaving me gaping at the notes I'd been making for this week's shopping list.

That was the one joy of this shit job—I didn't have to buy the food, nor did I have to clean up. I just made the meals, and the sluts did the rest. I considered that a massive win. Especially since there was an industrial dishwasher.

If they'd had to wash by hand, then I'd have done the dishes myself. Prejudiced? Yup. And proudly so.

In my defense, it was a wonder venereal diseases weren't airborne in this fucking place.

With an admittedly supercilious sniff, I left the thankless and never-ending task of cooking for a zoo behind.

Rushing out of the clubhouse, I ran over to the bunkhouse where my stuff was.

Of course, before I escaped, I saw someone having sex by the front door, and because I was getting used to it, I didn't even try to avoid seeing who was boning who, just let it float over my head as I bypassed them to make it outside.

When an arm shot out and grabbed me, I jerked in surprise.

The biker, a douche called Lever, was screwing Jingles—her tits had little bells dangling from her nips—and he thought he could touch me?

Ew.

Wanting to douse myself in bleach, because only God knew where his hand had been—just the notion made me break out in hives—I jerked out of his hold.

"What the fuck do you want?"

He licked his lips, fleshy, gross things that reminded me of the suckers on squids—with that mental image, who wouldn't want to fuck him?—and with a cocky smirk, told me, "I'd love a sandwich."

It was a request I was starting to hate. Everyone wanted a fucking sandwich, but if I didn't offer it in the kitchen, I sure as fuck didn't offer it out of it.

And certainly not with a guy who made Jack Skellington look cute.

Barely refraining from shuddering, I shot Jingles a truly sympathetic look. "I think you're lucky to be fucking Jingles. Don't get ahead of yourself."

He frowned, not understanding my meaning. "We should take this upstairs." His belligerent tone had me gritting my teeth.

"I think you should fuck off," I barked at him, and with my spare hand, I slammed the side of my palm down on his outstretched arm, at his elbow. It wouldn't hurt him, but his reflexes would work on my behalf so I could liberate myself.

Before he could complain, and well aware that that wouldn't be the first or last time he accosted me—wasn't that something to look forward to?—I mumbled to myself, "As if."

Some of the guys didn't seem to understand that I wasn't available, and to be fair, that said a lot about my father and his abilities and position in the MC. If he'd been in the council, or if his brothers had known to fear him, they'd have left me the fuck alone.

As it stood, I'd got some come-ons, enough to piss me off and make me grateful that my brothers had taught me self-defense at a young age.

"As if?"

For the second time in as many minutes, I jolted in surprise. Raising a hand to my chest, I sucked in a breath, then released it when I saw it was Nyx.

"What are you doing out here?" I grumbled, trying not to let on that my heart was beating like I was Bugs Bunny.

Okay, so I failed in that competition, because I sounded like I'd been running, and with my boobs, I didn't *run* anywhere.

"I told you I'd be waiting on you outside," he ground out, then his brow furrowed. "Why are you out of breath?"

"No reason."

A moan sounded right behind me, and I realized I could hear Lever boning Jingles right through the fucking front door.

God help me, I could even hear the bells on her tits!

He snorted at the sound. "Get a little flustered?"

"As if!" I spat, repeating my earlier declaration without meaning to. "Who's Jingles fucking?"

It was nauseating that he knew it was her too.

"Lever."

That had him scowling. I wasn't sure why, but it did. "Did he come on to you?"

"Maybe." My eyes widened when he moved toward me so fast, I thought he was going to slam me into the door.

Only, he didn't.

He grabbed the handle and went to open it, and when I realized what he was doing, I shoved myself between him and it, and sputtered, "Where are you going?"

"To smash his face in," he spat. "I've warned him about this."

"About me?" I shrieked. "Why the fuck would you be warning anyone about me?"

His top lip curled in a sneer. "About any fucking woman. He's a lecherous prick." He shouted the last two words, and when Jingles stopped squealing like a pig being killed, I shuddered, because apparently, the message had been rammed home.

I didn't want to think how.

When Nyx smashed his fist into the door, I scowled at him.

"Why do you let him stay in the club, if he treats women like shit?"

"He doesn't. Not when I'm around."

"When you're around." I sniffed at that qualifier. "So, you're the unofficial police around here?"

He cocked a brow. "You just call me a pig? Your insults are getting better." He bared his teeth. "Shame for you I'm losing patience. Go get your shit from the bunkhouse. I want to be on the road soon."

I glowered at him, but did as bid because I seriously needed to do something with my hand.

If Lever had fingered Jingles with the hand he'd used to touch me... Jesus, I knew from health class that you couldn't catch the Clap that way, but tell that to my arm.

Seriously, I was having a major issue in sitting down on any of the surfaces in that fucking place, because I knew everything was fair game when it came time to boning people.

And yeah, I said people, because not even the guys were safe.

This was an LGBTQIA friendly zone, apparently. Something that had stunned me almost as much as the fact that Nyx had saved my butt from my dad.

Hustling over to my sleeping quarters, I eyed the building, once again surprised it wasn't an outright dump, and headed inside.

When I heard moaning coming from one of the bedrooms, I cursed fate for landing me in an unofficial porn movie, and strode over to the place I'd staked out for myself.

If only temporarily.

This place was pretty sweet, and while it wasn't home, I loved that there was a connecting bath in my room, and the twin buttheads shared a full bath—one I didn't touch.

I figured Nyx's patience wouldn't last long enough for me to have a shower, but fuck, I really, really wanted one.

Lever's hand, the morning sweating over a pile of bacon... Was it vain that I didn't want to be on the back of Nyx's bike for the first time smelling like pig?

Because bacon, apparently, was his favorite perfume.

Not.

Snorting at the thought, even as I dithered over whether I had time or not, I raised my arm to grab my purse, and what I smelled? There was no way I was heading into a new job with interviews with reps from breweries and the like stinking.

Quickly shucking off my clothes, I headed into the bathroom and put the shower on full blast.

While the place was old, and the tiles a shocking shade of avocado, the water ran hot, making it my favorite place to spend a few minutes every morning and night.

As I leaped into it, I quickly lathered up and got myself squeaky clean. If I used three times the amount of soap on my arm, well, that was between me and the bottle of soap, wasn't it?

Shuddering at the thought of Lever even thinking he had a chance with me, I finished up, and hoped Nyx had...

What?

Wouldn't I have preferred for him to have gone to the bar without me?

Somehow, I was unofficially working with him. All this without even a word from Rex, who hadn't really spoken to me since that first day, except to ask me to pass him some condiments from the kitchen. Not that I'd spoken to many people since getting here.

Nyx was right.

I hadn't bothered trying to make friends, hadn't even tried to make friends with him... Which was evident in the conversations we'd had together, which consisted mostly of arguments.

Well, some of those had been kind of cool.

Cool.

Hah.

Everything about Nyx got me hot and bothered, not cold.

Maybe exhilarating was a better adjective to describe what went down when Nyx and I went head to head *conversationally.*

When I tried to drag the towel from the hook just outside the shower cubicle and came up with nothing, I grumbled, then opened the shower curtain and screamed when I saw Nyx standing there, towel in hand.

Grabbing the curtain and wrapping it around myself, I hollered, "You fuckwit. What are you doing here? You pervert!"

"Which part of 'I'm in a fucking rush' didn't you understand?" He leaned back against the bathroom wall, just beside the bright green toilet, and crossed his legs at the ankle.

Was this guy for fucking real?

Bitching at me for dicking around, then standing there like he had all the time in the world? What the fuck was that about?

"I had to wash Jingles off my arm."

He stared at me. "Why would you need to do that? She was boning Lever, not you." He cocked a brow at me. "Or did I miss something?"

I scowled at him, feeling hot and flustered as I wondered how much of an eyeful he'd caught of me.

The bastard.

As I calculated just how much of my tits had been visible in the sliver I'd revealed when I'd pulled the curtain aside, I gulped. "Lever touched me. He grabbed my arm. He could have been touching Jingle's pussy with those fingers. Ew." I glowered at his lack of reaction, until I started to get chilly, so I huffed, "Can I have the fucking towel? We could have been on the road by now."

He shrugged. "You're the one who messed with the program."

"No. Lever did." I blew out a breath and let the hair on my forehead flop forward. "If I'd wanted to jerk you around, I'd have washed my hair. But see? It's dry."

"Some consolation." When he tipped his head to the side, his gaze drifting up and down my body, I gritted my teeth.

The sticky plastic of the shower curtain clung to my moist skin, and I kind of hated that him, standing there, looking cool and like James Dean before shit had gone bad for the ultimate rebel without a cause, turned me on.

I was mad, truly outraged at his breach of my privacy, but this wasn't how Nyx usually worked.

Nyx scowled at the idea of another biker touching me.

He defended me against clubwhores with vendettas, and he stopped my dad from hitting me.

He wasn't making a move, had no intent to harm me in his head. That was why this was weird.

Anyone else? I'd have been scared for my safety. But this was Nyx. And even though I'd known him twelve days, I knew I was safe.

My throat felt tight at that, because safety was relative, wasn't it?

I'd already established that nothing about Nyx was good for me, and yet, he was the only person who'd made the effort to speak with me.

Even if it was to piss me off most of the time.

Licking my lips, I stared at him, until I whispered the one question that was at the front of my mind. "Why do you talk to me, Nyx?"

Was I surprised when he didn't come out with some blasé shit? That he didn't make a joke out of what I said? I'll admit I was. But his words stunned me nonetheless:

"I don't know."

I believed him.

He didn't know either.

For some reason, he let me insult him, talk smack about the people he cared about, and he gave me the benefit of the doubt when all the clubwhores, who he knew more than he did me, and I wasn't talking Biblically here, came whining over how I'd treated them.

Why?

Why did he do all that?

Why did he watch over me?

Why did he make me feel safe?

I knew that question was for me and not him, but still, it ricocheted around my head, until I had no choice but to whisper, "We're going to be late."

"They'll wait." His tone told me they'd wait forever if he said so.

And maybe forever wouldn't be enough. Not for the promise that had surged into being in his eyes, a promise that fucked with my head and my body and, worst of all, my heart.

"No, Nyx." But I wanted to say yes. I really did. There was something about him, something that invited me to be bad.

To be me.

And that was terrifying.

God, it was so scary that it shook me to my core.

I'd shown him my worst side. Everything about me had been rebellious, rude, and mean since I'd arrived, and why?

Because that first night, he'd pissed me off.

I'd tried to be kind, tried to make a good impression. But every attempt had been brushed off as he walked me and my brothers over to this very bunkhouse.

The next day, one of the brothers had tried to come on to me, and another had thought I was their slave because I was hired to make them breakfast, lunch, and dinner. And when the clubwhores had ganged up on me?

That was when shit had changed for real.

I'd become the bitch I'd been known for in high school, and ever since, I'd been drowning in the old me.

The one who my brothers couldn't stand—which was probably why I barely saw them. The one who'd had to protect myself from my stepdad... that was the Giulia standing here today.

Not the one who'd freed herself from that toxic household, who'd started community college back in Utah, who'd wanted to become something, do something more than her mother had done. I loved her, but I knew Lizzie Fontaine's flaws. She needed a man, as for me, I needed *not* to need a man.

"Why are you looking at me like that?" he inquired, and there was something in his voice that made me feel even safer.

What the fuck was it with him?

In the face of this shitty existential crisis, my eyes burned with the need to shed the tears gathering there, but I didn't let them fall, because I knew he'd misinterpret them. Knew he'd think I was scared of him, and somehow, more than anything, I knew the idea of me being scared of him would kill him.

Kill him dead.

And so, I whispered, "Why aren't I scared of you?"

He jerked back at that, his head bouncing off the shitty avocado tile behind him. "Huh?"

"You heard me," I replied, my voice becoming stronger now that I saw his confusion. "You heard me," I repeated, when a muscle in his jaw flickered. "I'm not scared of you. Everyone else is, but I'm not.

"You'd never hurt me. I know you wouldn't, but I know you're the worst thing for me. You want me, and yeah, I can see that, you want *this* me. This horrible, shitty Giulia who doesn't deserve—"

"A blind man would know I want you, Giulia," he rasped. "Doesn't take much."

I dismissed that, because I knew he was backpedaling. My telling him I wasn't scared of him was like another guy's equivalent of backtracking when a woman told him she loved him.

I got that.

I understood it.

It made sense to me, and what that said about my mental health, I wasn't sure.

"You'll hurt me down the line. Bikers aren't capable of love. Not really. They love the road, the club, and their bikes more than they can love pussy."

He blinked, but seemed to be aware that I was talking to myself more than him.

"You'll break me, wreck me, and yet, you want the real me. The true Giulia. How can that be bad? How can it be wrong?" I gnawed on my lip a second. "This is me," I whispered rawly. "I'm a cunt. I have an attitude. I'm not nice."

"Neither am I." He ran a hand through his hair, making the ragged mess even more tousled. "I'm a monster."

I knew, when he said that, he meant it.

He wasn't talking smack, wasn't just saying it to 'impress' me. He was one hundred percent being honest.

Were we trying to convince each other we were wrong for one another?

Or just that... *fuck*. If he could take me at my worst, what would he think when he saw me at my best?

"I'm not a monster, but I'm not nice." I held out a hand. "Can I have the towel?"

I let the curtain drop, because he'd seen all the flaws in my fucking soul, so how could him seeing my imperfect body be worse?

I wasn't like the clubwhores. Not being pneumatic with help from a surgeon's knife had never stopped guys from wanting me, but I had jiggly bits, and my ass wasn't perfect, my knees were kinda dimply, and my arms were too thick. But I stood there. Flaws and all, and waited for him to give me the towel.

He stared at me. His eyes on mine, until slowly, they drifted down my length.

It was warm out, so there was no reason for the shiver that rushed along my spine as I let him take a full look at my body.

"Some parts of you are nice," he noted thickly, his eyes on my tits.

"Thanks," I said dryly, making grabby hands with my fingers for the towel. "There's a draft," I complained.

When he stepped forward, he looked so dark in contrast to me. I wasn't pale. My skin was olive, thanks to my Italian heritage, and my hair was just that side of black on the chestnut scale. I was golden, I guess, nothing about me white. But in contrast to him? I felt like an angel being approached by a demon.

And maybe I was.

The worst I'd done in my life was get a few parking tickets, and hell, maybe some jaywalking shit on my record. Nyx? Even his name meant night. But Christ, I bet jaywalking was the least of his worries.

Fuck, everything about this was bad, and yet...

I could be me.

I knew that.

Even more than that, I knew I could let the other side of me come out. The side that liked hot milk. The one who really loved her goddamn Comfy, and the one who seriously had an issue with *Friends* reruns.

In his dark leather, denim, and soft jersey Henley, he was everything my mom had taught me to avoid—not just through lectures but by experience, and yet, I was a moth to his flame, because he got me.

Sure, he didn't know every inch of me, even if I could feel the trace of his eyes along my skin, but the worst parts of me hadn't made him back off, and that was weirdly important.

I bit the inside of my lip when his hand came out.

He didn't go for my tits like I'd expected. He didn't even cup my ass, or go straight for the gold between my legs—and trust me, I'd seen how he treated that bitch Cammie...

The thought of her had me stiffening. "Do you have something going with Cammie?"

He reared back like I'd slapped him. "God, no."

My jaw tensed. "You only fuck her."

"At the moment. I don't share," he stated.

I huffed. "Right."

"I don't. The others know to leave her alone."

"Why?"

His expression was dark. Ominous. "I told them to leave her alone, and they do."

"That sounds like you're exclusive."

"We're not." He tipped his chin up, like he was waiting to argue with me, preparing himself for it, and my God, I felt my legs turn to mush when I saw how ready he was for the fight.

Excitement whirred through me, excitement and arousal. Christ, out of nowhere, I was horny. I'd gone from feeling all trembly and shaky, to suddenly feeling exhilarated.

He wanted my ire.

My wrath.

He was waiting on it.

His hand, the one I'd expected to go to all the usual places a guy aimed for, had gone to my chin. His thumb had pinched the tiny line I had there, so I grabbed his wrist and told him firmly, meanly, "I don't share either. If you think I'll fuck you until after I can clean your cock with alcohol wipes—"

Now that had him blinking. "Fuck that."

"Tea tree oil then."

"Because that's nature's defense against STDs?" He barked out a laugh. "If you need me to clean my cock before you come around it, then I'm okay with that. But I'm clean."

"I've seen her suck you."

"I always wear a rubber." He pursed his lips. "Club rule."

"Yeah, and I'm sure you wear a dental dam..."

"A what?" He pulled a face. "I don't eat pussy. They're not there for that."

"That has to be the most disgusting thing I've ever heard a guy say."

"It's for their safety too."

"That's supposed to reassure me?" I slapped his hand away. "You guys are gross." I grabbed the towel and quickly wrapped myself up in it. But, as my attention was elsewhere, his hand slipped around my waist, and he hauled me against his side.

"I'm a Sinner, Giulia. I'm dirty. Filthy to the core. My soul is black, but my body is clean. The least of my problems is an STD."

"This is the most unromantic conversation I've ever had," I informed him flatly.

"Oh, I didn't realize you needed roses and candlelit suppers." He laughed—breaking my fucking heart in the process, because God, his laughter came few and far between. "Remind me next time, and I'll bring both with me when I come to ride your ass about being late."

I tensed. "We *are* late."

"I hate being late," he informed me. "Don't do it again."

A part of me wanted to be late on purpose from now on, and fuck, if the notion didn't make my pussy wet. Not as wet as being held against his body, of course.

I could feel every inch of him. And I wasn't talking about his lean torso or the long, powerful stretch of his legs, which were covered in scratchy denim that had been worn smooth in only a few patches.

When I said every inch, I meant it.

Fuck.

He was huge.

I released a shuddery breath and whispered, "This is stupid."

"Yes. It is," he replied, but he rocked his hips against me. "But I want it. I want you."

I closed my eyes as I turned my face away. Taking a moment to collect my breath, to get my head in gear, I tried to get my lips to form the words that would make him release me, but I couldn't.

I just couldn't.

Instead, I reached down and pressed my hand to his, then covered his fingers with mine. "Do you promise you're clean?"

"Yes. Fuck's sake, Giulia, I wouldn't come to you unclean."

I believed him.

God help me.

My safety was important to him. Why wouldn't it be on this score?

Even as a part of me felt shitty for Cammie, another rejoiced, and what that said about the feminist in me was another matter entirely.

This entire clubhouse was bad for the feminist movement, but that wasn't my problem.

At least, it wasn't my problem at the moment.

The future Giulia was going to regret this, every minute of it, but God, he felt so good against me.

So right.

And the worst part about this? I wasn't drunk, so I couldn't blame this on the bottle of vodka I hadn't downed. All my convictions were going down the crapper, because what he made me feel, sweet Lord, it had to mean something, didn't it?

It had to be worth *something*.

Even if it was only once, I needed to know.

Needed to understand.

When he splayed his fingers, letting the heat of his palm sink into my belly, I was a goner.

He'd pulled none of the usual tactics, had done nothing that supposedly 'good boys' did when they got around a naked woman. If anything, he'd done everything ass backward, and I appreciated that so fucking much.

With a sigh, I twisted in his arms and whispered, "This is a mistake."

"All the best things in life are."

I felt his resolve and knew he meant every word. Looking into those deep eyes, I murmured, "Kiss me?"

"I thought you'd never ask."

FIFTEEN

NYX

I KNEW SHE WANTED MORE, but I gave her a gentle peck on the lips.

The tiniest kiss, a soft brush of our mouths, tender enough to make her moan, to prove something to both of us...

To prove that she meant more to me than just a fuck.

I was surrounded by beautiful women on a daily basis. Women who'd spread their legs at my command the second I walked into a fucking room. Women who could have walked on goddamn catwalks they were so fine, but no one was like this bitch.

This fine mass of curves in my arms was more than just a body.

She was Lizzie's daughter, and if there was something that could put me off her, it was that. But it was what fucked with my head. Not because I'd admittedly had a crush on her mom as a kid, but because she was a cut above.

She wasn't even a townie, or a country clubber, she was Lizzie's.

I had to treat her right—Lizzie deserved no less.

More than that, *Giulia* deserved it.

She deserved *better*.

Which meant I should back away, but I couldn't.

That weird as fuck connection that sprang to life whenever she walked into a fucking room was reverberating through me like a jackhammer down my vertebrae.

I felt each and every hit, except, instead of agonizing pain, I experienced a blissful pleasure at the slick bundle in my arms.

Squeezing her tighter than before, gifting her another soft brush of our mouths that had our lips clinging to one another, I whispered, "Let's make the mistake together."

When she gulped, I knew I had her. But there was no smugness, no bluster about this score. If anything, it was a kind of relief that flickered through me.

This, I understood.

Lust, need, arousal? They made sense to me.

Passion and desire too. It all fit.

The sense that I needed to protect her was something I could explain away also. I wanted to protect every woman and child in my vicinity. I could hide from the fact that that need trebled around her, could dismiss it as unimportant.

With her in my arms, I could breathe easier.

Pressing my face into the curve of her throat, I inhaled her sweet scent and whispered, "You're going to fuck with my head, Giulia, but you're going to fuck with my body too."

"Is that a request or a question?"

I heard the amusement in her voice and was charmed by it. How couldn't I be?

She was everything and nothing I'd thought I'd ever want. I hated sass in a woman. Hated it with a passion. Snark was one thing, but Giulia was a bitch. She was hard as nails too. But I respected that, and damn if I didn't want to fuck the gall out of her, one screw at a time.

My dick twitched at the thought. "Both."

She snorted, then reached between us and cupped my dick. It was the first forward move either of us had made, and I let her do it and loved the way she moaned.

"Fuck, you're huge."

That the moan was a combination of distressed and delighted had me smirking against her throat, even as I parted my lips and began to flicker my tongue over the sensitive skin there.

"I'll make it good for you," I promised, knowing why there was hesitancy coming from her.

Big dicks were great when it came to an open locker room, but I'd grown past the days where measuring my cock with another guy was important. Mostly, they were pains in the asses. Bitches could never swallow me down like they could an average guy, and I could never bone someone too hard for fear of goddamn breaking them.

One of the reasons I liked Cammie was because she could deep throat three-quarters of my length. That alone was like having the Virgin Mary pop up in my bedroom every second Thursday of the month—a goddamn miracle.

"I'm sure you will," she replied. Again, she sounded amused, and fuck if I didn't like that I never knew where she was going with her moods.

I let my hands drop down to cover her ass, then, as I parted her cheeks, I dragged her against me, trapping her hands between our bodies.

After a final flutter of my tongue against her pulse point, I pulled back and drawled, "Are you ready to make a mistake?"

She blinked at me before her grin, not unlike the sun rising in the morning, began to grow.

Wider and wider, until I felt blinded by it.

"I'd love to," she retorted, then immediately squealed as I hauled her up against my chest.

She parted her legs and instantly hooked them around my waist, and taking advantage, I squeezed her butt again as I walked out of the bathroom that had needed a new look back in the eighties, and into a bedroom that contained a bed that was way too small for what I wanted to do to her.

But—and it was a huge but—I didn't need this shit getting around the clubhouse. Everyone knew I wouldn't share, but the second they knew Giulia was fucking one of the brothers, she'd be fair game, and as fucking terrified as everyone was of me, that didn't mean some bastards wouldn't tempt fate just to get a piece of something I wanted.

I wasn't going to claim her, and that put her in jeopardy.

Anyone who touched her would lose their fucking hands, but that wouldn't save her from the trauma.

God, my thought process was enough to make me pull back, and I probably would've done, if she hadn't reached up and connected our mouths.

The second she did that, I was lost. I couldn't even think, my brain was blown out, clean through the gaping hole in my skull after the hit to the head that was this kiss.

I felt it in my dick, my bones. Not even my soul escaped the power of this kiss. It was like a...

God, why was my mind filled with violent thoughts as I dealt with the repercussions of this kiss?

I didn't know, so I pushed it away, focused on the good, the joy that came from this simple connection.

Her mouth was tender, her kiss soft. So unlike the woman who made a hedgehog look like it had a Brazilian. She slipped her tongue into my mouth, hesitant at first, softly, then as they touched, tangled, she shivered, moaned, then hitched herself higher in my arms as though she was trying to get closer and couldn't do it.

I grunted as her stomach rubbed against mine, her heat delicious and delightful at the same time.

She thrust against my tongue, fucking me there like I'd fuck her later, but that wasn't for now.

Next time, I'd show her shit that would make her eyes widen.

This time, I had to prepare her.

My fucking bastard cock.

With a grunt, I pulled back before I lashed my tongue over her lips in apology. She moaned, then instantly traced the same path I took, her eyes drowsy as though I'd laced my saliva with alcohol.

That look got to me so fucking much that I had to take a second to get myself under control. I had to focus. Had to breathe. I couldn't lose myself in her. Not yet, if ever.

Revealing the real me wasn't going to work. Couldn't work. No one could deal with that.

No one.

Inside, the demon clawed at the control I tried to assert over it. It ripped at the cage it subsisted in, tore at it like it was made of paper, and then she moaned, ignored my silent dictate, and connected our mouths once more. That moan told me she couldn't bear to be apart a second longer, and neither could I.

I sank into that kiss. Drowned in her and us. And the monster? It calmed. It was soothed, and I shuddered with relief as I just focused on her and our connection.

Unable to help it, my knees buckled as relief bombarded me, and I staggered over to the nearest wall, needing support, needing to make sure I kept her upright without dropping her.

Her weight was inconsequential to me, but when I was being torn down the middle by the two opposing sides that wanted a piece of me, I just knew I needed some extra help.

As she began to tongue fuck me once again, I stopped worrying about shit I couldn't control, stopped thinking period. I just focused on her, and us, and what she made me feel.

With a groan, I dove into her as much as she dove into me, until our tongues were thrusting against each other's. I ate at her, and she ate at me, and it was the deepest, most intimate kiss of my life.

Bar none.

She exposed every raw part of me, brought the light to it, and blew my mind with her power as she went, because no one had ever affected me this fucking much.

I shoved her into the wall, grabbed her hands and pressed them on either side of us, not stopping until she was pinned there, splayed above and below.

When I tore my mouth from hers, she whimpered, her eyes beseeching as the lids lazily opened, and she arched forward, trying to reconnect us once again.

"I want you to know something."

"What?"

Fuck, her mouth was kiss sore, pink and red, the lines blurring in a way that made me want to lick them.

"I have piercings."

"Huh?"

"My dick is pierced. I didn't want you to run screaming from the room when you saw my hardware."

For a second, she just stared at me, then when she laughed, I shook my head.

"H-Hardware?" she sputtered.

Though I was amused at her amusement, I just arched a brow. "You haven't seen my cock."

She did as I'd wanted to moments before—licked her lips. Fuck, I could almost taste her. Sweet and soft, pillowy. Better than any fucking donut I'd ever eaten.

With my eyes trained on her mouth, her smirk didn't escape my attention, so I let my gaze drift to hers, saw the sparks in them, and muttered, "Are you going to run screaming from the room?"

"Someone did?"

"A country clubber who wanted a bit of rough on a weekend one night last year." I hated fucking non-regulars, but she'd been persistent, and the demon was hungry... so I'd relented and had regretted it.

"I think I need to see this monster cock for myself. I mean, I've heard the rumors, and I've seen peeks."

Inwardly, I winced, because women just couldn't keep their mouths shut. Maybe some pricks would think their egos were being stroked, but I liked my privacy. That was why I didn't share.

That Cammie had talked about me, about what I'd done to her, made me want to scream.

If I hadn't been sure that my attentions would be on this little spitfire for a good long while, I'd make a point of snubbing Cammie as punishment for sharing shit she had no right to discuss. As it was, I meant it. If I was fucking Giulia, then I was done with Cammie anyway.

"Whatever you heard, it's BS," I told her, aware my tone was like gravel.

"That pisses you off, doesn't it?" she mused, her head tipping to the side as she studied me.

"What? That bitches are talking about my cock?"

"Yeah." She hummed. "I think I like that."

I just grunted, then grabbed her hips in my hands and hauled her around so I could return to the bed.

When I crouched down so she could lay flat on the mattress, I moved to a standing position and let my hands drift to my belt.

A moan made itself known to me—one that wasn't coming from Giulia.

I frowned, then remembered what I'd heard as I'd headed into the bunkhouse. My eyes narrowed. "Who the fuck are they fucking? No one is supposed to sleep with the Prospects."

She knew what I was talking about. "Have you seen my brothers?"

"Unfortunately." I grunted, then I smirked at her. "That must be fun. Sharing with your family..."

"I'm used to it. Used to drive Mom insane, all the girls they'd bring back. Sometimes together, sometimes apart."

"Why doesn't that surprise me that they share?"

"All the time." Another shrug. "I'm used to it. I'm so far past thinking it's perverted that I'm on the other side of the fence."

"You should know that worse shit goes down in the clubhouse."

"Trust me, I've seen it. Seen too much of your cock, as it happens, but I never noticed any *hardware*."

"Because I was always covered in a rubber. It masks it."

She raised up on an elbow, and I saw the light of curiosity in her eyes as she murmured, "Show me."

Another moan whistled through from the other bedroom, and I frowned. "You screamed."

"When?"

"When you were in the shower."

"Yeah. You stunned me," she retorted, but she sounded like she wanted to laugh.

"Why didn't they come and see if you were okay?"

Her cheeks burned. "I scream a lot."

My brow puckered. "And they heard you come?"

"What?" She reared back. "No! I didn't mean that." She let her arms flop out from under her and covered her face with one of them as she muttered, "I'm not that loud in bed. Not that they know, dammit."

"Shame," I told her. "I'd have liked to hear that."

She squinted as she shifted her arm to glare at me. "I hate spiders, and insects, and—"

"I get the picture. So they don't come and save your butt from creepy crawlies?" I smiled at her, genuinely this time.

The idea of this hard-as-nails bitch who'd slam a clubwhore's face into the granite countertop without a second's thought, screaming at a spider in the shower stall just made me want to laugh.

For real.

She huffed. "No. The bastards. I had to get used to killing bugs myself when I moved away from home, but I can't stop the squealing."

"Let's see if we can make you squeal now, huh?" I teased, loving her laughter as she snorted out a huff before pealing into a giggle that tore my heart open.

Adoring the sight of her like this, I wanted more of her, more of it. Unbuckling my belt, I felt my heart pound. If she made a single comment about me missing my calling as a porn star, I wasn't sure I'd stay in the fucking room.

Unfastening the three buttons on the fly, I sucked in a breath as I pulled my dick out, and watched her eyes widen at the sight.

"Is that fully hard?" she whispered, her eyes and mouth rounding as she sat up.

"Semi." Thinking of her brothers ignoring her screams had made me soften up some.

"Jesus," she whispered, more under her breath than anything else. When she swallowed, I wasn't sure if she was going to run off anyway, then she sat up, and she went to eye level with my dick. "The female cervix can only take so much."

"Trust me, I know," I groused. "I have more intimate knowledge of cervixes and vaginas than a fucking OB-GYN." I rolled my eyes when she didn't even peer up at me to chide me.

"Why did you make it scarier?"

Brow arching, I asked, "Are you saying my dick is scary?"

At that, she finally stopped gaping at my cock and stared up at me. "You know it is. You're like the Terminator. You have a penis fit for a cyborg."

But she wasn't running off.

Thank fuck, because all her attention was getting me hard again.

"Hardly a cyborg. It doesn't shoot blanks," I joked, loving her laughter as she chuckled at my joke.

"Glad to hear it," she purred, sultrily enough to make my cock twitch. The sight had her eyes widening, then she reached out and rubbed her fingers over the various piercings that covered my dick. "Why did you get so many?"

"They're not for me," I told her truthfully.

"Huh? Then who are they for?"

I reached down and rubbed the two rings at the frenulum, one at the front and one at the back. "This feels good against your clit at first, then, when I'm inside you, it will rub up against your G-spot."

I fingered the Jacob's ladder that ran down the length on the underside. "This will make you come so hard, you'll cry."

She gulped. "Really?"

"Yeah. Really."

"Why isn't it all the way down to the base?"

I had it running from under the rim of my cock to about halfway down. "That's all I can usually get in."

"How does—"

Because I knew what she was thinking, and I hated it, fucking hated it all of sudden when before, I'd wanted to shove her face in the sight of Cammie giving me head, I grabbed her chin, and pinched it between thumb and forefinger. "Don't. And that's why I always use condoms too."

She bit her bottom lip. "I've never been with anyone as big as you."

"Then you're in for a treat, because the only way I'll get it in is if I make you feel good." I jacked off for a second, letting my hand rub along the length until I could feel myself getting a little too turned on thanks to her attention being exactly where I needed it to be, but also where I didn't, because focus was imperative.

"You gonna spread your legs for me, baby?" I rasped, watching as she hesitated a second before parting them and slowly, carefully, slipping back onto her elbows once more.

She eyed me warily, like she was waiting for me to hurt her, and because that killed something in my soul, I dropped to my knees and took away any threat I might inadvertently be transmitting.

The last thing I wanted was her fear, so with my cock in hand, and still on my knees, I approached the bed and said, "You being so far away ain't gonna do either of us much good, is it?"

The heat in her eyes burned me.

I loved seeing that, loved knowing I'd taken her concerns away, and when she shimmied toward me, her tits jiggling with the move, I eyed her pussy and saw her slickness, thanks to the fact she was trimmed. Not bare like I usually preferred it, but a little hair on her didn't put me off.

I made her work for it though, didn't stop studying her pussy until she was close enough for me to touch her without moving an inch. And she knew. Knew that I wasn't going to do dick until she came to me.

The second she felt my breath on her cunt, she released a shaky moan, and finally, I gave her eye contact.

She whispered, "Please?"

And, inadvertently, she asked for something she didn't mean. Had never intended on asking.

I dipped my chin, and with the point of my tongue, I let it drift down her folds, poking and prodding here and there, making her jerk, her ass tighten and relax, until I moved to her clit once again and began to flick over the surface of it, until her body was jerking too, the muscles twitching as I gave her what she didn't know she needed.

A man with a cock like mine got good at giving head. Even if I didn't bestow my talents on the sweetbutts, it wasn't something you forgot.

Within minutes, she was squirming on the bed, getting riled up, and had me smirking until I opened my lips around her clit and sucked hard.

She shrieked, her hands coming to hold my head, gripping my hair until the roots stung. Her legs clamped down around me, and she cried out as I carried on.

Sucking hard and fast, fluttering my tongue here and there, before I let go and thrust a finger into her.

My mouth was wet, my chin, jaw, and face too, thanks to the juices that were already flowing from her, and as I fucked her with that finger, I saw her glassy eyes and knew she wasn't expecting anything I was giving her.

With a moan, she stared at me, desperate already.

Fuck, she was new to this, maybe not *brand new*, but her lovers in the past definitely hadn't been high achievers in the orgasm department. I couldn't wait to teach her every fucking move I had in my repertoire.

With a grunt, I slipped another finger in, and another, until she was full with all four. In between, I rewarded her clit with a simple kiss, but mostly, I focused on scissoring my fingers, getting her used to being full.

When she took all four, I gathered spit in my mouth and let it drop over her clit. As she shuddered, I rubbed it with my other hand, then curved my fingers up and raked down the front of her pussy. I began to suck on her clit as I moved my fingers, and only when she was sobbing, begging me to let her come, did I suck down as hard as I had at the beginning.

When she cried out, screaming and moaning and sobbing, I felt triumph roar through me. I watched as she twitched on the bed as she came down from the peak, and though I wanted to growl, I answered her when she whispered, "I thought you didn't give head."

"I don't."

"You're too good," she whispered, rocking her head back and forth, side to side.

It pricked my ego, even if it was a compliment, that she could think of other bitches at a time like this.

Ordinarily, I figured I'd be glad. It meant she knew this was just a lay, but this wasn't *just* anything.

I didn't know what it fucking was, but 'nothing' wasn't it.

"I had a misspent youth," was all I told her about myself. "And if you're asking about Cammie, then I let another sweetbutt go down on her."

She swallowed at that, not in revulsion or pleasure, just like she was taken aback by my words.

Maybe she hadn't expected that answer, maybe I'd never fucking know...

In fact, I didn't want to know, so I bowed my head and punished her for asking something she shouldn't have asked at all.

Sucking down on her tender, hypersensitive clit, I didn't stop until she was sobbing, her body twisting around as she tried to escape and evade what we both knew she needed.

All the while, I kept my fingers inside her, spreading her apart because, fuck, she was tight. Even if I thought about doing this to punish her for thinking shit she shouldn't be thinking about, I'd need to do it because she was too small for me until I got her too fucked in the head to care, and she could take me easily because she needed to be filled.

I'd admit to being out of practice on the old tongue-fucking score, but what could I say? It was like riding a bike.

I made sure to touch her G-spot and thanked God for having long, slender fingers so I could tease her constantly. When I took her up to the peak twice more, and she was shaking like a leaf as she came, I pressed my wet mouth to her inner thigh and bit down on that fleshy piece of skin.

She jolted, but didn't do more than whimper, and that was my test. The one I'd learned long ago was the marker for if a bitch was ready.

So, when I knew she was, it made no sense that I went to the other thigh, bit her there too, then sucked down hard so she would wear my fucking mark for days to come. I sucked as hard as I had on her clit, raking down against the tissue until it was blushing blood-red. When she was anointed on both sides, I let my gaze drift to her, and smirked as I began to straighten up.

Grabbing my wallet from my jeans, I pulled out a condom as I eyed her.

She was splayed on the bed, her arms and legs wide open, her eyes closed, her mouth parted as she breathed heavily through her lips like she was panting.

Her pussy was bright pink, and under her ass, she had a wet spot from all the juices that ran from her core to grace the sheets.

As I pulled on the condom, for the first time in my life, I resented covering my cock. Why? Fuck if I knew. I just did. That tight cunt was going to be like a glove, and I wanted to feel every inch of her, every slick, delicious inch against every inch of me. She was going to feel like heaven and hell, and I couldn't wait to allow myself to fall into the temptation of her.

When I crawled onto the bed, my weight making the mattress shift, her eyes flared wide.

"I've never," she groaned, "never, ever, ever—"

My lips curved, but I didn't tell her I knew that already.

I wasn't sure if she'd *never* come, or if that was the first time someone had tongue fucked her into a stupor, but either way, it was a damn shame, and her ex-lovers needed a bullet to the brain for letting her down in the sack.

Although, maybe not, because if she was this dazed over what I'd done to her, maybe when I fucked her, she'd never think about fucking off to New York. She'd stay here, close to hand and— And what?

My jaw clenched, my smile fading at the thought of her leaving for New York, because that had been no idle threat.

The prospect had irritated me before, but now she was here, her juices on my tongue, her taste in my mouth, and her cunt wet for my cock, there was no way in fuck I wanted to think about her being anywhere but under me.

Maybe she saw the shift in my mood, maybe she thought something was different... That was because it was.

When I moved over her, my mind had twisted things. I'd never hurt her, and I figured she knew that, because she didn't run.

Giulia studied me, watching me warily like she knew I was a predator that was eying up its prey but she wasn't scared, and that made all the difference.

When her tits jiggled with her heavy breathing, I resented the fabric between us. Resented that anything parted us, and I reared up as quickly as I'd covered her and tore my Henley off and over my head.

The second she saw my chest, she reached up and let her fingers spread over my pecs. When the tips fiddled with the piercings in my nipples, she cocked a brow as she tugged at them, then questioned, "Why do you like to be so full of metal?"

"Don't worry, my bones are mostly calcium."

Well, except for the titanium plate in my skull. Courtesy of a bar brawl when I was nineteen.

But I didn't think she needed to know that.

I shrugged at her question. "Why not?"

Her lips twitched, and when I looked at her, all creamy and golden atop the worn sheets, I had to admit that I liked how bare she was. Her ears weren't even pierced for Christ's sake, and no part of her was inked.

I could no more stop myself from savoring her juices on my tongue than I could stop myself from dipping down and slipping the crest of her nipple between my lips and tugging on it.

As I bit down on that delicate tip, I mumbled, "It's only a little prick."

"Said no one to you ever."

Despite myself, I had to laugh, and then, I realized that was like the second or third time she'd made me do that today.

Fuck, was there something in the water?

She beamed at me, almost like a soccer mom whose brat had just scored at a meet, and then the fingers of one hand ran over my head, sliding through my hair, and when I wanted to close my eyes and savor the intimate touch, she both spoiled it and turned me on by grabbing a hold of said hair and tugging it.

Bringing me down so that we were on the same level again, her mouth and mine hovering closely, she grated out, "You going to stop teasing me, Mr. Terminator?"

I felt the demon inside me react to her tone, flaring wide and blazing brightly at her demand, and I let him rip.

I grabbed her thighs and hauled her up, so her pelvis was arched and not flat to the mattress.

Blindly, I grabbed for one of the pillows at the head of the bed, and in a minute flat, I had her slightly rearranged so her hips were higher, her ass was tilted forward, and her legs were spread wide as could be.

My mouth watered again at the sight of her juicy cunt, but I grabbed my sheathed dick, and pressed it to her heat.

The wet flesh looked so clean against the dirty lines of my cock. Not that it *was* dirty. But the sight of so many studs, so much metal, it was the opposite of the pristineness of her pussy.

I just knew that, even if she wasn't a virgin, she wasn't far off.

She'd let fuckers into this cunt, but they weren't me.

I was about to show her what it really meant to fuck a man.

As I rocked my hips, letting my cock slide through her juices, allowing the bumps of the piercings to notch against her, to rub and rock against her tender folds, I watched as her mouth began to work, as she started to swallow, and her fingers dug deep into the sheets, clawing at them because she couldn't claw at me.

When she began to twitch, I watched her stomach muscles ripple.

"You're going to take as much of this as you can, aren't you, baby girl?"

"Y-Yes," she concurred with a moan.

I held my shaft at the base before I slipped the tip against her entrance. As I pushed inside, I waited for her to adjust. A flash of discomfort crossed over her brow, and I let her take a second to catch her breath.

Reaching over with my other hand, I began to rub her clit, and within seconds, she was rocking up, her legs widening as she sought my touch. Pushing inside her, a few more inches at most, I watched her face for discomfort.

The second she began to feel the ladder against her tissues, however, her tits began to shake like Jell-O in an earthquake, and I could feel her arousal start to surge, which, in turn, made me want to blow my wad like a young guy who got his hands on a Playboy magazine for the first time.

Gritting my teeth, I carried on rubbing her clit, slowly but surely pushing in. The ladder was my measuring system too. It was usually what women could take without hurting them. Especially at first.

The second I was in to that final notch three-quarters down my dick, I stopped rubbing her clit, and leaned over her, pressing my hands to either side of her shoulders.

Hovering above her, I rubbed my pubic bone against her clit, rocking back and forth to make sure she had pressure there. Her eyelids fluttered as she dealt with the thickness, the change of pressure, as well as all the different textures inside her.

I went the extra fucking mile. My condoms weren't 'ribbed' for her pleasure. My whole fucking dick was.

As I began to arch my hips, I slowly rocked back and forth. I wanted to ease her into this, because there was no way in fuck this was one and done. If it was, then I'd fuck her hard and fast, and wouldn't give a shit about her pleasure. I'd be out that door so fucking fast, the condom would still be on my dick before I tossed it into the trash on the way out of the bunkhouse.

But I wanted this again.

And again.

Too many 'agains' for my sanity, honestly.

So I was careful, and I wasn't known for being careful. Well, not *this* careful, at any rate.

Releasing a shaky breath, I shoved all my weight onto my arms and focused on not coming, on not thrusting into her so hard, too hard. Sweat beaded on my brow, and down my spine, I could feel it prickling into being.

My lungs began to ache like I'd been running, and my heart was pounding with the excess adrenaline bounding around my system. The trouble was, the monster wanted to thrust and fuck. But I was keeping him in hand. Miraculously enough.

Then, she fucked everything up.

Her hands came to my waist, they slipped around, and she dug her nails into the bottom of my back where my rear abdominals were.

The second I felt that slight prick, I felt the blood rush to my head. Jesus, it happened so fast that I should have lost my erection, but instead, I lost all reason.

I moved.

Fast.

I thrust.

Hard.

And I fucked her.

Furiously.

I pounded into her, but all the while, I kept enough fucking sanity to stay half out of her. She clung to me though. Instead of pushing away, instead of screaming at me to get off her, she grabbed me with her arms and legs, not content until I was on top of her, no space separating us, nothing keeping us apart as I took us to another level.

She clenched down around me with no touching, with no teasing. She screamed in my ear, her sweat and heat and scent surrounding me as I burst into a fiery blast that decimated me to my core.

I felt the backs of my eyes turn black, and my lungs no longer just burned, they fucking stung with pain as I allowed the sheer pleasure to whirl through my system, cleansing me even as it renewed me, even as it brought parts of me back to life. Parts that had been dead for a long time.

In the heat of her passion, I found that those parts of me were reawakening.

Only time would tell if that was a good or a bad thing.

SIXTEEN

GIULIA

I WAS SORE.

Oh, God, was I sore. But fuck, it felt so good that even as I clung to Nyx's hips with my knees, I couldn't regret it as the throb of the bike beneath me seemed to massage all my sore spots.

Deep inside, I felt like he'd touched a part of me that had never been touched, and while it kind of hurt, it also felt epic. Like... shit, almost like the first time I'd had sex and had stupidly felt as though I'd gone from being a girl to a woman, thanks to that one act.

Okay, so he hadn't made a woman out of me, but Jesus, he'd done something.

Sure as hell, the next day, I'd be walking woodenly. Shit, I might even need help once we arrived and I had to get off the bike... the thought of which had me wishing that the journey from the compound into West Orange was farther than it actually was, a fact I knew had to piss off the affluent county to no end because, as we drove toward the main town, we passed so many swank houses, it was unreal.

I was a biker's daughter, not a biker's bitch, but I couldn't deny I found that amusing.

I could imagine the original Satan's Sinners had done that on purpose, snubbing their noses at society in the vicinity with joy in their hearts and malice in their minds.

To be honest, the bastards I'd met along the way who thought they owned the world because they were rich, made me quite pleased at the Sinners' address.

It was pretty around here too. We were surrounded by green. Trees were everywhere, little copses of them separating estates and individual houses. Rolling fields lined the roads, and they weren't just golf courses either.

I mean, I remembered the area. I'd lived here longer than I'd been away from it, but it was strange. Like, I remembered it as a kid, not as a woman. All my adult memories were based in Utah. And fuck, as we passed the green rolling hills, as we drove deeper into a town that I remembered in my bones, I realized how much I'd hated Utah.

Sure, you couldn't say you hated a state, only a town, but the second I'd driven into it, I'd just wanted to go home. In a way, it wasn't the state, just the fact that my mom had brought me there. Taken me and my brothers to another place, away from home and everything we knew just on a whim.

Of course, *now* I knew it wasn't a whim. She'd gone somewhere my dad couldn't get to her. Well, he could have if he'd given a shit, but he hadn't, so she'd gone just far enough for him to leave us alone.

But it wasn't him who I'd missed.

I'd missed the Old Ladies and the kids who were closer than friends, they were family.

And what sucked the most, and what had probably caused more of my shitty attitude than anything, barely any of them were still there.

Most of the kids had been my age, and they hadn't stuck around. It was a brutal life, so I wouldn't be surprised if they'd hightailed it to the city to get away from their past and to make something of their lives that had begun in a shroud of violence and death. As for the Old Ladies, most of them had either died or, like my mom, had realized being a biker's woman was no easy thing, and had pissed off somewhere else.

Hell, maybe my mom had even inspired some of them to take the bit between their teeth and get the fuck out of there, before any more shit could befall them.

So, even though I knew the Sinners' compound, and even though it was like a latent memory, I was missing so many old faces that it made it a wonder I wasn't more miserable than I already was.

Home wasn't home anymore.

My mom hadn't been home either.

And I'd been out in the cold for so long that I was starting to get frostbite.

I really didn't want to think about how, being close to Nyx, I was suddenly warm.

Putting anything into him, into any kind of relationship with him, was just asking for trouble, and I was not my mother. I had no intention of getting pregnant at a young age. Maybe if it was with a decent guy, but with a biker? Hell no.

I shuddered at the thought, and then grimaced when Nyx called over his shoulder, "You cold?"

"No," I hollered back at him, and squeezed his waist with my hands to make sure he understood.

I wasn't cold.

I was, if anything, the opposite.

I was hot in all the best places, and inside, I was warm too. Like I'd had a lot of hugs in a very short space of time, and each one had gone some way to easing pieces of my sadness.

Okay, that sounded like bullshit, even to me, so I focused on the corn fields, the bright white sun that shone overhead like a ball of gold that was intent on blinding me, and relished in the throb of the bike between me and the powerful biker who knew how to ride a beast like this.

I was, I feared, my parents' daughter.

I'd been on the back of my brothers' bikes more times than I could count. I was the only bitch, they claimed, who they'd allow on the back of theirs, and fuck, if I didn't love it.

After five orgasms—yeah, *five*, because Nyx was one helluva lover—I felt like screeching out, whooping, and basically doing a frickin' jig as elation whirled through me, casting out the shadows and making this day so much more fucking joyful than it had started.

Back at the compound, in his arms, I'd flown, but *this* was like flying for real.

The wind in my hair, whipping the ponytail around like nuts, the air blasting into my skin, whistling around me as the heat of the day hit me in a way it wouldn't if I was in a cage.

This was the fucking life.

As we made it into town, I was almost disappointed, because it meant I'd have to get off soon—my quivering, aching inner thighs be damned. Sure, I had the return journey to look forward to, but maybe not.

Maybe Nyx would disappear, leaving me at the bar, and I'd have to find another way home...

The Sinners would pay for a fucking cab if he didn't come and take my ass back, that was for damn sure. And if he didn't? If he *did* leave me here, he'd pay for it too.

Even as I thought about dosing Nyx's next meal with laxatives, preemptive planning for a strike in case he did attempt to dump me in town and then head on out without a backwards glance, I realized we'd passed the main street and were approaching a freestanding building that had my brows lifting.

The town had changed in the time I'd been gone.

No surprise there.

Big brands and huge names littered the streets, but in the center of it all, just beside a busy thoroughfare and a large parking lot, there was a chain of buildings, smaller than a mini mall but still impressive.

With four storefronts in total, I saw they were purpose built, custom-made for each business.

As central as it was, it made me wonder whose arm they'd twisted—or *broken*—to pull this one off.

A strip joint next to a diner next to a bar next to a garage? Horrific for the country clubbers, but for a biker's brat, I figured, because of how they decorated the front, it blended in well. All silver and chrome, the place was like something from *Happy Days*.

On one corner, the garage took up the most space, I guessed. It spat out onto the road at an angle, somehow keeping it distant from the other businesses, while still doing what it was doing.

There were a shit ton of bikes parked outside of it, and I had to wonder how that was possible, considering—from what little Nyx had shared—these places were all brand new. No staff, no one manning any desks, and no customers.

So why the fuck were there a dozen bikes out front and a couple of cars?

The strip joint was all black glass and more chrome. You couldn't see inside, but the doorway was in the middle of the front, and, I had to laugh, but it was a huge archway that look like a set of legs. Thinner at the bottom, curvier at the top, and with a distinct kind of 'pearl' at the apex.

It could have been art deco, if I knew these bastards didn't do everything with their tongue fixed firmly in cheek and the middle fingers of both hands raised to the world.

The diner was retro vintage chic. I almost wished I was working in there, but the bar was the piece de resistance. It had all kinds of shit on the sign, but it declared "Daytona" to the world, which was definitely a joke, seeing as these guys didn't race. Racing was beneath bikers, even if they took over the roads like they owned them and flew down highways without a care for paltry things like speed limits.

The background of the Daytona sign was black and white checkboard, but at the center, there was a kind of stack of wheels that propped up the name, and on either side of it were huge fenders from a vintage Cadillac. Bracketing them were models of Fender guitars. It was kind of messy, but it somehow fit.

The front was wooden, but it had more chrome touches, and it certainly didn't scream biker bar.

I had to wonder who they were going to aim their business at—locals, bikers, or the elite who lived around these parts and who, ordinarily, would stick their noses up in the air rather than frequent something that was owned by biker trash.

We pulled up, not unsurprisingly, outside the garage.

When Nyx tapped my leg, letting his hand stroke down the curve of my calf that was bared, thanks to the shorts I wore, I had to withhold a shiver as his callused palms brought nerve endings to life that had no business being awake.

He'd fucked them into a stupor earlier on.

I didn't mind the gesture, because he touched the leg that wasn't on show to the rest of the crowd that had gathered around the front of the shop.

There was nothing special about this place, not like with the other businesses that actually looked quite classy.

Not that I thought bikers weren't capable of being classy, just that...

Shit, I was digging myself into a grave with that train of thought, wasn't I?

Especially since I was biker spawn.

Wanting to smack myself in the face, I climbed off the back of the bike, and waited for him to kick off too.

As he did, I eyed the muscles in his form, muscles that were clearly visible, thanks to his Henley and the tight cut of his jeans. He wasn't a vain man, I knew that much. His hair was usually all over the place, even if he did try with some gel or other product that usually wore out after he'd messed with it enough. His jaw was stubbled more often than not, but not densely enough that I thought he never shaved, and his clothes were clean, even if he tended to wear the same stuff over and over again, just in different colors.

His boots were polished, he smelled good, and his nails rarely had shitty grease or motor oil down them like my dad always had, which had always made me shudder in revulsion.

No, all told, Nyx was a beautiful specimen for more than just his pretty face, and his clothes merely framed a delicious body I was grateful I'd seen semi naked.

A part of me wanted to pout that he hadn't stripped while I'd been totally bare, but I got it. He'd been trying to minimize my discomfort, and while he was big, he wasn't a fucking anaconda. I had to wonder what stupid bitch had given him a complex over his size.

Even as I felt myself getting overheated—both from the memories of that huge dick sliding inside me, and the fact that I really didn't want to know how many other women had creamed around that cock—I turned to him and asked, "Are you helping out in the garage too?"

He stunned the fuck out of me by grabbing my hand and clasping our fingers together.

For a second, I could do nothing other than gape at the union of our hands, then I tugged mine away from his and hissed, "What are you doing?" Quickly, eying the crowd, I saw no one had seen, and thanking God for small mercies, I spat, "Do you want me to be free game?"

I knew how the brothers ran.

It was a free for all, especially on something that was considered free game. Sure, I was a daughter of a biker, but that hadn't stopped a lot of daughters from becoming clubwhores over the years. They followed in their mother's steps, a lot of them...

Sluts.

Okay, okay, I knew I was being mean, especially when I'd just spread my legs for a biker too, but I'd grown up with a mother who *loathed* the sweetbutts. That kind of shit stuck with a girl, and to be fair, there was no sisterly camaraderie with those skanks anyway. They'd screw any biker, whether he had a ring on his finger or was dating someone else, or not. They deserved no sympathy because they'd fuck any Old Lady over without even blinking.

While Nyx scowled at me, he didn't argue and released his hold on my fingers without further argument. I wasn't sure whether I was relieved or sad at how he let me go. I sure as hell didn't want the other guys to think there was something between us, because if they did, I'd get more come-ons than I usually did, and after experiencing Lever's idea of flirtation, the fewer of those I endured, the better. But it had also felt good holding his hand.

Good to...

God, this was another stupid train of thought.

Stupid, stupid, *stupid.*

Wanting to punch myself in the face this time, because face palming wasn't enough, I blew out a breath and followed him as he trudged over to the garage without another word. Was it wishful thinking that I'd hurt his feelings? Not because I wanted to hurt him, but because if he had feelings, then I wasn't the only one in over my head?

Letting a breath gust from me, I followed him, eying up the people at the garage as I did so. I wore shitkickers, my usual gear, and a pair of shorts that covered up the fact I didn't have a thigh gap, and a loose flowing top that was comfortable.

Was it weird that I was second-guessing my usual clothes just because we'd had sex? Or was it normal, considering the crowd we walked into consisted of a group of club sluts that had me narrowing my eyes at them as they drooled over Nyx? They were with bikers, that was evident from how they clung to their guys, and I'd seen women wear more clothes at the beach.

Didn't they get annoyed with their panties stuck up their ass crack all the fucking time?

Just wearing a thong got me agitated, but this stuff made cheese wire look generous. They had those denim shorts that porn stars wore, with the front fly half undone, baring too much to the world. With huge tits that were covered in tees that would do well in a wet shirt competition, and high heels that made me worry for their future bunions, I felt like a frump. Which, you guessed it, didn't put me in the best of moods as I monitored the situation.

As Nyx walked straight into the circle of men and women who had gathered in front of the workshop, I saw him head for a guy with an earful of piercings that made me grateful I hadn't had mine pierced when I was a kid.

The cuts these guys wore were different. Black, sure, but the patches were weird, not like the ones the Sinners' had.

I realized how stupid I'd been then. Just because the bikers were close to our territory, didn't mean another set of riders hadn't invaded our space.

Even as I tensed up, unsure if this was some kind of declaration of war —because that wasn't the first time shit started this way—Nyx shook the other guy's hand.

"Razer," he boomed, but he was smirking. Which, for Nyx, was the equivalent of a welcoming smile. Except... something was different here. He was tense. Now, that was par for the course with him, especially after I'd just pissed him off, but he was definitely on edge. Which made me wish I hadn't followed him like I was a sheep and he was little Bo Peep.

"Nyx, my man. Just wanted to check out the shop."

Razer slapped Nyx on the arm, and it wasn't the kind that was a pissing contest. It was more of a greeting—if that was a thing, especially when it was strong enough to almost make Nyx stagger to the side.

I'd been on the other side of those muscles, so I knew it took some punch to get him to shift at all.

"Pretty, ain't it?" Nyx mocked, peering up at the storefront that was anything but pretty.

It was navy blue with a simple white sign that had, in blue letters, a detailed list of the services the place offered.

That was it.

Behind the large garage doors, I assumed there was the necessary gear to fix stuff, but if Nyx was here to open up, he didn't pull out a set of keys.

Something Razer picked up on. "You aren't opening up?"

Nyx shook his head. "I'm in charge of the bar."

Razer snorted. "Rex always was a smart bastard. Get the teetotaler behind the bar top, and you'll have dollars coming out of your ears."

One of the club sluts popped bubble gum, and I realized then how close she was to me. I didn't jerk in surprise, my focus on Nyx's conversation because I'd seen him drink, so why was Razer calling him a teetotaler?

Then the bitch murmured, "Who the fuck are you, fatty?"

I wasn't fat. I was curvy. *Bitch.* But I wasn't about to say that when she made a toothpick look plus-sized.

With one of our sluts, I'd have shoved my fist in her nose, but I wasn't about to start shit with another club.

Instead, I ignored the whore by gritting my teeth.

Nyx cut me a look, and when he looked relieved at my—what I assumed was—stoic expression, he released a sigh and stated, "I'm sure Link will be along soon. This place is his responsibility."

"The fucker's running late if he is," Razer ground out, but he didn't sound that pissed off.

If anything, he sounded cordial.

Which I trusted less than if he'd growled.

Nyx raised his hands. "You know how Link is. He's probably getting a BJ."

Razer's eyes flashed with genuine amusement. "This is true. Well, drop the bastard a line and tell him to get his quickly. Some of us have shit to do."

The heavy rattle of a bike pierced through the regular rumble of traffic, almost punctuating Razer's statement.

Nyx twisted to look over his shoulder. The move was weird, but I quickly understood why—he didn't want to show Razer his back.

Was it weird that I understood that?

Maybe.

I mean, I hadn't been raised in the club. Not really. Not like my brothers, who'd been dragged away from the Sinners' reckless lifestyle when they were beyond saving. It was why they'd whined all the time at being far from the clubhouse. They'd been destined to be bikers, or so they claimed. It was in their DNA.

Me?

I just hoped my DNA wasn't covering too much of the borrowed bed I was sleeping in at the compound.

My mom had made them promise they wouldn't become bikers, though, and when she'd died, I'd known almost immediately that the promise would be broken without her there to keep them in check.

It was why I'd traveled with them, because if I hadn't, I'd never have seen them again.

Yeah, they weren't the best brothers. They'd barely talked to me since we'd arrived here. More than anyone else, but asking me, "Where's the toilet roll?" and, "Make me a sandwich, Sis?" wasn't what I considered decent conversation.

So, that being said, having been raised to be a prissy girl, I really shouldn't understand why Nyx was on edge, but I did.

He had no choice but to be friendly with this unknown MC, but he wasn't happy about it. So why were these bikers here if it was without an invitation?

When a bike pulled up behind us, the crowd's attention veered toward the rider, and I took the chance of looking at the cuts the bikers around us were wearing and saw their sigil was a wolf with its teeth bared.

Rabid Wolves MC.

Not very original, was it?

Then again, neither was Satan's Sinners.

But at least my MC didn't sound like it belonged in the humane society shelter.

"Razer, sorry, man. Ran into traffic."

Nyx smirked when Link flipped him the bird as he elbowed his way into the crowd. Totally uncaring about who got whacked in the side as he did so.

The second he shook hands with Razer, then did that stupid hug thing that guys did, the one that included the shoulder clap while drawing them in for a half hug, Nyx slapped another biker on the side.

"Another time, Kit, and we'll get together for drinks."

"When the bar's ready," Razer declared, swerving out of his conversation with Link to focus on Nyx.

"Sounds good. I guess we'd best get some beer on tap then, huh?"

To some laughs that sounded fake to me, he retreated, and grabbed my arm as he headed out of the circle.

The sensation of being hauled didn't please me, but I let him drag me until we were about ten feet away, then I shook off his hold.

He pulled out his cellphone. "Thank fuck you held your tongue."

"I'm not an idiot," I spat, pissed that he thought so little of my brainpower. It didn't take a fucking genius to recognize that there were some people it was okay to insult, and another club's bitches weren't on that list.

As he shot off a text, he cut me a look. "She deserved for you to do what you did to Kendra."

"Like that, did you?"

"Well, 'like' is strong," he said dryly, "but I'm sure she deserved the chipped front tooth."

I laughed, unable to stop it from bursting free. "Wasn't my fault she moved when I aimed her face at the counter."

"I really shouldn't like how aggressive you are," he grumbled as he shoved his cellphone into his back pocket.

"No? Apparently, you like me just as I am," I reminded him, because if he didn't agree with Toothpick back there, it figured he liked my curves.

His eyes were enough to roast me from the inside out as he let his gaze drift over me when he said, "I do."

He grabbed my hand and folded his fingers over mine, glaring at me as he did before he tugged me into moving.

I didn't question the gesture, but I did ask, "Since when do MCs work together?" I cleared my throat. "Okay, that's a loaded question. Since when do two clubs who aren't chapters work together?"

"Club business." *And so it begins.*

I huffed out a disgusted breath. "Well, you didn't seem too happy to see them there."

"They weren't supposed to be on their way until we had shit up and running. It's rude they came early."

Rude.

I almost snorted. "Just as rude as Link being late?"

"Maybe." He cut me a look. "You know how this shit works, Giulia. I can't talk about this crap with you."

I shrugged, but inside, I'd admit to being stung. Stung enough to want to punch him in the gut, but I merely raised my chin and stormed toward the bar—I didn't even bother tugging my hand from his. Why give him that satisfaction?

The prick.

SEVENTEEN

LINK

"WHAT'S GOING ON?"

"With who?"

I rolled my eyes at Nyx's evident bluff. "Try that on with someone who doesn't fucking know you, man.

"Something has bitten you both on the ass. What is it?"

It was as clear as the nose on my fucking face that something was going down between Nyx and Giulia. If he thought they were hiding shit, then they were idiots, but even though Nyx was one of the smartest fuckers I knew, even he couldn't see the trees for the wood sometimes.

Dipshit.

Giulia had been gnarly from the start. In fact, she made a fucking cactus look fluffy, but Jesus wept, that was nothing to now. The looks she was aiming Nyx's way should have been enough to have him pissing blood. And Nyx? His glower made it clear that he wasn't a happy frickin' bunny.

"Nothing's going on, man. I don't know what you're talking about."

His bluster had me snorting. "How long have I known you again?"

He flipped me the bird. "Nothing's wrong." He completely twisted that around by muttering, "Sin, get me a shot of tequila?"

Sin's brows rose, but he did as bid, throwing the bottle from one hand to the other before pouring Nyx a shot, which he instantly downed.

After he'd finished pulling a face, I muttered, "Still want to tell me nothing's wrong?"

His nostrils flared and, ignoring me, he twisted around to face the room once more. The second Cammie shimmied over to us, I saw Giulia pinpoint the action like a heat-seeking missile.

Fuck, she'd be a beautiful woman if she didn't always look like she was sucking on goddamn lemons. But now, she looked like she had a lemon and lime medley going down in her mouth as Cammie pressed her hands to Nyx's chest and began giving him his own personal lap dance.

Stupid bitch.

Nyx didn't like public displays of anything.

Sometimes, he'd get his cock sucked in public, but that was mostly because he didn't want to take Cammie to his bed.

See that was how well I knew my brother, and here *he* was, trying to sell me a lie.

I watched Cammie put on a show. I wasn't sure if it was for Nyx's or Giulia's benefit, but it wasn't working.

Nyx looked like he'd taken a leaf out of Giulia's book and was sucking on a lime. He certainly wasn't appreciating having a gorgeous woman writhing all over him, that was for fucking sure.

Casting a look over Giulia's way, I saw her face had turned impossibly stony. Implosion was imminent, and I could see the countdown begin ticking down before my very eyes, like it was hovering above her fucking head.

On the brink of nudging Nyx to warn him that shit was about to go down, I knew he'd either reached his limit of Cammie's BS—she knew not to approach him like this, so she was doing the female equivalent of pissing all over him like he was a water hydrant—or he'd seen Giulia's reaction himself.

"Enough!"

The words were an explosion in and of themselves. The heaving crowd of bikers who were dancing with their slut of choice ground to a halt, someone even switched off the music, because when Nyx used that tone, everyone knew to back the fuck off.

Cammie jerked back like she'd been slapped, and for Nyx, that was about as violent as he'd get with a bitch. He hadn't had to lay a hand on her for Cammie to realize she'd pushed her fucking luck.

Just that one word and a glower was enough to have her twirling on her heel and staggering off into the crowd. I could hear her crying and knew it was because the bitch probably thought she was in love with the fucker, but hell, she should have known.

Bikers never made clubwhores their Old Ladies.

It never fucking worked.

And if she'd thought she was special because Nyx was giving her all his attention, she was wrong.

Looking over at Giulia, I didn't find any smugness in her expression. Mostly, there was surprise. But when Nyx twisted back around to face the bar, it didn't shock me to see a look of yearning written into her features.

Sometimes, the heart knew what the heart wanted, and the brain knew the heart was fucking stupid.

I clapped Nyx on the back. "I think you're back in her good books."

He sniffed. "You think my shouting at a slut who had no right to touch me, in front of the woman I actually want, is going to put me in her good books?"

When he put it like that...

"If you're done with Cammie, that mean I can have a go at her?"

I glowered at Sin's shitty timing. "Really, man?"

"She's hot." *Like that said it all.*

"I have eyes too, but there's a time and a fucking place, man."

"She never was mine anyway," Nyx grunted. "Have at her."

The words weren't loud enough to be heard over the crowd, but I knew enough people heard and recognized what that meant.

Of course, everyone but fucking Giulia recognized the significance of his words. But that fit. Both she and Nyx were difficult motherfuckers. Trust her to misunderstand.

She bowed her head over her can of Coke, making me wonder what she was even doing here. After all, she'd only just closed the bar up, and I knew she had to be exhausted because the place had to take a lot of work.

But here she was.

A glutton for punishment?

I slapped Nyx on the back again. "You know what you just did, right?"

"I did nothing," he denied.

"Yeah, you keep on telling yourself that."

He shrugged off my hand and powered off the bar in an explosive movement that had Giulia flinching. That her focus was so utterly on him, even though she didn't want it to be, was clear.

Because the two of them were no hopes, after Nyx headed off to only God knew where, I slouched over her way.

She cared for Nyx, anyone could see that, and the truth was, Nyx was my brother. I couldn't love him more if he was flesh and fucking blood.

Lighting up the second I was beside her, I laughed when she glowered at me and grumbled, "Feel free to poison your own air but leave mine free and clear."

"Shouldn't be sitting in here if you didn't want secondhand smoke."

She ran her fingertip over the rim of the can. "Didn't feel like sitting on my own."

I cocked a brow. "I thought you'd be fucking exhausted after what you've been doing at the bar."

"I am, but that doesn't mean I can get to sleep easily."

"You do know you catch more flies with honey than vinegar, right?"

She twisted her neck so she could grace me with her lemon-sucking expression. "Who the fuck said I wanted to catch flies?"

"Me." I smirked at her. "I've known Nyx a long time. You're smart enough to figure out that he doesn't like his business to be public. That's why Cammie's claiming went as bad as it could go."

"Yeah? So?"

"So, if you think he's the kind of guy that playing hard to get works on—"

She snorted. "Link, save your fucking advice. I'm not doing shit to entice Nyx. He's the one who reminded me of what he is."

I frowned at her. "What is he?"

"Just like my father."

And with that, she stormed off, leaving me gaping at her, because Nyx was nothing like Dog.

"Well, that couldn't have gone much worse."

Recognizing my Prez's voice without having to turn my head, I muttered, "You got that damn straight. What the fuck did Nyx do?"

"I'm not sure, but the first day she was at the bar, when you were late meeting up with the Wolves—"

"I'd like to know how you can be late for an appointment that didn't exist?" I grunted, because I was getting sick of defending myself on that score.

I'd known fuck all about the Wolves heading into our territory to check over the garage, but everyone, Nyx included, had blamed me for being late and for forgetting to inform the council that they were entering our city.

Rex just rolled his eyes and said, "Anyway, she had to get a cab back from town." He laughed. "She got a receipt and made me pay her back for the expenses."

"You like her," I said slowly, my eyes wide as I made that realization.

"I barely know her, but I like her for him. I think she's what he fucking needs. She isn't scared of him."

"Fuck off. No woman is scared of him. They all go to him when they want him to save their asses—"

"Physically, they know they're safe, but..." He tapped his temple with a tattooed finger. "Up here, they know to be wary of him, and you can't blame them for it. Their instincts are on point. But Giulia will give him shit, and that's exactly what he needs."

I thought about that a second. "Maybe she doesn't know what he is. What he's done."

"Undoubtedly. But the women don't really know."

"They watch the news," I said dryly.

"They think we're all involved. They don't know it's personal for him. They don't know it's his way of cauterizing old wounds." He reached for the shot glass Sin slid his way. As he stared into the liquid, he grunted, "You meant well, but they're both too prickly to accept any advice."

I winced at that, because he wasn't wrong. He saw my wince and smiled a little. "You always have to fix shit, don't you, bro?"

"If I can," I admitted gruffly.

I hated to see people suffering for no goddamn reason.

Sometimes, when you took a step back from the situation, only then could you see things that up close were blurred.

Fixing things for the people I gave a shit about was the only way I could help. If it meant they called me an interfering motherfucker, I'd take it because, hell, that was why I'd been given this road name.

Because I was the *link* between so many of the brothers here.

The person who knew all their secrets, and who'd die before I'd reveal a fucking one to any bastard—be they friend or foe.

EIGHTEEN

NYX

A FEW DAYS after our first afternoon together, Giulia was still mad at me.

I wasn't sure which had pissed her off most.

The fact that I couldn't tell her about why the Wolves had been on our turf without anyone losing a drop of blood, or the fact that I'd had to leave her at the bar, and she'd had to get a taxi back to the compound.

Rubbing my chin as I eyed her behind the bar, I'd admit that for someone who had no experience there, she fit.

With enemies on our turf, I'd been as useless as a coffee percolator made out of chocolate with the way my mind was focused on business rather than this place. But she'd made it work when I'd left her to deal with most things, as I concentrated on getting security to monitor the Wolves without being spotted.

Because I ran a tight security team, things had flowed like clockwork, and the Wolves had headed back to their side of the border with little fuss.

We'd never been *unfriendly* with them, never been at war because they ran shit differently than us. Girls weren't our thing. But going in together on this was a project that Rex wanted, and most of us didn't.

Sure, we were a democracy, and we ran everything by vote. Somehow, Rex had twisted Maverick, Link, and Storm's arms, and gotten them on his side, even though it made me cringe to think of having Wolves on our territory.

Sure, we were going to make a boat load of cash, and we were going to be tightening our links with the Five Points over in HK, but sometimes, money wasn't worth the loss in security.

But I guessed that was my past talking there.

In my absence, Giulia had somehow used that beautiful head of hers, and out of nowhere, we had a staff of two that was going to grow to four in the next couple of weeks as the takings were assessed and finances were assimilated, and she'd gotten a fully stocked bar as well as five different beers in. Beers that weren't damn bad. I hadn't expected her to have decent taste, but she'd gone for some great American lagers, then had picked up some fantastic bottled IPOs.

She'd also created some kind of bar snacks menu, and had begun conferring with the diner for them to make that stuff and bring it through.

Sure, it wasn't rocket science, but I knew that had never been the intention, because the diner was supposed to shut halfway through the bar's opening hours.

Not anymore.

The line chef was either loving or loathing her, but she was right.

People wanted to eat. And drinkers wanted something to snack on while they were listening to music or watching a game.

Rex, Storm, and Link had been the ones to kit this place out. I hadn't had any interest in making this shit look fancy. My biggest concern had been whacking them with the best alarm systems and security details that money could buy. It wasn't like we could use things like CCTV, not when business was bound to go down here, and the last thing we needed was the Feds piggy-backing onto our gear, so motion sensors, alarms, and all that were where I'd taken things.

Especially the strip joint.

It was the first in this particular area, and we had a feeling that even though the clients were going to be upper crust and willing to drop a fortune, they'd be brats and might get handsy from time to time.

Somehow, it was always the rich pricks who couldn't take no for an answer. So we had more doormen than strippers just to make sure that heads would roll in case some pricks decided to be overconfident.

Still, just because I could take no credit for how damn good this place looked, I could appreciate it as I skulked in a booth and watched the woman behind the bar confer with two servers who were too damn handsome for my liking. They were pretty boys with slicked back hair and way too many white teeth.

They were also more her age than I was.

Of course, I was older than her brothers, who weren't young, so what that said about me, I didn't know.

I refused to believe I was ancient, but fuck, I felt it watching pretty boy one try to cozy up to Giulia.

Even as I enjoyed watching her put their flirtations down with smiles that could only be called professional, I was more amused at how they tried to take charge, and that was the only time she'd ever look at me.

Yeah.

When she wanted backup.

Not when she wanted to shimmy up to me, place a hand on my arm like I'd seen some of the other girlfriends do, not even lean up on tiptoe to kiss me to stake a claim—to show the pricks she was taken. Because, duh, she wasn't, but that didn't mean I didn't resent the fact that was the only time she looked to me was for backup on her authority.

Most of the stuff she was doing was supposed to be my job, which left me sitting with my thumbs up my ass for most of the night, as the place went from being busy to busier to busiest.

Only at that point did she ever let me behind the bar, and the bitch of it was, she pulled a better beer than I did, and she had zero experience.

I'd already heard her jokingly tell a few of the patrons the same story about the brewery's rep having to show her what to do.

"I'd just bet he fucking had."

"You'd just bet who had what?" Rex asked.

I glanced at my Prez, who'd sidled up to me an hour ago, and who I'd been ignoring ever since.

I drummed my fingers against the table which, of course, was clean. Just like every other table in here, because Giulia ran a tight ship. A part of me had wondered if she was OCD or something, but when the beer line had sprung a leak and she'd been coated in it, she hadn't started screaming or demanding to use the shower in the strip joint next door.

Fuck, if that hadn't been torture watching her serve beers with her shirt all transparent...

Yeah, this had been a titty bar for the time it took for her shirt to dry out.

"Nothing."

"Well, fuck, Nyx, nothing about cuts it. You sulking with me or something? I know you're not happy about the Wolves—"

I instantly shot my scowl at him instead of Cody, the fucker behind the bar who kept brushing against Giulia, like he had some kind of internal compass malfunction. The guy needed glasses for how clumsy he was.

"*Sulking?* Do I look like I have a cunt?"

"No. I didn't think you had one, but Jesus, you've barely talked to me since I got in."

"Since when do we gossip?"

"We don't, but more than two words would be great," he grumbled.

"I'm not mad about the Wolves," I told him, balling my hands into fists as I watched Giulia laugh at something a guy with a hat that dwarfed his head told her. "I don't think it's smart, in fact, I think it's dumb as shit to get involved with them—"

"As you've already fucking said a thousand times."

I scowled at him. "Why do you want to talk to me again?"

"I don't fucking know. Why are you glowering at Giulia anyway? As far as I can see, she's sorted things out perfectly. Especially since you weren't around to watch over shit."

I heard the complaint in his voice and stated, "If you'd told me the Wolves were coming earlier than expected, I'd have been here."

"If I'd known, Link wouldn't have been late," he sniped back.

"And that's the reason why I hate working with the fuckers. They can't be trusted."

"But they're good at what they do, and with our new distribution up and going, we have the means—"

"I know." I grunted. "We don't need to talk about this shit here."

He grunted back at me. "You shouldn't need to tell me that, but damn, man, what's with the sour fucking face? I feel like your wife or something."

I flipped him the bird, then I flinched when I heard Giulia's laugh again.

Was she doing it on purpose?

I had hardly ever heard her laugh back at the compound, but here she was, chuckling all the fucking time.

As far as I knew, we didn't have nitrous oxide leaking in from the garage, so what had made her sense of humor make an appearance, I didn't know.

"You got the hots for her or something?"

"Is this grade school?" I countered woodenly, as I grabbed my bottle of Coke and took a deep sip.

"Maybe. Okay, definitely from the way you're scowling at the servers." He elbowed me in the side. "Don't be a prick."

"Why not? Why shouldn't I? They're supposed to be working, not fucking joking all the time. It isn't comedy hour."

"Christ, what's bit you on the ass? I know you're a miserable fucker but —" He tilted his head to the side, a thought evidently coming to him. "She put out for you?" When I didn't say anything, just clenched my jaw, he snorted. "I'm surprised she has your balls in a twist, considering I thought her cunt creamed vinegar."

That had me glaring at him. "Shut up, Rex. Don't fucking start."

He cocked a brow at me. "She really does have your balls in a bind."

"Stop talking about my fucking balls," I rumbled, aware that his arched brow was a warning.

Rex gave us all a lot of leeway, Mav and me more than most, but we all knew when to back the fuck off. Just because he came across as mellow didn't mean shit. Rex was as big a bastard as I was. I just had more kills ratcheted up on my scoreboard, and that was because of my past.

I hadn't been born an evil shit—I'd been made this way.

"She must have been crap in the sack if you're this mean in the aftermath."

"She's not talking to me, hasn't in over three days," I told him, really feeling like I was in grade school now.

"Why? What did you do? Give your class ring to someone else?" he mocked.

"No. I was supposed to handle most of the organizational shit for the bar, but I had to leave to handle things with the Wolves. Then, she had to get a taxi back to the MC. Ever since, she won't get on the back of my fucking bike."

I hated that I sounded like I was whining, but dammit to hell, I was used to bitches wanting to be on the back of my damn hog, not doing their best to avoid it.

"And you want her there?" This time his arched brow wasn't in warning, but in consternation.

"Yeah. I do."

"But you never ride with anyone at your back."

"Always a first."

"You have feelings for her? Or the fact that she's Lizzie's daughter get you—"

"Don't even finish that sentence. Fuck's sake. I had a crush on her. I was horny and she had massive tits. You telling me you didn't want to see them in the raw?"

He sniggered into his beer. "Okay, you got me there, but I don't want to fuck Giulia, and you do."

"Yeah, well, I like her. She's different."

"Different in that she isn't terrified of you?"

"That might have something to do with it," I muttered wryly.

"It's definitely a novelty."

"Everyone's scared of you."

"I wonder why," I mused, smirking at him.

"Yeah, I wonder," he replied, dry as the Sahara. "When are you getting your next tattoo?"

"Don't know."

"Thought you'd be all over that shit."

I shrugged, because usually I would be. But this wasn't 'usual.' I had bigger fish to fry than getting inked.

"Think that guy's coming on to her?"

Rex frowned. "Are you being serious right now?"

I shot him a look. "When am I not serious?"

"Fuck me." He scrubbed a hand over his face. "What are you going to do? Beat the fuck out of anyone who dares approach her?"

"Potentially."

"Then maybe I need to switch her job. She'd be safe in the garage."

"Face like that, she's safe nowhere," I predicted, aware I sounded grumpy, even more aware that Rex could try as much as he wanted, and he'd never get Giulia to do a damn thing *she* didn't want.

Which meant she'd be exiled.

Which meant she'd be on her way to fucking New York.

Goddamn women.

He grunted. "I'm not sure what to do with this information."

"Which information?"

"That you banged her, and that you want more. You never want more. Not from anyone who isn't a sweetbutt, and even then, it isn't really the bitch but the hole you fucking want."

I frowned at his description, which made me sound like a dick, then I saw the bastard at the bar laugh. He had blond hair, teeth so fucking white they glittered which he bared every time he goddamn smiled, and everything about him screamed that he was from Orange Hills, one of the swankiest subdivisions in the area.

His fucking shoes probably cost more than my bike, and everything had that cloying designer feel to it. From his white shirt to the simple jeans.

The dick screamed money, and I had to wonder if that kind of flash would appeal to Giulia. I didn't know her that well, after all.

Didn't know if she went for surface glitter over...

Over, what?

Biker grime?

"Fuck, I think I just grew a pussy," I said to myself.

"There's no *just* about it. You've been creaming yourself since you started watching her."

My nostrils flared at that. "Could you be any more..." I struggled to settle on a word. "*Vulgar?*"

"Vulgar? Yeah. If I tried."

Inwardly, I smiled. Outwardly, I flipped him the fucking bird.

"Seriously, Nyx. What the fuck is going on with you?"

"Nothing."

"Tell that to someone who doesn't fucking know you," he scoffed.

Because he did know me, and there was no evading that truth, I simply grunted, stating, "Fuck off."

"Can't fuck off. This is the table allotted to me." He arched a brow at me. "The Prez's table. That I'm deigning to let you sit at."

I rolled my eyes. "Want me to fucking bow and scrape my thanks? How about I tug on my forelock?"

"What the fuck is a 'forelock?'"

Waving my hand at that, I gritted my teeth when I heard Giulia laugh again, then I mumbled, "He *is* coming on to her."

"You said it yourself. With her face and those tits, she's never not going to get come-ons."

That he hadn't even looked in the same direction as me told me that he wasn't interested.

I scowled. "But he's more insistent than most."

"What are you going to do? Go and piss on her?" He snickered. "Please do that before I leave. I'd like to see what her reaction is."

Despite myself, I had to laugh, and of course that about stunned Rex, so that when he sprayed me with beer, I didn't even have it in me to glower at him.

Fuck, if I was him, and I'd heard me laugh for the first time in years, I'd have spat out my beer too.

❖

NINETEEN

GIULIA

I HEARD the laugh from all the way across the bar, and I knew where it came from and whom it belonged to.

My heart instantly began pounding like I was running, and though the place was busy tonight, and sure, I'd been moving fast from one end of the bar to the other, it wasn't enough to merit this level of response.

I didn't look at him, even though every part of me wanted to see him laugh.

He'd smirked, snorted, scoffed, and pshawed, but chuckle? Outright? Nope. That I hadn't seen often.

I knew he'd look beautiful. Bet the sides of his eyes crinkled, and his face, always so goddamn somber, lightened up some, just a tad, but not a lot because it wasn't in his nature to be effusive. I'd seen him laugh so few times, and already, the sight of him that way was burned onto my retinas.

"Babe, get me another Coors?"

I shot a grim look at the prick who'd been trying to charm me since he'd walked in with his royal flush of dicks an hour before. Trying to calculate how much time he'd spent on his hair was preferable to eying up Nyx and his fine ass.

His fine *dumb* ass.

I wasn't normally a red card and over kind of bitch in a relationship—be it fuck-buddy-esque, casual, or serious—but Nyx was working at a disadvantage. That disadvantage had a name–*Dad*.

I'd seen how my father treated my mother. More than that, I'd seen how bikers treated their women, and I wasn't about to turn up as another statistic whether he crawled or not.

And he hadn't exactly crawled by way of apology either.

He'd dumped me at the bar that day, and I hadn't seen him for dust. When I'd had to get a taxi home, I'd known that I was just another lay to him, and everything he'd done since hadn't proven otherwise.

Mostly, he just watched me. Glowering at me from that fucking table at the back of the bar that put him in my direct line of sight.

It was on a raised platform, a bench shaped in an open square that was surrounded by bikes on all sides, like they were fucking sentinels or something.

It was, oddly enough, like a throne, and it was the only place that was off limits to the clients. The one and only rule that Nyx had told me before he'd left me to deal with, ya know, *everything*, was that no one was allowed to sit on that dais other than Sinners.

Yeah, that was what he'd informed me.

Nothing important like the contact details of the breweries who were supposed to visit the bar, or the names of the reps who'd be bringing in soft drinks.

Nope.

Just that that area was verboten to the average Joe.

The prick.

When I told another prick the price of the Coors, he slid a ten-dollar bill over to me, and when I made to grab it, he pulled it back. Shooting him a look, I retorted, "Do you want the beer or not?"

"I'd prefer you, darlin'," he said with a smirk.

I was used to smirks, and this guy's was piss-poor. Having been raised around bikers, growing up with two dudes who wanted to be a biker more than they wanted to get their dicks wet—and that was really saying something—and then having fucked an Enforcer of the biggest badasses in the Tri-State area, yeah, I knew a good smirk, and this guy just didn't have it.

"I'd prefer you pay for your beer," I told him with a smile that was probably a little too small to be polite.

His eyes narrowed. "I can wait," he replied.

"For what?" I questioned, genuinely surprised by that answer. Hell, I was surprised by his interest.

Next door, there were over two dozen strippers swinging around poles, and in here, there were some cuties that I'd bang if I were gay. Why was he interested in me when I was...

I winced before the thought process could swell into being.

Fat.

Yup.

God, I hated being cliché.

I knew I was pretty, knew I had what it took to score, and I was genuinely happy with myself, but because Nyx had let me down, and because I'd been stupid enough to be let down in the first place, I was totally reverting to type.

Remembering the insults Lance had tried to scorch me with, recalling what the cheerleaders at school had said because I was popular with the Jocks, and they couldn't deal with the fact that a woman who actually ate could be wanted by the football team.

Juvenile?

Yeah, but any woman would be when they were constantly surrounded by naked women who were *perfect*.

To my left, there were strippers, and back at the compound, there were clubwhores who'd sink to their knees for any of the brothers. I'd seen more asscheeks and tits than I would at the beach, and all the while, it was easy to wonder why a guy like Nyx would want to fuck regular old me, when he could be screwing a pin up model.

"You can keep on waiting," I retorted, my tone colder, thanks to just thinking what I was thinking. "I have a boyfriend."

It was a lie, but fuck, what was I supposed to say? Guys did worse shit when they were humiliated, and at least this way, I saved his pride.

I was grateful for my sound reasoning when one of his dick friends slapped him on the back, whispered some shit in his ear that I couldn't hear over "Sweet Carolina"—Lord, I hated that song—and together, they slouched off to their booth.

He kept on glancing at me though. Smiling like he thought I was playing hard to get.

'No' really didn't mean 'no' to some guys.

It wasn't like that was news to me, but every time I came face to face with that fact, it always made me crabby.

Over the course of the night, I kept my eye on them because they were rowdy as hell.

One of the dicks was getting married next week from the way they were cheering him on as he chugged back tequila like it was water, and I got the feeling that they were building up to going next door.

As the guys I'd hired, cool boys who were working this side hustle to save up for community college—and I knew how hard that was—worked the bar, I did my own thing.

Ever since opening, we'd been busy, and since I was learning the ropes as much as they were, something that had given me trouble when they'd tried to take over at first, it wasn't easy keeping up with everything. Especially as I was using these nights as a means of, A, avoiding Nyx, and B, trying to calculate what we'd need for the official opening party which didn't have a date as of yet.

I wasn't sure what kind of weird ass logic had them throwing the launch party a couple of weeks after opening, but who was I to complain? I was gonna get paid double that night, at least, according to Nyx, who'd managed to corner me in the kitchen this morning as I was making breakfast.

It sucked to be me. Late nights *and* early mornings? I couldn't get my ass to New York fast enough.

Wiping down a couple of the tables was probably the quietest part of the job, and even though I'd tried to avoid the groomsmen's table, I failed when Chad, apologetically, had to ask me for help.

"There's too much shit for just me," he admitted with a grimace after the table placed another order.

"Go twice," I stated firmly.

I mean, I wasn't the boss, but he wasn't to know that, was he? I'd hired him, after all. And Nyx wasn't one for sticking his nose in, which I was almost grateful for if I wasn't pissed at him.

"I'll help."

I cocked a brow at the sound of *his* voice. "No, Nyx, you go and sit down," I told him sarcastically. "I'm sure you have lots and lots of business to deal with."

He narrowed his eyes on me. "Your mouth is going to get you into trouble one day, baby girl."

Those last two words were whispered in my ear as he swept toward the booth that was laden with empty glasses, dead beer bottles, and all kinds of crap that I was grateful I didn't have to pick up.

"Think it might be time you guys called it a night," he suggested, as he stacked bottlenecks between his fingers.

Now, that voice was the antithesis of friendly, but blond prick eyed up Nyx's cut, then spat, literally *spat*. "I don't think we're ready, are we, guys?"

The globule of saliva landed on the table. Just beside Nyx's hand where he'd been reaching for the next bottle.

His stillness would probably stick with me forever, because I could feel the sudden charge of fire slip into the atmosphere.

I'd never felt anything like it.

Ever.

In my life.

And violence wasn't something I was unaccustomed to.

Apparently, even in their drunken haze, the group of men appeared not to be totally fucking stupid, and they fell silent, their dopey giggles from too much tequila dying.

One of them, a man I'd forever be grateful to, offered, "I think he's right. We need to get back. I know Josie is waiting for me."

Blond prick mumbled, "Could you be any more pussy whipped?"

But with his shift of attention, Nyx relaxed a fraction. And when I said a fraction, I meant a fucking fraction.

The tension lessened by one-sixty-fourth, no word of a lie, and he carried on with his shit, staying quiet as he grabbed more bottles and retreated from the table, leaving the guys to gather their crap together which, thankfully, they did with only a few irritated mutters.

When Nyx approached the counter, I watched him warily, hating that I was turned the fuck on.

With each step he took toward me, I could feel the strength in him, the violence. It was leashed, but barely, and fuck me, I wanted that violence raining down on my body.

Not with a hail of fists, or a flurry of kicks, but with his body thrusting into mine. Overpowering me, making me take everything he had to give.

The aggression in him should have repelled me, should have made me want to avoid him, but it didn't.

If anything, it made me want him more, and considering I thought he was a douche for what he'd done to me that first day, I felt even more stupid than I already did.

There was heat in his eyes, heat that I knew was aimed at me, so I turned, went to stack up the fridge with more Coke, and let him move away, head on out to the plastic crates at the back of the bar where we stored the empties.

I felt like a coward, and that was probably one of the worst insults I could aim at myself, but fuck, I'd be stupid to get involved with him again.

Once?

Sure, it was worth it.

Twice?

That was like that whole 'fool me once, shame on you. Fool me twice, shame on me,' thing. This was more than shame. This was outright idiocy we were talking about here.

So, I avoided him, and unfortunately for me, I didn't count on the blond prick's stupidity as he swerved toward me at the end of the bar, which was closest to the door, and muttered, "Should have known you were a biker's slut." He sneered at me before I could say a word, then, just as he was about to leave, Nyx was there.

It was like something from a movie. A fucking action flick at that.

He put one hand on the bar, and with a strength that looked casual, but just couldn't be, he leaped over the counter and landed on the other side, as though he'd literally just walked through it.

Hell, that would have been easier to me.

I'd never been one of those people who could do cartwheels and hand-stands. That was probably another reason to dislike Nyx. For how goddamn fit he was.

Still, that was the least of it. When he grabbed the blond prick's hair, the hair that he'd primped and preened and coated with so much product that even after a night of drinks, it was still in pristine condition, he grabbed it and smashed his face into the door.

I didn't hear what he hissed in the guy's ear, didn't need to know. All around us, the bar went silent, and the guys who were friends with the dick simply froze, evidently not willing to fuck with Nyx, and damn, I hated myself for how badly that made me cream.

This man, this fucked-up shit, held the entire room hostage with his power.

Everyone knew to avoid him.

To evade his look, his touch.

Everyone except me.

He wouldn't hurt me.

Ever.

And dear Lord, how I wanted him for that, which was all kinds of messed up.

Jesus, I was just like my mom, except Nyx was a thousand times better than Dog. Not just with inherent power, but with looks too. Nyx was an eight. My dad? Even in his heyday, had barely scrubbed a six.

I gritted my teeth, trying not to be turned on at Nyx's defense of me, then I had no choice but to gasp—no choice, because it escaped my mouth before I could contain it—when Nyx pulled back and the blond prick fell to the floor.

I wasn't sure what had happened, why he'd crumpled that way, but when Nyx backed off, he cut the other guys a glower and ordered, "Get him the fuck out of here, and don't bring him back."

When they scurried to follow his bidding, I knew I was beyond wet. These guys were rich. And in this area, money came with power. I knew the sort, had known it from being a young kid. There were folk like me, then there were the country clubbers the Sinners so disdained, but they were in the majority around here.

West Orange was wealthy, and we were the blight on the area.

A blight that was gaining more power and wealth, thanks to whatever dealings the Sinners were mixed up in.

And for all that these men were those wealthy pricks who thought they owned the air they breathed, they still did as Nyx bade them.

In a few minutes, not a one of them remained, and the guy on the floor, who'd been bleeding out of his nose and looking more punch-drunk than ever—get it? Cue snort—had been chivvied out and into the parking lot across the way.

I didn't bother watching them go, instead, I watched Nyx.

I could feel my skin prickle with heat as he graced me with his focus, a ferocity in him that made me want to whimper.

He looked at me, and I at him, and as he walked toward the end of the bar, I had no choice but to follow.

I was no sheep, but damn if I was about to avoid Nyx when he was like this.

My skin prickled, and my stomach churned, but it wasn't with uncertainty, it was with need.

I wanted to harness his violence, wanted to have him burn it off inside me, and I knew he wanted the same.

"Clear the blood up," he commanded Chad, who instantly obeyed, something else that set me off, and without a second glance, he opened the door to the back room and held it wide for me to pass through.

I left behind a three-quarters' full bar that was loaded with clients who were stone-cold stunned at the violence they'd just witnessed, and I didn't care. Didn't give a shit. I just walked into the office, didn't stop until I was at the desk, and I placed my hands on the edge.

The door closed behind him, and I heard the thud of his boots as he took the same path I had.

I could feel the sweat beading on my upper lip, could feel it prickling down my back, and the heat? Jesus, I felt like I had central heating for a heart, because it was pumping an inferno around my veins.

When his hands came to my waist, I about died. My lungs almost ceased when he squeezed his left hand about my stomach, then, with his right, placed it in the center of my back, right between my shoulders.

Without a word, I leaned over, and when I had my elbows on the desk, he stuck his leg between mine and jarred mine apart.

A shaky breath escaped me, and excitement filled me, making me wait in agony as I wondered over his next move.

My tits shook, jiggling against the desk and the papers on there that I'd been dealing with earlier—papers I'd been bitterly handling as I figured this was Nyx's problem and not mine. But all that was forgotten as, finally, he reached for my skirt and began to tug it up until it was banded about my waist. The feel of his hands against my skin, his fingers, with those fucking calluses, dragging against sensitive tissues, had me flinching with just how on edge that simple touch made me feel.

I was on fire before he even managed to get his hands on my panties, and when he dragged them down, then used the toe of his boots to lower them to my calves, I released a low moan.

"You wet for me, baby girl?" he rasped.

A shaky whimper escaped me. Yeah, I whimpered. Sue me. "Y-Yes," I whispered back.

"Good." His fingers slipped through the folds of my sex, not stopping until I could hear how wet I was, never mind feel it. I closed my eyes, clenching them shut as I processed just how good it felt for him to be touching me this way.

I wanted to die, wanted to live, but whatever, I just wanted to feel this.

Feel him.

I shuddered as he nudged my clit, softly at first, before he began to outright rub it. Prickles of pleasure blossomed, morphing until I felt like I was being punched with just how wonderful it felt for him to touch me there.

With his spare hand, he slipped a finger inside me, and when he thrust it, back and forth, up and down, I rocked my hips, which he took as the sign it was.

Another finger appeared, and he did the same. I bowed my head, loving the pressure, needing more.

Another finger, then finally a fourth. I closed my eyes, just thinking about that massive dick of his and how four of his fingers in no way compared to his girth.

Shifting my legs, I parted them, widening them, then lowered my abdomen to the table, arching my ass up in the most liberating invitation I'd ever bestowed upon a man.

He didn't chuckle, didn't grunt, didn't even crow. He was quiet in his triumph, and I knew that was what had to be pouring through him.

I hadn't talked to him, not once, in just under ninety-three hours, yet here I was, welcoming him into my body.

The rasp of his zipper lowering had me shuddering, and when he rubbed his dick against me, finally, I felt all that metal, all that 'hardware' as he called it, and surged up onto tiptoe.

It was bizarrely warm and cold at the same time. Warm from his body contact, yet with the faint tang of metal that made my clit feel like it was... hell, I didn't even know. If I said it felt like it was on fire, that was way too close to a UTI symptom, but Jesus Christ, this was beyond good. The rub of it against me, one of those damn barbells touching my tender flesh, had tears weeping from my eyes.

Reaching up, I clung to the edge of the desk, needing to hold on for dear life as I accepted whatever he gave me.

The crinkle of the condom opening stunned me, because I hadn't realized he'd stopped touching me. Damn, where was my head? Knowing slick latex parted us, I almost mourned the intimacy of skin to skin contact, but shoved it aside to deal with the fact that I knew what was coming.

A groan escaped me as the tip found my gate. I tensed for a second, then jerked when he slapped me on the ass.

"You want me inside you?"

The harsh tone made it a wonder I wasn't gushing around his dick.

I didn't want him to be mean, but fuck, something about him, something with him in this mood, just about did me in.

"Y-Yes. I want you inside me," I answered truthfully.

"Then relax." He reached between my legs after he slid his hand under my stomach, and when he patted my clit, I jerked again, then rocked my hips as he worked the tip inside me.

I could no more stop myself from biting down around the fleshy part of my upper arm, than I could stop myself from taking my next breath. The pain felt good, just as good as him slowly working himself inside me.

I could feel every ridge, every bump, and though it was alien, it felt right. Like my body had been made to take him like this.

I shuddered as he worked his way into me, trusting that he wouldn't take things too far. He'd kept me safe before, had made sure he hadn't gone too deep for me to hurt the next day, not outside of the norm, at any rate, and I relaxed around him, wanting to take as much as I could, needing him to need *me* as much as I did him.

He grabbed my hips and dragged me back, not stopping until my tits were on the table, my stomach bare. His fingers gripped me there, and he grumbled, "Bear down."

The grumble should have been discordant, but it wasn't. I tried to give him what he wanted, but pulling the same move as when my OB-GYN shoved the speculum inside me for a checkup wasn't my number one way to get off.

I could feel sweat beading on my brow, felt the drum of my heart as I worked to give him what he needed, and when he thrust in another inch, then another, I whimpered, feeling slightly flustered at just how full I was.

Then, he stunned me.

He pressed a kiss to the top of my head as he bowed over me, giving me his weight, before he began to rub my clit.

The orgasm hit me hot, hard, and fast. I hadn't expected it, hadn't thought he'd let me come so soon—and yeah, the word 'let' was no joke. Nyx was in total control of my body, and I'd be a fool if I didn't recognize that.

I screamed, uncaring if anyone could hear me as my pussy clenched down around his thick length, and the pressure inside me, both from him and the pleasure of what he made me feel, made me wonder how I didn't burst open, implode then explode into a million lights as my energy transferred to the next dimension.

He took me somewhere, to another level, to someplace where I felt like I was going crazy with the ecstasy ricocheting through me. And then he moved. And I had no choice but to scream again.

He was cautious, I'd give him that, but his movement set off a welter of panic inside me.

"Too much, too much, too much," I half screamed, yelling the litany as I tried to deal with what was working its way through my system.

His thrusts were slow, too slow, yet too fast. His hips bucked into mine, our skin slapping, bodies clapping as we bounced off one another, and then he jerked upright, and he pulled half of his cock out.

Another scream escaped me, and I started to cry when he fucked me. I missed his full length, but I also didn't feel like having a bruised cervix, so I was half-delirious from the impending orgasm, and half overcome with gratitude at his care.

When he pinched my clit, I yelled, "You bastard!" It sounded choked, but then, that was me.

Choking on his dick.

In more ways than one.

I bowed my head and once again, gnawed on my arm to contain the pressure of what he was making me feel. When he placed his hands just below my ribcage, I almost melted when I realized it was to protect me from being hit in the stomach as he rammed into me.

Then, the damnedest thing happened.

His cock throbbed inside me, and because he was so big, and I wasn't, I knew what that meant.

My entire body responded to that pulsation, everything inside me starting to switch off to deal with the cataclysm heading my way.

And just as he came, a loud grunt escaping him as his hands squeezed my waist, his body moving faster to deal with the welter of pleasure hitting him, I felt my own orgasm blast into being.

And like that, I was a goner.

A fucking no hope, because, in that second, Nyx claimed me in a way that no man ever could.

Ever would.

And I was fucked.

In more ways than one, because I'd never be any biker's Old Lady, and he, damn him, probably didn't even want a girlfriend, never mind anything as permanent as branding me as his.

But my climax was too powerful to make any of my bittersweet thoughts overtake the joy of what he gifted me, so I threw myself into it like it was the deep end of a pool, and I drowned in him, in everything he had to give me, because this had to be enough.

Even if I knew, deep down in my heart, that it wasn't and never would be.

TWENTY

NYX

I HATED how right she felt on the back of my bike.

It actually fucking irked me. Her arms around my waist, her heat on my back, her legs cupping my hips. It was perfect. Sheer fucking bliss, and I didn't know why.

Didn't understand why.

How could I?

I wasn't used to these feelings, wasn't used to the warmth inside me—it was alien. All I knew was that I liked her there, and even that was too much.

The wind blasted us in the face, so I understood why she turned her head and burrowed into my cut. I understood, even as I bemoaned it, because I liked that too.

I liked how she cuddled into me, and I liked even more how, earlier on, she'd seen the monster come to life inside me, and she hadn't run away. If anything, she'd welcomed that beast with open arms.

I gritted my teeth as my cock started to get hard. She'd be too sore to take any more of me tonight, and not for the first time, I cursed my cock, because it was a serious impediment to a good fuck.

What was even more of an impediment?

I knew she was out for the count, and I still wanted to get into bed with her.

What the fuck did that mean?

As we drove down the highway and veered off into the valley where the clubhouse was situated, I saw the cop car in the nook where it waited on speeders, and raised a hand in salute. When they flashed their headlamps, I whirred on past, until I made it to the gates and found Jaxson waiting there to push the button that would open them up and let us in.

He nodded at me as I drove up the driveway, but instead of parking up by the garage where everyone did, I carried on over to the bunkhouse where Giulia was staying.

As I pulled up and cut the engine, she squeezed my waist, then hopped off the back. When I stared at her, she tipped her head to the side.

"What?"

I shrugged, because I didn't have an answer. Mostly, I was just wondering how she could look so good in both daylight and moonlight. It was a full moon, and her hair was dappled with silver strands that made the pitch dark of the chestnut locks seem even richer. Her skin gleamed too, and I wanted to see her against crisp white sheets as I fucked her in a pool of this light...

And then I asked myself again if I'd grown a cunt because what was I even thinking? Romance? I didn't do that shit. I didn't need to, never had and never would, and that I might even want to start with that BS made me distrust this entire situation all the more.

Not enough to head on back to the clubhouse though.

Fuck that.

She tugged at my hand in an attempt to get my attention—because, yeah, I hadn't been giving her enough of that recently—and she repeated, "What is it?"

"Nothing." I kicked the stand, got off the bike then straightened up.

As I walked toward her place, she stayed put, then she rushed after me. "What are you doing?"

I peered at her over my shoulder. "We're going to bed."

She bit her lip. "I'm sore."

She didn't have to tell me that. I was seriously a goddamn expert on vaginas.

"Then we did a good job tonight," was all I said.

A snort escaped her. "That's one way of putting it."

"And another is... I want to go to bed to sleep. I have a long day tomorrow."

"You do?" She pulled a face. "I have an early start and a late finish."

"All the more reason to hurry the hell up and get into bed then, yeah?"

She stared up at me, her eyes worried as she twisted the door handle.

When she pushed open the door, then released a sharp breath, I sensed her relief that her brothers weren't in, because the place was dark and there were no noises coming from the bedroom.

She didn't wait for me or invite me in, Giulia just headed straight for the fridge and, surprise surprise, grabbed a carton of milk.

As she poured some into a mug, I watched as she put it in the microwave, and I leaned against the doorjamb to watch that fine ass of hers as she moved around.

"You gonna stand there all night and let in that draft?"

I didn't reply, just edged out of the way and closed the door behind me.

Not bothering to move, though, I carried on watching her. Every now and then, she'd peer at me over her shoulder and huff before returning to staring at the milk in the microwave.

When it beeped and she pulled it out, she grumbled, "Anyone tell you it's rude to stare?"

"No one ever fucking dared."

A laugh escaped her, and she turned around, leaned back against the counter, and before blowing on her drink, muttered, "Why does that not surprise me?"

"People stopped telling me what to do when I was sixteen," I admitted.

Her eyes widened at that. "How come?"

There wasn't a second's hesitation in me, no doubt about answering with the truth—she deserved to know what I was and why.

A part of me feared she'd run, but I needed to know if she could take it.

If everything I had to give was too much for her, I needed to know *now*.

So, I told her, "That was when I killed my uncle."

She paused, mid-blow, and for a second, she just gaped at me. "You're joking, right?" Then, when she saw I wasn't fucking laughing, her brow puckered. "But... I don't remember hearing that about you, and I remember you."

Inside, I was pleased that she did. I couldn't say I'd remembered her, mostly because of the age difference, but also because at fourteen, babies hadn't been of that much interest to me.

Suddenly, I felt the fourteen-year age gap keenly. Not just the years, but also the experience. The shit I'd done. The blood on my hands... She was clean. Pure. I was anything but.

"You wouldn't have heard anything about it. Not even an urban legend over it. Rex's dad, Bear, covered it up."

"Why did you kill him?" she whispered, her milk forgotten as she placed the mug on the counter.

"He raped my sister. I had to protect her memory."

God, how I managed to get those words out was beyond me.

She had no fucking idea how hard it was to verbalize any of that, and if she did, she'd realize just how in over my head for her I was.

Her eyes looked like they were about to pop out. "D-Did he hurt you too?"

"He threatened me. Told me if I told anyone he'd rape me too." My jaw worked. "She begged me not to say anything, begged me to let her protect me, because she knew he'd do it, and she knew no one would believe me if I told the truth."

"What happened?"

"She killed herself, and I had no choice but to make him pay for it."

Giulia, blinking all the while, crumpled down until she was sitting on the floor, her back to the counter. She looked like I'd punched her in the gut, but she wasn't eying me with fear, didn't look like she was on the brink of calling the cops. If anything, she looked confused. "Why are you telling me this?"

"Because I'm not good for you, and you'd be wise to toss me out of here."

My tone was calm, my words informative, and I projected just how rational and level-headed I was.

My kills were badges of honor, but the rage inside me made me the monster I was. But I'd never hurt her. Ever. And I needed her to know that, even if she did throw me out, even if she did think I was deranged, I needed her to know that she was safe from me, and from any other fucker in the vicinity.

I wasn't sure why it was important that she knew that, just that it was imperative.

"How did you kill him?"

The demon, which was leashed after that delicious fuck back at the bar, tore at its leash. "Shot him."

Her head twisted to the side. "I'm kind of disappointed."

My mouth worked, but the only word that would come out was, "Eh?"

"Bastard deserved to have his dick cut off while he watched. Shooting him seems like the punishment wasn't up to the crime." I stared at her long enough for her to shrug. "Guess that isn't PC of me, huh?"

"I didn't want to go to juvie. I made it look like an accident."

That caught her interest. "Really? How did you do that?"

"You gonna go to the cops?" I didn't think she would, but her reaction surprised me enough to ask anyway.

She smirked. "You should have thought about that before you tried to warn me off, and anyway, do I look stupid? You'd come baying for *my* blood before I even had the chance, and I have no intention of going into WitSec, or dying before I'm at least sixty-five."

Well, that was one way of looking at this situation.

Clearing my throat, I confessed, "He used to hunt. A lot. I fucked with the barrel on his shotgun. The pellets backfired."

"Seriously?"

Fuck me, did she sound impressed?

I rubbed a hand over my face, because this conversation hadn't gone down the route I'd expected. "Yeah."

"Guess your family didn't opt to have an open casket, huh?"

Okay, it was a sick joke, but fuck, I couldn't stop myself, couldn't withhold it.

I laughed.

I laughed like I'd never laughed before, and my stomach ached as I let my amusement swirl inside me, because damn, that was a *good* one.

She beamed at me when I'd finished hiccupping, and when I stopped, propping myself up by shoving my hands against my knees, she announced, "I like seeing you laugh."

"Don't get used to it," I said dryly, rubbing my stomach where a weird ache had gathered from laughing so hard.

"You just never had much to laugh about before." She got to her feet. "Whatever we are, Nyx, I'd like to think of you as a friend." *Friend?*

The demon practically screeched inside me in outrage.

'Friends' wasn't enough. It would *never* be enough.

But I dipped my chin, because two fucks didn't make her mine.

When she moved toward me, her hand outstretched, I stared at it, then peered at her. She beckoned me with her fingers, and I reached over and slipped mine into hers.

"Now we're done with story time," she commented ruefully, "I'm ready for bed."

As we walked toward her bedroom, she shut off the light when we crossed the threshold. The second the door was closed behind her, she flicked on a bedside lamp before she began to strip.

When she was in the raw, she reached for a shirt that was draped over the foot of the bed. Everything inside me cringed at the man's tee she wore, and when she saw me eying her up, and in what I assumed wasn't a good way, her lips twitched.

"Easy, Tiger. It's my brother's."

Though that was marginally more acceptable, it still pissed me off.

Quickly, I shucked off my cut and Henley. Passing her the shirt, I demanded, "Wear that instead."

"You're taller than me, but you're not the Hulk. This isn't going to cover my pussy."

"Be grateful I'm letting you wear anything at all," I groused, as I carefully folded up my cut and placed it on the chair that sat in the corner of the room, beside the bathroom door.

Though she huffed, she didn't argue. From the corner of my eye, I saw her lift the shirt to her nose and take a cautious sniff.

At first, I thought she was checking to see if I stank, then when she sighed and smiled, I realized why, and fuck if that didn't make me feel like King Dick.

I twisted around to watch her pull on the Henley, and she wasn't wrong. Her pussy and ass were on display.

"Best. Idea. Ever." I eyed her cunt.

Fuck, I wished she was messy from my cum, and the idea of fucking her bareback made everything inside me clench with need.

She pshawed at me, however, unaware that my cock was aching once more, even though she'd blown my mind back at the bar.

She tugged down the sheet, then scrambled into bed before she curled onto her side, facing the portion where I'd be lying and not the wall like I'd half expected.

As I peered around, saw how neat it was, I didn't feel right just dumping my shit on the floor. Though my place was neat, before bed, it was anything goes. Instead, I folded my pants over the chair, too, after I toed off my boots and neatly lined them up against the wall.

When I strode over to the bed, I flicked off the light beside the nightstand, and climbed in. Her heat wasn't something I was unaccustomed to. Cammie often crashed beside me in bed before I tossed her out in the morning, but she was usually drunk, and stank of it as well.

Giulia smelled of flowers, and she was wearing my Henley, so I could also smell my aftershave, as well as a faint whisper of sweat that came from having fucked her back at the bar.

I stared up at the ceiling, eying the lights that flashed over it when bikes began to pull into the compound, the curtains not preventing that intrusion from invading our space.

It felt good to lie here, to just breathe and be. No expectations, nowhere to go, nowhere to be. Mostly, it was good to have her by my side.

She confused me, or to be precise, my feelings for her confused me, but

I'd rather be bewildered and with her than back in my room wondering where her head was at, as I'd been doing the last couple of nights.

"Why did you tell me that?" she whispered into the darkness, breaking into my thoughts.

"I told you why."

I let my head roll on the pillow so I could look at her. She was cuddled up, not in fear, just readying herself for sleep. Her hair was tossed everywhere, some strands even reached out to connect with me.

I kind of wished she was closer, close enough to touch, but I'd never ask her to move nearer. I'd feel stupid making such a request.

"You meant to frighten me off?"

My lips curved in the darkness. "Most people wouldn't invite a serial killer into their bed."

She fell quiet again. "How many people have you killed?"

"A lot."

Her hand came out, and she touched my arm. "Don't you dare say it's club business."

"It isn't. It's personal."

The club made it their business for my sake, but it wasn't. Not really.

They spared my sanity, and as a reward, they had the most dedicated Enforcer in the States.

Because I was so vigilant, we had very few deaths. To the point where we'd hardly lost anyone to anything other than natural causes since Rex had become Prez and had promoted me to Enforcer.

As for losing people to jail, that wasn't something I could control as much, but I tried to keep everyone flying down the highways and not locked up in a fucking cell.

She gripped my bicep, her nails digging in slightly. It was unintentional, as was the delight that speared me in the gut from that tiny prick of discomfort. "What's the tattoo on your back?"

"You noticed that?"

"Couldn't really miss it," she whispered.

I thought about the tattoo that covered every inch of my spine. Some of it was colored in, some of it was shaded, some of it was waiting to be marked. I knew it would never be complete, because there were too many sick fucks waiting to feel my wrath.

"Nyx? What is it? What does it mean?"

The devil was between my shoulders, his horned head smirking out at the world. The lines of his face reminded me of the Iron Man helmet, but

I'd had this on my spine long before Robert Downey Jr had worn that particular suit.

Lucifer's arms hugged decapitated skulls that were bleeding from the eyes and mouth. Twenty-eight skulls, to be exact, because I was waiting on my twenty-ninth tattoo.

Satan was blood-red, bringing the black and white skulls, and the blood on them, into sharp relief.

"Each skull is a man I've killed."

"Why?"

"Why did I kill them?"

"No. I can figure that out."

"Oh, you can?" I demanded, turning onto my side so I could look at her. In the shadows, I couldn't see much, but my eyes had adapted to the minimal light, and that irritating flash of headlamps helped me see her expression.

Her eyes were closed, and her features weren't pinched like she was terrified. If anything, she looked relaxed.

I wasn't sure who was more astounded.

Me, or the fucking demon who lived inside me.

"They're pedophiles, right? You hurt them so they can't hurt anyone else."

She sounded so accepting that, for a second, my throat felt choked. Christ, was I about to cry?

Everyone here accepted my need to inflict pain on these sick fucks. They helped me, facilitated me, and even let our business deals revolve around my forays into murder, but this level of ease wasn't something I'd anticipated.

And then it hit me.

Fuck.

It hit me hard.

"Someone hurt you."

It was a blanket statement. Blanket because the rage that pooled inside me made me want to tear this room apart.

"Someone *tried* to hurt me."

"Who?" I grated out, not appeased by the qualification.

Her hand smoothed down over my arm. "It's okay. I hurt them first," she soothed.

Soothed.

She soothed *me.*

For a second, I wondered if I'd wandered into a parallel universe, then she derailed my thoughts by murmuring, "My stepdad. But he tried and failed."

My brain whirred at that, and then I asked, "Lizzie divorced his ass, right?"

"Nope." The word popped from between her lips. "She didn't believe me, so I stopped believing in her." And that was it.

Her attitude.

It made sense.

If anyone could understand, it was one victim to another.

I could no more stop myself from reaching for her than I could stop my heart from taking its next beat.

I hauled her into me, not stopping until she was tucked in my arms, her chest to mine, our limbs tangled. I pulled her closer until I could feel the gentle rise and fall of her tits against my chest, as I felt the pulse of her heart against my being.

"No one will ever hurt you again," I vowed between gritted teeth.

"You can't promise that," she said with a sad laugh. "I thank you for it, though."

"You don't have to. I mean it. Every fucking word."

"I know you do."

I thought of her in New York, where she was too far away to protect, and I almost tore through my tongue as I stopped myself from asking her not to leave. To stay here where she'd always be safe, because I'd make fucking sure no one ever got their hands on her again.

She released a sigh, and her hand came up to cover my heart. When she nuzzled into me, I wasn't sure what to do with myself. I'd never slept this close to another human being before, but it felt right with her.

She yawned then, and I realized she wasn't far from falling asleep.

"Aren't you frightened of me? Now that you know the truth?"

The words were ripped from my soul, my very fucking being, because Christ, I'd be scared of me.

I'd made myself a reputation that stopped anyone from getting too close, that kept me at arm's length from anyone who dared approach. Yet, here she was, tucked up against me.

"Seems to me it's everyone else who should be scared."

The words were mumbled, and I realized, yet again, she was close to falling asleep. That was how chilled she was.

"Why's that?" I whispered, needing to know, to understand.

"Because you just threatened anyone who meant me harm, which means I'm safe. Even from you."

And like that, she floored me. Her logic was resolute, impossible to argue, and somehow, that fucking monster inside me settled, because she was right.

And he knew it too.

TWENTY-ONE

GIULIA

A FEW NIGHTS LATER

THE PRESSURE of his hand against my stomach, sliding down over my curves and toward my pussy, woke me up.

His fingers were calloused, and they felt so damn good against my tender skin, that it was no wonder I'd awoken at the faint touch. My body knew who he was, even as my mind registered it.

Nyx.

Always him.

I shivered, deep inside, my pussy clenching as I waited on his next move, and when he hummed against my throat, his face buried there, I felt the faint vibration and sighed with delight. "You always smell so fucking good."

"Is that a complaint I hear?" I half-teased, my voice a low rasp that morphed into a groan when his fingers finally swept down to between my legs.

My brow puckered in both delight and agony as he rubbed over me, letting the tips just hover over my clit.

I knew I was wet. Knew it, and felt no shame for it. Maybe with another man, I might have done, but this was Nyx. He was dark and dirty, and he liked me to be the same.

Plus, he was massive, so being wet around him all the time just facilitated things.

"Never a complaint, just a..." He broke off a second, before admitting on a mutter, "distraction."

I blinked. Whatever I'd expected him to say, it wasn't *that*.

"Thanks. I think."

He snorted at my dry words, then shut me up by raking his teeth over the fleshy part where my throat connected with my shoulder. I bit on my bottom lip to contain the cry that started to escape me, and then I didn't bother when he graced me with the faintest pressure on my clit.

I was past caring that my brothers might hear me, had long since stopped giving a fuck, and instead, I threw myself into the revelry, lifted my leg and cocked it over his thigh to give him more access.

He chuckled, and the sound was better than his grunts of pleasure when he was coming. I was addicted to that sound because it was so rare, and I loved that he seemed to be gifting me more and more of them, as though he knew he could be himself around me.

My heart melted, more than it usually did when I was around him. I knew what was happening to me, knew it, and had even started to embrace it, just as I was embracing the fact that I had to be fucking insane.

Nothing had changed.

Nothing.

He was still a biker, and I was a biker's brat who'd been burned after years of watching my parents butt heads, but fuck, I didn't care. I just couldn't care. I needed him. In a way that I'd never needed anyone before. Shit, in a way that I'd never allowed myself to need anyone, either.

A shaky sigh escaped me as I forced myself to recognize what I was feeling for him. Sure, it was fast. Sure, it was crazy. And sure, it made no sense, but that meant nothing in the grand scheme of things. What I felt was honest, real, *pure*. And I had a feeling that what he felt for me was exactly the same.

His cock was there, a solid presence between my thighs. It rested against my inner thigh, in fact, and I could feel the pre-cum dripping from the tip, could feel my sticky juices starting to mix with his, and the notion about made my eyes cross.

I wanted nothing more than to let him inside me with nothing between us, wanted to feel all that hardware against my soft inner tissues, but Jesus, was that taking things too far down the rabbit hole? This was more than just my heart that was at stake, this was my body. My health.

"Reach into your nightstand drawer."

I knew why, so I didn't argue, but when I did as bid, I didn't feel the crisp foil of a condom, instead, I felt paper.

"Knew it was a big deal for you, so I had the full works, and I got it done express."

"What are you talking about?"

"I'm clean."

I reached for the paper and peered at it in the semi-dark. My mind wasn't really thinking about STDs at that moment—talk about a buzzkill—but I gnawed on my lip and forced myself to read the letter. When I saw the results, I cleared my throat.

"You did this for me?"

"Wasn't going to do it for anyone else, was I?" He pressed his lips to my throat. "Know you're protected."

I hummed. "I am."

"You gonna let me inside you bare?" he rasped, his voice and the words telling me how badly he wanted that. And fuck, I wanted that so badly too.

I clenched my eyes closed, so overwhelmed at that moment that I felt sure I was going to overheat and simply melt on the sheets.

Not only was my heart pounding with the realization he'd actually gone to the clinic and paid extra to have the results rushed, but he'd done so for me.

For my sake.

For my benefit.

I didn't doubt that he knew he'd reap the rewards, but that had to mean something, didn't it?

He wanted me. And not for just a roll in the hay, because why would he have gone to all that trouble, unless it was for my benefit?

My heart started pounding, beating until I could hear it in my ears, and I whispered, "Come inside me, love."

That was one word I hadn't planned on using, because it ran too close to home, but he didn't stiffen at it. At least, not in any way that I didn't anticipate.

When his cock twitched, I gnawed on the inside of my cheek, and moaned when he began to rock his hips against me, letting me feel all those delicious textures, all that hardware and metal. Just thinking about feeling his Jacob's ladder deep inside me, with nothing between us, had my eyes crossing.

He rubbed my clit and focused on my throat equally. I knew I'd bear a mark in the morning, but I couldn't find it in me to care. I loved his hickies, even if they were primitive—and I loved his bites on my inner thighs even more, truth be told.

"I want you to feel every fucking inch of me, Giulia. Can you do that for me?"

"I-I don't know," I whimpered, moaning as his words hit me right at my core. "I-I'll try."

"I want you to know me, Giulia. You want that too, don't you?" he asked as he dragged my folds apart, exposing my clit to the air.

I moaned and whimpered, "Y-Yes, I d-do."

"That's the right answer, baby girl." He nipped at my throat, then his hand moved down so that the heel of his wrist was grinding into my clit, even as he was moving his cock, shifting it so that the tip was against the entrance to my body.

I tensed up, then forced myself to relax because that made things easier, and with a breathlessness that had me nearly hiccupping, I waited.

And waited.

Until finally, his heat, with those odd barbells, began to penetrate me.

It was completely and utterly different to feel him bare, to not have the slick slide of the condom between us. It was, I'd admit, also easier with the condom, but I far preferred this. I loved the intimacy, loved that he was tucked against me in the depth of the night, loved that he was at my back, my body curled about his as he made me his for real.

The piece of paper was like the Declaration of Independence lying beside me, fluttering with each breath I expelled, and I ignored it, even as much as I loved it for what I thought it represented.

As his tip pierced my gate, I gulped, released a shaky sigh, then pressed my hand to the bed to use as balance. Arching my hips back, I began to rock, needing to move, always needing the option to shift slightly because I always felt faintly panicked when he was working his way inside me.

When he nipped at my throat, hushing me once more, I gulped, then he ground the heel of his hand into me again, and my clit exploded with sensation.

I gushed around him, my muscles alternating between clenching deeply and relaxing totally, and he used that to his advantage.

Within seconds, he was inside me, and my eyes flared wide as I muttered, "N-No, that can't be."

He laughed. "You did it, baby girl."

He sounded impressed, but even better, he sounded fucking happy, hell, he sounded faintly drunk himself. And when he didn't move, I knew he was relishing the fact that I was taking him, all of him, and that his entirety was cosseted by my pussy.

Was it stupid to feel pride? Stupid when I knew, in the morning, I'd be aching like a bitch? It was even stupider than that, really, because he wasn't going to be able to fuck me like this—he'd goddamn wreck me.

But I knew it felt good, and that made *me* feel good.

Deliriously so.

I shuddered when he rocked his hips, and like I'd known he'd do, he pulled out until the final piercing at the halfway point of his dick, was rubbing against the entrance of my body. That was his measure, and I was both grateful for it and resentful, because sweet fuck, it felt different bare like this.

When he began to rock his hips again, a gurgle escaped me, and I twisted my head to the side, reached for the pillow, and bit down as he began to fuck me.

He was careful, I'd give him that. But the feel of all those textures inside me?

Mind.

Blowing.

My hand clawed at the sheets, and I reached back to dig my nails into his thigh, to let him share in this feeling, to let him know how overwhelmed I was. How overwhelmed *he'd* made me feel.

When he began to massage my clit and sped up, I knew I couldn't last. It was impossible. No one could sustain this level of anticipation, of delight, without imploding, and with each thrust, I was seeing more than just sparks, I was seeing fucking flames.

The scream that escaped me might have woken up my brothers, hell, it might have even woken up everyone on the compound, but did I give a fuck?

Nope.

Not one bit.

As the pleasure reamed me, those piercings rasping against confused tissues that weren't sure whether they were proffering bliss or torment, my body felt like it was folding in on itself, and I released another sharp scream, one that twisted in tangent with his low grunts and harsh curses as he exploded into his orgasm too.

I felt him, then. All wet and warm, sticky and slick. He filled me, every inch of me, his cum pouring inside me even as he thrust his hips in deep, not letting a drop escape as he plugged me up with his full length.

And God help me, it felt right.

It felt *perfect*.

I released a gusty, if shaky breath, and maybe that was the perfect moment for the sheet of paper on the bed to fly off the side, to float to the ground.

To disappear into the ether.

Just as I did.

Hazy from the pleasure he'd gifted me, and exhausted, I fell asleep in his arms.

TWENTY-TWO

GIULIA

A WEEK LATER

"LATE NIGHT?"

I shoved North in the arm, and grumbled, "Fuck off. Like you'd know over all the noise you make."

"Sisters are allowed to hear brothers during sex. Brothers aren't allowed to hear sisters."

My brow crumpled at that logic. "What the fuck are you talking about?"

Hawk merely sneered at me. "You really don't want me to do an impression of you when you're coming, do you?"

Maybe other women would be icked out by this conversation, but I wasn't other women, and I'd grown up around this place and these two fuckwits all my life.

"I always thought I was quiet in the sack," I told them, my tone musing.

North pulled a face, but I saw his gaze drift to my throat that, as was getting to be a regular thing, was sporting a hickey. "TMI, Giulia. Too much fucking information."

"You're the one who started this conversation. Not me. And with the amount of women you've fucked, against the rules I might add, you're lucky that—"

Hawk scowled. "You threatening us?"

"Depends," I retorted. "You got anything worth blackmailing over?" I eyed their scruffy jeans and the tees that looked like they needed a couple of weeks in the laundry before they'd be clean again. "As far as I can see, you don't."

North rolled his eyes. "You're all heart."

"No, I just see nothing worthy of bribing you over." I shot him a grin, then twisted around and returned to the bacon and eggs I was frying.

If there was a spring to my step, then so be it.

I was, I'd admit, happy.

Yeah, I wasn't used to the feeling either.

Whether it was because Nyx was boning me enough to make me cock-drunk, or I was just enjoying my current status quo, I couldn't say.

Having never been cock-drunk before, it wasn't something I was used to feeling, so my inexperience was shining through, but aside from being tired from work, play, and fucks, yeah, everything was currently coming up roses.

I didn't think it would last, but that didn't mean I couldn't enjoy it until it was over, did it?

"I can't believe you're still not cutting Dad any slack."

With my mind on the food, I'd missed half of North's complaint, but the second he said the word 'Dad,' that turned my smile upside down.

Gritting my teeth, I stated firmly, "If he won't cut me any slack, why should I cut him any?"

I hadn't told them about him trying to slap me that first week. I saw no reason to wreck their relationship with him, even if it totally merited it. Dad was a violent bastard, and it wasn't in a way that I could get behind.

Nyx was like a grenade with the fuse halfway pulled out. He was ready to blast, and I knew that. But it would only be something worthy of his violence that would take him to the edge.

My dad? Not so much.

Control. That was the difference between Nyx and my father, and that was why I didn't and never had trusted him.

"I have no desire to be in his life, and just because I'm here, under the same roof as him, I see no need to talk to him." To me, he deserved as little attention as the club sluts.

"He's our dad, Giulia," North muttered, and from his stern frown, I figured I was about to get a lecture.

"You might want him in your life, but I don't want him in mine."

"He's fucking lucky he's in your lives. Period. I almost had Rex toss him out the week you arrived after that stunt he pulled with your sister."

North and Hawk tensed the second Nyx had arrived, and I couldn't blame them. They were, after all, Prospects, which meant they were way down low in the pecking order, and Nyx, even if he was a terrifying motherfucker who collected skulls on his back to go with the souls of the men he'd taken—I'd have to ask him if he was an equal opportunity murderer and went for women pedophiles too—he was also the Enforcer.

And that meant a fuck ton to the MC.

"What did he do?"

Hawk's belligerent tone didn't altogether surprise me, not when his back was to the wall. Hawk hadn't been given that much charm, instead, North had gotten the lion's share of it in the womb.

"Slapped her."

"*Tried* to slap me," I corrected with a frown, not pleased with him sharing this story when I'd wanted to keep it to myself.

"That supposed to make it better? A second later, and his hand would have connected with your face." He glowered at me, even as he carried on walking around the counter, not stopping until his hand was on my ass.

That was how he greeted me every day.

Like we hadn't just woken up in bed together.

Like he hadn't just eaten me out before making me scream down the house as he fucked me before I had to make breakfast.

His 'hello' was a hand on my butt.

It surprised me by how unoffended I was by it.

Any other fucker, and I'd have squeezed their balls in retaliation. I didn't like invasions of privacy, but Nyx was one big invasion, and I kinda liked it.

I was even going to miss it when he went on the run tonight.

I didn't know what was going down, didn't know when he'd be back—there was too much déjà vu for my liking, because it just reminded me of when I was a kid, and I hadn't known when my dad was coming back home or *if* he'd be coming home at all—but, oh, the irony, it was just a part of the life.

And I couldn't believe I'd allowed the thought to cross my mind.

Fuck, I hated it when my mom had said that to me, and I was using that BS to console myself now.

Jesus Christ.

"What did you do to make him want to slap you?"

The question didn't surprise me, but it had Nyx's biceps bulging in a way that didn't bode well for my older brother.

Sure, it was a dick question to ask, but Hawk *was* a dick.

"Do you think women deserved to be slapped if they backtalk?" Nyx asked, his tone quiet, but Hawk would have to be a fucking moron if he didn't hear the deadly poison dripping from each word.

"No, but Dad..." North sighed and scrubbed a hand over his face. "That's how Dad works."

"And that's how domestic violence passes through the generations," Nyx growled. "If I hear of you beating any of the women, slapping them around, I'll have your fucking guts hanging out on the front lawn to feed the opossums."

"I didn't know opossums were carnivores." If my tone was musing, then so be it. I was curious.

"That's all you have to say to that threat?" North sputtered.

I shrugged. "I hope he does it too. Dad's a dick, but that doesn't mean you two can be dicks as well. Whatever's left of you after Nyx slaughters you, I'll piss on. How about that for a neat and tidy bow?"

"Opossums are carrion-eaters," Nyx inserted, his tone helpful now that my brothers were gaping at us both like we were the next episode of *American Horror Story*.

I could deal with that.

I'd always been the bloodthirsty one. It was why my stepfather had resorted to bitching at me about my weight after he'd tried making a pass at me.

My kick to his balls had been hard enough to rupture his testicle, and after a lot of surgery, and many doctor's appointments, he'd had one removed.

That was why my brothers knew to be wary around me.

I was a ball buster.

And proud of it.

"Anyway," I carried on, "he was bitching at me for not coming around to meet his new Old Lady." I huffed. "Like I was even interested in meeting her."

"Katy is cool. Cooler than Dog. And if that's how he takes rejection, then I'd better visit her and find out if he's treating her right."

"She seemed happy enough when we met her." North wriggled his shoulders.

"How anyone could be happy with him is beyond me." I sniffed, then flipped the bacon once more to make sure it was extra crispy, the way Nyx liked it.

Double whipped.

Sheesh.

"Does he know about Lance?"

Hawk's question had me snorting. My brother was digging as well as trying to shit stir. "He knows of the situation, yes."

"Bet he doesn't know you're more than capable of defending yourself."

I didn't bother shooting him a warning look, because that would just fire him on all the more.

"You say that like it's a bad thing," Nyx retorted.

"It isn't. We helped teach her, we just taught her too well."

"Is that possible? If she's good at defending herself, then that's—"

North raised a hand to stall him. "No way she told you all about Lance."

"I saw no need to discuss his surgery," I said with a grumble.

"Surgery? And who is Lance, anyway?" Nyx demanded, finally moving his hand from my butt so he could fold his arms.

I didn't think he was scared off because he didn't back away, just leaned against the fridge and waited, impatiently, for my brothers to tell their story.

And hey, who was I to butt in?

I wasn't ashamed of the tale, but I half expected he'd be running away by the end of the conversation.

My brothers always looked queasy when they talked about this, and for some reason, they talked about it a lot. I figured they were, in a weird way, proud. But male camaraderie meant they had to be grossed out by it too.

"Lance is our stepdad. He's a dick," North replied, pulling a face.

"If he's a dick," I butted in, "then he's a small one." I waggled my pinkie finger. "The smallest of the small. We're talking micro penis."

Hawk snorted. "You'd know more than us."

Sure, it was an insensitive thing to say, but when Nyx growled, stalking forward like a puma on the hunt, I quickly grabbed his arm and stopped him from slamming my brother's head into his knee.

"It's okay. He didn't mean it that way," I insisted quickly, glowering at my dick of a sibling all the while. "I kneed Lance in the balls when he tried to touch me."

He grunted, "Good." But he was still throbbing with tension, and I knew he really wanted to smack my shithead of a brother.

"She didn't just knee him," North corrected. "Deservedly," he tacked on, his hands raised in surrender at the stone-cold killer glare Nyx aimed at him. "She ruptured his fucking testicle. Bastard had to have it removed."

Nyx stilled, then he shot me a look. "How did you do that?"

"Well, I kneed him in the balls," I repeated warily.

"You're forgetting the stiletto," Hawk chimed in.

"You stabbed him in the nuts?"

Okay, so I definitely wasn't mishearing the appreciation in his voice now.

Some of the tension I'd been feeling since my twin brothers had decided to be dicks eased. "Not with a knife. With a stiletto heel. I kneed him hard, then when he was on the ground, I stood on him. I had a good aim."

Nyx grinned while my brothers still looked pretty green around the fucking gills.

"Pussies," I hissed at them, as Nyx curved his arm around my shoulder and hauled me into him.

Of course, I was too flustered to appreciate the first PDA we had.

Not too flustered, however, to appreciate Cammie's stunned expression when she wandered into the kitchen a second later.

If my smile was smug when I turned the stove off, then it was smug.

Fuck it.

Nyx was mine.

For the interim.

And I didn't mind if people knew that. Especially not if the shit about Lance's nut got out. Hell, I'd be safe as houses.

❖

TWENTY-THREE

NYX

WHEN WE SET off down the interstate, I'd admit to being uneasy.

I didn't know why I was uneasy, or at least, I knew why, but I wasn't happy about it.

This was the only night in twelve days that I hadn't been watching over Giulia at the bar, and it was the first time that I'd be away on a run.

That was what I didn't like.

Even if news of her abilities in castrating a man did ease my mind, I was still on edge about leaving her when I knew how many come-ons she fielded every fucking evening.

If I had the right, I'd have demanded she stay back at the compound, but she wasn't my Old Lady, and the MC wasn't a charity. The bar was a good business, just like Rex had predicted, and it needed its team to be working at full steam ahead.

Even if it did put the Satan's Sinners' MC in a piss-poor mood.

Truth was, all the new storefronts were booming with business, even if the country clubbers weren't happy about the type of locale we'd intro-duced into the town, it didn't stop them from spending their dough with us.

The strip joint was busy every night, and I knew Storm was finding it hard to get enough girls to cover all the shifts, especially as personal lap dances were proving particularly popular.

The garage was busy, thanks to our mechanics' expertise, and throw in the custom jobs we were rolling out, we'd already had interest from people all over the country who knew of Link's skills where that was concerned.

He and Steel were working together on that project, with Steel behind the scenes in the chop shop, and I was glad, because the garage was pivotal to our money laundering and distribution plans, and I had enough on my hands at the minute.

The diner was packed every day, something else Steel had his hands on, and the bar was crammed at night with the diner running late to cover the bar food we'd started serving under Giulia's direction.

Business was definitely booming, but it was all a front. We still had shit to do, and that was why I was away when I didn't want to be.

The Enforcer—me—and the Road Captain—Link—went on every run. As we headed into the city to pick up the merch that would have our group splitting up, one heading back home with Link, and the other going up to the Canadian border with me before Link joined up with us again, I had to admit that taking off into the night was both exhilarating and irritating.

Exhilarating because there was nothing like being on the open road, the wind in your face, the moon overhead, the throb of the engine between your legs as you drove on, what was essentially, your commute to work.

But it was also irritating because I knew that Giulia would be working at the bar, and I'd gotten used to watching over her.

Sure, she did all the work, but I got things done too, during the early hours and the later ones, when the booth wasn't filled with brothers taking advantage of the discounts they had on drinks.

It was a good place to watch the men, to monitor the lay of the land on Rex's behalf. Mutiny—even in a well-run, well-oiled MC—was rife, and I wasn't about to let that happen on my watch.

Listening to the fuckers get drunk, complaining about their jobs or praising the council for the recent additions to the books, was a good way to ascertain the status quo.

Especially as the recent changes were coming into being.

One of said changes was where we were headed now.

The deal with the Five Points wasn't something that I was easy about. Mostly because it involved dealing with the Rabid Wolves, who were a Quebec City-based MC.

I understood the Five Pointers' perspective though.

They wanted maximum bang for their buck all over the upper North Eastern seaboard, and by joining with us and merging with the Wolves— even if they were rabid by nature as well as by name—they'd be getting into Canada, as well as gaining reach as far west as Montana and as far south as Oklahoma, thanks to our sister chapters, who were getting involved in the distribution too.

The idea was simple, and although I wasn't a simple man by nature, I did like my business to be of that variety, especially when we were going to be crossing state lines with a few products on board.

The Pointers would handle the actual gathering of the merch. We weren't interested in that side of shit. They dealt with stealing the cars which, over time, would drift to our garage in West Orange, where we'd chop them into smaller parts, then load them up with drugs, which we'd use to transport across the country.

See? Simple.

What I wasn't including there, of course, was the fact we had to get the drugs from their main warehouse in Hell's Kitchen, and cross from New York and into New Jersey before we even got shit started.

Still, no one ever said making a cool two-hundred-thou a run was easy, but I was on red alert, and even if Link was as laidback as any of the brothers were, he was tense as well.

This was too big a deal to lose, but there were a lot of variables that could go wrong. It was the nature of the game, and normally, I enjoyed it. Shame for me that nothing was normal in my life right about now.

It took just over thirty minutes to get from our compound to Hell's Kitchen, and the worst part was Lincoln Tunnel. Of course, that was only compounded by heading into the city itself, because, fuck me, I hated how close everything was.

West Orange wasn't in the middle of nowhere. Not even Giulia would call it Buttfuck, New Jersey, but there was a shit ton of green everywhere, and I liked that. I liked to feel as if I were surrounded by nothing but trees, because the notion of being surrounded by people just suffocated me.

I wouldn't say that I hated people. If I did, it was weird that I chose a life that put me in the heart of a community of men and women who chose to live together. But I *did* hate the societal bullshit that came from one-upping the Joneses, as well as the pressure of the rat race. Some folk were made for that, and I wasn't one of them.

The streets were busy, even at one AM, and I'd admit to missing how, in West Orange, shit was closing down for the night at this time.

There was nothing better than being on my bike on an empty road, but now, I was trapped between a Buick, a fifth wheel, and a fucking Porsche. Not my favorite kind of sandwich.

When we approached the main warehouse where the initial pick up was going down, I eyed the security setup and would admit to being impressed.

The place was arranged like a prison, with high gated walls that had barbed wire for trimmings around the top. I had no doubt that in the light of day, broken glass would glint on the surface as well.

In fairness, it looked exactly like what it was—somewhere that shady business went down.

It didn't put me at ease thinking some federal agents were taking shots of my ass as we drove through the gates and into the compound, but that was the nature of the business.

And for myself, it was just part one of tonight's escapades.

We drove into the outer keep, and thirteen of us parked toward the main doors. The building was the architectural equivalent of a brick shit-house. It was square, red brick with white plaster that had chipped away over the years. There were windows, but they were shuttered up with metal frames, and the only way in and out was that one large door.

It was almost like a castle, except castles hadn't been built to current safety standards. Saying that, as I eyed the distinct lack of fire safety specs, I recognized that this place hadn't either.

As our engines died, the doors opened, and two guys walked out. I recognized one of them—Declan O'Donnelly.

Mean bastard, and he had a wicked temper, as far as I remembered.

He wasn't the brains of the outfit, but he was more than just the fists.

He was good at organizing shit, and half of today's run had been keyed in by him, which was unusual, but the Five Points were on our side, and they were running point with the Wolves, because MCs didn't usually play nice together.

The guy at his side wore a slim-fitting suit that screamed tailoring. In contrast to Declan's jeans, white wife-beater, and leather jacket, he looked like he was heading into the city to offload a fuck ton of orange juice futures.

When, glowering at Declan, he turned away, I caught sight of his face full blast because of the spotlights that snapped on, and my brows instantly lowered because the stranger looked like the patriarch of the line, but at least thirty years Aidan Sr.'s junior.

Another O'Donnelly sibling?

I thought I'd met them all when Rex had come up to the city to finalize the deal with the Five Points, but maybe I hadn't.

With the rest of the brothers hovering by their bikes, waiting on orders, Link and I strode forward, shoulder to shoulder, as the Five Points' guys headed toward us.

When Declan held out his hand to me, I shook it, then he greeted Link.

He turned to the stranger and stated, "Finn, this is Nyx and Link. They're Sinners' councilors."

Finn shot us a tight smile as he shook both our hands. "I'd say it was a pleasure to meet you guys, but my wife's in the hospital, so I'd like to keep the conversation to a minimum so we can get the fuck on."

Because personal talk was the last thing I'd expected, I blinked at him. "Is she okay?"

"Expectant dads," Declan mocked. "Worse than expectant moms."

Finn glowered at him. "I'd like to get this shit underway so I can get to Mount Sinai in time for my heir to be born." Had he really just called his kid his heir?

When Declan laughed, I figured it was a joke so, uneasily, I shot Link a look, and was relieved to note he looked just as fucking wide-eyed as me.

Personal business was exactly that. *Personal.* Was this a move they were pulling? Sure, they were on our side, but I didn't take chances when my family was involved.

"We have everything ready for you," Declan replied, his tone hardening as he did as Finn requested—got on with shit. "The two loads are prepared."

I dipped my chin, relieved to be back on solid ground. "I'm heading to Quebec and Link is taking the other back to base. He'll catch up with us once he's made the drop."

"Good. We've paid officials to turn a blind eye, but once you get to the border, the Wolves are in charge, and it's down to them."

My ears pricked at the irritation in his voice. Was he not happy with the other MC?

"We only have to get the merch to the border, yeah?"

Finn nodded. "Then it's on them whether they get caught or not. They have the contacts on that side."

"What about our cut?" Link questioned.

Declan looked at him. "You'll get it when we get ours. If they fuck up, we're all fucked."

"Well, that's reassuring," I muttered, but I had to admit, I appreciated his honesty.

"Rex called and told me about their visit. Out of the blue, wasn't it?" Declan declared grimly, his biceps bulging beneath his jacket as he folded his arms across his chest.

"I don't know what their fucking game is, but if they screw us over—"

Declan didn't let Finn finish the sentence. He clapped him on the back, then gripped his shoulder and said, "Let's not borrow trouble. There are bound to be issues the first time anything goes down.

"At least we know the Sinners have our backs." With his spare hand, he raised his fist and Link bumped knuckles with him, before I was extended the same greeting.

We'd been dealing with Declan for a while now on other shipments. Mostly some guns that we'd been taking down to Oklahoma every two weeks.

The Five Points relied heavily on loyalty, and with us, that came from the fact we'd been tied into the mix by a marriage. I wasn't sure why the Wolves were being trusted, and truth be told, I wasn't sure I wanted to know either.

They were a part of the transaction, and that was it.

I was just glad we didn't have to cross the border into Canada with our gear. That shit went with double digit prison time, and while that was a risk in our line of work, I didn't feel like serving time right about now.

"How's Mary Catherine doing?" Finn queried, his eyes lighting with the glint of a warning that put me on edge.

The Old Lady could have been bitching at her mom for all I fucking knew, and if that was the case, we'd probably just walked headfirst into a trap.

I didn't have to answer though, because Link said, "Digger told me she's pregnant."

"There's something in the water. Aside from being pregnant, is she okay? She's never been that far away from home." Declan winced at our surprised glances. "She's extended family. I give a damn."

I shrugged. "I never see her at the compound. I'd meant to introduce her to a friend of mine. Someone who grew up in the club, but it never worked out."

Because I'd started boning Giulia and between the bar, cooking, and me, her spare time was at a zero.

Priorities.

Never let it be said I didn't have them.

"I think they're okay," Link stated, making me wonder if he was lying or if he'd really fucking asked Digger how his marriage was. *I'd have paid to see that conversation go down.* "Digger's still sappy whenever you mention her name."

Finn clapped Declan on the back. "There's hope."

"Watch him. I want to know if he fucks her over. Do you hear me?" Declan warned, and though the threat got my back up, I totally understood.

"Nyx is every woman's champion, Declan. I wouldn't worry about her.

I'd worry about Digger. Second he hurts her, Nyx hurts him." Link's cocky tone had me inwardly snorting.

Though the O'Donnelly son absorbed that without even the blink of an eye, he merely replied, "More ways to hurt a woman than with just fists." He scrubbed his hand over his jaw. "Finn's right. He needs to get going, so let's get this underway."

Because there was no arguing with that, or the fact that he turned on his heel and backed off, we spent the next forty minutes making sure everything was in place, and as the vans were being driven by Pointers' men, we really were just making sure that we were getting what we'd been told.

There was an element of distrust in scanning over the logs, making sure shit lined up with the content on board, but fuck, we were the ones who'd be doing the time if we got caught with our asses hanging out because a Pointer had badly stored a baggy of drugs.

So, we scanned, checked shit over... well, I said 'we,' but I meant the others. I just stood there and watched the men earn their cut. I also watched O'Donnelly and his buddy, Finn.

With each minute that passed, the other guy got more and more agitated, and no matter what Declan said to calm him down, it didn't work.

I got the feeling they were close, though, and more than just friends, especially with the familial resemblance.

As I monitored them and their interaction, watched Finn start to pace the outer yard where the trucks were parked and we were looking into shit, I tried to imagine what he was feeling, and what stunned me the most was that I got it.

I thought about Giulia, and I thought about how I'd started worrying about her, and I thought about how I'd feel knowing she was in the hospital and my not being able to go to her.

Business always came first in our world. It had to, because it could mean life or death, could be the difference between a lot of good men being lost to jail time if someone didn't pull their weight.

I scratched my chin, finding myself utterly sympathetic for Finn's predicament, because I understood why he was here, even as I understood why it was killing him.

Maybe it was a dick move, maybe it was smart. Maybe my brains and my balls were suddenly being overruled by something that I had no idea how to control, but I moved toward the two men.

Declan saw me first, and I got the feeling that right there was the state of Finn's distress—he didn't pick up on my movement until Declan tensed.

See, that was the thing about business.

Even when you were dealing with guys who were on your side, you had to be wary.

I raised my hands, wanting them to see that I had no intention of causing them harm. I was probably more dangerous than anyone in this fucking space, no matter that there were around two dozen Points' men aiming semi-automatics at the floor as they secured the area, but I genuinely meant them no ill.

When Declan eyed me, his brow furrowed, I stated, "Finn doesn't need to stick around. We'll be done soon. Let him go be with his wife." I had no right to make the statement, but that was how badly my head was messed up right about now.

Women... they fucked with more than just your cock.

"I appreciate the concern, but my place is here," Finn replied, but I could sense that was duty talking. And not the duty he had to his wife.

"We both know that's BS. Your place is with her."

His chin tipped up as he narrowed his eyes at me. "You got a woman?"

I hesitated. Not only because I wasn't sure if I did, but because Giulia wasn't the sort to appreciate that kind of claiming.

Reaching up, I rubbed the back of my neck, and when Declan laughed, I frowned at him.

"Yeah, he's got a woman. You can always tell when a man's got his dick tangled with—"

"You call Aoife a cunt once more, and I'll break your goddamn neck."

Declan sneered. "You and whose army?"

"Seems like Nyx would be on my side in this fucking fight."

Then, he sighed, popped his own neck, and sighed again when it clicked. "How much longer for you to look over shit?"

"You know how it works. Got to make sure things are copacetic for the ride home and the ride north. I'd say it won't be long though."

"I get it." Finn blew out a breath. "I'm needed here."

"You're needed there too."

Maybe he heard my sympathy, maybe he realized I was being genuine, because his eyes darted to mine before they shot to Declan.

"You're no use to me here. Fuck off to Aoife's side and let me know if it's a boy or a girl," O'Donnelly grumbled.

Finn's lips snarled in a twisted smile. "Why, Dec, I didn't know you cared."

That had the other guy rolling his eyes. "I try not to."

Because none of this conversation was anticipated, I cleared my throat and thrust out my hand for him to shake.

"Hope things go well for her and the baby."

Finn returned the gesture and stated, utterly heartfelt, "Me too," before he darted off, yelling orders at the guards securing the area.

When a car swerved out of nowhere, barreling toward him, he didn't stop running until he was in the backseat, and then the massive gates were opening and he was roaring out and toward his woman.

"Pussy whipped, but Aoife's got a heart of gold, so I can't blame him." The insight had me cocking a brow, then scowling when he murmured, "Seems you're pussy whipped too, considering you ain't said two words to me in all the months we've been dealing together, but you come over to help Finn the first night he's here and moaning about Aoife being in labor."

My first instinct wasn't always violent, but I didn't particularly like the derogatory tone. Finn evidently cared for his wife, and by the sounds of it, Declan thought she was good people too, so his bitching made me wonder if he was just bitter.

I knew how that worked.

Love sucked when it burned you. Maybe Declan had been burned, and then, I realized Rex really was right.

I wasn't whipped, just growing a cunt.

"No point in him being miserable. This shit takes how long it's going to take, you know that, and I'd be on edge thinking my wife was about to give birth too."

"So, common courtesy, hmm?" Declan snorted as he shoved his hands into his pockets. "If you say so." Then, his gaze drifted over my men, and he muttered, "If the Wolves give you any trouble, tell me. I'll cut that line faster than you can blink."

"Would you cut us too?"

"Oh yeah, if you fucked up."

"The Wolves know you're close to cutting them free?" That knowledge could change loyalties, and it could fuck us over in the long run.

"Them traveling to your territory and eying up your garage makes me think they're getting too big for their britches, as my Da likes to say." He jerked a shoulder. "We're running point on this, you're just distributors. Seems like they didn't get that memo.

"Fucking French Canadians. Never let it be said they're all polite and shit. The ones I've dealt with are always in my face."

I had to laugh. "Everyone literally says Canadians are the politest folk out there."

"Yeah, well, something goes wrong with their bikers. And they have prisons and shit too, so they're not all fucking nice. At least with you, I know you're a bunch of fucked-up maniacs."

My brows rose at that. Maybe some would consider it an insult, but not me. "You prefer to deal with insanity?"

"Your variation of it, sure." He bared his teeth. "You're getting quite a rep. Angel of Mercy... maybe that tattoo on your back shouldn't be Satan but—"

I frowned. "What the fuck are you talking about?" Tension invaded my limbs, but I wasn't going to act first without thinking.

"You and I both know what we're talking about." He smirked. "Why do you think my dad likes you so much? Always insists you're on the job when the Sinners come up on runs."

"I'm the Enforcer, it makes sense for me to be here." That wasn't a lie. I was always on runs. *Always.*

Declan sniggered. "Yeah, tell yourself that." He clapped me on the back, then began to walk away when his cell buzzed. "But you've come to the attention of a select few people, Nyx. Whether you wanted that or not, doesn't matter." As he turned his back on me, I saw his cell, saw him pause before he hit the green button, then he twisted to look at me over his shoulder and asked, "Want to know if it's a boy or girl when I find out?"

When I didn't reply, he smirked at me. "I'll save you the bother of making a decision now and will text you with the news." He winked, then with a brogue so dense it was like he'd just stepped off the boat from Ireland, said, "Go with God, my child."

And if that wasn't one of the most bizarre conversations I'd had in a good while, then I wasn't sure what fucking was.

❖

TWENTY-FOUR

GIULIA

IT WAS strange not having Nyx glowering at the customers who dared talk to me.

Well, the male customers.

I'd grown quite accustomed to his stare, his intent regard, and I missed it. Yeah, missed it.

What that said about me, I wasn't sure. Maybe I was as fucked up in the head as he was, all I knew for certain was that I missed it, missed him, and disliked the fact he'd set a brother on me to watch over shit.

I knew Sin was there for that reason too, because he'd been drinking Coke all night.

Yeah, *Coke.*

And the brothers who were hanging out, getting drunk, weren't giving him any crap over it.

Clue two.

Sin certainly wasn't Nyx, and in truth, I thought the bar did better because of it. Nyx brought the dark dangers of the night with him. Fitting, considering his name. It added a heaviness to the atmosphere that I was getting used to, but it was intense for the walk-ins. Like walking into clouds, almost. Well, either that or fog.

Inside fog.

As I pondered which fit more, I focused on my remaining duties and not my phone, which was back in the office. Nyx couldn't exactly send me a text every ten minutes when he was on the back of his bike, but it hadn't stopped me from checking my inbox and being disappointed when I didn't see anything from him.

So, even though I really wanted to see if he *had* sent me something, pride insisted that I carry on cleaning up for the night as the dwindling customers began to get ready for home.

This working behind the bar gig wasn't as bad as I'd thought. I didn't like cooking for the MC too, at least, not at breakfast, but I kind of enjoyed being in charge. The bossy bitch inside me appreciated being able to do whatever the fuck I wanted, and I could... not just because I was boning Nyx, but because Nyx wasn't interested *at all* in the bar.

I wasn't even sure why Rex had given him the option, because he didn't give a fuck about anything other than watching me. Maybe that would have been different if we hadn't started this... relationship?

Could it be called that?

I figured we were past fuck buddy stage, even though it had only been three weeks, because you didn't share shit about murder unless things were intense, right?

I highly doubted Nyx had engaged in homicidal pillow talk with Cammie, and yeah, I knew I was seriously twisted when I was pleased about that.

But fuck, violence was in my blood, I guess it had to run free at some point.

As I watched Chad mop the one side of the bar that was clear of all customers, I began to take a small inventory of the cans we had up front. I'd sent Cody home an hour ago when things had taken a quiet turn as a popular girl at the strip club next door caused a mass exodus.

As I counted cans, I thought about hiring some more help, because I knew I was tired, so it figured that Chad and Cody were exhausted as well.

Since Nyx had given me free rein to do what I wanted so long as the bar was bringing in the money to do it, I thought about hiring two more people. That had been my initial plan, but I was cautious by nature, even if it wasn't my money I'd be wasting, and I'd admit that a part of me wanted to impress Nyx and Rex. Not only with my work ethic, but also that, even if I had zero experience, I had a brain between my ears.

Learning the ropes had been hard, but it wasn't rocket science. Neither was the work, but that didn't mean it wasn't tiring. So while I knew the guys needed money for college, I didn't need them dropping dead from the late shifts either.

By the time I was done with the inventory and wondering if it was the right time to hire some staff, I saw that Chad had finished, so I motioned him over and said, "It's okay, you go on home."

"I'll come in twenty minutes earlier to clean those two sections tomorrow," he offered, and his earnestness was so sweet that I had to smile.

We were the same age, and yet I felt a thousand years older.

I knew why too.

I was MC born and bred. My years away didn't change me that much, and the MC reared old souls, ones that knew about the harsh truths in this world. We weren't raised with Santa creeping into our living rooms. If some fucker broke in on Christmas morning, we shot them, we didn't give them cookies and fucking milk.

Plus, I liked the two guys I hired. They didn't have an attitude with me anymore. They could have, considering everyone knew that Nyx was fucking me—if he'd tried to keep things on the down low, he'd failed, because he growled at anyone with a dick who dared talk to me for more than three minutes—and the fact that I was a woman who was their boss no longer fazed them.

Yeah, it sucked that that was a 'tick' for them, but hell, I'd take it.

"Sure, that's fine. You look tired, and I know I am."

He peered back at the few stragglers and asked, "Want me to stay?"

I knew he didn't want to, could practically see him withholding a yawn as he stood there gripping the damn mop, so I smiled at him and shook my head. "Nah, it's all good. See you tomorrow."

"Thanks, Giulia!" He cut a look at the door. "That guy left about ten minutes ago. Did you know that?"

I twisted around to see that Sin had, indeed, left me on my own.

I wasn't nervous, not when the stragglers were all couples, but still, I knew Nyx would castrate him if I told him the guy had wandered off.

"I didn't see him leave."

"I think he went next door. It's getting crowded. You can hear the cheers in the storeroom."

I shrugged. "He'll be back soon, I'm sure. He's the one giving me a ride home."

Chad looked relieved. "Oh, good. I'm glad to hear it."

I shot him another smile and told him, "You go on. Catch some Zs."

"You too, Giulia, thanks." He disappeared to grab his shit, then waved at me as he left.

Deciding to be nice, I mopped the second section, which was all the incentive the stragglers needed to go.

Within twenty minutes, there was only one more section for the guys to clear tomorrow, and I could count the till before getting ready to leave.

As I considered the likelihood of me having to drag Sin out of a crowded strip joint, I headed over to the door to lock up.

Sighing as I thought of my to-do list, I wished Nyx was here.

Which was stupid. Because he was more of a disruption than anything else. Counting up the profits always took twice as long when he was distracting me with those damn come-to-bed eyes of his.

Shrugging off the weird melancholy that overset me, and well aware that it was way too soon to miss someone this much—especially when that someone was a biker whose life involved long road trips that were couched in secrecy—I straightened my shoulders and made to turn around.

As I did, I saw him surge toward me from the direction of the bar, and my eyes flared wide in surprise.

When recognition hit, I found myself blinking. That blond hair that probably took him hours to style, the smirk that revealed teeth his dentist had to be proud of, a little tape on a patrician nose that had recently been broken, and the designer jeans and shirt that instantly classified him as a country clubber—it was the guy from a few weeks back. The one Nyx had made an example of, who'd classified me as a biker slut, because I had zero interest in him.

Frozen, I processed all that in a second, before I recognized what was in his hand and registered what his next move was going to be. Then his face twisted with rage, and I defrosted.

The glass bottle arched down, slicing through the air toward me. I ducked, punched the blond bastard in the gut, and went to raise my knee to get him in the balls. He jerked two seconds before I could connect, and instead, his free hand snapped out to grab my wrist. With one clean twist, he broke it.

Agony sliced through me, but rage unfurled first. With my free hand, I went for his nose and was glad when he howled as it spurted blood. I really fucking hoped I undid the healing that had taken place since Nyx's original hit.

"Slut!" he spat, the hiss sibilant with his rage and loaded with his pain.

That this was revenge was clear. What wasn't was how far the fucker was going to take this. From the malice in his eyes, I had to figure it wasn't going to end well for me, but I couldn't think about that right now. I just had to focus on the fact that I wasn't about to go down without a fight.

Even with blood spurting everywhere, and me twisting around like a wildcat, he managed to get the bottle high enough to clout me on the head with a force that had my knees buckling, but the hit wasn't bad enough to stop me from punching him in the nuts on my way down.

Nobody, no-fucking-body, could ever accuse me of not being a fighter, and this guy wasn't here to give me some fucking roses. Not with that bottle in his goddamn hand.

Another howl escaped him, but he cursed, "You fucking bitch," and managed to evade my clawing hands to raise the bottle high enough to gain some real momentum.

The second it collided with my temple, I knew I was fucked.

And not in a good way.

More than fear, I found I was furious. So fucking angry. So mother-fucking wrathful that I knew, point-blank knew, that when Nyx killed this motherfucker, I was going to be there, stripping his organs alongside my man.

It was what kept me going as the cunt dragged me across the floor as though I was a bag of trash. He was limping from what I'd done to him, and I could only hope that my ball-busting capabilities had preceded me, and the fucker wouldn't be able to get it up with the way I'd punched him.

"He's going to slit your throat, and I'm going to bathe in your blood," I slurred, as I made sure I was a dead weight.

I wanted, more than anything, to kick his legs out from under him, but I was seeing stars. The way he dragged me had my head connecting with the ground every goddamn step, too.

The agony wasn't something I'd felt before, and the truth was, I wasn't sure if I was going to be sick. But if that was going to happen, I was totally going to vomit all over him.

I willed my stomach to stop churning until the moment was right. Fuck, I hoped it was projectile, and I hoped like shit that I got him square in the fucking face.

The anger inside me kept me going, burning hotly like it usually did. I wasn't a nice person, and I knew that, had embraced it a long while ago, but at that moment, I knew what I was capable of.

I wasn't the kind of person who flew in a fight. I stuck around and got shit done. Even as dazed as I was, I thought about what he was doing, and how I could counter it to make him hurt, but I'd admit, his silence in the face of my threat, and what he was doing, dragging me instead of just raping me in front of the door where I lay, concerned me.

He had a game plan, and I had no intention of letting that come to fruition.

I cursed Sin for leaving to go see some bitch take her clothes off, when there were a dozen sweetbutts wandering around naked back at the compound, and managed to kick my leg out in the vain effort of trying to slow the bastard down. Maybe if I could keep him from doing whatever he'd planned, Sin would come back, and he'd save me from this absolute dick.

Was it weird that I was pissed about not knowing his name? Or for forgetting it? I wanted to humanize the piece of shit, remind him that I was a real fucking person, and to do that, I needed his name. Essentially, I was a hostage, and I'd seen enough crime shows to know that shit wasn't going to end well unless I turned the tables.

For the first time, a slither of fear whispered through me. I thought about Nyx, and everything I still wanted to do with and *to* him, and I thought about how he'd feel when he found out about this.

He'd said he'd keep me safe, and on the first run out of the district, here I was, being assaulted.

Seriously, the man's luck was bad. Mine was worse.

But... if the cunt managed to hurt me, permanently, Nyx would never forgive himself.

Jesus, I'd never forgive *myself* if I was about to be a crime statistic, and did nothing to save myself.

Fuck, that made the fear slide out of the building as I gathered my strength and kicked my leg out once more. When it connected with his knee, I thanked God, Jesus, Buddha, and every other deity I could remember from Wikipedia when the dick crashed to the floor.

The second he collided with it, his intention changed. He scrambled over to me a second after he hit the ground and pinned me down. "Cunt, stay down," he spat at me, and spots of saliva slathered over me.

I had little Tweety Birds floating around at the edges of my vision, but that didn't stop me from laughing in his face. "Yeah, I'm just gonna let you rape me, fucker." I twisted in his hold, shifted so I could elbow him in the face. Luck was back on my side, because I hit his nose again.

A wail escaped him, but even as the pain hit him, the rage came next. When he punched me, I knew I was more fucked than before. The Tweety Birds had started a chorus movement by now, and even as I tried to unseat him, tried to buck him off me, it just wasn't going to work.

He dragged down my jeans, and I was glad I'd gone for the skinny ones that were a real pain in the ass to get on and off, because he struggled... Until he pulled out a knife and sliced them and my panties off me.

When the blade connected with my skin, I whimpered. The sound was weak, so frail, and I hated it. *Hated* it.

That was not me.

It wasn't.

I blinked when his finger was there, touching me, touching where only I could choose to have someone touch me.

He thrust it inside me and laughed. "Nice and dry, just how I love it."

I twisted again, but it wasn't like before. I felt like I was being tossed about in the middle of a storm, but I wasn't moving that much, and when my motion barely affected him, I started willing myself to puke because that had to fuck with anyone's arousal, right?

As I focused on anything other than that invasion, than the sound of his zipper coming down, I saw something at the back end of the bar.

A light.

Oh, God, was it Sin?

I cried out in relief, and the sound had the bastard atop me jerking around to look in my line of sight.

When he did, I was doubly relieved to see him react to the stranger's presence, because I figured I was seeing shit. Losing my mind.

That couldn't be who I thought it was.

Could it?

I gazed dopily up at the brother, and watched as my attacker got to his feet, his knife in front of him as he started to defend himself, but whatever he was doing, it wasn't enough.

The intent in the Sinner's face told me all I needed to know.

I was safe.

My attacker *wasn't*.

In the end, it was anticlimactic.

The brother grabbed the knife and stuck it straight between his ribs, right in the cunt's chest.

As the fucker crumpled to the ground, his hands flailing around like newly caught fish as he bled out, the Sinner came to me and started rearranging me, pulling my jeans back together like that would help.

He caught my eye, and I caught his. It was then I knew I wasn't imagining things. More than the blood seeping out of my attacker, more than his life blood puddling on the floor close to me, it was the look in his eyes and the way he raised his finger to his lips in a plea for silence.

I nodded, then cried out as the ache in my head made itself known.

"I'll call the police," I whispered, not even knowing why I was whispering, just knowing that I had to.

"You need an EMT."

"I know." I closed my eyes. "Go."

"Thank you."

I laughed, then regretted it when my stomach started churning. "You're the one I need to thank," I slurred.

"You'll be all right?"

"Just dandy." When my vision wavered, I bit out, "Go! So I can get the cops in."

He got to his feet and rushed out of the bar. I had the wherewithal to notice that he went out the back, and the second I heard the door snick as it closed, I let my rebelling stomach release its poison.

For a second, I just lay in my puke, and the stench of it was enough to keep me conscious. I used it to get some strength, to force myself into acting. Even though I didn't want to, even though I just wanted to pass out, I knew I couldn't.

So, exhausted, I patted down my pockets and remembered I'd dumped my phone back in the office because I'd gotten sick of checking to see if Nyx had sent a message. Wanting to moan in distress, I felt tears prickle my eyes as I knew I'd have to get the bastard's.

As I slid across the floor, I slipped in his blood. My stomach almost protested but I knew I had to act, to move.

It was my first instinct to want to call Nyx, but wherever he was, he'd be no use to me. A scream escaped me when the bastard jerked as I patted down his jeans and found his phone.

It was one of the new iPhones, and I held it up to his face to open it. When his eyelids fluttered open, I saw how dazed he was, and then I registered that the phone hadn't opened.

It needed a goddamn passcode.

My stomach churned as I thought about moving over to the office, and it was a no brainer to reach over and grab the hilt of the knife in the bastard's chest. Before I did anything, I whispered, "What's your phone's passcode?"

When no answer was forthcoming, I stared into the bastard's eyes, saw the hatred mixing with the pain, and I twisted the knife. His hoarse cry wasn't music to my ears, but it certainly made my heart pound in satisfaction. Actually, it made me feel woozy. The shift of power was making me lightheaded.

"Stop!" he cried out, but I carried on.

And on.

"423," he rushed out quickly, and I stopped twisting the knife. "341," he slurred out the six-digit passcode, his tongue thick as blood gushed from his mouth.

The sudden stench of piss and shit releasing from his body was enough to make me scuttle out of his way before any more of his poison connected with me, and I groaned as my bones protested the move, but I had the wherewithal to know I had to do two things.

Firstly, I went to his settings and changed his passcode after I logged in. I muttered the number over and over again, refusing to let my addled brain forget the six digits. When that was done, I changed it to six zeros, then shifted his Face ID to recognize my own.

That took more energy than I had, but I wanted his phone. I wanted it because I knew, like fate was holding my hand, that this had happened for a reason.

And the only reason I could think of was here in my hand.

"Nice and dry, just how I love it."

That was what he'd said, and it resonated with me on a level I couldn't even begin to define. Maybe that was stupid of me, to put so much into those words. Bad shit just happened sometimes, and it was my unlucky day, but I had to embrace that, or I'd start to cry.

Yeah, stone-cold, knife-twisting bitch that I was, and I wanted to cry.

Fuck, more than that, I wanted Nyx, I wanted him so badly, but I couldn't have him, so I had to woman up. He wasn't here to save me. He was only God knew where, and I had to look after myself.

Like I'd been doing since forever.

Wishing we weren't on the small dance floor in the middle of the room so I could prop myself up against a chair or something, I let myself cascade to the floor as I keyed in 911.

When an operator picked up, I whispered the address of the bar, then said, "I-I've been raped."

He'd finger-fucked me. Was that rape or sexual assault?

For a second, I just lay there, blinking, until her voice broke into my dark reverie.

"Ma'am? Is your attacker still on the premises?"

I knew I had to come up with some story that would satisfy the police, but my brain had been pushed to the limits by having to think about changing the passcode on the phone I was holding.

Because I was fading, I whispered, "I killed him. I-I'm going to pass out now."

I heard her sharp, "Ma'am, stay with me," but it was no use.

Clinging to the phone in my hand, I prayed that the next time I woke up, I wouldn't be lying in my own vomit, covered in his blood, and there'd be no scent of piss and shit around me. More than that, I prayed Nyx would be there, because if he wasn't... I didn't know how I'd cope.

TWENTY-FIVE

NYX

TWENTY MINUTES AWAY FROM BLACKPOOL, just before the border, I got the call.

Five hours away from my woman, and I got the fucking call.

I'd never been gladder that Link had caught up with us because the second my cell buzzed with the ringtone only Rex used, I stopped at the side of the road, pulling off instantly.

Sometimes, he had intel that he'd feed to me before we made a drop, so I knew not to avoid it anyway, but this time, I was doubly glad I pulled over to answer.

Five hours... it took *five* motherfucking hours to get back home, and I made it in three.

Each of those hours killed me, slashed at the demon inside me until it was a bleeding mass of wounds that endured because it, too, suffered on Giulia's behalf.

I felt like I was dying, and only the fact I needed to stay awake and aware when I was riding at a hundred-miles-an-hour and more kept me going.

She'd been attacked.

At the bar.

Hurt.

On Sinners' territory.

I wasn't sure who I was going to kill first.

Sin, the motherfucker I'd left to keep her safe, or the bastard who thought he could hurt a Sinner's woman.

My woman.

Mine.

As rage throttled me, urging me on, even though I'd been riding for nine hours by this point, I made it back into town and headed straight for the hospital.

I'd never been more grateful to be a Sinner because, like they knew, and as they were aware of how I was, my brothers didn't say shit to me when I made it inside the clinic, but they were there.

One at the entrance, another at the end of the hall, each one a marker I had to follow like some fucked-up trail of candy for Hansel and Gretel.

The receptionist didn't fuck with me, instead, the second she saw me, she bowed her head to avoid looking at me, and I ignored her, intent only on following the trail my brothers had made for me.

There were eight of them in total, and each of them dipped their chin at me without saying a word.

The tension in their faces put me on edge, because... Rex had only said she'd been attacked.

Their response told me it was bad.

Really bad.

Was she dying?

Was another woman in my life... Had I failed her?

Failed her like I'd failed Carly?

The thought was like a punch to the gut, and I almost buckled as I made it to the ward where Rex was standing guard. He was grim and tense, his face resolute, and his eyes wary as he opened the door for me.

I didn't even greet him, just headed inside, and what I saw made me realize I hadn't just let her down, this went beyond failure.

I didn't deserve to even see the state of her, and she *was* a fucking state.

Her eyes were bruised, her nose broken. She had one hand and arm in a cast, and from the bulk beneath her hospital gown, I could tell she had bandages in places I couldn't see.

She was cut and scraped everywhere, and I wasn't sure if that was from a knife or... hell, I didn't even know what I was looking at.

My back hit the wall opposite the bed, and I stared at her, stared and stared, trying to process how this had happened.

It had to be because I'd been staking a claim on her time. This had to be retribution because no one fucked with Sinners' property, and that was a fact I'd helped hammer home every year I'd been an Enforcer.

Needing answers, because dealing with how badly I'd failed her was fucking with my head to the point I wasn't sure if I was losing it, I just knew that I needed to make someone pay.

I needed to avenge her. I needed to do something because the thought that I hadn't helped her get her gun license throbbed through my brain. I'd been thinking with my cock, not her safety, and never in my goddamn life had I felt more ashamed of myself than I did now.

Because I felt like I was going to destroy something, I knew I needed answers, which Rex would have. He would be able to explain this to me, so I went to leave. But the second my hand connected with the door handle, she whispered, "Stay."

The one word was softer than a murmur, and yet, it had the same effect on me as a bullet to the brain.

With my back to her, I let my heart and soul, fuck, the *demon* bleed into my voice. "I don't deserve to stay. I let you down."

When she didn't say anything, I closed my eyes, hating that she agreed. Even if I knew it already. Even if I knew I didn't deserve to breathe the same air as she did.

Then, she whispered, "Don't you think I deserve to be the one who decides that?"

"I told you I'd keep you safe."

"You tried."

I pressed my face into the door. "Not hard enough."

A shaky sigh escaped her. "Please. Don't leave, Nyx." The quiver in her voice when she'd always been so strong, so fucking resilient, had me tensing even more. "Stay."

Because her needs mattered more than my own, I pushed off the door. When I heard her sob, I knew she thought I was leaving anyway, but I twisted on my heel and swerved toward her, not stopping until I was at her side.

She looked so small on the bed, and it took me a few minutes to reconcile that this was her. Because while she *was* small, short, and curvy, she had so much presence that it was easy to think she was bigger.

This diminutive figure wasn't the woman I knew.

I shoved the thought aside, because if I started thinking that, then I was fucked. Rage was always making my brain whirl, and throw in exhaustion after the long ride and no sleep, well, I wasn't firing on all cylinders.

The mustard-colored chair was on the same side as her cast-covered wrist, so I hauled it up and moved it around to the other side of her.

I wanted, so damn badly, to hurl it at the wall, to watch the destruction rain down, but I didn't.

Couldn't.

She needed me.

I wasn't sure if I'd ever been needed before, not really, at least, not by anyone other than the MC, and that was different.

She needed me in spite of my having failed her, and that meant something.

I wasn't sure what. But it did.

When I took a seat in the chair that was way too small for me, I looked at her, saw her injuries up close, took in her red eyes and wet cheeks, and whispered, "I'll kill him."

Then she stunned me even more—she smiled. "I did that already."

My brows rose. "You did?"

"Yes."

"How?"

"Knife to the heart." A shadow cast over her eyes, one I didn't understand. She couldn't possibly feel guilty for killing the fucker, could she?

"He deserved worse."

"Well, that was all I could manage."

Was she teasing me? Fuck. She was. That little smile about did me in.

"Shame," I whispered. "I'd like to make him pay."

She didn't let her eyes drift from mine as she murmured, "I would too."

At that moment, I recognized the demon in me had found its mate, but before I could focus on that, she whispered, "oooooo."

I blinked at her. "Huh?"

"My cell phone is in the cabinet there." She pointed to a solid unit that was for housing personal effects.

I frowned. "Why do you need me to know that?"

She just stared at me, unblinking, focused only on making me do as she wanted. "Get it."

Not understanding, but wanting to, I reached into the unit and pulled out a cell phone that definitely wasn't hers. She had a smaller iPhone that was about two years old, and this was one of the newer ones.

I pocketed it and asked, "Want me to take it home?"

"Yeah." She closed her eyes and whispered, "I want to sleep now. They keep coming in and waking me up."

So she had a concussion, and the notion of her being hit hard enough to trigger that made the rage start to burn inside me once more. The demon was awake, and it wanted vengeance. *Needed* it.

Maybe she saw that, maybe she felt the change in me, because her eyes flared wide. "Don't go," she begged, slaying me with the request.

"I won't. I promise. Sleep. I'll be here when you wake up," I vowed gruffly, melting inside when she released a sigh, nuzzled into the pillow that should have been my shoulder, and let herself fade out.

I placed my hand on hers, argued over climbing into bed beside her, and instead, shoved my hand into my pocket and fingered the phone.

It had to be her attacker's. Had to be.

But why had she taken it?

Why had she given it to me?

I wasn't averse to her stealing a phone that cost a couple grand. Hell, she more than deserved it, but Giulia didn't really give a shit about stuff. She didn't have many friends, and considering how prickly she was, I knew why. She seemed to tolerate her brothers, and aside from them, she was content with only talking to me.

It made me feel weird, deep inside, to know that. For whatever reason, I was in her circle. She'd trusted me enough to be there, and I'd failed her.

My jaw clenched, and I gently lifted my hand when she released a soft snuffle that told me she was sleeping, then carefully got to my feet after I toed out of my boots. The second my socks connected with the floor, I shuffled over to the door and opened it.

When I saw Rex was still there, leaning against it, I muttered, "Thanks for hanging around."

"Like I was going anywhere else." His eyes were fixed on mine. "How are you doing?"

"How do you think?" I snapped, then instantly regretted the harshness in my voice. It wasn't his fault, and the last thing I wanted was to wake Giulia.

"Sin's been punished."

"Tell him he'll wish he was dead when I'm through with him."

Rex shook his head. "No. I sent him to Oklahoma."

My brows lifted, nostrils flaring wide with anger. "What?" If I spat out the word, then so fucking be it.

"He fucked up, but he doesn't deserve for you to kill him, just because she got to the fucker before you could."

I hated that he knew me so well. "I'd have fucked him over, not killed him."

"You're too ugly to pout."

"We both know that's a lie," I retorted, but my scowl held less fire than before. Until I thought about what my woman had suffered through, endured, and all because he'd... what? I needed to know, even though I was aware the truth would fuck with my head even more. "What happened?" I rasped.

"I don't really know." Pinching the bridge of his nose, he explained, "Sin was there all night, until he left before closing. When the cops and ambulance pulled up, he was nowhere to be found."

"Motherfucker."

"It was the guy you had a problem with that night. The rich blond bastard."

Instant recognition hit me, and I wished, then and there, that I'd done more than break his goddamn nose. If I'd broken his fucking legs, he wouldn't have been able to do shit to my woman.

"I remember."

"I didn't think you'd forgotten," Rex grumbled, then he reached up and rubbed his eyes, and I realized he'd be just as exhausted as me. The bar closed late, and if this had happened at closing, well...

"He's from a prominent family, Nyx. We're going to get shit for this."

"The police are in our pockets," I dismissed.

"Yeah, but they have to ask questions."

"He was attacking her."

"Yeah. He was. Her injuries fit that profile."

My throat closed. "Did he rape her?"

"No. But he did something. I didn't want to ask. They gave her a rape kit, but—"

"He penetrated her with something but didn't come in her?"

"I think so. At least, that's from what I gathered thanks to the chatter." He shot me a look. "I'm sorry, Nyx."

"Don't be. She's alive, and she hurt him worse than he hurt her." I had to take comfort in that. I had to, or I'd lose my mind.

Maybe I already was losing it, maybe the demon thought about taking charge of me, but—and it was a massive but—she needed me. Nyx. Not the demon. And that, and only that, had me clinging to my sanity.

I fingered the cell phone in my pocket, and murmured, "All os. She gave me this." I passed it over. "She wanted me to take it home."

He studied the expensive phone. "His?"

"Think so."

"Why did she want us to have it?"

"Don't know. Find out." I scraped a hand over my face, then cut her a look, made sure she was still sleeping, and stated, "She said she killed him by stabbing him. That's..."

"Unlikely? Lucky? Yeah. Someone was watching over her."

Not me.

That was for fucking sure.

I'd let her down.

God...

I rubbed at my eyes, not really understanding what had gone down, but knowing that I wouldn't be going on a run for a while.

Not until she was back on her feet, not until I... *Fuck.*

I scraped a hand over my face. "You here because she's Dog's girl, or because she's mine?"

Rex snorted. "What kind of dumb fuck question is that? Technically, you ain't claimed her, but I knew she was yours before you even figured it out yourself. Nyx, you're many things, but—"

"But what?" I demanded when he broke off.

"You care too much. That's your trouble. Technically, I'm here because she's Dog's. You know we don't protect bitches unless they're Old Ladies."

"That's why I asked."

"You gonna change that?"

"I'm no good for her."

"Maybe not. Let her decide for herself though, yeah? She might say no."

"After tonight? Who could fucking blame her?" I rubbed the back of my neck. "Have her brothers been in?"

"Yeah. They were drunk, so I sent them home."

"And they went?" My estimation for them dropped at that.

"They were escorted," Rex said dryly. "Dog didn't come. Said he'd upset her more if he visited than if he left her alone, and because he isn't wrong, I didn't push it."

"Good thinking." I shot her another look. "She in overnight?"

"Yeah. For the concussion. She hasn't really explained what happened, so the cops are antsy to know." Rex hesitated. "I really need you to not lose your shit when that conversation goes down, Nyx. I don't need you in a jail cell."

"I know." My tone was sullen enough to make me wince.

"Broken wrist and nose, sprained ankle, and she has bad lacerations on her upper thighs." He clapped a hand on my shoulder and squeezed—I knew why too. I could feel the wrath swell inside me once again, making me burn like a fucking fire. "Don't fuck this up, Nyx."

I cast him a look. "What would you know about fucking up?"

"You have to ask me that?" His mouth pursed. "She knows what the tattoos mean?"

"Yeah."

"And she wants you anyway. Don't screw this up," he repeated firmly. "She might be the only thing that stops us from losing you to that twisted shit inside you."

Because I didn't want to deal with this conversation, I just grunted and retreated into the room. When the door closed behind me without another word, I knew he was going to let me escape.

Unfortunately for me, Giulia wasn't.

"I like your twisted shit."

Her mumble had me sighing. "Thought you were asleep."

"I was. Until you started shouting." She squinted at me. "Don't you know you're supposed to be quiet in hospitals?"

"I didn't get that memo."

"That doesn't surprise me." She sniffed. "Anyway, what twisted shit? In particular, I mean?"

"You know what he's talking about," I said bluntly.

"Maybe. It all seems rational to me."

"Well, that means you're as fucked up as I am."

She smiled, and somehow, it was all the more ungodly for how she kept her eyes closed.

"Meant to be," she countered with a laugh. Her eyes popped open. "I made him hurt, Nyx. You'd have been proud of me."

My throat closed, and it was hard for me to say, "Even if you hadn't, I'd be proud of you. You survived, baby girl. That was all I needed you to do. I can fix what's broken, but I can't repair what's—"

She stared at me like I wasn't the monster I was, and then, after blinking a few times, whispered, "Is that what hurts the most? That you can't repair Carly?"

My jaw worked. "She was too broken. He'd done it for so long that she wasn't... right. The writing was on the wall for a while, and I knew that, and I still didn't say anything."

"You made him pay."

"Too late."

"Never too late."

Now wasn't the time to argue, so I just grunted. She held out her good hand, and told me, "When the cops come, you don't have to stay with me."

"Of course, I do," I grated out. "What the hell do you think I am? A pussy?"

"No. I don't want you to get arrested is all. I need you with me, Nyx. The last thing I want is you in a cell."

Because Rex had just said that too, I rolled my eyes. "I have more control than either you or Rex think."

"I know that. But I also know that something about me makes you want to protect me... you can't protect me from the cops."

"Just fucking watch me." And she did.

The next afternoon, when the pigs came to question her, she kept her eyes on me all the while they asked her to recount every fucking detail, until I wasn't sure if I was going to lose my shit and break my promise to her.

The demon that burned inside me wanted to let it rip, wanted to maim anyone and everyone in sight, but the fucker who needed to pay was already dead.

She'd done that.

She'd made him pay, and I couldn't resent her for that, because she needed the closure more than me, but damn, I wished I'd done it. Wished I'd been the one to skin the fucker alive, and...

"He just attacked?"

Detective Cole was looking to get a fist in his face if he wasn't careful.

"Yes, Detective," she ground out. "He just attacked. I didn't ask for it. I didn't wave my ass in his face and beg him to cut my clothes off and hit me over the head with a bottle. I assure you, he did that all on his own."

From the corner of my eye, I saw Cole turn bright red, but she didn't. She didn't see because she was looking at me.

"If we had camera footage to back this up, things would be easier," the other detective, Bradley, muttered disapprovingly.

I wasn't sure if the disapproval was over our lack of CCTV footage, or the fact that Cole had asked such an insensitive question.

Either way, I'd had enough.

"Are you disappointed that my woman managed to survive and her rapist didn't, Detectives?"

"Of course not!"

"I don't appreciate your tone—"

The sound of a voice clearing behind us had me breaking the connection I had with Giulia. She looked at the doorway too, and when she spied Rex and a woman I knew she didn't know, she frowned.

I headed over to Rachel Laker with my hand held out. "Thanks for coming, Rachel."

"My pleasure." She shot the detectives a look. "Is this really the line of questioning you want to take? To a woman who's been beaten and sexually assaulted by Luke Lancaster?" She reached up and tapped her chin with a manicured nail. "I think I can see the headlines now. *Cops Take Rapist's Side in Shock—*"

"Enough," Cole growled. "We have all we need."

"For the moment," Bradley tacked on.

"Be sure to contact my office to schedule an appointment first. Remember, gentlemen, my client is the *victim*. The Lancasters might be trying to portray this a whole different way, but my client's injuries attest to the truth. We have no compunction in going public too."

The detectives glared at her first, then shared their charm with Rex and me before storming out without even an apology to Giulia.

Before I could get too mad, Giulia murmured, "Since when do I have a lawyer?"

"Since the Lancasters decided to spin what happened last night."

Giulia frowned at Rex. "How have they done that?"

When she glared at me, I shrugged. "I don't know. I've been in here with you."

Rex tossed a paper at me. I eyed the headline, and my mouth twisted at what I read.

"*Lancaster Heir Dies in Suspected MC Attack.*"

When I held it up to Giulia, knowing she wouldn't let me get away with shielding this from her, she blanched. "My God. They can't get away with that."

"Oh, we're suing," Rex told her, sounding borderline cheerful. "Don't worry about that. We're a legitimate business."

Rachel reached for the paper. As she perused the headline, she scoffed, "Yeah. Like that's true."

Rex just grinned at her, then shot Giulia a concerned look. "Don't worry, Giulia. We have things in hand."

I scrubbed at the stubble on my jaw. "Those detectives weren't ones I recognized."

"Was hoping you'd know them."

I shook my head at him. "Could Lancaster have brought in his own team of cops? Is that even possible?"

"You're the one who knows more about law enforcement than anyone," Rex pointed out.

"It's breaking jurisdiction in more ways than one, but—"

"If the family can put a slant like this on the story," Rachel interjected, shaking the paper in her fist, "then who knows what they can do."

"They're new to the area," Rex inserted. "I've never heard of them until recently. They cut up a stink about the permits on our mini-mall, but we had enough friends in local places to get our licenses."

My brain whirred as I tried to figure out what was going on, but fatigue and lack of sleep weren't helping me. All I knew was that if the scumbag's family could bring in cops of their own, something wasn't right. And if we couldn't rely on the pigs on our payroll, then shit was more than in the wind —we'd have to take steps to make sure we didn't get caught in the spray.

"Are you okay?" Rachel's concerned question had me flinching and turning my attention to Giulia. Where it should have been all along. But fuck, breaking the habit of a lifetime of putting club business *first* was hard to stop. Didn't mean I wasn't going to keep on goddamn trying though.

"I've been better," she mumbled, and I strode over to her, grabbing a firm hold of her good hand.

"They'll be sending you home soon," Rex informed her with a small smile, but I saw his gaze drift to our hands, and I dared him, with my glare, to utter a fucking word on the subject.

"Good." She blew out a breath. "Are you going to introduce me?"

Rachel flushed. "Sorry. I learned quickly to attack first where the Sinners and the cops are concerned." She stepped closer to the bed and held out her right hand so Giulia, once I relinquished my hold on her, could shake hers with her left. "I really hope you get better soon."

"Thanks." She gnawed on her split bottom lip, not seeming to care that her skin was broken. "Will I need your help?"

"You shouldn't. It was self-defense, and everything about your current status backs that up, but the Lancasters are rich and powerful, so we're just evening the odds." She patted Giulia's shoulder. "Don't worry. Please. Just concentrate on getting better."

Her smile was wan, and I couldn't blame her. This was bullshit. Total and utter bullshit. But as much as we owned the police, there was a difference between slipping through with a smuggling charge and a carrying without a license charge and murder.

"I-I don't know if I can afford a lawyer," she admitted, and I could hear how badly that stung her pride.

Rex sniffed. "You're a Sinner, Giulia. We look after our own."

She cut him a look, and I hated how her mouth quivered, knew she was holding back tears, but she managed to control them before she nodded and choked out, "Thank you."

"No thanks needed," he rebuffed. "We'll deal with this shit, and make sure the Lancasters are tied up in knots over it. You did good taking out the trash, Giulia. Well done."

She frowned, but her head tipped down to the side as she asked, "My phone?"

Rachel cleared her throat. "I don't think I need to hear this."

"No one does," Rex stated grimly. "But we'll deal with it later. I'll see you out, Rachel." He cut me a look. "We'll talk when you're back at the compound."

I nodded, but I'd admit that I wasn't as curious as Giulia evidently was.

I wondered if she knew how at the very center of my focus she was.

At that moment, all I could see, hear, and breathe was her.

I wasn't sure if she was ready for that intensity, didn't know if she'd be able to deal with it in the aftermath, so when the door swung shut behind Rex and the club's attorney, I moved to the armchair that made an Iron Maiden looked comfortable, and sat myself in it. Tilting my head back, I closed my eyes and tried to relax.

She tutted. "How can you sleep when he left it like that?"

"Nothing we can do until we're home."

She bit her lip. "Home."

I let my lids open a sliver. "Yeah. Home."

Her head bobbed for a second, then she whispered, a little more firmly, "Home."

And though I couldn't say I was cheerful, not exactly, that went a million miles closer to making me feel a helluva lot better.

TWENTY-SIX

GIULIA

THE SCREAM WOKE me up first. Then I realized why I was screaming.

A nightmare.

Dammit.

I hated nightmares. I mean, I guessed they weren't anyone's idea of a good time, but still, they were a weakness, and I...

God, I hated being weak. Being weak got you nowhere fast, but the bitch about your subconscious was that you couldn't exactly control it, could you?

When the bed beside me shifted, I stopped rubbing my eyes, and peered over at the poor bastard who'd been woken up every night this past week. He was armed, a sight I was getting accustomed to, and he was concerned—a sight I wasn't.

When a tap sounded at my bedroom door, I grimaced, because that alone was further proof that things were still weird.

I screamed, and usually, my brothers ignored me.

Now when I screamed, they came to check up on me, to make sure that I was okay.

Well, I *was* okay, but I was just having a few issues with some things, and I really didn't need them to be on tenterhooks around me. That just reminded me that things were strange.

Eying the glint of metal that came from Nyx's piece—real hardware, not just of the genital variety—I huffed, "It's okay, guys. Just a bad dream."

"Okay. Get some sleep," Hawk called out.

"I'm trying. Asswipe." Sheesh, even when he was trying to be nice, he pissed me off.

Flopping back onto the mattress, I watched as Nyx, as silent as ever, maneuvered around on the bed and placed his gun under his pillow.

It comforted me to know it was loaded. But it comforted me more having him here in bed beside me, having him there ready to shoot the second I screamed out in the middle of the night.

Without a word, I turned on my side, and he hauled me against his chest. He pressed a kiss to my shoulder and, like every other night so far, he stayed quiet and began to rest.

I liked that he didn't want to talk. I liked that he was okay with letting me process things the way I needed to. Of course, it fit that tonight, I didn't want that. Tonight, I wanted to explain. *Had* to.

Six nights of successive nightmares? It was starting to look like a pattern was forming, and even if it was, I needed him to know that it wasn't a regular pattern. I wasn't loaded with regret, didn't feel shame or guilt. That was why the nightmares didn't make sense. I felt none of that shit.

And I refused to believe it could be fear. Fear that someone else had shown me how precarious my security was. Fear that, once again, someone could overpower me and—

That train of thought was taking me nowhere. Fast. So I blurted out, "I don't feel guilty."

Technically, I had no reason to. But I didn't want him to know that, did I? Not the specifics, anyway.

"Nor should you," he assured me softly, his voice telling me that he was wide awake, even if he'd been going through the motions of falling asleep again.

It made me wonder if, every other night, he'd done the same. As I'd rested, he'd stood guard, and if that wasn't enough to make any woman's heart melt, then said woman's heart was just plain mean.

I was talking Cruella de-fucking-Vil mean.

"I just didn't want you to think I felt bad."

"I didn't," he denied, sounding so calm that I believed him.

"Good." I gnawed on my bottom lip, then muttered, "I tortured him."

He tensed. "How?"

I could hear his surprise, not his disgust. "I needed the passcode to his phone. I twisted the knife in his chest to make him give it to me."

A soft snicker escaped him, and it had pride winging its way through me at the sound. "Good girl."

"I was rather proud of myself too," I admitted wryly, then I swallowed, and asked about something I was desperate to know more of. "Why won't you tell me what was on the phone?"

He didn't have to move a muscle for me to feel the tension in his body. A tension that appeared every time I broached the subject.

A part of me, and God, I knew how stupid this was, but I felt sure that was why I couldn't settle. That, and the fact that the cops were still investigating Lancaster's death.

Rachel assured me there'd be no repercussions, not with the injuries I sustained, but it was like a shadow was hanging over me.

The investigation was just adding insult to injury, literally, and I'd be glad when I could just shove everything behind me. Lawyers weren't always right, and I really didn't want to be spending time in jail for a murder I hadn't actually committed, but for a man who'd been on the brink of harming me more than just by rape.

I wasn't sure what Lancaster's intent had been that night, but I just knew it wasn't only rape.

How I knew that, I couldn't say. And instinct wasn't something you could hand over to a lawyer and expect them to get you off the hook with. It didn't help that Nyx was uneasy about the investigation.

When I'd seen him almost cocksure about every other aspect of his life, in this, he was hesitant. Specifically around the cops, and I knew it was because he wasn't sure whose pockets they were in anymore.

Which, of course, put me at even more risk.

Yay!

"You don't want to know."

His words were so long in coming, I almost forgot what I'd asked him. Because he was pivotal in my pre-sleep schedule, I didn't kick him off the bed and send him to the couch in the living room. Instead, I asked, "Ever think that I need to know enough that it's messing with my head?"

"What I saw really would be fucking with your head, Giulia. You don't need that on top of all this other shit you've got going on."

"Shouldn't I be the one to make that decision?" I kind of liked that statement. I'd been using it a lot since the hospital, and as he'd done then, he conceded with a long-suffering sigh.

"Yeah, you're the one who should be making that decision, and normally, I'd have no problem with it. It's not like this is club business, but you have to trust me, baby girl. I'm doing this for you."

Because I was touched, I wriggled around until I was facing him. "I know you are, and that's why I'm not getting mad."

He snorted. "You're all heart."

"I know." My wry tone had him barking out a laugh. And the sound made something inside me settle, because those laughs were few and far between, but they were making more and more of an appearance, even with the aftermath of the episode at the bar.

"Please?" I whispered, pressing my forehead into his chest, and letting the few whorls of hair tickle me there.

He hesitated, long enough for me to think he wouldn't answer, then he stated, "He had videos on there."

My heart plummeted, sinking through my stomach and just plopping right onto the fucking bed. It didn't take a mind reader to know what kind of videos a sick fuck like the Lancaster prick would have on his phone.

With my mind feeling like it had been in a Vitamix, I whispered, "Want to know something weird?"

"Sure?"

"I had to use his cell to call the cops. That was why I needed his passcode, and I changed it to all the zeros. But the second that I had it in my hand, it felt like that was why I'd gone through what I had. So I could get my hands on his cellphone. Strange, huh?"

"Maybe, maybe not." He cleared his throat. "The videos were of what he'd done to other women."

"What he'd have done to me if he could?"

"Yeah." He grunted as his arm squeezed tighter about my waist. "You had more of an escape than you even know, Giulia."

"Trust me, I'm grateful." I pushed my forehead harder into his chest and whispered, "Come on, hit me with it. What aren't you telling me?"

"W-We think..."

"You think what?" I prompted, when his voice broke off.

"Fuck. We more than just think. We *know* he was holding two women somewhere. We're trying to find them."

He sounded so stoic, but I knew that staunch tone was hiding a multitude of emotions. Emotions that were probably cutting him up inside, thanks to his past.

"So, it did happen for a reason," I stated bluntly.

"That you can even think of it that way pisses me off," he grated out.

"I'd prefer for you to be pissed off and for you to know there are two women being held hostage somewhere, in a prison that... God, it's been six days since he died, Nyx. That's at least six days they've been without food." I swallowed, and any sense of peace I'd found in his arms abated as I surged upright. "They'll die soon."

"Maybe."

His wooden tone told me how bad the footage he'd seen was. It also told me that he was dying inside too.

My Nyx was a protector, and he'd not only failed to save me, but there were another two women out there who might die soon, two women who would lose their lives, even though our attacker was beyond us all.

Back bowed, I slumped over so I could press my face into my hands. What I'd gone through was nothing in comparison to what those women were enduring now, what they'd endured.

The thought of them just rotting away...

I scampered to my feet and pounded on the floor as I rushed to the bathroom. The second my head was over the bowl, I purged my stomach.

The act was violent, and my body ached with the dry heaves that came after, but it wasn't anything likened to the poison still flooding my veins.

A gentle hand collected my hair into his fist, and I felt him comb it off my sticky forehead, making sure I didn't get it in the bowl as I carried on heaving long after my belly was emptied.

When, eventually, I put down the lid and cautiously reached for the flush, I wiped my mouth with the back of my hand and whispered, "I want you to do me a favor, Nyx."

"The entire club is pooling all our resources to find them, Giulia. You don't have to worry about that." He sighed. "We don't know if we can trust the cops. The detectives sniffing around you are dirty as fuck, and I don't know what lengths they're willing to go to in order to cover up for the Lancasters—"

Before he could say another word, I interrupted, "I wasn't worrying. I already knew you would be doing everything you could to get to them before it was too late."

I blew out a breath as I shifted on the floor, my knees protesting as they rubbed harder into the tiles before I managed to get to my feet. When I washed my hands, I bent down to rinse my mouth out, then I looked at him through the mirror and whispered, "My favor has nothing to do with Lancaster..." With our eyes locked on one another, I stated, "Don't you ever call yourself evil again."

He reared back. "What?"

"You heard me," I said, aware that I sounded fervent, but that was because I was.

He wasn't evil.

I *knew* evil now.

It had touched me.

Been inside me.

And Nyx? He was twisted, sure, but he wasn't that.

I let him process my words while I reached for the mouthwash. Wanting to bathe in the stuff, I rinsed out my mouth again, then began to wash my face.

After, and feeling marginally better, I held out my hand for his and tugged him from the room, back toward the bed.

As we climbed atop the mattress once more, I muttered, "I'm ready to get back to my regular schedule in the morning."

"It's too soon—"

"I know what's too soon for me, Nyx, and I want to be normal again. I'm a little bruised, some stuff is sprained, but he didn't break me. I'm okay." I grunted. "I put my alarm on for seven-thirty."

"So, this is a courtesy conversation?"

I smiled into the pillow as he pressed his hand to my stomach and hauled me back against him. "Exactly. You know me too well."

And that wasn't a lie.

For two people who'd only been around one another for just over a month, he knew me better than even my brothers, because while there was a history we hadn't shared, two separate lives we hadn't had a chance to reveal to one another, deep inside, I got him, and he got me.

His demons were mine, and mine were his.

And that?

Fuck, that signified more of a union than a wedding ring could ever dream of.

The next day, with him glowering at me from the counter, I began to cook breakfast. It wasn't that hard, but cracking eggs was, and he had to help me out.

Because I wanted to go easy on myself, I decided to make omelets. If the guys wanted to grumble, then they could grumble, and they could swivel on the birds I'd send them as they complained.

It felt good to get back to my regular routine. Sure, I hated cooking, but it was nice to hate something normal again. Just to be bitching at ungrateful bikers and stoves that didn't get hot enough was a joy because it was bland, and sweet Lord, bland tasted mighty damn good right about now.

Yeah, my arm ached, my wrist felt like it had been twisted off entirely at the joint—which wasn't the case—and my body was one big bruise. The constant headaches I'd been dealing with had only just stopped being as strong as migraines, and my concussion was something I was going to have to be careful with for the next month or so, but... I was alive.

I was free.

I was able to make breakfast for a bunch of badass bikers who cared more for the plight of victims than the authorities did.

Nyx was, I realized, right.

The compound was home, he was home, and this was my place—bitching over bacon fat that spattered me while grunting at Nyx as he told me to take it easy and to come and sit down if I got too tired.

Did I look like I was about to turn ninety-five?

"Can I help?"

The voice intruded upon our bickering over my taking a quick break, and when I peered at the door and saw Cammie of all fucking people hovering there, I wasn't sure what stunned me more. The fact that she was the one offering to help, or the fact she was wearing clothes that actually covered her body.

In fact, scratch that, it was definitely the latter that surprised me the most.

Of all the clubwhores, ironically enough, she was the only one I hadn't gotten violent with, and now Nyx and I were unofficially together, something the clubhouse couldn't *not* know, considering he was like my goddamn shadow, I'd expected there'd be bad blood between us. So her offering to help made me wonder if she was a Trojan Horse.

Ever cautious, I mumbled, "No. It's okay."

"Thanks, Cammie. Yeah, you can take over," Nyx stated firmly, overriding my words with a glare at me. "You know your hand is aching as much as I do."

I glowered at him. "You in my body now?"

"No, but you know I will be the second your head doesn't have a jackhammer living in it."

His purr had my nostrils flaring, and I glowered harder at him. "I don't have a headache."

He chuckled. "Oh yeah? Tell that to someone who hasn't had a concussion before."

I happened to glance at the one woman I was probably jealous of most in the entire compound.

For some reason, Nyx had picked her to fuck, and she was the exact opposite of me. She was blonde and thin, had massive *perky* tits that told me they were silicone rather than natural, because natural tits did *not* bounce like that, and she was all lean and lithe, whereas I was forged on pasta. Plus, she was pretty, and she smiled and didn't appear to have a shitty attitude.

Unlike me.

At that moment, again unlike me, she was gaping at Nyx, and I knew why.

He'd chuckled.

Yeah.

It was still rare enough for me to pause when I heard it, but I was getting used to the sound, which always came out rusty, like his body had forgotten what a laugh was.

Seemed like this was Cammie's first time hearing him sound happy...

I really shouldn't have felt so smug about that.

It didn't take her long to shake off her surprise, because she stepped into the kitchen and offered, "Giulia, I'm not that great with cooking, but if you'd like to show me what to do?"

I frowned, wondering what her game was, then Nyx gently tapped me on the ass and said, "If you don't want her to burn your eggs, you'd better show her."

Grunting at his prompt, I twisted around to shoot him a nasty look, then headed over to the burner.

I pointed to the bowl of eggs. "Omelets are easy. You just whisk the eggs together and—"

Which began an impromptu cooking lesson that made me feel less like Giulia Fontaine and more like Julia Childs.

I ignored the sad looks Cammie kept on sending Nyx, because he was totally oblivious to them. With his focus on his phone, he wasn't interested in her, and when he did look up, he instantly cast his gaze over me, making sure I was all right, before he went back to whatever it was he was doing.

It was weird being cordial with her, but because he didn't make me feel insecure, it wasn't too bad.

I wondered, then, if my mom and dad would have had a better relationship if Dog had done shit like this. Reaffirming the connection he had with his woman, rather than acting like the—

My mouth opened as the thought blasted me square between the eyes. "Nyx?"

"Hmm?" he asked, his focus on his phone.

"Is my dad called 'Dog' because he's a manwhore?"

Nyx blinked at me, and I swore he blushed. "Well, I mean..."

"Fuck, that *is* why." His non-answer was all the answer I needed. My brow puckered. "Mom never had a chance, did she?"

"Probably not," he agreed, but his mouth turned down at the sides.

I stared at him, and he at me, and I felt the silent promise slither between us. It was like we made a vow to each other that we'd never be like them. That we'd do things right, do things *better*.

When I smiled at him, he smiled back, and the gesture was so unlike his usual smirk that I wasn't surprised when Cammie, about ten minutes later as guys began to traipse in for breakfast, half whispered, "He seems happier."

With his attention elsewhere, it was easier to talk, and I'd thought she'd take the chance to be a bitch, to slate me or something, and instead, she talked about Nyx.

The guy she evidently loved.

It bothered me that I felt bad for her, because I'd been raised to think nothing but bad juju about sweetbutts, but it was clear that her feelings for Nyx were one-sided, and that sucked for anyone.

Unrequited love was a bitch.

A bigger bitch than even myself.

"I think happy is too strong a word. He's unsettled. We all are."

Cammie fluttered her unnaturally large lashes at me as she stated, "You heard about the girls?"

"Yeah. I did." My jaw tensed, and I looked away from her.

She stunned the shit out of me by pressing her hand to mine on the countertop. "He'll find them, Giulia."

I didn't want her touch, didn't want her care, but I didn't pull back, instead, I just muttered, "I know he will."

And I did, because for the first time in my life, I had faith in someone.

I had faith in Nyx.

❖

TWENTY-SEVEN

NYX

WATCHING her approach the bar like someone had tossed grenades in it pissed me off, because it was so unnecessary that she be here. I didn't even know what game she was playing, why she was rushing shit, but that was Giulia. Headstrong to the end, and it wasn't like I wanted to change her. So I had to just put up and shut up.

She was weird, but I liked that.

It was what had my dick twisted into a knot, after all.

Each step she took toward the premises, though, made me grit my teeth.

It was clear to me that this was some kind of closure. Like she needed to prove to herself that she could do this, and for all that she claimed everything was well with her, and that she was A-okay, her nightmares told me otherwise.

But that was fine.

That was natural and normal.

As a kid, I'd been to enough shrinks to know that—something Bear had insisted on after he helped cover up my uncle's death—so I let her do it.

An hour later, after she'd forced herself to walk inside the bar, run an inventory that was beyond half-baked, I watched as she shot a strained smile at me and said, "I think I'm ready to go home now."

Home.

The magic word.

I hadn't gone to the booth that was my usual haunt. Instead, I'd stood by the front door, waiting on her to come to her senses.

At her words, I held out my hand, watching as she approached me, taking each step like she was walking toward her doom.

I figured it was because she wanted to run out of the bar, but her pride wouldn't let her, and because some days, I'd felt like my pride was the only thing keeping me glued together, I knew that gifting her with the notion that I believed she was okay, that I didn't see through the illusion, was the kindest thing I could do.

After we were outside, she took a deep breath, probably the deepest she'd taken in a while. When she tightened her fingers about mine, gripping them to the point of pain, I let her, and carefully guided her back to my bike.

She'd refused to drive in a cage, even though I'd made the offer, and later on, I figured she'd pay the price for being stubborn with a banging headache, but I actually had something for her, something I knew she wouldn't like, but something that I needed to scratch off my personal bucket list.

When I veered in the opposite direction away from the compound, she didn't yell in my ear, just tightened her arms around my waist as she cuddled into me.

It astonished me, just like it had the first time, how right that felt. How fucking perfect she was there, riding bitch behind me.

It made me wonder if she was the reason why I'd never let another woman behind me. If, deep inside, I'd been waiting on her. It seemed like a fanciful notion, but fuck, what else was love if it wasn't goddamn fanciful?

All it did was confirm what I was doing was right.

I steered us into Verona, the next town over, and when I parked us outside Indiana Ink, she propped her chin on my shoulder and asked, "Time for tattoo number twenty-nine, huh?"

I nodded. "No time like the present."

"You sure you want me to be here?"

I frowned at that, then twisted around to ask, "Why wouldn't I?" I couldn't see that much of her face in that position, but I felt her shrug.

"I don't know. It's like a pilgrimage for you, I think. I don't want to get in the way of it."

I snorted at her, then said, "Get your ass off the bike."

"Yes, sir," she retorted sweetly, but when I climbed off the bike, she punched me in the arm.

"I knew submission was too much to ask for from you." I grinned at her, shaking my head as I absorbed that her punch packed some weight to it, then I grabbed her hand and tugged her along.

The storefront was crafted from carved teak, and the lettering in the sign reminded me of a Wild West font. For all that it looked old world, it wasn't though.

As soon as we stepped inside, the buzz of the needles echoed along the soundwaves, and I watched as Giulia peered around, taking in the bright yellow walls that were covered in Indiana's tattoos.

She was Algonquin, and her style reflected her heritage. She'd made a name for herself with animal tattoos and tribal work, but she was great at mandalas too—three of which, huge back pieces, were blown up and took up half the walls of the reception area.

As Giulia gaped at them, I led us to the half desk where her assistant, David, sat behind a computer.

When he saw me, his polite smile strained some, because my rep preceded me most places, but as Indiana had done the last fourteen of my tattoos, I was more than just a regular to him now, so his agitation only pissed me off.

"She'll be with you in ten minutes," David squeaked when he caught sight of my scowl.

I nodded and steered Giulia toward one of the low brown leather sofas that lined the back wall.

"He's scared of you," she murmured, sounding amused.

"Everyone is."

"Apart from me."

I heard the pride in her voice at that, and had to hide my smile. "Apart from you," I confirmed, almost laughing when she squeezed my hand.

"How many tats do you get a year?"

I shrugged. "Depends on what happens."

"On how many you find who do bad things?" she queried, keeping her words clean for anyone who might be listening in. Not that anyone was in here other than David, but she knew to watch her mouth. "Yeah."

"How many did you get these past twelve months?"

"Two."

She whistled. "Two too many."

I eyed her, sober to the last. "Exactly."

When she settled back into the couch, relaxing some, I was surprised when she rested her head against my arm. She wasn't very affectionate, at least not outside of bed, but I knew why she was being a little more touchy than usual—going to the bar had drained her.

I wanted to growl at her over that, over pushing herself too hard, too fast, but what could I say? In her shoes, I'd have been chomping at the bit to get back to normalcy too.

I didn't bother talking with her, didn't even bother grabbing my cell. I just sat there with her, in silence, letting the buzzing of the needles calm me.

This was my version of meditation. As fucked up as it was. But, over the last few days, I'd had a lot to think about so this helped me process my thoughts.

Somewhere in the area, that Lancaster piece of shit had hidden away two innocent women who were going to die if we didn't find them soon.

We couldn't approach the cops, because they'd not only ask *why* Giulia had stolen Lancaster's phone, but they could even execute the threat to the Lancasters by finding the women and disposing of them before they had a chance to speak out.

Not only that, but my woman had been attacked, and was still under investigation because some billionaire held power in the area.

And, more than that, I'd been coming to terms with changes I wanted to make in my life.

The desire to provide Giulia with more security had led me to make this decision, but in the end, I only made it because I needed her.

Big, bad Nyx, the Enforcer that was feared from Oklahoma to NYC, needed his woman. Not just in bed, but in his fucking heart.

Maybe another brother would have been nervous at this point. But I wasn't. I was resolute. She could argue, she could run kicking and screaming from the ink parlor, but she wasn't leaving this place without my brand on her. Even if I had to spank her to get her to agree, I'd do it, because she was mine, and it was about time she knew it.

Eight minutes after David had told us ten, Indiana appeared in the doorway to her station. She was leading a woman over to the front desk, and from the looks of her chest and the bandages there, as well as the way her shirt sat against her body, I had to figure Indiana had been giving her a tattoo on her mastectomy scars.

That was something else she was getting a name for, as well as the fact that she did it free of charge.

Glad I'd arrived early to see that, because I'd cover whatever it cost—no way was I going to let Indiana foot the bill on her own—I stayed quiet until the woman left. To no avail. As she moved toward the door, she froze at the sight of me before she scuttled away, like a frightened mouse.

"Good thing she saw you after the tattoo," Indiana told me dryly.

"Consider me crowd control."

"That's one way of looking at it." Her gaze cut to Giulia who was, I realized, dozing at my side.

Though I was startled by that, even though it made sense when I thought about how she'd pushed herself today, Indiana wasn't, and her gaze softened as she looked at her. "She's been through the wars."

"Yeah, she has, but don't tell her that. She considers it only a battle."

Indiana blinked. "There's a difference?"

"Of course. Lots of battles in a war."

Indiana chuckled at her, then said, "Sorry if we woke you."

"I was just resting my eyes."

"You were close to snoring. Admit it," I teased.

Giulia sniffed. "I admit to nothing, and admit to everything, which leaves you in ignorance."

Because she was a contrary pain in the ass, I grinned. "Time to get inked."

She snuggled her butt into the sofa, and murmured, "I'll be fine here."

"No, you won't," I informed her gruffly. "You're getting inked too."

At that, her eyes flared wide open. "Huh? I'm not getting a tattoo! I don't want one."

My lips curved. "You'll want this one."

She tensed, then glared at me. "Are you being serious right now?"

"Is Nyx capable of being anything other than serious?" Indiana queried wryly.

Giulia glowered at her. "Are you close or something?"

She laughed. "Um, yeah? He's my brother."

If her eyes had been wide before, they were as round as an orange at Indiana's statement.

"Huh?"

"She's my sister," I told her, feeling kinda nervous now the truth was coming out.

This was just one of many facts about me that she didn't know, but I wanted her to.

Fuck, I wanted her to know everything.

The good, the bad, the goddamn ugly.

"But I thought she was..."

"She is. That was Carly." I reached up and touched the songbird on my neck. "Indiana is my baby sister."

She licked her lips, then shot Indiana a look. "I don't understand."

"Nothing to understand. Our mother had sex at least four times in her life," Indiana announced seriously. "I'd like to think it was less than that, but..." As her words waned, she shot me a look. "She doesn't look ready to be branded."

Giulia gulped, and her hand went to my knee. She squeezed it, not enough to cause me discomfort, but more like she was clutching at something to ground her.

I liked that she used me and not the sofa to do that.

"Nyx, this isn't something you can take back," she whispered, her tone wary.

"I know it isn't."

"I won't be like my mom," she warned. "You'll be stuck with me for life. I'll fucking haunt you, and if you cheat on me, I'll chop off your dick and make the Sinners eat it for breakfast."

"Bloodthirsty, *nice*," Indiana observed with a whistle.

I glowered at her, saw she'd leaned against the wall to take in the show, and just rolled my eyes at her when she beamed at me.

"There's a lot of meat there," Giulia said seriously. "It's gonna make a great omelet—"

"Ew, I didn't need to know my brother has a big dick," Indiana squealed, then made a dash for her booth, a dash that, with a squeak of his own, David quickly mimicked.

She smirked at me. "Women are so squeamish."

I snorted. "You did that for some privacy?"

"You bet your ass I did."

"You didn't like your brothers knowing you scream when you come," I pointed out.

"That's completely different."

It totally wasn't, but I wasn't in the mood to argue with her.

Not over that anyway. For our future? Sure, I'd argue to hell and back with her. If I had to.

I reached for her hand and told her, "Giulia, I want this."

"You want this now."

I shook my head. "What about me is transient, Giulia? Everything about me is permanent. Including you."

"Nothing's permanent in an MC," she muttered sadly, and I saw, deep in her eyes, that she *was* sad. I knew then that I had her. Her past was making her doubt something she knew she didn't have to. We were linked, her and I. Bound.

"I'm not an ordinary man, Giulia, and it fits that the woman for me isn't ordinary either.

"You can take the monster in me, can handle it and deal with who I truly am. That takes guts, and if you think I'm stupid enough to tangle with a woman who I know is perfectly capable of severing a man's testicle with a shoe, then you're the crazy one. Not me."

When she snickered, it was like the sun rising after a long winter night. Her fingers tightened around mine again.

"Isn't it too soon?"

"Life's short. We have to take each day we're given, live them to the fullest. I want to do that, with you riding bitch at my back."

A quiver whispered down her spine at that, and when she reached over, cupped my chin, and told me, "There will come a day when you ride bitch, Nyx, you do know this, don't you?"

Her words only gave me further confirmation she was the woman for me.

Even if there wasn't a cat in hell's chance that I was ever, in a million fucking years, letting her control my hog.

Now that *was* crazy fucking talk.

TWENTY-EIGHT

REX

THE SECOND NYX walked into the clubhouse with Giulia's name tattooed on his throat, there wasn't much more of a declaration required.

I had no doubt that her brand would be somewhere only he could see, because he was a possessive bastard, and the way his arm was around her shoulders reminded me of shit Jocks pulled with their girlfriends as they walked down the hall in school.

My lips curved because Nyx had worn no letters at school, none other than F.U.C.K O.F.F, and I couldn't see Giulia wearing a Letterman jacket.

Not in this eternity, at any rate.

For all that I could have rolled my eyes at my brother's antics, I had to admit I was happy. Happy for him, happy for her, happy for the club. It was about time shit changed around here.

The council were all in their mid-thirties, with only Storm having an Old Lady, until he'd fucked shit up with Keira a couple of months back.

The place didn't have any of the vibe it'd had when I was a kid, and was more porn movie studio than what the Satan's Sinners should be—a community. We were family, and, one of the perks was to have pussy on hand, but fuck, in my dad's day, the two hadn't been mutually exclusive.

But to get that, we'd need an Old Lady with brass balls.

Somehow, I thought we had that in Giulia.

She wouldn't have a problem in telling the clubwhores what to do, and I'd let her reign over the women until I picked a woman for myself.

Well, that was a lie.

I'd already picked the woman, but convincing her was going to be a long project. I had time, so did Rachel, and because of this messed up situation with Lancaster, we'd be working together more than ever.

Rachel was normally disapproving of our methods, but she knew about that cunt's phone, knew what we'd found on there, and knew—more so than any of us—how the police investigation was skewed in the Lancasters' favor. To the point where if those detectives on the family's payroll started saying Giulia had raped Lancaster, I wouldn't be fucking surprised.

Link cheered at the sight of Giulia and Nyx together, which triggered a wave of cheers because, to be frank, no one knew how to respond to most of the shit Nyx did. It didn't surprise me that Link was the one who'd guided him in the right direction. I knew it would either have been him or Steel.

Digging my elbows into my knees as I sank back into the sofa that everyone knew not to fuck on because it was mine, I tipped my chin so I couldn't see them. They'd wander over here eventually, after Nyx had shown off his tat, and for the moment, I needed to think.

I'd already sent off JoJo and Tink, and I knew Jingles would be on her way to see if I was okay.

The clubwhores weren't all bitches. Not like Giulia evidently believed, but we had a lot, and they did need corralling. I had neither the time nor the desire to do that, but I figured my 'honeymoon' present to Giulia would be the gift of kicking them into line. And fuck, she'd need something to occupy her while this investigation was underway.

A part of me didn't doubt she'd be exonerated. But another part was on edge.

The Lancasters were new around here, but they were rich enough to have some clout with the mayor, which told me they'd funded his re-election campaign.

That clout meant the sheriff, who was in our pocket, wasn't leading the investigation, and the detectives on the case had a slant for everything that had gone down. They were gearing up to accuse Giulia of all kinds of charges—I had a feeling in my fucking bones they were going to say she hit *him* up, and then attacked him with the intent to steal his gear.

It didn't help that his iPhone hadn't been found—wouldn't be, not when it was hooked up to our computers as Mav used it in our hunt for more of Lancaster's victims—but what was on her side was that his wallet had been untouched and he'd had just over six hundred dollars in there. *Dipshit.*

What the police were tossing around was the level of bruising and injuries on Lancaster's corpse, and as for the hit itself, I could understand their skepticism because Giulia, whether she'd handled a knife before or not, would never have attacked like that.

Not when she was a short ass.

Which meant she was telling lies about how Lancaster's death had gone down.

Which put holes in her story.

I wasn't sure who she was protecting, or why, but the sneaky cameras we'd had installed in the bar itself were no fucking use.

I'd had Mav scan them, and he'd pulled up nothing but blank tape for the minutes of the attack. Any brother had access to the camera equipment, anyone could have switched them off, but the question was why?

Why switch off equipment that the police didn't know existed?

It showed a level of premeditation that I didn't understand.

There was no hiding from the fact that Giulia had been raped. The state of her? The bruising? The sexual assault? It was all real. And her fear of the bar was such that I knew we'd lost our bar manager for a good long while. So, that was *real*.

But the lie had to be who'd helped her.

Why hadn't they told me?

"Prez?"

Nyx sounded a little nervous, a lot exhilarated. Enough that I had no choice but to stare him in the eye and grin at him.

I bounced onto my feet and hauled him into a hug that showed how tight we were as friends. More than just brothers in an MC, brothers IRL.

I slapped him harder on the back. "Glad you fucking listened for once."

His laugh in my ear was something I'd never forget, because I'd heard it so rarely in my life.

Nyx?

Happy?

My mom would be probably doing the tango in her grave.

"I always listen when you make smart suggestions."

Giulia eyed us both, then, unsurprisingly—because the attack had shaken her but not zipped up her mouth—demanded, "What did you suggest, Rex?"

"That I don't fuck this up." Nyx hauled her into his side once more. When his hand went to a high part on her waist and she flinched? I knew that was where her brand was. Just underneath her tit.

Nyx was predictable as fuck sometimes.

I smiled, genuine in my happiness for my brother, as he pressed his mouth to hers, and I took a seat, knowing they'd be sitting with me for a while.

When they huddled together on the sofa opposite, their hands clinging, their bodies touching, the yearning between them real, I knew I wanted what they had. Knew I was ready to feel something more than just the drudgery of life.

And even if she didn't realize it, regardless of the lies she was telling, I'd keep Giulia and the brother she was protecting safe—it had to be one of the twins, didn't it?—just to preserve *this*.

A smiling Nyx.

A lighter Nyx.

A *happy* Nyx.

So long as he looked as though his demons were at rest, she'd have my back.

No matter the consequences.

TWENTY-NINE

NYX

WHEN I FELT her slick heat against my cock, I let my eyes drift open lazily. Her movements were unhurried, relaxed, and that was how I felt.

Sure, there was an urgency stirring inside me, sure, I wanted to come, but more than that, I liked that this was the first time she'd taken the initiative.

Adored that she wanted me enough just to lazily ride me like this.

Loved, even more, that she was getting over what that bastard had done to her, and was starting to own her body once more.

"Morning, baby," she rasped, her voice still husky from sleep.

"Morning, sweetheart," I greeted her back, letting my hands come up to cup her waist, not to steer or to stop her, just to hold on to her.

With each rock of her hips, she was coating my cock in her cream, and each time, her clit came into contact with the piercings on the tip.

And every time she bit her lip harder, I knew the feeling was electric, and I knew, just as much, that the laziness would disappear and be replaced with the fire that always consumed us.

The inferno that would devour us until our last breath left our lungs, and we were nothing more than the ash our passion had forged.

I sighed with relief when she grabbed my dick after a good few minutes of this delicious torment, and sighed again when she pressed the tip to her entrance.

This part was always agonizing, and it was particularly excruciating with her, because she was so fucking tight.

In all the time we'd been together, she'd never ridden me, never managed it, and I wasn't sure she'd be able to today either.

Her tits shook as she tried to get me inside her, and I reached up, cupping the underside of one that showed her brand.

She had "Property of Nyx" tattooed in cursive under there, but it was the devil's head that I truly appreciated. It was a match to the one I had on my back, only instead of the blood and the gore that I had on mine, hers was decorated in Indiana's signature mandalas.

It was quirky rather than gruesome, but that was more of a brand than anything else.

My touch inspired her to rub my own mark. Brothers didn't usually get branded, but I was one and done, and I wanted her to know that.

I had a past, and it was dirty and grimy. I'd fucked more women than most men could dream of, but I wasn't about to let what we had be tinged by the bitterness that could be stirred from my history.

So I wore her mark with pride.

Carly's songbird on my throat had a partner now, a mirror image that reflected Giulia's importance in my life.

"I can't get it in," she grumbled after another minute.

"I know," I told her dryly, wondering how sex could be funny with this woman. It had always been a need, an urge, but now? It had taken on a life of its own.

"Aren't you going to do something about it?" she demanded with a huff, her glassy eyes and pink cheeks telling me she was more than ready for me to take things further.

"I thought you'd never ask," I growled, and grabbing her, I twisted us around so that she was on her back and I was above her.

Her squeal was badly timed. It meant I missed the sharp knock on the door, but after her giggle died down, I heard the pounding fist and, cursing, I pressed my forehead to hers and shouted out, "Who the fuck is it?"

"It's me. Rex."

Growling under my breath, I grated out, "I'm sorry, babe."

Though she was pouting, she knew the score as only a brat reared in the club ever could.

I grabbed the PJ shirt she'd tossed onto the floor this morning before she'd attacked me and used it to cover my junk. I opened the door a sliver so Rex could only see my glowering face as I answered his call.

"What is it?" I groused. "Church isn't for another few hours."

His face was tense, his eyes loaded with strain as he told me, "We've found Lancaster's hostages."

THE NEXT BOOK IN THE SERIES IS NOW AVAILABLE ON KU!
Carry on to read the first two chapters!
www.books2read.com/Link

LINK

A YEAR EARLIER...

LILY LANCASTER

Blood.

Lots of it.

Whether it was mine or yours, it should have been inside us.

Soaring through our veins and arteries. Keeping us alive.

It shouldn't be seeping from us.

Draining out of us.

Stolen from us.

I blew out a breath as the ache in my body made itself known, and using a few sheets of toilet paper, I rolled it in on itself, creating a tiny barricade I hoped would hold. Shoving it between my ass cheeks was enough to bring on a panic attack, because I hated my ass. Hated. It.

Not for any normal reason, like because it had cellulite. Not because it was just a smidgen too much of a bubble butt. Not because it was bony or flat. I didn't give a crap about how it looked. I hated it because *he* used it.

Shuddering as I stood, the paper lodged there, collecting blood he'd spilled, I dragged my panties up high and lowered my skirt.

When I approached the vanity, I looked at myself and was, as always, surprised to note I looked normal. So fucking normal. Not like I'd just been used—*abused*. Not like the walking wreckage I was.

My body was one big ball of pain as I washed my hands and launched myself into an upright position. Smile firmly fixed in place, I headed on out, then winced when I saw Tiffany, my best friend, had let herself in. She was flat on her stomach on the bed, phone in her hand, her legs swaying from side to side.

"Did you see what Lourdes just posted on Instagram? I mean, my God, did she get dressed in the dark?"

My lips twitched. "Maybe she did."

Tiffany scowled at me, her eyes squinting as she processed my remark and judged whether I was joking or not. Then, because she couldn't tell—I had a damn good poker face—she grumbled, "Who gets dressed in the dark?"

I shrugged. "It would explain the past few choices she's made."

"Fashion disasters you mean." She huffed, rolled off her stomach, and straightened up into a standing position. Her eyes drifted over me. "You look like you're in pain." Her brow puckered. "Got another headache?"

That was the excuse I used when I was feeling this way. "Yeah. I'll be okay though." My smile didn't display just how fragile I felt. I'd had a lot of practice in making certain I looked normal.

That was like my family's secondary talent. Looking normal when, underneath it all, we were the exact opposite. The primary talent, of course, was making money.

Lots, and lots, and lots of money.

I'd exchange it all for the ability to lead a regular goddamn life.

"You sure?"

"Positive."

She hummed under her breath as she gave me another scan, then she shrugged. Not because she didn't care—she did. Sometimes I was positive she was the only person who gave a damn about me period—but because she knew me well. We'd gone to St. Lawrence Academy in Manhattan together and had been through thick and thin as friends.

She knew I wouldn't let anything stop me. She just didn't know why I was that way. It wasn't because I was forthright and indomitable. If only it were. But no, it was because the punishment never fit the crime, and I'd learned to adjust my behavior accordingly.

"What's this party about anyway?" she asked, her attention still on our friend Lourdes' post.

"Didn't your dad tell you?" I questioned, amused despite myself.

I headed over to my dressing table and picked up my favorite scent. As I dabbed it behind my ears and along my décolleté, I stared out at the yard where, beneath a blanket of string lights, amid thousands of perfumed flowers and the stirring music from a string quartet, a hundred people were moseying together, appreciating my father's largesse. One thing could be said about my bastard father—he knew how to throw a party.

"Oh, he did, but I didn't listen." She beamed at me, her green eyes twinkling as she straightened up her tie and sorted out a few flyaway strands of hair. Unlike me, who always wore a dress for these events, she wore pantsuits with ties. Sure, she looked like a sexy newscaster, but hell, she rocked it. "You know I make it my job to ignore my dad on the regular."

I rolled my eyes. "Lies. You're a daddy's girl. Face it."

She stuck out her tongue. "I'm not. He's making us move."

"You're twenty-two, babe. If you want to stay in the city, you can." There was no envy in my tone, even if inside, I was a wriggling, writhing ball of jealousy over her freedom.

"Nah. Not if you're moving there too." Unlike Tiff, I didn't have the freedom of choice. "Might as well see what New Jersey has in store for us." She made a puking sound. "Never thought we'd leave the city."

"Well, that's what happens when people as rich as our parents get tax breaks for moving states," I said dryly. With another glance out the window, I looked around the crowd, trying to ensure I had the name-to-faces down pat. Then, I frowned when I saw someone I didn't recognize. "Who's he?"

She hummed as she bent forward, peering into the ornate mirror and smoothing her finger around her lips in an effort to keep the line of her lipstick crisp. "Who's who?"

"The guy with the guards." As I stared at the man I didn't recognize, a shiver rushed down my spine. He was in his forties, surrounded by men in black suits that were, quite clearly, packing heat. They had more bulges in odd places than a drug trafficker. "That one," I stated, pointing to him when she peered out the window too.

She shuddered. "Gianni Fieri. Isn't he creepy?"

Creepy wasn't the word. He was, truthfully, quite handsome. In a young Al Pacino kind of way. But he was dark on dark. Black hair, black eyes, black shirt, black tie, black suit and shoes. He was like a walking shadow, for Pete's sake. And the way he stood there like he ruled the roost? It put me on edge.

No one did that in my father's presence.

Not without living to tell the tale, and yet he was permitting it. As I watched, my father even wandered over to him, laughing at something before evidently getting down to business as they both sobered up. Well, Father did, Fieri's lips hadn't so much as twitched at the bad joke he'd just heard.

"Whoa, he isn't ass-licking your dad," Tiffany whispered, sounding just as shocked as I felt, and for a reason.

Everyone licked my father's ass.

Everyone.

That's what ninety billion in the bank did to you. Got you rimmed on the regular.

"No." An uneasy feeling settled in my stomach. "That's weird."

"Weird? It's unheard of." She hummed again. "Wonder why he's here."

"He must have invested in your dad's property development."

She frowned. "I guess. Shit. I wish I'd listened in on all those boring conversations over dinner now."

Even though I was so envious of her that I couldn't contain it sometimes, not just because she had loving parents and a familial relationship that looked like it belonged in a rich man's version of *The Walton's*, I had to smile at her. "You should listen anyway. You know your father wants you to go into the business."

"All the more reason to ignore him." She pulled a face. "What use would I be in property development? I'm a therapist."

"You'd be fantastic at anything you put your mind to." Tiff, though I loved her, was one of those annoying people who got A grades all the time without even studying.

"Prefer to be married to the property developer. Would save me wrinkles in the long run," she joked, elbowing me in the side. Though she hadn't meant to, she connected with one of my bruises and I winced. "Sorry, love. God, your head really is killing you, isn't it?"

I gave her a faint smile even as I rubbed my side, pretending that was what hurt. "Yeah. It's all good."

I looked down at my father then jerked when I saw I had Fieri's attention. He was glowering at me to an extent that I jolted back in surprise, which set off a tsunami of aches in my battered body. His glower deepened, then he grabbed my father's arm, whose attention flashed up to me.

The second I felt his focus, I drifted back and away from the window. The last thing I wanted was to be in his crosshairs.

"Luke's making a fool out of himself," Tiffany pointed out, her attention having drifted. Something I was glad for.

"When doesn't he?" I muttered.

"True. Not sure why your dad puts up with him." She trembled again—which put Fieri and Luke in the same league in her mind. Jesus Christ. What that said about Fieri, I didn't know. As for Luke? He was a psychopath. Pure and simple.

"He's the golden boy," I mumbled, staring at myself in the mirror one last time to make sure I looked perfect before I stuck on a smile. "Ready?"

She whistled as she turned to give me a quick scan. "You look hot. In pain, but hot." Then she squinted. "You sure you're okay to do this? Nothing worse than feeling shitty when you have to talk to these morons for an entire evening."

Tiff was right. I wasn't in the mood for it, but my choices, my wishes, weren't important. Never had been.

Never would be.

So I gritted my teeth and got on with it.

I'd have my day.

"I'm fine. Promise." I tucked my arm through hers. "Let's get this over with."

She snorted. "Preach, sister. Preach."

ONE

LILY

I winced the second the beauty blender collided with my cheekbone. The wince morphed into an extended hiss as I let the pain flush through my system, only to be bombarded by it yet again as I carried on patting on the foundation.

The bruise was shockingly bright against my creamy skin, but I was pretty good at hiding the aftermath of a run-in with my father's fist now and could hide it with the clever application of makeup. What I couldn't hide? How his ring had torn into the skin, leaving behind the faintest cut, which stung every time I touched it.

There was no hiding that.

A fact, I was sure, that would irritate him to no end. But then, I irritated him period. Always had, always would.

And I would never *not* be proud of that.

Ever since I'd learned the truth, I lived to irritate my scum-sucking father.

I burned for it.

I took his wrath and let him reap it on me, because I loathed him and he loathed me, but I was blood, and now I was his only heir. It was just time that would make that official, and I couldn't wait for that day.

Wincing yet again as I dabbed on the makeup, my attention was caught by my screen lighting up in the corner of my eye. I'd set notifications on Google for anything related to my brother's case, and the fact that the cops were in my father's pockets and were trying to spin it so the woman my brother had tried to rape was somehow the attacker hadn't escaped my attention.

I just didn't know how to go about rectifying things.

Which was why I was hiding a bruise caused by my father's fist. I'd tried, and failed, to put things in some semblance of order, and he wasn't having it. But then, he'd always thought that prick walked on water. Just because Luke was a boy, he'd received an automatic free pass to do whatever he wanted.

And when you had money like we did, *whatever* took on a different connotation.

Luke was sick. Rabid. I was glad he was dead, because it saved me from having to do it at some point in my life. The past twenty-two years had been spent working up the courage to kill my father and my brother, and I was ashamed I'd achieved neither.

In another world, in another life, I'd be a good daughter and a good sister, but this wasn't another world, and this was my life. My family was evil. My father was one of the malicious, fat white men who ran the world from his ivory tower, and my brother had been born in his image. They were both bastards, and even in death, Luke was being one.

Quickly scanning the news alert, I saw the victim, Giulia Fontaine, had been brought in for questioning. Again.

My mouth tightened, even as I focused on covering up the bruise. It took me an extra forty minutes to achieve what I could usually do in ten, but when I took a step back from the vanity, I was impressed despite myself.

I looked as I always did.

Pristine except for that tiny cut, which I could reason away with ease. I thought an accident while playing tennis would easily explain it. I tripped and fell against the grass, and there was a tiny shard of glass there. At that point of the conversation, if someone asked, I'd laugh and tell them I'd fired a gardener over their inattention to detail, and everyone would laugh with me.

Because that was the world I lived in.

In that world, it was okay for fathers to beat daughters and for daughters to come up with random excuses that everyone accepted even though they *knew* what said father was like.

Donavan Lancaster was the biggest cunt around.

Everyone knew it.

But he had ninety billion in the bank and, therefore, he got away with murder.

Literally.

That was why my mom was in the family mausoleum back in Manhattan, because he'd murdered her when she'd done the impossible and had asked for a divorce.

I gnawed on my bottom lip as I stared at the bouncy blonde waves that danced around my shoulders, took in the blue eyes I'd enhanced with a dark slash of navy eyeliner in the corners, and the cheekbones I'd sharpened with bronzer that led to ruby red lips which gleamed in the light above the vanity.

Taking a step back, I looked at the neat dress that clung to all my slim curves, accepted that the black did things for my skin tone and hair that made me look even more attractive, and sucked in a breath.

I knew I looked like a china doll, and it was an image I played up to. I'd continue to do so until I found my way in and, through that, found my way out.

Today was a step toward that path.

An exit that involved my father's death and not my own because, and this was the God's honest truth, the only way out of this family was through death, and I didn't intend to die. Not for a good long while.

The bathroom around me was a study of marble. The light beige counter was dotted with open makeup bottles, and the floor beneath my Louboutin heels—that added a good four inches to my height and did wonders for my ass—was a darker gray. The walls were covered in a creamy white stone that had gold striations throughout which, oddly enough, made my hair appear gold rather than blonde. As I contemplated the contrast, I realized I looked like my mother.

The thought had me twisting my lips as I turned away from my too pretty features and stepped over the mass of towels I'd left on the floor. I was messy, and I'd admit to it, but that was one thing allowed of me in this household. I had staff who'd clean up after me, and I took advantage of that.

When I returned later on tonight, this place would look like it was a showroom once more. Now? Well, it just looked as if a Tasmanian Devil had whirled around the place, knocking stuff over, and leaving chaos in its wake.

I ignored the rest of my suite and headed over to the patio doors at the front of my room. I had access to the grounds from here, thanks to a set of steps. It was how I was supposed to reach the pool, but I used it to sneak out.

Not that my father cared what I did on a daily basis so long as I followed his rules, returned here every night and slept in my bed, and didn't give my security detail too much of a run around, but I didn't want to come across him even accidentally before I got out of here.

The magnificent vista slipped by me. I didn't even see it as I headed down the steps. My heels sank into the thick grass, but I strode on toward the garage. It was a little awkward to approach this way, but it was worth it. I had to step around the pool house where my brother had lived—a pool house that was like a mini mansion because Donavan Lancaster's son deserved only the best—and slip between the two tennis courts.

The ten-minute walk in four-inch heels was one I knew well. Though we were relatively new to the area, I'd left the house this way every day of the three months we'd been here.

If there was a chance I'd run into my father, I'd find a way around it. Meeting him usually ended up with me slathering on foundation to cover a bruise on my face, and while I was adept at it, I wasn't a masochist.

Staying out of his way was the key to surviving this hellhole.

When I reached the garage, my heels tapped against the concrete floor. Spotting Luke's Lamborghini, I sneered as I let my fingers drift over the sleek lines.

I was tempted, oh so fucking tempted, to take that car out, but if the news hit my father's ears, I'd have matching shiners. So, instead, I went for another sports car. One my father didn't mind me driving—a Porsche Carrera. It was a few years old, and that was why I was allowed to drive it.

My father believed women drivers were a plague, so we weren't to be trusted with the best in his stable.

Chauvinistic asswipe.

I leaped behind the wheel and reversed out, driving past twenty million dollars' worth of cars on my exit, and only when I was through the gates did I release a sigh of relief.

Getting out of there always felt like I was escaping a looming storm cloud. It was a weight off my chest that made me feel like I could breathe properly for the first time since I'd made it back here the night before.

When my security detail pulled up behind me, I ignored them. They were always watching, always following, so I just pretended they weren't there. Tonight, however, I'd need to find a way to make sure they weren't as on the ball as usual.

That would mean endangering their jobs but, truthfully, they were dicks anyway. I didn't care if their careers were in the can after the moves I was going to pull tonight. My brother had security too, and they *knew* what he was up to.

Knew it because they followed him just like they followed me.

Bastards.

Of course, they were probably dead bastards by now. My father had undoubtedly paid someone to wipe them off the face of the Earth, lest they ever think to blackmail him for the shit Luke had pulled.

My hands tightened around the wheel as the ever-present rage washed through me, flooding me with more emotion than I knew what to do with. I'd been locked up tight since my mother's murder, and subsequently Luke's death—and the shit I'd inadvertently discovered about him—was creating holes in my control. Emotions were spluttering toward me, and I couldn't deal with them. I only knew I had to do something, *anything*, to help.

Making it into town was easy. We lived just on the Caldwell-West Orange border, but the ride was always smooth, and I enjoyed the wind in my hair and the loud music I let blare through the speakers. It was still ringing in my head as I cut the engine when I was parked and, humming to the beat, I climbed out after I grabbed my purse. Once I was standing, I stared at the bar up ahead.

My father had been very vocal in his fight to stop a local motorcycle club from gaining the required licenses to open this particular mall but, for once, he'd lost. I was curious how that had happened, because it meant the MC had more tokens with local councilors than my dad did, and *that* was impressive.

If I had a hat on my head, I'd take it off to them because, yikes, beating Donavan was nigh impossible.

Dear old Dad had been particularly pissed the day he'd heard of the licenses going through, and he'd been doubly pissed when, barely six weeks later, the club had managed to get some of the businesses up and running. That, right there, told me they had money to burn. Nobody got several businesses functioning that quickly, not unless they were willing to hemorrhage cash.

There was a diner, a strip joint, a garage, and a bar. It was the latter, Daytona, that was my intended destination. The place didn't look trashy. Sure, it wasn't swank, not like the bars at the country clubs I usually haunted, but I wasn't here to get drunk. Wasn't here to have fun. There was a method to my madness, a method I was praying someone within the confines of those walls could help me with.

Sucking in a sharp breath, I took off, crossing the road with such purpose that I almost missed the car that was pulling around the corner. The sharp honk of the horn had me jerking to a halt, and I was on the receiving end of a glower and a fist shake as the driver, a woman in her seventies, passed me by.

Heart in my throat at my stupidity for not checking for traffic, I tried to ask myself what the fuck was going to happen if I died before the shit I knew could be passed on to people who'd help.

There'd be blood on my hands, that's what.

Blood that would haunt me even into death.

Breathing deeply, I carried on after looking right, then left, and made it, *safely*, to the other side of the road. Not messing around, I moved into the bar and, once I'd checked it out and had spied a kind of area that was cordoned off with bike parts—what the hell was that about?—I couldn't fail to notice all the men in leather cuts, jeans, boots, and Henleys. It was like a uniform or something. Only a few had on wifebeaters that were surprisingly white.

As I wondered if they did their own laundry, or if it was totally like *Sons of Anarchy* and they had women who did it for them, I headed to the bar and placed an order. "Can I have a vodka, please? Neat."

Though my request got me a funny look, the server just shrugged when I shook my head at his, "Not on the rocks?" and within a few minutes, I'd chugged down the clear liquid and felt it going to my head in a manner I seriously needed.

While I burned from the alcohol, my mouth tingling from it in a way that loosened my tongue, I caught the bartender's eye again and leaned forward to say, "I need your help."

Frowning, the guy leaned into me and asked, "What's wrong?"

I shot him a tight smile. "Two men are going to come into the bar soon. They'll order lagers. I'll pay you a hundred dollars to pour two shots of vodka into each of their drinks."

"You know that's illegal?"

My mouth tightened further. "They're my security detail. I need to divert their attention."

"I'm not going to lose my job just to help some rich bitch lose her guards—"

"You work for the MC here, right?" I jutted my thumb toward the seating area behind me. "I have information for them. Information I think will help them. I can't give it to them if my guards are watching." Of course, that was half a lie. The MC might not give a damn about some innocent women's plight, but I was hoping they'd help just to get dirt on my brother. Boy, dirt didn't even begin to cover it.

Almost to punctuate my comment, the doors swung open, and I

didn't have to turn around to feel the stares of the two guards who followed me around. They weren't supposed to drink at all, but Paul and Alix knew I was, relatively speaking, a good girl. I never got into trouble, never stirred shit, so they could relax. When I went to the country club, they took it in turn to be DD, while one always got hammered on my daddy's dime.

The bartender's eyes cut to my security detail, and then his gaze flashed over to the guys in the MC, who were seated in that odd concoction of bike parts.

The place was half Western saloon and half parts shop. I didn't particularly like it with its coarse wooden tables and sleek banquettes, but I didn't have to like it, did I?

This wasn't about to become my local haunt.

"Make it two hundred, and I'll dose them up," the server whispered, as he poured me another shot of vodka.

I'd have paid a grand to get Paul and Alix off my back. "Okay. Make it three shots then. I'll double the money if, every time they order, you do the same."

He hitched a shoulder in what I took to be agreement, then moved forward when he saw me slide some money under my empty glass.

Eyes connected, we both nodded as I retreated, heading over to a corner booth. I watched as Paul took up a table at the opposite side of the room, his gaze on the door, while Alix put in an order. The bartender must have told him he'd bring their drinks over, because he soon joined Paul. I found a spot in the mirror behind all the liquor on the back wall of the bar where I could watch them without seeming like I was.

I gnawed on my bottom lip as the server poured their beer. I couldn't see anything from over here, not in the dim lights anyway, and I hoped three shots would be enough to impair them. They were big men but, as far as I knew, they only drank lager. Would three shots make them tipsy? I had to hope it would. Even better, I had to hope it would give them a thirst for more.

Once the drinks were served and Paul and Alix had sipped at them, I stopped studying them in a mirror. Though they'd pulled a face at the first sip, it hadn't stopped them from downing the rest of their beer and, thank God, putting in another order. Tonight's designated driver had evidently decided it was time to get hammered.

The bartender smirked at me as he filled some beer mugs for them, and I darted my gaze away from the bar just in case they thought my interest in their order was suspicious. As I watched a couple shuffling around a space that was for dancing, I learned two-stepping to Guns and Roses wasn't impossible.

My mouth quirked up in a smile, though, as I took in the couple's tight embrace. They looked happy, relaxed in one another's company, and I'd admit to feeling jealous. I'd never felt like that around another person. Not even my mom, and I'd loved her more than anyone else on this planet. But trust wasn't something you could have in my family. We were all backstabbers, myself included.

I gnawed on my lip as sentimental nostalgia, undoubtedly aided by my second shot of vodka, made me teary-eyed. I shouldn't have to do what I was doing tonight, and yet, here I was, trying to get my guards drunk and all so I could speak to men who were the type of guys I actually needed protection from.

The MC brothers were loud, raucous, and rude. That much I'd seen in my forty minutes at Daytona. They drank too much, laughed too hard, and swore like sailors on coke. I didn't like them, but they were my only hope.

There were around ten of them in the booth, and every now and then I'd let my gaze drift around the red, laughing faces, trying to figure out who was the best to approach for help.

Each time, I caught sight of the guy in the corner because everything about him was like metal to my magnet. He had his arms slung over the back of the booth on each side, and he was slouched down. Though he laughed, his eyes were alert, and twice he'd caught my gaze with his own, his mouth twitching in a smile a split second before I looked away.

He wasn't drunk, even though I'd seen him down two bottles of beer and a couple of shots, and from the heat in his eyes, I figured he thought I was trying to work out which of the men I was going to fuck.

My stomach churned at the prospect. I knew from my own circle of friends that they'd often come here to, as they called it, 'rough' it. Fucking one of the Satan's Sinners appeared to be a rite of passage in these parts, but I wasn't here to fuck anyone. The last thing I needed was one of these bikers thinking I was here for a quickie in the restrooms.

Gah, just the notion made me scowl into my vodka.

I'd never understood the desire to have sex in a public restroom. Not only were they gross, but ugh, it was filthy and loaded with germs. I wouldn't have sex in *my* bathroom, and I knew for a fact that Conchita steamed most of my quarters to keep me happy.

When a loud bray of laughter burst out from the other side of the room, I first thought it was one of the bikers. They'd been making weird noises for a while now, so it fit, but when I glanced at them, they were cutting a look in another direction—my guards.

Paul and Alix were wasted. Alix was snorting out a laugh as Paul was slapping the table with the palm of his hand as he, too, snickered at whatever inside joke they had going on.

I studied them for a few minutes, watched as they turned toward one another and began arguing over something. It was a friendly argument though, and I figured it had to do with sports. I knew they both supported the same football team and had often heard them discussing stats and the like when they were on detail.

Getting to my feet, I decided to try and make a move. The restroom was my first port of call, just to see if they noticed I'd gone. I'd taken note of the signage the second I'd taken a seat so, as I walked past them, maneuvering my way through the roughly hewn tables that were made out of slices of trees, I hitched a breath as I wondered if I'd made it.

When they didn't snap out a hand as I brushed past them, I knew I was good to carry on with my plan.

The second I made it to the hall that led to the bathrooms, I almost crumpled as relief hit me. For a second, I just leaned against the wall, ignoring the picture frame that dug into my back as I did so. Pressing my hand to my forehead, I sucked in a breath, calmed myself down, then straightened up. As I did, I jerked in surprise.

The brother from the booth was standing there. Inches away.

Watching me.

I gulped, tense from surprise and uneasiness.

He was close. Too close. In my space, and I couldn't move back.

He tilted his head to the side, his eyes catching mine before they drifted down to my mouth. He was big. Huge, in fact. And even though he was handsome, as handsome as the Devil himself, he was scary. But I was used to that.

My father wore a mask for the public. He donned expensive suits and watches that cost more than some people's homes, and he'd wave at the photographers, a big ole smile on his face as he beamed at the world because he owned it. Or, at least, a chunk of it. The world was his bitch, and he rode it hard and wet.

It was only when he came home, when the front doors were closed, that things changed. That smile turned dark. Twisted. It was even worse when he'd grab my hair and slam my face into his fist. Worse still when he'd pushed my mom down the stairs that night, all with that cruel smile on his face.

This man?

He wore no mask, yet there was something going on with him.

He was white blond, but it was natural. Not from a bottle. It was kind of like mine, but more strawberry, I guessed. He had it slicked back in a loose, stubby ponytail that dragged most of it off his face. It would be, I knew, a tousled mess that waved around his jaw when released, and it looked like silk. Honest to God silk.

He had a broad brow, with dark gold eyebrows that accentuated his bright green eyes. His nose was strong, and it led to a set of lips that would have made a saint want to sin. Around that wicked mouth, he was stubbled from his moustache to the rest of his jaw. He wore the leather cut all the MC brothers did, a white wifebeater, and a pair of jeans that, from that one quick glance, I knew he filled out well. Around his neck he wore, of all things, a rosary.

To say the sight surprised me was an understatement. It had wooden beads on it and a crucifix. All of it was rough, and any polish came from him worrying it with his hands.

But for all that he was beautiful, those green eyes of his?

They disturbed me.

I couldn't say why, just that they did.

"What do you want?"

Those four words should have come from me, only they didn't. Hadn't. He asked them, and sweet Lord, his voice was just as beautiful as the man himself. It was raspy and deep, and it seemed to sink into my bones, settling there like mercury, weighing each of my senses down until I had no choice but to press my back harder into the wall behind me.

Turning into a puddle of goo in front of a man like this would do me no favors. I'd been around enough men like him to know what he was—a predator.

He might think I was prey, but I wasn't. I was a predator too, but I knew how to play a part. I was a wolf in sheep's clothing, and I would only reveal that when I was ready.

I cleared my throat. "Why are you asking?"

"Because Cody behind the bar told me what you're paying him to do."

My head tilted to the side at that. I hadn't seen Cody approach the booth. The other server had though. But he'd said Cody, and I distinctly recalled the button on the shirt of the bartender I'd dealt with. "When?"

His lips curved and fuck, what that did to those eyes? Holy shit. It was like looking into a cat's eyes. They were kind of blank, yet somehow managed to transmit exactly what he was thinking which, I knew, was a paradox. But still. Maybe that was this man. Paradox with a capital P.

"Ever heard of the miracle of phones?" He arched a brow at me. "Text messages are a miracle, aren't they? Now, what do you want?"

My throat tightened as I realized, inadvertently, I'd gotten my wish.

I was speaking to a Satan's Sinner brother, and all without Paul and Alix being able to report it to my father.

For a second, my vocal chords froze. Words I'd been planning on uttering for days in the aftermath of Luke's death seemed to choke me. I had so much to say, so goddamn much, but I was speechless.

Until the guy stunned the shit out of me and murmured, "Take a breath."

I stared at him, wide-eyed, then he stunned me further. He blew out a breath then slowly inhaled, and I stared at his mouth, rounded and perfect, and followed his lead.

At that moment, everything grounded to a halt. The world itself seemed to stop spinning on its axis. The music blaring behind me, the noise of a toilet flushing in the near distance, the raucous crowd who was spending the evening getting drunk...it all faded into the ether.

I saw nothing but him.

Felt nothing but him.

His peace in the face of the chaos of my life.

His calm in the presence of the turbulence that brought me here.

I could hear the breath rasp from between my lips, heard his as it gusted from his mouth, and slowly, my heart stopped racing, my lungs stopped burning, and time clicked back into being.

After around thirty seconds of the deepest intimacy I'd ever had with another person, I let my gaze drift to his eyes and whispered the stark, horrendous truth. "I know where Luke kept them."

He tensed, his body turning rigid in front of me. Distance appeared between us, a distance of my own making, especially when those weren't the words I'd wanted to say, but they were all I was capable of. And the space that suddenly pushed us a state apart made me want to sob. I longed to reach out, to grab his hand, to get that connection back. The link where I felt the beating of my heart as much as I'd sensed his own, but that was gone now. I'd cauterized it with my family's evil.

His words confirmed what I'd hoped—the MC had been looking into Luke's past to find a way to undermine my father's desire to pin a murder charge on Giulia Fontaine. "His captives?"

I nodded. Once.

"Who was he to you?"

My mouth twisted, and my throat choked as reality punched me there. "My brother," I spat, speaking those two words like the curses they were, and he reared back, either because he was surprised I was related to Luke or because my vitriol for that bastard had come through loud and clear.

"Where are they?" he demanded, his voice low, rough. Raspier than before. But now wasn't the time to be caught up in how his voice made me tingle in places *no one* had ever made me tingle before.

Now, I had to think about those poor women. Those poor women who my bastard of a brother had—

Fuck.

I couldn't even think about that.

I just had to get them out of the hell he'd placed them in.

"Give me your phone number," I ordered, my voice sounding more like mine again.

I couldn't believe I'd shown weakness to a man like this, but hell, even I was overwhelmed at the depravity my brother had waded through in his short lifespan.

Knowing someone was evil and seeing it?

Two separate matters entirely.

The guy narrowed his eyes at me but reeled off a number which I quickly input into my phone. I found the email where I'd stored all the information I'd found when I was sneaking through Luke's stuff, copied it into a text, and sent it to him.

"That's all I know."

He frowned as he stared down at his phone which lit up with my text. "How long have you known?"

My throat grew tight. Not just at the horror at what my brother had done, but at the threat in the MC brother's tone. I was grateful I didn't have to lie. "A few days. I didn't know where to turn." I sucked in a breath. "My father would let them rot, and the cops are in his pocket along with the mayor."

"The sheriff isn't." When my mouth worked as I tried to figure out what to say, since I hadn't known that was the case, he merely shook his head. "Why come to us?"

"Because Luke attacked one of your women." My smile was tight. "You protect your own."

He tipped his chin up. "You should have come to us sooner."

"Not as easy as you think when you have security following your every move. They'll report to my father." My throat grew tight again. "I'd hurry. If he decides he needs to get to them first…"

The guy didn't stick around to hear my conclusion. He just walked off, his boots silent against the ground as he disappeared as quickly as he'd appeared. A breath escaped me as I pressed back into the wall.

My task was over. I just hoped I wasn't too late.

TWO

LINK

"I believe her."

"She had tits and ass. Of course, you believe her," Steel muttered, snorting as he began shuffling a deck of cards. It was a nervous tic of sorts, a new one. That damn deck was in his mitts at all times, had been ever since we'd found out about Luke Lancaster's little harem from hell.

I figured it had to do with the prospect of some innocent women being imprisoned somewhere in the United States of America. Starving to death...

I blew out a breath.

Yeah, no wonder he had a nervous tic. I was getting that way myself. When I closed my eyes at night, I thought about those poor bitches, locked up, not knowing when the cunt who held the keys to their prison would return. Not knowing that he'd never return. I thought about how hungry they must be. How cold. How fucking alone, and yeah, I ended up *not* sleeping.

I was a callous son of a bitch. By nature and nurture. You couldn't do what we did and have a big heart, but even the cold stones lodged in our chests were flopping like dying fish at what those women were going through.

Even so, I resented Steel's words. You made one fucking mistake as a teenager, and these bastards never let it drop.

"Could be a trap," Rex concurred, breaking into my irritation, rubbing his chin as he eyed up the way Steel was shuffling those damn cards.

"Doubt it. She was nervous as fuck. Paid Cody behind the bar to dope up her guards' drinks with vodka. Then was antsy all night waiting on them to get drunk. Plus..." I flinched as I dragged my pointer finger along the curve of my cheekbone. "She'd been beaten. All covered up. Well, too. Not the first time she's been hit with makeup skills that good."

Steel's jaw clenched. "She put herself at risk."

At his words—words that were a statement and not a question—I muttered, "Yeah. I think so."

"We can afford to send out a couple of brothers to check this shit out," Rex decided. "Even if she's blowing smoke up our asses, I'd rather be safe than sorry. Don't think I'd be able to fucking sleep at night if we didn't at least look."

Steel winced. "Yeah."

Rex clapped him on the back. "You're watching out for the MC, brother. That's what your job is."

"Feel like a cunt."

"We all do," I retorted, shrugging my shoulders uneasily. "We're all hyped up. Worrying about Giulia, worrying about Nyx worrying about Giulia, and wondering when he's about to break and go on the fucking rampage." I let a breath whistle out from between my teeth. "Then there's those women." I gulped. "Dunno about you, but I've slept like shit for the past week."

Rex dipped his chin. "Yeah. I'm going to go and tell Nyx."

"You know he's going to want to come along for the ride," Steel pointed out.

"Which means Giulia's coming too," I said dryly. "No way in fuck he's gonna take his eyes off her."

Rex grimaced. "Because taking her to some fucked up prison in the middle of nowhere is his idea of a date now. Jesus Christ." He scraped a hand over his head. "Last thing she needs to see is that."

"Bet she wants to go. She'll want to help. And fuck, she knows what it's like to be vulnerable to that cunt. Maybe it will help them?"

"Won't help her though, will it? And I have to think of Nyx."

Despite myself, I had to snicker. "You worry about him too much. He's not as vulnerable as you think he is."

"I don't think he's vulnerable," Rex denied instantly, but his glower told me I'd hit a nerve.

"Yeah, you do. He ain't," I countered. "Bro's got brass balls, and even if he was fucked up, Giulia's straightening him up some."

Steel's snickered. "How did you say that without busting your gut laughing? Last thing that bitch is gonna do is straighten a guy like Nyx out. If anything, she'd encourage him."

"Two psychopaths in sweet harmony," I joked, leaning back against the wall and digging my heel into the drywall as I did so. "Did you hear about what she did to her stepfather? Good thing Nyx's balls *are* brass. That's the only thing that'll keep them safe if she goes nuclear."

My words got my brothers smiling, just as I'd intended, then I reached forward, gripped Rex's shoulder, and urged, "Hustle, Prez. We need to get them girls out."

"If they're even there," Steel said.

"Don't be negative," I chided. "Let's hope they *are* there, then maybe we can sleep again."

Rex grunted but moved down the hall to Nyx's room, where he and Giulia were probably sleeping. He knocked and I heard a few thumps as Nyx made it to the door. When the door slammed shut a few minutes later, and I heard more thumps, I knew he was getting ready.

Steel cut me a look. "You think this is true? Not BS?"

"Fuck knows. I just hope she wasn't lying."

"I'll slit her throat myself if she is. What kind of sicko—"

Before he could continue, I mumbled, "She's related to Luke Lancaster. A guy who rapes for fun? Let's hope being a psycho isn't a genetic trait in her family."

Steel huffed but shoved the deck of cards away in his jeans' pocket.

About twenty minutes later, Nyx and Giulia were on his hog, Steel was on his, and I was climbing onto the back of mine. A quick glance at the clubhouse told me everyone was watching, even though this was supposed to be under wraps, and I mock saluted those peering at us from behind the curtains before I kick-started my bike into action.

The roar of the trio of hogs made my blood sing, and even though our end destination might be the definition of a nightmare in the flesh, I felt energy flood my veins as we began the roll down the driveway.

The gates opened the second the Prospect saw us, and we sped up, flying out of the compound like we were using winged chariots.

As the wind smashed me square in the face, I let out a holler, and wasn't surprised when a feminine version that matched my own came next. I twisted around and saw Giulia was clinging to Nyx, but her hair was whipping around in the wind, her face was tilted to get it full frontal, and her eyes were closed as she gloried in the moment.

If I hadn't known that she came from biker stock, I had proof then and there. This shit was genetic. Passed down from generation to generation.

We were born to ride these beasts, just like our ancestors had lived on horse-back. Some people were meant for the constraints of city living, of the rat race, then there were folks like us. Folks who lived on the fringes of society. Who led their lives the way they wanted, not the way the government did.

The three-hour journey was broken up by two breaks at a pitstop. It was late already, none of us had been sleeping right anyway, and Giulia was sore after what that fucker had put her through. We each downed a large cup of coffee which, of course, necessitated the next stop.

Fucking coffee.

Lancaster's little sister didn't realize how lucky she'd been coming across me. As Road Captain of the Satan's Sinners' MC, it was my fucking job to lead my brothers into chaos. She hadn't just caught the eye of any brother, she'd caught mine.

But then, looking like she did, I knew every fucker with a dick had seen her walk into the bar when she had. No one could have failed to spot the elegance she exuded. Everything about her screamed money. More than that, it screamed 'hands off,' which of course, was more of a challenge than anything else. Especially to a fucker like me.

The coordinates to our end destination were on my phone as I led us to hell, but along the way I thought about her, thought about how she'd looked around Daytona like it was dog crap on her expensive heels. Then, I thought about the vulnerability in her eyes when I'd had to help her breathe through her panic. At first, I just thought she was scared of me. Lots of country clubbers approached the MC, wanting to get laid. Wanting to get fucked hard by the local scum. I'd thought she was one of them until Cody had shared her intentions with us, then I'd learned otherwise.

She'd entered my world with a purpose.

A purpose that saw me driving straight through the heart of New Jersey and close to the Pennsylvanian border. The reason it was so far from the MC was because of a windy motherfucker of a road that brought us to the town itself and took a goddamn age to traverse.

Stewartsheim, according to Google anyway, was home to less than three hundred souls. I had to assume the women being held against their will weren't included in the census so, yeah, more like three hundred plus.

My mouth twisted into a grimace as we approached the township. Lancaster's sister had given me fucking coordinates. How the hell she knew them, I didn't know, but I wasn't about to look a gift horse in the mouth, especially when we went off road, driving onto a field, and approaching a body of water I had to assume was a reservoir, seeing as we were in the middle of the goddamn country, and I didn't know about any lakes in this part of the state.

The early morning sun made the body of water gleam and glitter where it hit, but it was still dark enough for me to see that, in the distance, there were rows of homes where the good folks of Stewartsheim lived, and who were slowly starting to wake up.

The coordinates took us past the township, past the reservoir—if that's what it was—and onto slightly higher ground that was surrounded by trees.

When we reached our destination, I didn't even fucking realize it. The sun had started its rise, sure, but we were surrounded by a chaos of trees that kept us in the shadows. Only when I braked to a halt did my brothers join me, and Nyx was the one who called out, "Where the fuck are we? Why did we stop?"

"These are the coordinates," I stated firmly, peering at the map and wondering if Siri had failed me. Again.

"Looks like that bitch was toying with us," Steel muttered.

I glowered at him, aware he'd see my expression because of the glow from my phone. He grunted at the sight, and I bit off, "We can't see for shit. There could be a fucking creepy ass cabin right in front of us and we wouldn't know it was there."

"We have our lights on," Steel retorted, as he folded his arms across his chest.

Fucker looked like he was settling in for a fight.

I opened my mouth to give him what he was asking for, then Giulia whispered, "Did you hear that?"

She sounded shaken, and I knew the difference. She hadn't been around the clubhouse that long, but she was a weirdo who I quite appreciated. She was snarky, usually a bitch, and had a wicked right hook. I actually liked that she'd managed to bust her stepfather's ballsack because with a fucker like Nyx in her bed, she'd need to be ready for anything.

Not that *he'd* hurt her, but living our life the way we did? Shit got real *and* weird, fast.

"What is it, babe?" Nyx rumbled, his voice low. His leathers squeaked as he twisted to face her, giving her all his attention.

The second he did, she released a sigh, like she could breathe or something because he was looking at her, *seeing* her. I wasn't sure why that would help, but it did. Hell, it had helped Lancaster's sister this evening too. Breathing with her, calming her down, it had felt oddly natural. But then, I'd done it often enough with my ma, helping her climb out of her panic-fogged stupor, for me to be at ease with it.

"I don't know," Giulia admitted. "It was like a cry."

"Probably the wind," Steel muttered, earning himself a glare from both me and Nyx as well this time.

"Why are you trying to be awkward?" I groused. "You want them found as much as we do."

He gritted his teeth. "'Course I fuckin' do."

"Then don't be so damn difficult." I turned my focus to Giulia once more. "I didn't hear anything. The bike's engine is still whistling in my ears."

"Mine too," she admitted, "and it was faint." She reached up, tugging slightly in a way that made me realize Nyx had somehow managed to grab a hold of both her hands. She ran the one he released over her face. "Maybe I'm losing my mind."

Nyx snorted. "No way, baby. You're not losing shit. I'll find you every fucking time. You hear me?"

Her lips curved in a dry smile, and she surprised me by raising their joined hands and brushing her mouth over his knuckles. That small act of tenderness probably gained more of a reaction from me and Steel than her getting naked would have. Women didn't do shit like that around us, but Giulia had because, it figured, she wasn't like any of the women we usually had at the clubhouse.

And weirder still?

Nyx didn't mind.

He didn't pull back. Didn't pull away. Didn't even shoot us embarrassed looks.

Fuck, he loved her.

He actually fucking loved her.

I mean, I guess it made sense. He'd given her his brand, she wore his patch. But still. I hadn't thought about love. Love wasn't a thing in this world of ours.

On edge at what I was witnessing, I kept quiet. I didn't want to be on the end of Nyx's fist tonight, not when there might be some women who needed our help around here. Last thing they needed was to see their saviors bruised and bloodied after getting into a stupid fistfight. But I wanted to speak. Fuck, I wanted to ask questions.

How did it feel to be in love?

Was it weird? Was it nice? I'd never felt anything like that myself and I was curious, even if I probably shouldn't be. Badass bikers didn't fall in love...*supposedly*. Nyx had, though. And shit, he was the biggest, baddest motherfucker I knew. Demons would cower before Nyx, that was how messed up he was.

The shit I'd seen him do to those sick fucks who messed with kids?

Yeah, I couldn't see Satan himself not feeling squeamish at the shit Nyx did in his spare time.

Giulia sighed, catching my attention once again, and I saw that their hands were lowered and she'd pressed her forehead to Nyx's arm.

Was she crying?

I cut Steel a look again, saw he was just as uneasy as me.

A noise whispered through the trees as I was about to clear my throat, trying to get shit moving. It was quiet. Like a shushing sound, but it was high-pitched too.

I tensed and so did my brothers, and my brother's woman, who scrambled off the bike at the noise. Nyx had her back a second later.

"What was that?" I rasped, even as I started to climb off my bike too. I pulled off my helmet and hung it from the handlebars as I straightened up.

Steel, peering through the trees where only the faintest of light was bleeding through, said, "I heard it too."

"Well, if you heard it, then it must be real," I snarked at him, earning myself the bird he flipped my way.

I took another look around, sweeping my phone's flashlight in the area. Steel, evidently doing the same, mumbled, "Some kind of truck has been here. SUV maybe. Something heavy."

I stared where his light was directed and saw what he was seeing and agreed, "SUV. I recognize those tires."

"Of course, you do," Giulia mocked.

Nyx tapped her leg. "Link runs the garage for a reason, babe."

My lips twisted. "Just 'cause I hate cages doesn't mean I don't know how to fix them." I knew how to fix them too fucking well. Meant most of our customers wouldn't be coming back as often as they should because I knew my shit.

Of course, I'd tried not to work at the garage. When Rex had dumped the MC's new businesses on the council's shoulders, I'd hoped some other fucker would want to run it. No dice. I was stuck getting engine oil in my asscrack for the rest of my natural life.

"That bodes well though, doesn't it? If there are tracks that means someone's come here recently." The hope in Giulia's voice was painful to hear.

I sucked in a breath. "Could be anyone. Could be hunters."

To counter my words, there was that noise again.

I whipped around, my phone with me, trying to fucking see where that goddamn sound might be coming from.

"Never heard a bird sing like that before," Steel complained as he slowly turned, his gaze drifting along the tree line. "Something's here."

"If that isn't the creepiest thing you could have said," Giulia retorted, shuddering as she wrapped her arms around her waist. "This is like the setup for a horror movie."

Nyx snorted and hauled her into his side. "You're safe with us."

"Yeah," I teased. "Giulia, ain't you realized it yet? We're the boogeymen."

Her only response was to huff, which either meant she thought I was full of shit or she was agreeing. Never could tell with Nyx's bitch.

"We're going to have to go into the woods," Steel stated grimly, and I knew he was just as freaked as Giulia but he wouldn't say shit.

I'd have goaded the motherfucker for being a pussy but hell, it *was* creepy. It reminded me of the opening scenes of a horror movie too. When the director was setting shit up to get the audience in the mood. Even the lighting wasn't on our side. It was bleak and there was a haze to the air. Plus, knowing that some women might be held in captivity around here didn't exactly make the place fucking cheerful.

Grunting at my thoughts, which were goddamn stupid, I strode forward. The crunching of grass beneath my feet was a giveaway—there was more crunching when my brothers and Giulia joined me. Three more streams of light joined mine as we pushed between the trees and began walking over the soil. It was pretty peaceful in here, but there was a low mist that made it hard to see the ground.

Okay, so this place was beyond creepy as shit.

I'd admit it.

Even if it was only to myself.

As we walked, our feet making too much noise as we stomped through the forest, it was a miracle we heard that weird ass sound again, but we did.

And we all froze.

I thought about what it sounded like, and could only compare it to the clank of a wrench or something clanging against the body of a car. Metal against metal. A dull whine.

Ears pricking up, I peered through the mist, then groaned with relief when a shard of light from the sinking moon pierced the trees.

Giulia whispered, "Oh my God, over there."

I followed the direction where she pointed with her finger and grimaced at the sight of a shack. Fifteen by fifteen, minimum.

As we processed its sudden appearance, we took off at a run. The sound echoed again, and my belief that it was metal ringing against metal was reiterated as the dull, shrill whistle seemed to be on repeat.

My heart began to race with hope. Someone who was being held captive, who'd managed to hear someone in the vicinity, who was trying to call for help...they'd make that kind of noise, wouldn't they?

I heard the click of a gun behind me and dug into the back of my jeans where I kept my weapon. Knowing Nyx had armed himself made me want my gun in my paw too, and when I heard Steel's safety snick off, I knew we were all feeling the same vibe. The same hope. The same concern. Especially as we slowed down the second we got to the shack.

It was made of wood, almost entirely, except for a window beside the door—four dirty glass panes held together by a cross, loaded with spiderwebs and filth. There was guttering around the roof that quivered when a gust of wind whispered through the trees.

"Shit, did we bring anything with us? Food? Fucking clothes?"

Steel's remark had me jerking in surprise. I twisted around to glower at him. "You serious right now?"

"Yeah. If there are women in there, we need to help them."

"Yeah, by not shooting the shit," I ground out, even as I strode forward and pulled the door. It was, not surprisingly, locked. "There are space blankets in each of our saddlebags as well as water and protein bars," I informed him absentmindedly. The door rattled and shook under my grip, the padlock old and rusty, but there was some wear around the hinges that told me it was used.

"When did you do that?"

"When you were taking a leak before we set off," I muttered. Twisting to Nyx, I ordered, "Hold the light steady so I can shoot off the padlock."

The second the stream of his flashlight hit it, I angled myself so it wouldn't ricochet into my damn face and shot it off. That clanging sound appeared again, confirming that someone was behind it.

Someone in the fucking shack.

Breathing in sharply, I pulled open the door, and the second I did, the stench hit me.

I was a hardened criminal. I'd killed. I'd watched Nyx torture fucking pedophiles. I'd helped torture them. I would kill and kill again for my MC, but that smell? It had me staggering back with my hand to my face to try to cover it.

"Holy fuck!" Nyx spat, and Steel's curse echoed at the same time.

I wasn't surprised when Giulia dashed off and the sounds of her puking soon followed.

That stench?

It was death.

We were too late.

Too fucking late.

Then the clanging sound came again and fuck, I realized someone had to be alive in there.

Someone had been *living* with that goddamn stench.

The prospect of heading toward the smell made my stomach roil like I'd eaten ten ghost chili peppers, but step forward I did. I tried to breathe through my mouth, tried not to inhale the scent, but it was impossible. And then the humming started.

"Coffin flies," I muttered, the words coming out nasally.

"Sweet fuck, someone's down there with a corpse," Steel rasped.

His words shouldn't have been the catalyst, the stench and the flies should have been, but his statement kicked us in the ass. As one, we stepped into the shack, peering around and seeing jack shit. We swept our lights over the ground, saw the cellar door, and rushed over.

The clanging sound came again, softer this time. Weaker. Like someone who'd either given up hope or who'd lost the strength to carry on.

Heart fucking melting, I scrambled to find the handle, but if the gloom outside was bad, in here it was worse. And with the stench making my eyes water and the flies fucking with my ears, it was a wonder I could do anything.

"Stand back," I roared, the second I found a smaller padlock in the bottom corner of the opening. Giving whoever was down there a few seconds, I shot the lock off as I braced myself for what I was about to see.

But even as I prepared myself, even as I told myself to man the fuck up and deal with whatever chaos Lancaster had left behind, nothing could have prepared me for what I saw.

Nothing.

Seeing the shit Nyx could do to sick fucks was *nothing* in comparison to this.

It coated all five of my senses. In comparison to the sight, the smell, the fucking *taste*—I could *taste* it. The sheer evilness, the fucking horror of what I was witnessing drowned all five of them, making me falter for a few seconds as I tried and failed to process it.

Only seeing the girl slumped over, with some kind of pipe in her hand, twitch, jerked me into action.

As I staggered down the few steps into that pit of hell, I realized there were four cages down here. Four fucking cages I wouldn't have put a goddamn pit bull in. They were half the size of a single bed in both length and width, and how the fuck the one out on the floor had escaped was beyond me.

"Go get the blankets and food, Giulia!"

Nyx's command had me jerking in surprise, and it had the women in this pit jolting too. A woman, filthy, so filthy I didn't even see her eyes at first because she was covered in shit and piss—fucking shit and piss—moaned as she slumped onto her back.

My mouth twisted into a snarl as the desire to string Lancaster up by his balls, to eviscerate him, filled me.

I forced my thoughts away from violence and tried to focus on the women. One of them, at least, was dead. That smell, those flies? Someone had to be dead in here.

I flashed my light over the cages, cringing when I saw more fluids, more insects, more of everything no one ever wanted to see, and finding relief when I heard two sets of moans as the women reacted to the light. Only one didn't flinch. The four cages were lined up in a row. The one to the far left, against the wall, didn't move, and when I trained the light on her, Steel doing the same, I saw—

My stomach roiled once again, and how I didn't puke, I'd never fucking know.

Staggering down the stairs, feeling dazed, I made it to the woman on the floor. Hauling her up, I lifted her into my arms, wincing as she pretty much goddamn rattled in my hold. She was a bag of bones, and I passed her up to Steel who I knew would pass her to Nyx.

With her out of the way, I approached the cages. My boots had them flinching, and I whispered, "Luke Lancaster is dead. My brother's woman killed him. It was slow. She twisted the knife, made sure he *hurt*, but no amount of hurt is payment for this. My name is Link." I pointed to Steel. "He's Steel, and my brother upstairs is called Nyx, and his woman is Giulia. She's the one who ended that cunt's life."

"He's dead?"

The voice was softer than a whisper, and it was the spookiest shit I'd ever heard. Ghosts were louder than this poor creature.

"Yes. We're here to help."

A cough came from the cage beside the ghost. "Too late for Sarah. Almost too late for us."

"Too late for Sarah, but just in time for you. What's your name?" I asked, even as I stepped into the puddles of human waste and tried to find where the openings to the cages were.

"I'm Tatána," one woman replied, her voice stronger than the ghost's. "She's Alessa, and the one you carried out is Amara."

I hummed at her words, trying to split my attention as I sought a way out for them. It took me longer than I'd like, but there were tiny padlocks keeping them barred. When Steel stepped forward, I cut him a look, saw he had something from only the fuck knew where, and he smashed it into the padlock. On the brink of telling him that wouldn't work, it worked, and he handed it to me.

It was a brick.

A fucking brick.

The occupant jerked when I slammed into the metal, and maybe fortitude was on my side too, because within five slams, the padlock was broken and I could open the door.

I crouched down, then peered inside. "You're going to have to crawl out, honey. I can't get you out. It's too small for me." It was too small for her too. She was crouched on her side in a fetal position, but her legs were relaxed in a way that told me this was as far as she could stretch.

"Too tired," she mumbled.

"You're not too tired," I countered, my throat thickening with tears. Tears! Me. I hadn't cried at my momma's goddamn funeral, yet here I was, ready to bawl. "We just got here. You gotta help me help you."

I flickered a glance at Steel and saw he was chivvying the other girl out. Grabbing her arm, he was half dragging her out of the cage, and although I wanted to shout at him, I knew these women were on the brink of death. If they couldn't help themselves, we'd have to do the heavy lifting.

Wishing there was more fucking light in here so I could see what I was doing, I reached in, grunted when I touched something wet, and tried not to think about it.

Fuck.

Every moment of these past five minutes were going to stick with me for a lifetime, so there was no forgetting any of what was currently going down.

Shoving the thought aside, I grabbed something soft and frail, and started hustling the woman, Alessa, toward the opening. She cried out in pain, and I understood, I did, but fuck, what choice did I have? I had to get her out of there.

Sweat beaded from every single pore as I strained to get her out. She wasn't struggling, but she was a dead weight, making the job ten times harder. When I managed to maneuver a part of her out of the opening, I wanted to crow with delight, but she slumped, and suddenly, I knew what a deadweight truly felt like.

My heart in my throat, I shook my head, unable to believe we'd come so close only to fucking lose her.

Rage filled me, it burned me from the inside out, and though I was pretty strong anyway, a level of power I'd never tapped into hit me at that moment. It helped me haul Alessa out of the tiny space, helped me drag her onto the filthy floor, and it helped me carry her out of that poisonous prison and into the outside world, where there was only the vague scent of death, rotting flesh, the pungency of a mass wave of insects, and human shit.

Giulia was there immediately, and I wasn't surprised when she retched, even as she held open the space blanket so I could wrap Alessa in it.

"I-I think she's dead," I bit off, even as I pressed the bundle to the ground.

"No. She just fainted," Giulia rasped, as she pressed a hand to Alessa's chest. "Feel. There's a slight vibration. She's breathing."

Hope swirled inside me. "She needs help."

Giulia nodded, but after she licked her lips, she whispered, "But how?"

These women needed medical attention, but I knew why Giulia was at a loss. If we got involved, somehow the cops would make it so that we were the ones who'd abducted the women. They'd squirrel into our lives, into our world, ruining it because they could Capone us—get us on a charge that had nothing to do with our business to shut down our operation and jail us, even if we'd done nothing wrong to these women.

"Can you drop us off somewhere?"

I jerked in surprise at the ghost's voice. It was a gentle susurration of sound that whispered along my ears, filling me with relief that she was awake again. "You're too weak to move. You need help. A lot of it."

The ghost's laugh was eerie. "You'd be surprised what we can do. We've survived this far."

Gutturally, I responded, "I know you have. You're warriors, but now's the time to heal. You've done the fighting, now you need to rest."

"I know your MC. I heard of them when I was working over in Newark." She smiled, her brutally thin lips pulling taut against her jaw. That smile told me she knew something about us, something she probably shouldn't know.

I twisted around so I could look at her, and when her eyes caught mine, there was a stillness there that, oddly enough, calmed me.

Whatever had happened to her in that pit, and it didn't take much fucking guessing, she knew that sometimes, self-confessed sinners weren't all in possession of midnight souls.

"I have a burner phone," Nyx inserted from his crouched position at Amara's side. "We could place you somewhere and you could make the call for help."

Steel disagreed, "No. We need to keep this shit under wraps. Giulia's already in enough shit because of that Lancaster cunt. Last thing we need is to have the cops sniffing around us over this. You know as well as I do that they'll pin this shit on us." He sucked in a breath, one that sounded oddly shallow. "We need to bring Stone in."

My eyes widened at that. "Fuck me, has the world just come to an end?"

He scowled at me. "What?"

"You heard me. Thought the only time you'd even fucking breathe her name was if Bruce Willis was stuck on a meteorite above us." I peered up at the sky. "Where's Aerosmith? They gonna burst into song?"

He flipped me the bird. "Fuck you."

I just shrugged. "Too many ladies want to fuck me for me to waste my fine self on my fist."

A soft snort escaped the ghost, and I peered down at her and grinned. Maybe now wasn't the moment for a conversation about classic movies— and fuck yeah, I considered *Armageddon* a golden oldie classic—and maybe I shouldn't be joking when these women had been laying in their own shit for only fuck knew how long, but Christ, that smile on the ghost's face? I knew Steel was right.

Stone could help.

If she'd agree to come to the clubhouse, that is. We all knew Steel and Stone hadn't parted ways as friends.

He slipped his phone out of his back pocket. The screen lit up and he put in the code—don't know why he bothered. Everyone knew he used Marilyn Monroe's birthday for all his fucking passwords—and started scrolling through his contacts.

"You don't have to do this, brother," Nyx rumbled, sounding, as usual, dark as fuck.

"Yeah. I do. For the MC."

I pulled a face at that, because even if it was best for us, I wasn't sure if it was best for the women. "Stone can't do all that a hospital can for them," I pointed out softly, and I wasn't even joking when I said, "Save the sacrifice for another time, bro. These ladies need proper medical attention. They're starved, their bodies are—"

"Please. Don't take us to a hospital."

Ghost's words had me rearing back in surprise. If anything, I'd have thought she'd want to go back to civilization. "Huh?" I asked, dumbfounded.

"Please." When she started shifting on the ground, moaning as she moved, I realized she was trying to sit up. "Don't take us to the hospital."

I considered myself a dumbass because, just that second, I heard the accent. "You're an illegal, aren't you?"

She sagged against the ground. "We all are."

"That changes things." Nyx cut Steel a look. "Get Stone on the line. I'll talk to her."

"Ain't no one gonna mention that it's fucking weird as shit you still have her number?" I questioned.

"I keep an eye on her," Steel rasped, even as he connected the call and put it on speaker.

"Have pigs started flying? Or has hell frozen over? As far as I know, that was the only time you said you'd talk to me again."

Steel's top lip snagged into a snarl, but he turned his face away at the sound of Stone's voice and left it to Nyx.

Never thought Nyx would be the rational one in a situation like this, but fuck, these were trying times.

"Stone, it's Nyx."

"Nyx?" Stone sounded confused. "Oh my God," she rasped. "Oh, God. I'll be right there! Don't you let that fucker die, do you hear me? I'll drag him back from hell if I fucking have to. Do you hear me, Nyx?" she screamed, making the ghost jolt on the ground in surprise.

"I hear you, honey," he replied, tone soothing as he shot me a wry look. "We'll keep him going until you get here."

"Good," she barked, then cut the call.

I blinked at Nyx before we both turned to Steel.

"She thinks I'm dying?" Steel growled. "And that's the only way she'll come back?"

"Look on the bright side, she doesn't want you to die."

He didn't appreciate my help because he glowered at me.

"At least she's coming to the compound."

"Because she thinks I'm dying," he reiterated.

"Some men would think that was a compliment," the ghost whispered, but again, I heard a sliver of amusement in her voice.

How the poor woman could find anything humorous about this fucking situation, I didn't know. But sweet fuck, I was just grateful she wasn't sobbing and was coherent.

"Stone always did know how to fucking insult me," Steel grated out.

"Not sure it's an insult. She doesn't want you to die, bro," I pointed out. "I mean, she wasn't all, 'let me roll up so I can spit on his grave.' She wants you to live. Ghost's right, that's pretty much as big of a compliment as someone can give to another person."

"If she's on her way, we need to be on ours too," Nyx stated, putting an end to the conversation with a firm tone. Just because the dude was a sick motherfucker didn't mean he wasn't the bomb at being the Enforcer.

"They can't ride on the back of a bike," Giulia breathed weakly, and I cut her a look, unsurprised to see she was close by but had propped herself up against a tree.

This situation would traumatize *anyone*. But someone who'd only recently been traumatized? Fuck, it was a wonder she wasn't catatonic.

When Nyx glanced at her, I knew he saw that too and his face darkened in a way that, usually, he dedicated to the bastards he slaughtered. This one was only softened by the love in his eyes.

Yeah, the love.

Giulia didn't burn to nothing at the sight. Didn't disappear into a puddle of ash at the foot of the tree. If anything, she shot him a shaky look and rasped, "I'm okay."

"You're not," he instantly countered.

"I'll *be* okay then." She blew out a breath. "We need transport. The MC is too far away to help."

"It's three hours away, Giulia. Not Mars."

"Look at them and tell me we have time to fuck around?"

Ghost cleared her throat. "If we could just eat something, maybe that would help?"

Steel winced. "Don't you need, like, fluids or something?"

"You got sports drinks in those Mary Poppins bags of yours? Or just water?" Nyx questioned.

"Just water," I hissed under my breath. "Dumb of me to forget."

"Water would still be nice," the ghost whispered.

I flinched, because of course it fucking would be.

"I'll go get the bags."

"Nyx brought them already," Giulia murmured, as she began to riffle through the saddlebags that were at her side. Bags I'd only just seen.

In my defense, it was still gloomy as fuck around here. Couldn't see for shit, and trust me, there was enough shit around this place for that to be true.

The dawn light was too weak to make that much of a difference on the forest, and it was a reminder that even though I felt like I'd aged a good two years since I'd first entered these woods, it had probably only been sixty minutes from start to finish.

Sixty minutes from hell, and fuck, if a Satan's Sinner said that?

He meant it.

Need more?
Read on here: www.books2read.com/Link

UPDATE 2022: THE SERIES IS NOW COMPLETE!!

This isn't my first MC. That loony tune train started back with ALL SINNER NO SAINT, but I've been a major fan of MC romances for a looooong, loooooooooooong time. It's pretty much an obsession. So, I figured, it's my turn to write one. My turn to truly get into the nitty gritty.

Well, you just read it. What do you think? What say YOU? :P Let me know by either leaving an honest review (because they're an author's lifeblood and I'll fucking love you forever if you do that shit for me, MWAH,) or by chitchatting with me in my Diva Reader group on FB.

In the middle of the book, you met Finn and Declan O'Donnelly. This isn't their first rodeo. Finn has his own book, FILTHY: www.books2read. com/FilthySerenaAkeroyd. Where you can meet Aoife and read about their story. It's one of my personal faves, so be sure to check that out. It's on KU. Then, Eoghan has his story out in FILTHY RICH, and Declan's tale is revealed in FILTHY DARK, with Brennan and his FILTHY SEX out now too.

For a comprehensive reading order of the crossover universe:

FILTHY
NYX
LINK
FILTHY RICH
SIN
STEEL

FILTHY DARK
CRUZ
MAVERICK
FILTHY SEX
HAWK
FILTHY HOT
STORM
THE DON
THE LADY
FILTHY SECRET
REX
RACHEL
FILTHY KING
THE REVELATION
THE ORACLE
FILTHY FECK

I love you, guys. Thanks so much for letting me allow my batshit imagination to go wild. You're probably saving me from an asylum! :D
Love,
Serena
Xoxo

UNIVERSE READING ORDER

FILTHY LIES
FILTHY TRUTH

RUSSIAN MAFIA
Adjacent to the universe, but can be read as a standalone
SILENCED

FREE BOOK!

Don't forget to grab your free e-Book!
Secrets & Lies is now free!

Meg's love life was missing a spark until she discovered her need to be dominated. When her fiancé shared the same kink, she thought all her birthdays had come at once, and then she came to learn their relationship was one big fat lie.

Gabe has loved Meg for years, watching her from afar, and always wishing he'd been the one to date her first and not his brother. When he has the chance to have Meg in his bed—even better, tied to it—it's an opportunity he can't refuse.

With disastrous consequences.

Can Gabe make Meg realize she's the one woman he's always wanted? But once secrets and lies have wormed their way into a relationship, is it impossible to establish the firm base of trust needed between lovers, and more importantly, between sub and Sir...?

This story features orgasm control in a BDSM setting.
Secrets & Lies is now free!

CONNECT WITH SERENA

For the latest updates, be sure to check out my website!
But if you'd like to hang out with me and get to know me better, then I'd
love to see you in my Diva reader's group where you can find out all the
gossip on new releases as and when they happen. You can join here:
www.facebook.com/groups/SerenaAkeroydsDivas. Or you can always PM
or email me. I love to hear from you guys: serenaakeroyd@gmail.com.

ABOUT THE AUTHOR

I'm a romance novelaholic and I won't touch a book unless I know there's a happy ending. This addiction is what made me craft stories that suit my voracious need for raunchy romance. I love twists and unexpected turns, and my novels all contain sexy guys, dark humor, and hot AF love scenes.

I write MF, menage, and reverse harem (also known as why choose romance,) in both contemporary and paranormal. Some of my stories are darker than others, but I can promise you one thing, you will always get the happy ending your heart needs!

Made in United States
North Haven, CT
09 March 2024

49764023R00178